Love Kills
. . .

Love Kills

. . .

Edited by Ed Gorman and
Martin H. Greenberg

Carroll & Graf Publishers, Inc.
New York

Carroll & Graf Publishers, Inc.
260 Fifth Avenue
New York, NY 10001

Library of Congress Cataloging-in-Publication Data

Love kills / edited by Ed Gorman and Martin H. Greenberg. —
1st Carroll & Graf ed.
  p.   cm.
  ISBN 0–7867–0426–8
  1. Detective and mystery stories, American.   2. Detective
and mystery stories, English.   3. Love stories,
American.   4. Love stories, English.   I. Gorman,
Edward.   II. Greenberg, Martin Harry.
PS648.D4L68   1997
813'.087208—dc21

                                          96–53912
                                             CIP

Manufactured in the United States of America

CONTENTS

■ ■ ■

Afraid All the Time   *Nancy Pickard*   1

The Girl Friend   *Morris Hershman*   15

Predators   *Edward Bryant*   23

The Second Coming   *Joe Gores*   40

The Lost Coast   *Marcia Muller*   51

Night Freight   *Bill Pronzini*   74

Cat's Eye   *Larry Segriff*   83

The Midnight Train   *John Lutz*   92

I'm Not That Kind of Girl   *Marthayn Pelegrimas*   99

The Main Event   *Peter Crowther*   109

Obeah, My Love   *Barbara Collins*   117

Cracked Rear View   *Jerry Sykes*   132

Pretty Eyes   *Evan Hunter*   143

Graveyard Shift   *James Reasoner*   151

Amy Gdalla   *Jim Combs*   155

A Matter of Principle   *Max Allan Collins*   165

Famous Blue Raincoat   *Ed Gorman*   177

Morning Call   *Brian Lawrence*   190

The Case of the Locked Room Nude   *Maxim Jakubowski*   202

That Summer at Quichiquois   *Dorothy B. Hughes*   214

Alas, My Love   *Ron Goulart*   236

Firetrap   *Greg Cox*   253

The Calculator   *Joe Hensley*   276

A Soda for Susan   *Richard Deming*   288

Hot Eyes, Cold Eyes   *Lawrence Block*   295

He Loved Her So Much   *Sandra Scoppettone*   303

Midnight Promises   *Richard T. Chizmar*   312

The New Girl Friend   *Ruth Rendell*   319

The Quiet Room   *Jonathan Craig*   330

My Heart Cries for You   *Bill Crider*   339

The Best-Friend Murder   *Donald Westlake*   362

INTRODUCTION

■ ■ ■

Love kills.

Not a nice thing to say but love *does* kill. Sometimes, anyway.

The husband who bludgeons the wife. The mother who smothers the child with undue attention. The boyfriend who kills the other boyfriend the girl has been seeing.

Love kills.

We've collected here an anthology that expresses and examines this theme in many, many different ways.

There is the thoughtful, reflective take on the theme by Dorothy B. Hughes. The wry and sad take by Nancy Pickard. The unexpected and chilling take by Richard Deming. And the soul-weary, almost Simenonesque take by Donald Westlake.

And many, many more.

Here you'll find some of your favorite writers at their absolute best, writing about the one thing most of can't live without.

Love.

The greatest of all reasons to live.

And die.

Love Kills

AFRAID ALL THE TIME

Nancy Pickard

Nancy Pickard's "Jenny Cain" books are among the most successful and critically acclaimed mystery novels being published today. Mystery Scene magazine noted that she has "managed to combine elements of the cozy with elements of the modern noir." No small feat.

Here is Nancy Pickard at her very best in this somber story of love turned hateful.

"RIBBON A DARKNESS OVER ME . . ."

Mel Brown, known variously as Pell Mell and Animel, sang the line from the song over and over behind his windshield as he flew from Missouri into Kansas on his old black Harley-Davidson motorcycle.

Already he loved Kansas, because the highway that stretched ahead of him was like a long, flat, dark ribbon unfurled just for him.

"Ribbon a darkness over me . . ."

He flew full throttle into the late-afternoon glare, feeling as if he were soaring gloriously drunk and blind on a skyway to the sun. The clouds in the far distance looked as if they'd rain on him that night, but he didn't worry about it. He'd heard there were plenty of empty farm and ranch houses in Kansas where a man could break in to spend the night. He'd heard it was like having your choice of free motels, Kansas was.

"Ribbon a darkness over me . . ."

■   ■   ■

Three hundred miles to the southwest, Jane Baum suddenly stopped what she was doing. The fear had hit her again. It was always like that, striking out of nowhere, like a fist against her heart. She dropped her clothes basket from rigid fingers and stood as if paralyzed between the two clotheslines in her yard. There was a wet sheet to her right, another to her left. For once the wind had died down, so the sheets hung as still and silent as walls. She felt enclosed in a narrow, white, sterile room of cloth, and she never wanted to leave it.

Outside of it was danger.

On either side of the sheets lay the endless prairie where she felt like a tiny mouse exposed to every hawk in the sky.

It took all of her willpower not to scream.

She hugged her own shoulders to comfort herself. It didn't help. Within a few moments she was crying, and then shaking with a palsy of terror.

She hadn't known she'd be so afraid.

Eight months ago, before she had moved to this small farm she'd inherited, she'd had romantic notions about it, even about such simple things as hanging clothes on a line. It would feel so good, she had imagined, they would smell so sweet. Instead, everything had seemed strange and threatening to her from the start, and it was getting worse. Now she didn't even feel protected by the house. She was beginning to feel as if it were fear instead of electricity that lighted her lamps, filled her tub, lined her cupboards and covered her bed—fear that she breathed instead of air.

She hated the prairie and everything on it.

The city had never frightened her, not like this. She knew the city, she understood it, she knew how to avoid its dangers and its troubles. In the city there were buildings everywhere, and now she knew why—it was to blot out the true and terrible openness of the earth on which all of the inhabitants were so horribly exposed to danger.

The wind picked up again. It snapped the wet sheets against her body. Janie bolted from her shelter. Like a mouse with a hawk circling overhead, she ran as if she were being chased. She ran out of her yard and then down the highway, racing frantically, breathlessly, for the only other shelter she knew.

When she reached Cissy Johnson's house, she pulled open the side door and flung herself inside without knocking.

"Cissy?"

■   ■   ■

"I'm afraid all the time."

"I know, Janie."

Cissy Johnson stood at her kitchen sink peeling potatoes for supper while she listened to Jane Baum's familiar litany of fear. By now Cissy knew it by heart. Janie was afraid of: being alone in the house she had inherited from her aunt; the dark; the crack of every twig in the night; the storm cellar; the horses that might step on her, the cows that might trample her, the chickens that might peck her, the cats that might bite her and have rabies, the coyotes that might attack her; the truckers who drove by her house, especially the flirtatious ones who blasted their horns when they saw her in the yard; tornadoes, blizzards, electrical storms; having to drive so far just to get simple groceries and supplies.

At first Cissy had been sympathetic, offering daily doses of coffee and friendship. But it was getting harder all the time to remain patient with somebody who just burst in without knocking and who complained all the time about imaginary problems and who—

"You've lived here all your life," Jane said, as if the woman at the sink had not previously been alert to that fact. She sat in a kitchen chair, huddled into herself like a child being punished. Her voice was low, as if she were talking more to herself than to Cissy. "You're used to it, that's why it doesn't scare you."

"Um," Cissy murmured, as if agreeing. But out of her neighbor's sight, she dug viciously at the eye of a potato. She rooted it out—leaving behind a white, moist, open wound in the vegetable—and flicked the dead black skin into the sink where the water running from the faucet washed it down the garbage disposal. She thought how she'd like to pour Janie's fears down the sink and similarly grind them up and flush them away. She held the potato to her nose and sniffed, inhaling the crisp, raw smell.

Then, as if having gained strength from that private moment, she glanced back over her shoulder at her visitor. Cissy was ashamed of the fact that the mere sight of Jane Baum now repelled her. It was a crime, really, how she'd let herself go. She wished Jane would comb her hair, pull her shoulders back, paint a little coloring onto her pale face, and wear something else besides that ugly denim jumper that came nearly to her heels. Cissy's husband, Bob, called Janie "Cissy's pup," and he called that jumper the "pup tent." He was right, Cissy thought, the woman did look like an insecure, spotty adolescent, and not at all like a grown woman of thirty-five-plus years. And darn it, Janie did follow Cissy around like a neurotic nuisance of a puppy.

"Is Bob coming back tonight?" Jane asked.

Now she's even invading my mind, Cissy thought. She whacked resentfully at the potato, peeling off more meat than skin. "Tomorrow." Her shoulders tensed.

"Then can I sleep over here tonight?"

"No." Cissy surprised herself with the shortness of her reply. She could practically feel Janie radiating hurt, and so she tried to make up for it by softening her tone. "I'm sorry, Janie, but I've got too much book work to do, and it's hard to concentrate with people in the house. I've even told the girls they can take their sleeping bags to the barn tonight to give me some peace." The girls were her daughters, Tessie, thirteen, and Mandy, eleven. "They want to spend the night out there 'cause we've got that new little blind calf we're nursing. His mother won't have anything to do with him, poor little thing. Tessie has named him Flopper, because he tries to stand up but he just flops back down. So the girls are bottle-feeding him, and they want to sleep near . . ."

"Oh." It was heavy with reproach.

Cissy stepped away from the sink to turn her oven on to 350°. Her own internal temperature was rising too. God forbid she should talk about her life! God forbid they should ever talk about anything but Janie and all the damned things she was scared of! She could write a book about it: *How Jane Baum Made a Big Mistake by Leaving Kansas City and How Everything About the Country Just Scared Her to Death.*

"Aren't you afraid of anything, Cissy?"

The implied admiration came with a bit of a whine to it—*any*thing—like a curve on a fastball.

"Yes." Cissy drew out the word reluctantly.

"You *are*? What?"

Cissy turned around at the sink and laughed self-consciously. "It's so silly . . . I'm even afraid to mention it."

"Tell me! I'll feel better if I know you're afraid of things, too."

There! Cissy thought. *Even my fears come down to how they affect you!*

"All right." She sighed. "Well, I'm afraid of something happening to Bobby, a wreck on the highway or something, or to one of the girls, or my folks, things like that. I mean, like leukemia or a heart attack or something I can't control. I'm always afraid there won't be enough money and we might have to sell this place. We're so happy here. I guess I'm afraid that might change." She paused, dismayed by the sudden realization that she had not been as happy since Jane Baum moved in down the road. For a moment, she stared accusingly at her neighbor. "I guess that's what I'm afraid of." Then Cissy added deliberately, "But I don't think about it all the time."

"I think about mine all the time," Jane whispered.

"I know."

"I hate it here!"

"You could move back."

Janie stared reproachfully. "You know I can't afford that!"

Cissy closed her eyes momentarily. The idea of having to listen to *this* for who knew how many years . . .

"I love coming over here," Janie said wistfully, as if reading Cissy's mind again. "It always makes me feel so much better. This is the only place I feel safe anymore. I just hate going home to the big old house all by myself."

I will not *invite you to supper,* Cissy thought.

Janie sighed.

Cissy gazed out the big square window behind Janie. It was October, her favorite month, when the grass turned as red as the curly hair on a Hereford's back and the sky turned a steel gray like the highway that ran between their houses. It was as if the whole world blended into itself—the grass into the cattle, the roads into the sky, and she into all of it. There was an electricity in the air, as if something more important than winter were about to happen, as if all the world were one and about to burst apart into something brand-new. Cissy loved the prairie, and it hurt her feelings a little that Janie didn't. How could anyone live in the middle of so much beauty, she puzzled, and be frightened of it?

∎ ∎ ∎

"We'll never get a better chance." Tess ticked off the rationale for the adventure by holding up the fingers of her right hand, one at a time, an inch from her sister's scared face. "Dad's gone. We're in the barn. Mom'll be asleep. It's a new moon." She ran out of fingers on that hand and lifted her left thumb. "And the dogs know us."

"They'll find out!" Mandy wailed.

"*Who'll* find out?"

"Mom and Daddy will!"

"They won't! Who's gonna tell 'em? The gas-station owner? You think we left a trail of toilet paper he's going to follow from his station to here? And he's gonna call the sheriff and say lock up those Johnson girls, boys, they stole my toilet paper!"

"Yes!"

Together they turned to gaze—one of them with pride and cunning, the other with pride and trepidation—at the small hill of hay that was piled, for no apparent reason, in the shadows of a far corner of the barn. Underneath that pile lay their collection of six rolls of toilet paper—a new one filched from their own linen closet, and five partly used ones (stolen one trip at a time and hidden in their school jackets) from the ladies' bathroom at the gas station in town. Tess's plan was for the two of them to "t.p." their neighbor's house that night, after dark. Tess had lovely visions of how it would look—all ghostly and spooky, with streamers of white hanging down from the tree limbs and waving eerily in the breeze.

"They do it all the time in Kansas City, jerk," Tess proclaimed. "And I'll bet they don't make any big deal crybaby deal out of it." She wanted to be the first one in her class to do it, and she wasn't about to let her little sister chicken out on her. This plan would, Tess was sure, make her famous in at least a four-county area. No grown-up would ever figure out who had done it, but all the kids would know, even if she had to tell them.

"Mom'll kill us!"

"Nobody'll know!"

"It's gonna rain!"

"It's not gonna rain."

"We shouldn't leave Flopper!"

Now they looked, together, at the baby bull calf in one of the stalls. It stared blindly in the direction of their voices, tried to rise, but was too frail to do it.

"Don't be a dope. We leave him all the time."

Mandy sighed.

Tess, who recognized the sound of surrender when she heard it, smiled magnanimously at her sister.

"You can throw the first roll," she offered.

■   ■   ■

In a truck stop in Emporia, Mel Brown slopped up his supper gravy with the last third of a cloverleaf roll. He had a table by a window. As he ate, he stared with pleasure at his bike outside. If he moved his head just so, the rays from the setting sun flashed off the handle bars. He thought about how the leather seat and grips would feel soft and warm and supple, the way a woman in leather felt, when he got back on. At the thought he got a warm feeling in his crotch, too, and he smiled.

God, he loved living like this.

When he was hungry, he ate. When he was tired, he slept. When he was horny, he found a woman. When he was thirsty, he stopped at a bar.

Right now Mel felt like not paying the entire $5.46 for this lousy chicken-fried steak dinner and coffee. He pulled four dollar bills out of his wallet and a couple of quarters out of his right front pocket and set it all out on the table, with the money sticking out from under the check.

Mel got up and walked past the waitress.

"It's on the table," he told her.

"No cherry pie?" she asked him.

It sounded like a proposition, so he grinned as he said, "Nah." *If you weren't so ugly*, he thought, *I just might stay for dessert.*

"Come again," she said.

You wish, he thought.

If they called him back, he'd say he couldn't read her handwriting. Her fault. No wonder she didn't get a tip. Smiling, he lifted a toothpick off the cashier's counter and used it to salute the man behind the cash register.

"Thanks," the man said.

"You bet."

Outside, Mel stood in the parking lot and stretched, shoving his arms high in the air, letting anybody who was watching get a good look at him. Nothin' to hide. Eat your heart out, baby. Then he strolled over to his bike and kicked the stand up with his heel. He poked around his mouth with the toothpick, spat out a sliver of meat, then flipped the toothpick onto the ground. He climbed back on his bike, letting out a breath of satisfaction when his butt hit the warm leather seat.

Mel accelerated slowly, savoring the surge of power building between his legs.

■   ■   ■

Jane Baum was in bed by 10:30 that night, exhausted once again by her own fear. Lying there in her late aunt's double bed, she obsessed on the mistake she had made in moving to this dreadful, empty place in the middle of nowhere. She had expected to feel nervous for a while, as any other city dweller might who moved to the country. But she hadn't counted on being actually phobic about it—of being possessed by a fear so strong that it seemed to inhabit every cell of her body until at night, every night, she felt she could die from it. She hadn't known—how could she have known?—she would be one of those people who is terrified by the vastness of the prairie. She had visited the farm only a few times as a child, and from those visits she had remembered only warm and fuzzy things like caterpillars and chicks. She had only dimly remembered how antlike a human being feels on the prairie.

Her aunt's house had been broken into twice during the period between her aunt's death and her own occupancy. That fact cemented her fantasies in a foundation of terrifying reality. When Cissy said, "It's your imagination," Janie retorted, "But it happened twice before! Twice!" She wasn't making it up! There *were* strange, brutal men—that's how she imagined them, they were never caught by the police—who broke in and took whatever they wanted—cans in the cupboard, the radio in the kitchen. It could happen again, Janie thought obsessively as she lay in the bed; it could happen over and over. *To me, to me, to me.*

On the prairie, the darkness seemed absolute to her. There were millions of stars but no streetlights. Coyotes howled, or cattle bawled. Occasionally the big night-riding semis whirred by out front. Their tire and engine sounds seemed to come out of nowhere, build to an intolerable whine and then disappear in an uncanny way. She pictured the drivers as big, rough, intense men hopped up on amphetamines; she worried that one night she would hear truck tires turning into her gravel drive, that an engine would switch off, that a truck door would quietly open and then close, that careful footsteps would slur across her gravel.

Her fear had grown so huge, so bad, that she was even frightened of it. It was like a monstrous balloon that inflated every time she breathed. Every night the fear got worse. The balloon got bigger. It nearly filled the bedroom now.

The upstairs bedroom where she lay was hot because she had the windows pulled down and latched, and the curtains drawn. She could have cooled it with a fan on the dressing table, but she was afraid the fan's noise might cover the sound of whatever might break into the first floor and climb the stairs to attack her. She lay with a sheet and a blanket pulled up over her arms and shoulders, to just under her chin. She was sweating, as if her fear-frozen body were melting, but it felt warm and almost comfortable to her. She always wore pajamas and thin wool socks to bed because she felt safer when she was completely dressed. She especially felt more secure in pajama pants, which no dirty hand could shove up onto her belly as it could a nightgown.

Lying in bed like a quadriplegic, unmoving, eyes open, Janie reviewed her precautions. Every door was locked, every window was permanently shut and locked, so that she didn't have to check them every night; all the curtains were drawn; the porch lights were off; and her car was locked in the barn so no trucker would think she was home.

Lately she had taken to sleeping with her aunt's loaded pistol on the pillow beside her head.

■　■　■

Cissy crawled into bed just before midnight, tired from hours of accounting. She had been out to the barn to check on her giggling girls and the blind calf. She had talked to her husband when he called from Oklahoma City. Now she was thinking about how she would try to start easing Janie Baum out of their lives.

"I'm sorry, Janie, but I'm awfully busy today. I don't think you ought to come over . . ."

Oh, but there would be that meek, martyred little voice, just like a baby mouse needing somebody to mother it. How would she deny that need? She was already feeling guilty about refusing Janie's request to sleep over.

"Well, I will. I just will do it, that's all. If I could say no to the FHA girls when they were selling fruitcakes, I can start saying no more often to Janie Baum. Anyway, she's never going to get over her fears if I indulge them."

Bob had said as much when she'd complained to him long-distance. "Cissy, you're not helping her," he'd said. "You're just letting her get worse." And then he'd said something new that had disturbed her. "Anyway, I don't like the girls being around her so much. She's getting too weird, Cissy."

She thought of her daughters—of fearless Tess and dear little Mandy—and of how *safe* and *nice* it was for children in the country. . . .

"Besides," Bob had said, "she's *got* to do more of her own chores. We need Tess and Mandy to help out around our place more; we can't be having them always running off to mow her grass and plant her flowers and feed her cows and water her horse and get her eggs, just because she's scared to stick her silly hand under a damned hen. . . ."

Counting the chores put Cissy to sleep.

·   ·   ·

"Tess!" Mandy hissed desperately. "Wait!"

The older girl slowed, to give Mandy time to catch up to her, and then to touch Tess for reassurance. They paused for a moment to catch their breath and to crouch in the shadow of Jane Baum's porch. Tess carried three rolls of toilet paper in a make-shift pouch she'd formed in the belly of her black sweatshirt. ("We gotta wear black, remember!") and Mandy was similarly equipped. Tess decided that now was the right moment to drop her bomb.

"I've been thinking," she whispered.

Mandy was struck cold to her heart by that familiar and dreaded phrase. She moaned quietly. "What?"

"It might rain."

"I told you!"

"So I think we better do it inside."

"*Inside?*"

"Shh! It'll scare her to death, it'll be great! Nobody else'll ever have the guts to do anything as neat as this! We'll do the kitchen, and if we have time, maybe the dining room."

"Ohhh, noooo."

"*She* thinks she's got all the doors and windows locked, but she doesn't!" Tess giggled. She had it all figured out that when Jane Baum came downstairs in the morning, she'd take one look, scream, faint, and then, when she woke up, call everybody in town. The fact that Jane might also call the sheriff had occurred to her, but since Tess didn't have any faith in the ability of adults to figure out anything important, she wasn't worried about getting caught. "When I took in her eggs, I unlocked the downstairs bathroom window! Come on! This'll be great!"

■   ■   ■

The ribbon of darkness ahead of Mel Brown was no longer straight. It was now bunched into long, steep hills. He hadn't expected hills. Nobody had told him there was any part of Kansas that wasn't flat. So he wasn't making as good time, and he couldn't run full-bore. But then, he wasn't in a hurry, except for the hell of it. And this was more interesting, more dangerous, and he liked the thrill of that. He started edging closer to the centerline every time he roared up a hill, playing a game of highway roulette in which he was the winner as long as whatever coming from the other direction had its headlights on.

When that got boring, he turned his own headlights off.

Now he roared past cars and trucks like a dark demon.

Mel laughed every time, thinking how surprised they must be, and how frightened. They'd think, *Crazy fool, I could have hit him. . . .*

He supposed he wasn't afraid of anything, except maybe going back to prison, and he didn't think they'd send him down on a speeding ticket. Besides, if Kansas was like most states, it was long on roads and short on highway patrolmen. . . .

Roaring downhill was even more fun, because of the way his stomach dropped out. He felt like a kid, yelling "Fuuuuck," all the way down the other side. What a goddamned roller coaster of a state this was turning out to be.

The rain still looked miles away.

Mel felt as if he could ride all night. Except that his eyes were gritty, the first sign that he'd better start looking for a likely place

to spend the night. He wasn't one to sleep under the stars, not if
he could find a ceiling.

· · ·

Tess directed her sister to stack the rolls of toilet paper underneath the bathroom window on the first floor of Jane Baum's
house. The six rolls, all white, stacked three in a row, two high,
gave Tess the little bit of height and leverage she needed to push
up the glass with her palms. She stuck her fingers under the bottom edge and laboriously attempted to raise the window. It was
stiff in its coats of paint.

"Damn!" she exclaimed, and let her arms slump. Beneath her
feet, the toilet paper was getting squashed.

She tried again, and this time she showed her strength from
lifting calves and tossing hay. With a crack of paint and a thump
of wood on wood, the window slid all the way up.

"Shhh!" Mandy held her fists in front of her face and knocked
her knuckles against each other in excitement and agitation. Her
ears picked up the sound of a roaring engine on the highway, and
she was immediately sure it was the sheriff, coming to arrest her
and Tess. She tugged frantically at the calf of her sister's right leg.

Tess jerked her leg out of Mandy's grasp and disappeared
through the open window.

· · ·

The crack of the window and the thunder of the approaching
motorcycle confused themselves in Jane's sleeping consciousness,
so that when she awoke from dreams full of anxiety—her eyes
flying open, the rest of her body frozen—she imagined in a confused, hallucinatory kind of way that somebody was both coming
to get her and already there in the house.

Jane then did as she had trained herself to do. She had practiced
over and over every night, so that her actions would be instinctive.
She turned her face to the pistol on the other pillow and placed
her thumb on the trigger.

Her fear—of rape, of torture, of kidnapping, of agony, of
death—was a balloon, and she floated horribly in the center of it.
There were thumps and other sounds downstairs, and they joined
her in the balloon. There was an engine roaring, and then suddenly it was silent, and a slurring of wheels in her gravel drive,

and these sounds joined her in her balloon. When she couldn't bear it any longer, she popped the balloon by shooting herself in the forehead.

■ ■ ■

In the driveway, Mel Brown heard the gun go off.

He slung his leg back onto his motorcycle and roared back out onto the highway. So the place had looked empty. So he'd been wrong. So he'd find someplace else. But holy shit. Get the fuck outta here.

■ ■ ■

Inside the house, in the bathroom, Tess also heard the shot and, being a ranch child, recognized it instantly for what it was, although she wasn't exactly sure where it had come from. Cussing and sobbing, she clambered over the sink and back out the window, falling onto her head and shoulders on the rolls of toilet paper.

"It's the sheriff!" Mandy was hysterical. "He's shooting at us!"

Tess grabbed her little sister by a wrist and pulled her away from the house. They were both crying and stumbling. They ran in the drainage ditch all the way home and flung themselves into the barn.

Mandy ran to lie beside the little blind bull calf. She lay her head on Flopper's side. When he didn't respond, she jerked to her feet. She glared at her sister.

"He's dead!"

"Shut up!"

■ ■ ■

Cissy Johnson had awakened, too, although she hadn't known why. Something, some noise, had stirred her. And now she sat up in bed, breathing hard, frightened for no good reason she could fathom. If Bob had been home, she'd have sent him out to the barn to check on the girls. But why? The girls were all right, they must be, this was just the result of a bad dream. But she didn't remember having any such dream.

Cissy got out of bed and ran to the window.

No, it wasn't a storm, the rain hadn't come.

A motorcycle!

That's what she'd heard, that's what had awakened her!

Quickly, with nervous fingers, Cissy put on a robe and tennis shoes. Darn you, Janie Baum, she thought, your fears are contagious, that's what they are. The thought popped into her head: If you don't have fears, they can't come true.

Cissy raced out to the barn.

THE GIRL FRIEND

Morris Hershman

This story should be studied by all people who write, or would like to write, short stories.

It is a unique way of dealing with material that would otherwise be merely sensational. And it certainly remains with you long after the telling is over.

Morris Hershman has been a professional writer for many years. This is one of his very best pieces.

"FOURTEEN YEARS OLD!" BANNER'S VOICE WAS HOLLOW. HE held up the pocket snapshot that had just been passed to him. "A face like a dream, pretty blonde hair and all."

Mill dropped his feet from the desk, swivelled back in his chair and nodded slowly. "An average case as far as I'm concerned. You're going to prosecute it, Mr. Assistant District Attorney, so you might as well get the facts straight."

"What did she do, this girl?"

Mill crossed one foot over the other and rubbed it with thumb and forefinger. "It's quite a story. We had to ask a lot of questions to get the real answers. We wanted to know *why* she did it. Maybe you'd like to know about the why, first." He sighed. "Being a cop is such a rough job on the nerves because a cop can't afford to have nerves."

Mill liked to make little speeches about what it took to be a cop. In the years that Banner had known him, four or five, it happened at least once whenever they met. They weren't close friends; Mill couldn't talk about much but a cop's job. He seemed to have no outside interests at all.

"If you look this over," Mill said, pointing to a number of typewritten sheets clipped together, "you'll get some idea. What you got to know about a girl like this is that it's not all her fault, no matter what kind of nasty thing she did."

Banner picked up the sheets and settled them in his lap. They were in question-and-answer form. The girl's name was Alice King.

Q: How old are you, honey?

A: Fourteen. Fourteen, last December.

Q: What school do you go to, Alice?

A: Marley Junior High.

Q: You get good grades?

A: B's and B-plusses.

Q: Do you have a lot of boy friends?

A: No!

Banner frowned at the pocket-size photograph. "Good-looking kid. Why's she so quick to say she hasn't got a lot of boy friends?"

Mill scratched his foot again, then the back of an ear. He lit a cigar and puffed until it was drawing nicely. "Nothing else she could say. Of course at the time I didn't know it, myself. Don't forget we had just picked her up a little while before."

It had grown dark, and Mill flicked on the desk lamp. In the building, on three sides of them, men scurried back and forth. Outside the window, a pink dot could be seen far away, apparently the bathroom of a private home. Close to it was a larger window with blinds down, and bright light glaring out through a wider slit at the top.

"That kid," Mill said suddenly. "She ought to have been having the time of her life, going to proms and things. At that age, a girl's just finding out that she *is* a girl, and she sure as hell likes the idea."

Banner shrugged, then looked down to the sheet that was now on top.

A: No!

Q: Did you ever have a job, Alice?

A: You mean a job where I worked outside my house?

Q: That's right.

A: Only part-time. I worked in a department store for a while, but the job didn't last.

Q: Why not?

A: They were stingy—cheap, you know—and they kept me

working after hours and wouldn't pay me extra for that. My mother said it was practically white slavery. She told them off.

Q: And after your mother told them off, you left the job?

A: I was fired.

Q: What kind of a job did you get then, Alice?

Banner looked up, frowning. "The mother sounds like a louse. Alice doesn't want to talk about her."

"If you ask me," Mill shrugged, "the mother's a good-natured, hearty, heavy drinking, foolish woman. Maybe that's why the kid— go on reading, Ban, you'll see."

Q: What kind of a job did you get then, Alice?

A: In a dress shop, but just about the same thing happened. So my mother said I ought to work for her. She said she'd pay me ten dollars a week if I'd keep the house nice and clean before she—uh, worked.

Q: Sounds like a soft touch.

A: It was okay, for a while.

Q: What went sour?

A: I might as well tell you. Usually, mother kept me away from the house till half-past twelve at night. I'd stay over at a girl friend's place. But sometimes I had trouble with some of the customers. One of them, a Mr. Dail, sees mother twice a week. He happened to come in a little earlier once when I was cleaning. Mr. Dail took one look at me and said to mother: "I'd pay twenty dollars for just a half hour with her."

Q: What did your mother say?

A: She said no. She said she wouldn't let her kid do that. But Mr. Dail, he kept talking about it and after a few minutes, mother said that the rent was coming up in a few days and she was paying more than usual for protection. To the cops, I mean.

Q: So you went into the bedroom with Mr. Dail?

A: Mother said I wouldn't have any trouble. When Mr. Dail and I, the two of us, were finished, she was making jokes about it. All the time we were in there, though, she sat outside sobbing a little.

Banner, looking up, caught Mill's drily amused eyes. He avoided them, stood and walked to the window. The pinkish bathroom light far away had been put out. The sounds of routine police business had increased in tempo.

Finally, after swallowing quickly, Banner asked: "Did Alice King turn pro?"

The cop, openly pleased by Banner's interest, pointed to the sheets. "Read the q-and-a, you'll see." He added thoughtfully, "You know, I don't think you can imagine what the kid was like. Very refined, always smoothing down her skirt. When she asked for a glass of water she tacked on, 'please.' Never blamed her crime on circumstances or said she was victimized. In fact, a good kid. Like your daughter would be, if you had one."

Q: Did you do it with other men, Alice?

A: Sometimes. Mother always told them I was twelve and a virgin. She always charged more money for me than for herself. Up to twenty-five dollars. After it was over, she would give me five dollars for myself. Mother wouldn't let me do it more than twice a week.

Q: How many men would you say you've slept with, Alice?

A: I don't know.

Q: Ten? Is it that many?

A: I don't know.

Q: Twenty?

A: I don't know.

Q: Thirty? Forty? Fifty? Give me a number that's close to the truth, Alice.

A: Fifty, maybe.

Mill said, "You can skip the part where she gives names. The Vice Squad boys have picked up the ones she remembers, and they're in for a bad time. Your boss, the D.A., he'll see to that."

Banner said quietly: "At least I know now what you're holding the girl for. Delinquency. An easy case to prosecute. In her set-up, it could have been something worse."

"It was. It is." Mill looked intently at the tip of his cigar, talked slowly to it. "A hell of a lot worse."

In spite of himself, Banner lowered his head.

Mill added: "Alice King has good stuff in her, as a person. You take the average fourteen-year-old girl and put her in that spot and she becomes like the mother, you know—shiftless, lazy, vain, a stupid slob. Alice didn't."

Banner glanced at the snapshot.

"I don't mean just for looks," Mill said a little impatiently. "There's other things in a kid's life. Alice King kept up her grades at Marley Junior High, even improved them in one case. She started to appreciate ballet and modern dance. She did some dating. Normal, in other words, except for what she did twice a week."

Banner looked a little sadly at the picture. Suddenly he stiffened and set it face down on the desk. He was flushed.

Mill smiled. "Thinking you'd like to jump the kid yourself, I bet!" More seriously he added, "One of the hard things about being a cop is that you can excuse the bad in most people because it's in you, too . . . Give me the sheets, will you, for a minute?"

Banner slowly handed them across. The cop turned four pages, his wet thumb driving a crease into every one, then a fifth.

"Here it is. Where she meets Ronald Hutchinson."

Banner's lip curled. "Another customer?"

"Another kid. Fifteen, in fact. I found out a lot about him. A big wheel at Marley Junior High: baseball team in summer and football in winter, editor of the school paper, member of Arista, student president of the G.O. And rich, too. Lot of dough in the family. Old man is president of a chain of supermarkets."

"The kid sounds like a snob."

"No." Mill shook his big head determinedly, and tapped a crown of ash off the cigar. "Nice, healthy kid with a lot of girl friends. A good-looking kid with nice manners."

Q: How did you come to meet Ronald Hutchinson?

A: I went out for the school paper.

Q: Oh, you volunteered to work for it.

A: That's right. I thought I wanted to be a reporter when I grow up, so I took a crack at it. Ron was the student editor. We hit it off, all right. We liked each other. We laughed at the same things and had a lot in common. I always think that's very important with a boy and girl.

Q: Tell me what happened between you two.

A: Nothing did, at the start. I knew he'd want to take me out, but I didn't rush him. He waited two weeks. There was going to be a dance in the gym at school on Saturday night and he asked me to go with him. I said I would.

Q: Did he call you at home?

A: No, I never want boys to call me at home. It can get confusing.

Q: How did your mother feel about your taking off Saturday night?

A: Mother said it was fine, because she wants me to have good times. She doesn't want to interfere with my social life.

Q: That's for sure. So you and Ron Hutchinson hit it off, I suppose.

A: The first date, at the dance, was very sweet. Ron couldn't samba, so a bunch of us showed him. It was a lot of fun. After that, I saw him in school. It got so that we used to hold hands over the lockers in our "official" rooms. That means the rooms where students do things as a class, you know, according to what the principal wants.

Q: You were dating Ron pretty heavily?

A: We had a few cheap dates, first. We'd meet at the ice cream parlor and he'd buy me a soda and we'd sit and talk. We had an awful lot in common. Once in a while we'd go see a movie and hold hands. Then he'd walk home with me and say goodnight a block from the house. I never let boys call for me at the house.

Q: You didn't mind the cheap dates?

A: No, they were fun. Ron said that the whole town knew about his being rich, so he didn't have to impress girls by flashing a roll. A *bank*roll, he meant.

Q: In other words, you had nothing against Ron Hutchinson.

A: That's right, nothing.

Q: No grudge of any kind.

A: Of course not.

Q: Did you think you were in love with him?

A: I suppose so.

Q: You were serious about him, then?

A: Yes. Almost praying I could keep him interested till I was eighteen, so we could get married. That shows you what a fool I was!

Q: Why a fool?

A: On account of what happened.

Q: How many times a week did you see him?

A: Two, three.

Q: How did your mother feel about that?

A: At first she thought it was very nice and she told me not to give away anything, if you know what I mean. Then she said I ought to be home at nights, to work if I had to. She said expenses were going up and I ought to be paying a bigger share of my upkeep.

Q: How did you feel about that?

A: I wanted to get a job in a store, instead, but my mother didn't want that.

Q: The two of you argued?

A: Yes. I started to get sick when I had to use the bedroom with one of the customers. Sometimes I'd throw up or say that I had cramps.

Q: Tell me about last night—Saturday night.

A: Mother was a little under the weather. She wanted me to stay with one of our customers. The man came in, Mr. Cameron, and I just got sick when I saw him. I started to cry. Mother got angry, but when she saw she was licked anyhow, she told me to go.

Q: You had a date with Ron?

A: We were headed for a party over a friend of his' house.

Q: How about the knife, Alice? How come you took a pocket-knife along with you on a date?

Banner caught his breath.

A: My mother thinks its a good idea to bring one, in case a girl gets into a spot where she needs a little help. Mother isn't like most people, you know, and she always tells me to be very careful when I go out on a date and never go beyond necking. When we're alone, she calls the customers animals. She always warns me that men are after one thing and a girl has to use any way possible to keep—well, you know.

Q: And you believe that?

A: Mother's had more experience than me.

Q: So you took a pocketknife along on every date?

A: Most of them. It came in handy for little things, you know, like cutting open envelopes. I never had to use it to scare off a boy. Not till last night, that is.

Q: Ron made a pass at you?

A: We were at Baker's Lane. You know, a lot of cars stop there

for couples to neck in peace and quiet. Ron had borrowed his
dad's car for the date. He said to me. "What about it, honey?"
He put a hand under my dress and started slowly unbuttoning it
from behind. Like one of the customers does, Mr. Strawbridge,
that is. Anyhow, I tried to stop Ron. I said: "I'm not one of those
girls." And to make a joke out of it, to show I meant it for a joke,
I pulled out the pocketknife and said: "Better not." Of course I
said it in such a way he was sure it was a joke.

Q: He didn't give up trying, did he?

A: No. He was very calm, very patient, very sure of himself and
sure what would happen. Like a customer. Any customer. I was
sitting there with my knuckles in my mouth to keep from making
a sound. Then Ron fumbled with something in his breast pocket
and brought out a wallet and spread it open. He said very seriously: "I hope you'll let me buy things for you, and make life easier
for you. A girl and her mother alone always have a rough time,"
he glanced down at my dress, my best dress, "and I'd be glad to
help. The money doesn't mean a thing to me." And all the time
he was running a thumb over the bills in his wallet just like one
of the customers before he pays. Just like Mr. Dail. The exact
same . . .

Q: All right, all right! We'll pick up the questioning later on.
The way you're crying, a person would think I'd belted you one.
Strike that!

Mill said thoughtfully: "She was in love with rich-boy Ron and,
when he offered to buy her, just like one of the customers would,
she acted blindly with the knife."

One of Mill's hands stiffened in a fist; he stuck out a forefinger
and stabbed it suddenly against his heart.

Banner stared at the finger, then quickly looked away.

PREDATORS

Edward Bryant

"While She Was Out" was probably the best crime story published in the 1980s.
This one, in a completely different way, is just as good.
Ed Bryant has long been celebrated as a science fiction writer, bringing fresh approaches to the field and its conventions.
But for some, his dark suspense fiction is even better.
This is a first-rate story of urban horror.

HER NOSTRILS WERE CHOKED WITH THE STENCH OF BUS FUMES and all the other myriad odors crushed down into the streets by the winter inversion layer. Another day of looking for work in the city . . . Still no luck.

Lisa Blackwell's first reaction to the person who'd moved in upstairs was bewilderment. She could smell the fresh Dymo label on #12's mailbox in the downstairs hall. It read "R. G. Cross." Evidently the moving in of furniture and whatever other personal belongings had taken place earlier in the day, while Lisa had been hitting the job agencies for interviews.

The afternoon hadn't gone well. Lisa didn't like the cold, cloudy October weather—it looked as if it was going to snow. Worse, she didn't think she had uncovered any good employment leads. It had been weeks now, and the money the missionaries had given her was running out. She didn't want to check the balance in her new checking account. It was so important to make it here . . . Lisa wanted her parents to be proud.

Her apartment had been restful, a quiet refuge, with no one living upstairs. But now she had a neighbor. The first thing she learned about him—Lisa assigned him a gender upon no particularly firm evidence—was his taste in music. It was raucous and simplistic. She felt the vibration as soon as she entered her own apartment and shut the door. Then he punched the volume up. The bass line predominated. From time to time, a buzzsaw treble would slice through the bass. Lisa thought she could see the ceiling vibrate. Her ears hurt.

She decided to endure it. Surely he would get tired, leave, go to sleep, choose a more interesting album. Lisa understood that what she was listening to second-hand was heavy metal. She had learned that she preferred jazz. She loved the intricate rhythms. If worse came to worst, Lisa knew she could call the building managers and complain. That privilege had been explained to her when she'd moved in.

The next thing she discovered about her neighbor was the fact of his sexual activity. At about seven o'clock, Lisa was taking a pound of ground beef out of the refrigerator. The heavy, sweet odor hung in the air. She felt—as well as heard—the stereo upstairs turned down. Then she heard heavy steps clump out onto the third-floor landing and descend. On the ground floor, the foyer door squeaked open. Two sets of footsteps ascended. She heard voices—a treble piping mixed with the bass rumble. The door to apartment 12 banged shut.

It wasn't, Lisa thought, as though she was truly eavesdropping. The building was about fifty years old; the construction, thin to begin with, was loosening up.

The music from above started again, though the volume wasn't as loud as it had been in the afternoon. At eleven, Lisa lay sleepless on her Salvation Army Thrift Store mattress. She needed her rest. Bags beneath her eyes at job interviews . . . no! She had just decided to throw on a robe and go upstairs to ask her new neighbor to turn the volume down when the stereo abruptly shut off. Lisa curled up in a warm ball.

The respite was brief. Sounds began again from upstairs. Since the apartment layouts were identical from floor to floor, her neighbor's bedroom was directly above Lisa's own. R. G. Cross's bedsprings were not subtle. She tried to ignore the rhythm, then pulled the ends of the pillow around her head when she heard private cries.

After a time, the squeaking stopped and the thumping began.

In spite of herself, Lisa wondered what *that* noise meant: a steady, muffled *flump*, *flump*. Something that sounded liquid spattered on the floor above. How weird *was* R. G. Cross?

She didn't wonder long. The sounds stopped for good. Exhausted, homesick, a little lonely, wondering when she would ever get a job in this strange, new city, Lisa fell asleep.

She dreamed of a warm, lazy, savanna summer, and of lush sun-dappled foliage. It was all green and golden and smelled like life itself. She wanted to be again with everyone she'd left, Lisa thought fuzzily. Mama . . .

■   ■   ■

The next day was Saturday. Lisa had no interviews, but she did have a sheaf of application forms to fill out. She hadn't gotten up until noon. Between mild depression keeping her in bed, along with the simultaneous feeling of stolen luxury, she dozed away the morning.

When her eyes finally flickered open for good, her mind registered the time as 11:56. Digital clocks amazed her with their precision. Lisa rolled over on her back and remembered vaguely having been awakened earlier in the morning by angry voices from upstairs. She slowly and luxuriously stretched, then padded toward the bathroom.

Lisa brushed her hair and cleaned her teeth. Then she put on her gloves, terrycloth robe, and slippers, and went downstairs to collect her newspaper. The stairway was chilly, as though someone had left the outer door propped open.

She encountered a tall, blond stranger in the front hall. Lisa scented him before she actually saw him. He smelled of some sharp, citrus cologne.

"Hi, there." He shoved a large, tanned hand at her. "You're my downstairs neighbor, right? I'm Roger."

Lisa glanced at the mailbox and back at him. "R. G. Cross."

"That's me." He grinned widely. For a second, all Lisa could see was the array of flawless white teeth. "Mighty nice to meet you."

His hand overpowered hers. She withdrew her fingers, sensing he could have crushed down much harder. Roger leaned back against the wall and hooked his thumbs in his jeans pockets. He was more than a full head taller than she, though Lisa could stare level into the eyes of most of the men she'd met. He had an athlete's powerful physique. He probably works out every day, she thought. His jaw was strong. Roger's eyes were a bright, cold blue; his hair, tousled and light. His grin didn't seem to vary from second to second by a single millimeter.

Roger unhooked one thumb to gesture at the mailbox. "You must be L. P. Blackwell."

Lisa nodded politely and started to turn toward the steps with her paper.

"What's it stand for?"

"Lisa Penelope."

Roger stuck out one long leg so that his foot partially blocked her exit. "Oh yeah? Could stand for a lot of other things."

Unsure what to do now, Lisa paused at the foot of the stairs. She examined her options. The list was short.

Roger said, "Could stand for Long Playing . . ."

She stiffened, feeling a chill of apprehension.

"Like with a record album." He chuckled at his own joke. "Long playing, all right. Stereo too, probably." He smiled at her expression, then looked slowly and deliberately down the front of her to the floor, and then back up again.

"Excuse me, but I need to get upstairs." Lisa made her voice sound as decisive as she could.

"So what's the hurry?" His voice remained warm and friendly.

"I need to fix breakfast." She regretted saying anything the moment the words came out, but by then it was too late.

"I haven't had breakfast yet either," Roger said. "You like breakfast? I know I do. Best way to start the day."

Lisa looked straight ahead, up the stairwell. She sighed and said nothing. She didn't want this to mean trouble.

"We could do it together," said Roger. "Breakfast. What sort of meat do you like in the morning?"

"Please move your leg." He slowly, with great deliberation, evidently savoring the power of the moment, withdrew his foot from her path. "Thank you." Lisa resisted the impulse to bound up the steps two at a time.

He called after her, "Hey, don't mind me, L. P. I'm feeling good today. Great night, last night. Now I'm just high-spirited, you know?"

Lisa fumbled with her keys. She heard slow, steady steps ascending the staircase. She practically kicked the door open when the latch clicked. Once in the refuge of her apartment, she closed and locked the door. Then she turned the dead-bolt home. She did not want trouble. She had enough on her mind already.

"Damn it," she said under her breath. "Damn them. Why are they like that?"

■   ■   ■

Lisa spent Saturday afternoon filling out job application forms. Unfortunately she recognized her employability problems, not the least of which was her inability to type. After two hours of laborious and exquisitely neat printing, she took a break and made a pot of rich cambric. In rapid succession, she turned on a TV movie, switched if off, picked up a new paperback mystery she'd bought at Safeway, then put it down when she realized she wasn't concentrating on the plot.

Someone knocked at her front door.

Lisa hesitated.

Her building dated back to the late 'twenties or early 'thirties. Lisa's managers had told her that with some pride. This was a building that hadn't been razed to make room for a modern and characterless highrise. Some of the Art Deco touches still remained. About half the renovated apartments had glass spy-tubes in the front doors so that the tenants could scrutinize whatever callers stood on the other side. Lisa's door had something that antedated the tubes. She could open a little hinged metal door set at face height, and look out through a grill of highly stylized palm trees cast in some pewter-colored metal.

If she opened the little door. She hesitated.

There was a second, more insistent knock. She heard the floorboard creaking of someone shifting his weight. She could hear breathing on the other side of the door.

Lisa reached for the latch of the small door and pulled it open. She looked into the apparently eternally grinning face of Roger Cross.

"Oh, hi," he said nonchalantly.

"Hello." Lisa made the word utterly neutral.

"Hey, listen. I want to apologize for sort of coming off the wall before. You know, stepping out of line." Roger met her gaze directly. He reached up with one hand to scratch the back of his head boyishly, tousling the carefully styled blond hair. "I didn't mean to come across as such a turkey. Honest."

"It's all right," said Lisa. She wasn't sure what else to say. "Thanks for saying that."

"Say, could I come in?"

He must have seen something in her expression. Roger quickly added, "You know, just for a little while. I thought maybe we could sit down and talk. Get acquainted. You know, I really want to be a good neighbor." The grin became a sincere smile. "And friends."

Lisa said nothing for a few seconds, trying to get a handle on this. "Not—now, thanks, I'm not ready. I mean I wasn't expecting company and—"

"I don't mind a mess," Roger said. "You should see my place. A real sty."

She momentarily noted his vocabulary and wondered that he knew a word like "sty." He definitely didn't seem rural. But then, she thought, she knew she had never met anyone like this before. "No. Really. We—I can't."

He switched tracks. "Hey, L. P., you living on your own for the first time?"

Startled, Lisa said, "How'd you know that?"

"I thought so. You look pretty young. Going to college?"

She couldn't help responding. "No. I haven't had much formal schooling."

"Neat accent," he said. "I can't quite place it. From the South?"

She nodded. "A ways." *Dappled sunlight on the leaves.* Lisa felt a sudden stab of homesickness like an arrow piercing her side.

"Great winters here. You come north to live so you could ski?"

"No." It had never occurred to her to ski.

"That's why I came here. That and work. I've got a great job with an oil company. Marketing."

Floundering, Lisa said, "That must be . . ."

"Oh yeah, real interesting. Get to work with the public. Meet people." The sincere smile became more engaging. "Say, you come out here to get away from your family?"

"Uh, yes," she said. Lisa felt more pangs, equally painful. *Food, warmth, security, all provided. Her mother's satiny touch.* She suddenly and desperately wanted to see her parents again. She wanted so much to be on her own, but she also needed to be stroked and reassured. For the thousandth time she regretted leaving home.

"I know what it's like," said Roger earnestly. "I've been on my own for a long time. Never knew my father. Mother died when I was real young. Really I've got no family." His voice lowered. "I know it gets real lonely here in the city."

"Yes," said Lisa. "It does."

"Let me make things up," he said. "You want some hot coffee? I've got some great Colombian grind up in my place."

"I drink tea."

"Got all the Celestial Seasonings flavors. Or black, if you want it."

"No thanks," she said. "I just made a pot." Lisa turned her head and glanced across the living room at the pot of cambric slowly cooling beneath the quilted cat-print cozy. "It'll be getting cold, so I'd better go." She thought of the skim forming on the surface of the milk. Lisa turned toward him again. "Excuse me, please."

"Wait!" he said, seeming a little frantic now. "This is important—"

"Yes?"

"Listen, how's your laundry?"

"Beg your pardon?" What *was* he talking about?

"Don't you do your laundry on the weekend?"

"Well, yes." Lisa had lived in the apartment for little more than a month, but already discovered that she hated the laundry room. It was a dark, dank cell in the basement beneath the house next door. The laundry served both buildings, as the two were owned by the same company. The room contained two sets of coin-operated washers and dryers. All the machines were usually in use all the weekend daylight hours. It was a secluded and uncomfortable place at night.

The closest commercial Laundromat was more than a mile away, and Lisa had no car.

"I'm gonna do a load sometime tonight," said Roger. "If I don't, no socks and underwear for Monday morning. If you want to come along and do a load too—" He spread his hands. "I could escort you, make sure no freako jumps out and grabs you. We could get in some civilized conversation down there. Don't you need to wash some clothes?"

Of course she did. Lisa had been putting off the laundry room expedition. She really did need clean clothing for Monday. "Thanks anyway," she said. "I've got to stay in tonight and work. I've got a lot to do."

"I think you're lying," said Roger quietly.

"I really do have—"

"*Lying!*" Roger slammed the heel of his hand against the door. It jumped and rattled in its frame. Lisa involuntarily stepped backward.

"So what's wrong with me, you black bitch?" Roger shoved his face forward so that he blocked the entire opening. It occurred to Lisa that this was like looking out of a wild animal's cage—or into one. There was a fixedness to his eyes that she wondered might be madness. She had done nothing to bring this on herself. *Nothing!*

"Listen, I'm sorry," she said, stepping forward and flipping the little metal door firmly shut. She heard him outside, now speaking to the closed door.

"These doors are old. Not stout at all. I could kick this one down in just two seconds. Just like the big bad wolf . . ."

"Please go 'way," said Lisa. "I'll call the manager."

"You think you're gold, don't you?" His voice was low and intense. She could hear him working into a frenzy. "You think *it's* gold."

"Go. Please."

"You know who I am, Lisa? I'm the boogey man. And I eat up little girls just like that."

Lisa decided that perhaps if she didn't answer him any more, he'd go away.

"So don't answer. I know you're there."

She still said nothing.

"You know who you are?" Roger's chuckle decayed to something horrible. "You're a puckered little prude. I think maybe you need to be loosened up."

Lisa tried to back away from the door quietly, hoping none of the boards in the hardwood floor would creak.

"I hear you! You know what else you are, L. P.? You're a real fruitcake."

She continued to step quietly away from the door.

Roger laughed, almost a giggle. He said, "You're *so* weird, girl. Right out of the sticks—or is it off the plantation? Who else would wear gloves with a terrycloth robe. You—"

He said a string of things she didn't want to hear, including a few she didn't understand. Finally he seemed to run out of obscenities. Roger evidently turned away from the door and his voice became muffled. His deliberate, slow steps clumped upstairs. She heard his door open and slam shut.

Even though he was gone, she still tried to move as quietly as she could toward the couch and the tea cozy. The pot was still warm, so she poured herself a cup of well-steeped cambric. The milky, soothing scent filled the living room.

Lisa Plackwell had never before encountered anyone like Roger Cross. She had heard of them—creatures like him. A danger to their kind. She said to herself softly, "What is wrong with him?" And was confounded by the inexplicable.

■ ■ ■

Later that evening, Lisa heard Roger go out. She listened to the sound of him descending the back stairs, past her kitchen door. Something trailed his footsteps with a series of soft impacts. It made her think of something large and dangerous, dragging its prey. Almost against her will, she went to the kitchen window and looked down as the building's rear door swung open. Roger emerged, dragging a laundry bag.

So he does have a load to wash, she thought. Not that it made any difference. The man was clearly disturbed, a defective individual. Roger rounded the corner of the adjacent house and was lost to sight.

Lisa went into the living room and looked at the number she'd written on the piece of paper taped beside the telephone. She called the managers, a married couple who lived in the house above the laundry room. She got it wrong on the first attempt and had to dial again.

Joanne, the female half of the managerial team, answered the phone and Lisa identified herself.

"Right," said Joanne. "You're in number ten. What can I do for you?"

Lisa hesitated, then gave the woman an abbreviated account of her encounters with Roger, leaving out most of the things he'd said that she didn't want to repeat. It was still enough to kindle concern in Joanne's voice.

"You might be interested in knowing," the manager said, "that you're the second complaint. I heard from the tenant in number two. Our studly friend gave her a come-on too. Nothing as jerk-off as his thing with you, but it was still scummy enough for her to mention it to me." She hesitated. "I only talked to the guy a little when he first came to look at the apartment. He seemed harmless enough then."

Lisa said nothing.

Joanne volunteered, "Listen, if you're really upset tonight, you're welcome to come over here. Joe and I have a couch you can use. You won't have to worry about that guy sneaking around your place."

Lisa considered it. "No," she finally said. "Thank you very much, but no. I'd have to go home sometime. Anyhow, I'm probably just overreacting. I'll go ahead and stay here tonight and keep my door double-locked."

"You're sure? Really, it's no problem if you want to come over."

"Thanks again, Joanne. I'm sure." No, she wasn't sure, but she wasn't going to admit it. If she were going to be on her own in the city, then she'd just have to learn to cope. Breaking free. That's what she had come here for. Roger G. Cross wasn't going to spoil it for her.

"I've got an idea," Joanne said. "The owners'll be back from vacation Monday. First thing Tuesday morning, I'll get hold of them and explain about you and the other tenant that jerk hassled. Maybe the owners can find grounds to evict the son of a bitch, okay?"

Lisa thanked her and then kept the phone pressed to her ear long after Joanne had set down the receiver. She listened to the indecipherable whispers of the dead line, then the click and dial tone. Finally she hung up and sat there, not moving and blindly staring at the knotted fiber wall-hanging her friends at home had given her.

She realized she was tired, very tired. Stress. She had read articles about it. It was not a condition she was accustomed to in her old home. It did not please her.

In bed, she felt the cold desolation of being alone and lonely in a strange place. The feeling hadn't changed in all these weeks. She reminded herself she would keep trying.

After a long time, and not until she heard the telltale sounds of Roger Cross returning from the laundry room and closing his door, Lisa fell asleep.

She dreamed of traps.

■   ■   ■

In the morning, she woke tense, the muscles in her shoulders tight and sore. She awoke listening, straining to hear sounds from the upstairs apartment. She heard nothing other than the occasional traffic outside and the slight hum of the clock by the bed.

Lisa lay awake for an hour before uncurling and getting out of bed. There was still nothing to hear from upstairs. Finally she put on her robe and gloves and went into the living room, hoping for sun-warmth from the east windows. It was another cloudy day.

She almost missed the scrap of paper that had been slipped beneath her front door. Lisa gingerly picked the thing up and examined it curiously. It was a heart cut from a doubled sheet of red construction paper. The heart bore the inscription in wide, ink-marker slashes: "R. C. + L. P." She set the thing down on the coffee table and stared at it a while. Then she crumpled the Valentine into a ball and dropped it into the kitchen trash sack.

Lisa returned to the front door, opened the spy panel and looked out. Nobody. She opened the door a crack. No one lurked outside on the landing. She quietly and quickly descended the flight to the foyer. No one confronted her when she claimed her Sunday paper from the skiff of snow sifted on the front step. Roger didn't ambush her when she returned to her own door. The building was still and quiet, just as it had been every other Sunday Lisa had lived there.

The telephone rang as she closed the door. Lisa picked up the receiver and heard Roger's voice say, "Listen, Lisa, please don't hang up yet, okay?"

This confused her. She hesitated.

"Did you get what I left you?"

"The heart?" she said, still feeling she was lagging.

"I know you must have found it—the Valentine. I didn't want to knock and wake you up."

She wasn't sure of an appropriate response. "Thank you."

"I'm really sorry about yesterday. Sometimes I get into moods, you know? I guess I was sort of on the rag." He chuckled.

Lisa didn't answer.

"Did you like the Valentine?"

"It's—early, isn't it?"

There was an odd tone in his voice. "You're worth anticipating, Lisa."

"I'm going to go now," she said.

"Don't you dare," he said quietly. "I need to talk to you. I want to see you."

This was more than enough. "Goodbye." She set the phone down.

Lisa fixed a light breakfast—her ordinarily healthy appetite was diminished—and read the newspaper while she ate. She discovered she was reading the same headline paragraph over and over. She flipped to the comics section.

The phone rang. This time she let it ring half a dozen times before answering.

Roger. His voice was coldly furious. "Don't you *ever* hang up on me, Lisa. I can't stand that."

"Listen to me," she said. "Don't bother—"

"*Never* do that!"

"—me again," she finished. "Just. Go. Away."

There was a long silence. Then it sounded like he was crying.

Lisa set the receiver down. She realized she was gripping the handpiece as though it were a club. She willed her fingers to relax.

She paced the perimeter of the living room until she decided there were more productive outlets for her nervous energy. For part of the afternoon, she scrubbed out the kitchen and bathroom. By sundown, she'd begun to relax. Roger was apparently not home. Either he impossibly wasn't moving so much as an inch, or he'd gone out before she had awakened. The hardwood floor didn't squeak up there. No sounds filtered down from the bedroom. The stereo was mute.

When the telephone rang, Lisa stared at the set as though it were a curled viper. She allowed it to ring twenty times before answering. It could be an emergency. It could be Joanne or some-one else. She picked up the receiver and said, "Hello?" Nothing. "Hello," she said again. Someone was there. She could hear him breathing. Then the other receiver clicked into its cradle. In a few seconds more, Lisa heard the hum of the dial tone.

Roger Cross was a new listing in directory assistance. Lisa dialed the number the computer voice intoned. When she held the re-ceiver away from her ear, she could hear the telephone ring up-stairs. No one answered.

By early evening, Lisa found she was ravenous. She fixed herself a splendid supper of very rare steak and ate every morsel. She wondered if Roger were in some suburban singles bar picking up easier prey. While washing the day's dishes, she began to contem-plate the unpleasant possibility of having to move to another neighborhood. It wasn't fair. She wouldn't go. She *liked* this apart-ment.

The phone rang. Lisa ignored it. Ten minutes later, it rang again. And ten minutes after that. Finally, she picked up the re-ceiver with a curt *"What."*

"Hey, don't bite my head off." It was Joanne. The manager hadn't seen Roger all day either. She was calling to check on Lisa. Lisa told her about Roger's harassment.

"You could try calling Mountain Bell."

"Maybe I will," said Lisa.

"Listen, the offer's still open if you want to stay over here."

Lisa felt stubborn. Territorial. "No," she said. "Thank you."

"Hang in there and I'll talk to the owners on Tuesday," said Joanne.

Lisa thanked her and hung up.

By eight o'clock, Lisa was again immersed in comfortable clean-ing routines. She swept all the floors. Then she gave the shower curtain a scrub-down. She dusted the shelves in the walk-in closet and put down Contac paper. Finally she returned to the bathroom and considered running a hot bath. It occurred to her she was out of clean towels. In fact, she was out of *everything* clean.

It sank home that she didn't really have anything clean and neat to wear in the morning. Lisa knew it would be an error to appear at interviews in limp Western shirts and grubby blue jeans.

She had one good wash-and-wear outfit. Her first interview was at nine; that meant she would have to catch the bus before eight. Something had to be done about the laundry tonight. Since coming to the city, she'd been called *too* clean, *too* neat. She couldn't help it.

Lisa didn't relish the idea of taking her dirty clothes and soap and bleach into that very cold night and descending to the laundry room next door, but there seemed to be no alternatives. Lisa cocked her head and glanced at the ceiling. She still had not heard a sound from upstairs. Maybe Roger had got lucky at some bar and no longer concerned himself with her. Perhaps he had drunk too much and fallen in front of a speeding truck. That thought was not without a tinge of hope.

It wasn't getting any earlier. She would need a full night's sleep.

Lisa stuffed everything she would need into the plastic laundry basket and unlocked her rear door. The back staircase was dimly lit by exit signs on each landing. The light cast her shadow weakly in front of her on the yellowed walls.

She counted. Seven steps down to the landing. Turn a blind corner to the left. Seven more steps to the first floor. Before opening the outer door, she belatedly fumbled for her keys. They were in her hip pocket.

The night was just as cold as she had anticipated. She felt the goose flesh form. The fine hairs rose on the back of her neck. The cracked concrete slab sidewalk extended the length of the apartment building. Lisa walked toward the alley, her stride faltering for a moment when she noticed the door of the garage across the alley hanging open. She thought she saw something move within the deeper darkness of the interior. She heard nothing. Probably just imagination. Probably.

She followed a branching path to the right, around a pair of blighted and dying elms. Now she was at the rear of the house where her managers lived. The building was an elaborate Victorian which had been converted into apartments sometime in the 'fifties. The original brickwork was plastered over and painted green. All the windows in the rear of the house were dark.

The long, straight flight of cement steps led to the basement and the laundry room. One, two . . . She realized she was counting the steps under her breath . . . five, six . . . The temperature

Lisa listened to the distant sirens, the drone of an airplane, a sharp noise that might have been either a backfire or a gunshot.

The city disturbed her.

She wished she felt safe.

THE SECOND COMING

Joe Gores

Jack Kerouac and his merry band were the only writers much interested in the Beats of the late fifties and the early sixties.

It was a social and literary phemononen that seemed to have little appeal to other types of writers. One would have thought that suspense fiction, ever conscious of trends and societal shifts, would have produced several novels that linked Beats with the world of the criminal. Only two, Malcolm Braly and John Trinian, found the connection in novels.

Joe Gores found the connection in the following short story. This is a definitive piece on middle-class Beatniks in the early sixties. It is not only a frightening story, it is also a valuable social document.

"BUT FIX THY EYES UPON THE VALLEY: FOR THE RIVER OF BLOOD draws nigh, in which boils every one who by violence injuries other."
THE INFERNO OF DANTE ALIGHIERI (Canto XII, 46–48)

■   ■   ■

I've thought about it a lot, man; like why Victor and I made that terrible scene out there at San Quentin, putting ourselves on that it was just for kicks; they were a thing with him. He was a sharp dark-haired cat with bright eyes, built lean and hard like a French skin-diver. His old man dug only money, so he'd always had plenty of bread. We got this idea out at his pad on Potrero Hill—a penthouse, of course—one afternoon when we were lying around on the sun-porch in swim trunks and drinking gin.

"You know, man," he said, "I have made about every scene in the world. I have balled all the chicks, red and yellow and black and white, and I have gotten high on muggles, bluejays, redbirds, and mescaline. I have even tried the white stuff a time or two. But—"

"You're a goddamned tiger, dad."

"—but there is one kick I've never had, man."

When he didn't go on I rolled my head off the quart gin bottle I was using for a pillow and looked at him. He was giving me a shot with those hot, wild eyes of his.

"So like what is it?"

"I've never watched an execution."

I thought about it a minute, drowsily. The sun was so hot it was like nailing me right to the air mattress. Watching an execution. Seeing a man go through the wall. A groovy idea for an artist.

"Too much," I murmured. "I'm with you, dad."

The next day, of course, I was back at work on some abstracts for my first one-man show and had forgotten all about it; but that night Victor called me up.

"Did you write to the warden up at San Quentin today, man? He has to contact the San Francisco police chief and make sure you don't have a record and aren't a psycho and are useful to the community."

So I went ahead and wrote the letter because even sober it still seemed a cool idea for some kicks; I knew they always need twelve witnesses to make sure that the accused isn't sneaked out the back door or something at the last minute like an old Jimmy Cagney movie. Even so, I lay dead for two months before the letter came. The star of our show would be a stud who'd broken into a house trailer near Fort Ord to rape this Army lieutenant's wife, only right in the middle of it she'd started screaming so he'd put a pillow over her face to keep her quiet until he could finish. But she'd quit breathing. There were eight chicks on the jury and I think like three of them got broken ankles in the rush to send him to the gas chamber. Not that I cared. Kicks, man.

Victor picked me up at seven-thirty in the morning, an hour before we were supposed to report to San Quentin. He was wearing this really hip Italian import, and fifty-dollar shoes, and a narrow-brim hat with a little feather in it, so all he needed was a briefcase to be Chairman of the Board. The top was down on the Mercedes, cold as it was, and when he saw my black suit and hand-knit tie he flashed this crazy white-toothed grin you'd never see in any Director's meeting.

"*Too much*, killer! If you'd like comb your hair you could pass for an undertaker coming after the body."

Since I am a very long, thin cat with black hair always hanging in my eyes, who fully dressed weighs as much as a medium-sized collie, I guess he wasn't too far off. I put a pint of José Cuervo in the side pocket of the car and we split. We were both really turned on: I mean this senseless, breathless hilarity as if we'd just heard the world's funniest joke. Or were just going to.

It was one of those chilly California brights with blue sky and cold sunshine and here and there a cloud like Mr. Big was popping Himself a cap down beyond the horizon. I dug it all: the sail of a lone early yacht out in the Bay like a tossed-away paper cup; the whitecaps flipping around out by Angel Island like they were stoned out of their minds; the top down on the 300-SL so we could smell salt and feel the icy bite of the wind. But beyond the tunnel on U.S. 101, coming down towards Marin City, I felt a sudden sharp chill as if a cloud had passed between me and the sun, but none had; and then I dug for the first time what I was actually doing.

Victor felt it, too, for he turned to me and said, "Must maintain cool, dad."

"I'm with it."

San Quentin Prison, out on the end of its peninsula, looked like a sprawled ugly dragon sunning itself on a rock; we pulled up near the East Gate and there were not even any birds singing. Just a bunch of quiet cats in black, Quakers or Mennonites or something, protesting capital punishment by their silent presence as they'd done ever since Chessman had gotten his out there. I felt dark frightened things move around inside me when I saw them.

"Let's fall out right here, dad," I said in a momentary sort of panic, "and catch the matinee next week."

But Victor was in kicksville, like desperate to put on all those squares in the black suits. When they looked over at us he jumped up on the back of the bucket seat and spread his arms wide like the Sermon on the Mount. With his tortoise-shell shades and his flashing teeth and that suit which had cost three yards, he looked like Christ on his way to Hollywood.

"Whatsoever ye do unto the least of these, my brethren, ye do unto me," he cried in this ringing apocalyptic voice.

I grabbed his arm and dragged him back down off the seat. "For Christ sake, man, cool it!"

But he went into high laughter and punched my arm with feverish exuberance, and then jerked a tiny American flag from his inside jacket pocket and began waving it around above the windshield. I could see the sweat on his forehead.

"It's worth it to live in this country!" he yelled at them.

He put the car in gear and we went on. I looked back and saw one of those cats crossing himself. It put things back in perspective: they were from nowhere. The Middle Ages. Not that I judged them: that was their scene, man. Unto every cat what he digs the most.

The guard on the gate directed us to a small wooden building set against the outside wall, where we found five other witnesses. Three of them were reporters, one was a fat cat smoking a .45 caliber stogy like a politician from Sacramento, and the last was an Army type in lieutenant's bars, his belt buckle and insignia looking as if he'd been up all night with a can of Brasso.

A guard came in and told us to surrender everything in our pockets and get a receipt for it. We had to remove our shoes, too; they were too heavy for the fluoroscope. Then they put us through this groovy little room one-by-one to x-ray us for cameras and so on; they don't want anyone making the Kodak scene while they're busy dropping the pellets. We ended up inside the prison with our shoes back on and with our noses full of that old prison detergent-disinfectant stink.

The politician type, who had those cold slitted eyes like a Sherman tank, started coming on with rank jokes: but everyone put him down, hard, even the reporters. I guess nobody but fuzz ever gets used to executions. The Army stud was at parade rest with a face so pale his freckles looked like a charge of shot. He had reddish hair.

After a while five guards came in to make up the twelve required witnesses. They looked rank, as fuzz always do, and got off in a corner in a little huddle, laughing and gassing together like a bunch of kids kicking a dog. Victor and I sidled over to hear what they were saying.

"Who's sniffing the eggs this morning?" asked one.

"I don't know, I haven't been reading the papers." He yawned when he answered.

"Don't you remember?" urged another, "it's the guy who smothered the woman in the house trailer. Down in the Valley by Salinas."

"Yeah. Soldier's wife; and he was raping her and . . ."

Like dogs hearing the plate rattle, they turned in unison toward the Army lieutenant; but just then more fuzz came in to march us to the observation room. We went in a column of twos with a guard beside each one, everyone unconsciously in step as if following a cadence call. I caught myself listening for measured mournful drum rolls.

The observation room was built right around the gas chamber, with rising tiers of benches for extras in case business was brisk. The chamber itself was hexagonal; the three walls in our room were of plate glass with a waist-high brass rail around the outside like the railing in an old-time saloon. The three other walls were steel plate, with a heavy door, rivet-studded, in the center one, and a small observation window in each of the others.

Inside the chamber were just these two massive chairs, probably oak, facing the rear walls side-by-side; their backs were high enough to come to the nape of the neck of anyone sitting in them. Under each was like a bucket that I knew contained hydrochloric acid. At a signal the executioner would drop sodium cyanide pellets into a chute; the pellets would roll down into the bucket; hydrocyanic acid gas would form; and the cat in the chair would be wasted.

The politician type, who had this rich fruity baritone like Burl Ives, asked why they had two chairs.

"That's in case there's a double-header, dad," I said.

"You're kidding." But by his voice the idea pleased him. Then he wheezed plaintively: "I don't see why they turn the chairs away—we can't even watch his face while it's happening to him."

He was a true rank genuine creep, right out from under a rock with the slime barely dry on his scales; but I wouldn't have wanted his dreams. I think he was one of those guys who tastes the big draught many times before he swallows it.

We milled around like cattle around the chute when they smell the blood from inside and know they're somehow involved; then we heard sounds and saw the door in the back of the chamber swing open. A uniformed guard appeared to stand at attention, followed by a priest dressed all in black like Zorro, with his face hanging down to his belly button. He must have been a new man, because he had trouble maintaining his cool: just standing there beside the guard he dropped his little black book on the floor like three times in a row.

The Army cat said to me, as if he'd wig out unless he broke the silence: "They . . . have it arranged like a stage play, don't they?"

"But no encores," said Victor hollowly.

Another guard showed up in the doorway and they walked in the condemned man. He was like sort of a shock. You expect a stud to *act* like a murderer: I mean, cringe at the sight of the chair because he knows this is it, there's finally no place to go, no appeal to make, or else bound in there full of cheap bravado and go-to-hell. But he just seemed mildly interested, nothing more.

He wore a white suit with the sleeves rolled up, suntan that looked Army issue, and no tie. Under thirty, brown crewcut hair— the terrible thing is that I cannot even remember the features on his face, man. The closest I could come to a description would be that he resembled the Army cat right there beside me with his nose to the glass.

The one thing I'll never forget is that stud's hands. He'd been on Death Row all these months, and here his hands were still red and chapped and knobby, as if he'd still been out picking turnips in the San Joaquin Valley. Then I realized: I was thinking of him in the past tense.

Two fuzz began strapping him down in the chair. A broad leather strap across the chest, narrower belts on the arms and legs. God they were careful about strapping him in. I mean they wanted to make sure he was comfortable. And all the time he was talking with them. Not that we could hear it, but I suppose it went *that's fine, fellows, no, that strap isn't too tight, gee, I hope I'm not making you late for lunch.*

That's what bugged me, he was so damned *apologetic*! While they were fastening him down over that little bucket of oblivion, that poor dead lonely son of a bitch twisted around to look over his shoulder at us, and he *smiled*. I mean if he'd had an arm free he might have *waved*! One of the fuzz, who had white hair and these sad gentle eyes like he was wearing a hair shirt, patted him on the head on the way out. No personal animosity, son, just doing my job.

After that the tempo increased, like your heartbeat when you're on a black street at three a.m. and the echo of your own footsteps begins to sound like someone following you. The warden was at one observation window, the priest and the doctor at the other. The blackrobe made the sign of the cross, having a last go at the condemned, but he was digging only Ben Casey. Here was this M.D. cat who'd taken the Hippocratic Oath to preserve life, waving his arms around like a TV director to show that stud the easiest way to *die*.

Hold your breath, then breathe deeply: you won't feel a thing. Of course hydrocyanic acid gas melts your guts into a red-hot soup and burns out every fiber in the lining of your lungs, but you won't be really feeling it as you jerk around: that'll just be raw nerve endings.

Like they should have called *his* the Hypocritical Oath.

So there we were, three yards and half an inch of plate glass apart, with us staring at him and him by just turning his head able to stare right back: but there were a million light-years between the two sides of the glass. He didn't turn. He was shrived and strapped in and briefed on how to die, and he was ready for the fumes. I found out afterwards that he had even willed his body to medical research.

I did a quick take around.

Victor was sweating profusely, his eyes glued to the window.

The politician was pop-eyed, nose pressed flat and belly indented by the brass rail, pudgy fingers like plump garlic sausages smearing the glass on either side of his head. A look on his face, already, like that of a stud making it with a chick.

The reporters seemed ashamed, as if someone had caught them peeking over the transom into the ladies' john.

The Army cat just looked sick.

Only the fuzz were unchanged, expending no more emotion on this than on their targets after rapid-fire exercises at the range.

On no face was there hatred.

Suddenly, for the first time in my life, I was part of it. I wanted to yell out STOP! We were about to gas this stud and *none of us wanted him to die!* We've created this society and we're all responsible for what it does, but none of us as individuals is willing to take that responsibility. We're like that Nazi cat at Nuremberg who said that everything would have been all right if they'd only given him more ovens.

The warden signaled. I heard gas whoosh up around the chair.

The condemned man didn't move. He was following doctor's orders. Then he took the huge gulping breath the M.D. had pantomimed. All of a sudden he threw this tremendous convulsion, his body straining up against the straps, his head slewed around so I could see his eyes were shut tight and his lips were pulled back from his teeth. Then he started panting like a baby in an oxygen tent, swiftly and shallowly. Only it wasn't oxygen his lungs were trying to work on.

The lieutenant stepped back smartly from the window, blinked, and puked on the glass. His vomit hung there for an instant like a phosphorous bomb burst in a bunker; then two fuzz were supporting him from the room and we were all jerking back from the mess. All except the politician. He hadn't even noticed: he was in Henry Millersville, getting his sex kicks the easy way.

I guess the stud in there had never dug that he was supposed to be gone in two seconds without pain, because his body was still arched up in that terrible bow, and his hands were still claws. I could see the muscles standing out along the sides of his jaws like marbles. Finally he flopped back and just hung there in his straps like a machine-gunned paratrooper.

But that wasn't the end. He took another huge gasp, so I could see his ribs pressing out against his white shirt. After that one, twenty seconds. We decided that he had cut out.

Then another gasp. Then nothing. Half a minute nothing.

Another of those final terrible shuddering racking gasps. At last: all through. All used up. Making it with the angels.

But then he did it *again*. Every fiber of that dead wasted comic thrown-away body strained for air on this one. No air: only hydrocyanic acid gas. Just nerves, like the fish twitching after you whack it on the skull with the back edge of the skinning knife. Except that it wasn't a fish we were seeing die.

His head flopped sideways and his tongue came out slyly like the tongue of a dead deer. Then this gunk ran out of his mouth. It was just saliva—they said it couldn't be anything else—but it reminded me of the residue after light-line resistors have been melted in an electrical fire. That kind of black. That kind of scorched.

Very softly, almost to himself, Victor murmured: "Later, dad."

That was it. Dig you in the hereafter, dad. Ten little minutes and you're through the wall. Mistah Kurtz, he dead. Mistah Kurtz, he very very goddamn dead.

I believed it. Looking at what was left of that cat was like looking at a chick who's gotten herself bombed on the heavy, so when you hold a match in front of her eyes the pupils don't react and there's no one home, man. No one. Nowhere. End of the lineville.

We split.

But on the way out I kept thinking of that Army stud, and wondering what had made him sick. Was it because the cat in the chair had been the last to enter, no matter how violently, the body of his beloved, and now even that feeble connection had been severed? Whatever the reason, his body had known what perhaps his mind had refused to accept: this ending was no new beginning, this death would not restore his dead chick to him. This death, no matter how just in his eyes, had generated only nausea.

Victor and I sat in the Mercedes for a long time with the top down, looking out over that bright beautiful empty peninsula, not named, as you might think, after a saint, but after some poor dumb Indian they had hanged there a hundred years or so before. Trees and clouds and blue water, and still no birds making the scene. Even the cats in the black suits had vanished, but now I understood why they'd been there. In their silent censure, they had been sounding the right gong, man. *We* were the ones from the Middle Ages.

Victor took a deep shuddering breath as if he could never get enough air. Then he said in a barely audible voice: "How did you dig that action, man?"

I gave a little shrug and, being myself, said the only thing I could say. "It was a gas, dad."

"I dig, man. I'm hip. A gas."

Something was wrong with the way he said it, but I broke the seal on the tequila and we killed it in fifteen minutes, without even a lime to suck in between. Then he started the car and we cut out, and I realized what was wrong. Watching that cat in the gas chamber, Victor had realized for the very first time that life is far, far more than just kicks. We were both partially responsible for what had happened in there, and we had been ineluctably diminished by it.

On U.S. 101 he coked the Mercedes up to 104 m.p.h. through the traffic, and held it there. It was wild: it was the end: but I didn't sound. I was alone without my Guide by the boiling river of blood. When the Highway Patrol finally stopped us, Victor was coming on so strong and I was coming on so mild that they surrounded us with their holster flaps unbuckled, and checked our veins for needle marks.

I didn't say a word to them, man, not one. Not even my name. Like they had to look in my wallet to see who I was. And while they were doing that, Victor blew his cool entirely. You know, biting, foaming at the mouth, the whole bit—he gave a very good show until they hit him on the back of the head with a gun butt. I just watched.

They lifted his license for a year, nothing else, because his old man spent a lot of bread on a shrinker who testified that Victor had temporarily wigged out, and who had him put away in the zoo for a time. He's back now, but he still sees that wig picker, three times a week at forty clams a shot.

He needs it. A few days ago I saw him on Upper Grant, stalking lithely through a gray raw February day with the fog in, wearing just a T-shirt and jeans—and no shoes. He seemed agitated, pressed, confined within his own concerns, but I stopped him for a minute.

"Ah . . . How you making it, man? Like, ah, what's the gig?"

He shook his head cautiously. "They will not let us get away with it, you know. Like to them, man, just living is a crime."

"Why no strollers, dad?"

"I cannot wear shoes." He moved closer and glanced up and down the street, and said with tragic earnestness: "I can hear only with the soles of my feet, man."

Then he nodded and padded away through the crowds on silent naked soles like a puzzled panther, drifting through the fruiters and drunken teenagers and fuzz trying to bust some cat for possession who have inherited North Beach from the true swingers. I guess all Victor wants to listen to now is Mother Earth: all he wants to hear is the comforting sound of the worms, chewing away.

Chewing away, and waiting for Victor; and maybe for the Second Coming.

THE LOST COAST

Marcia Muller

Marcia Muller is frequently described as the woman who founded the modern school of female private eye writing. And that's true enough.

What's not pointed out so often is how much she's grown as a both a storyteller and a social observer.

When you compare the early Sharon McCone novels with the current ones, you see almost unimaginable differences in style, poise, and depth. A good journeyman has grown into a great artist.

Here is one of Marcia's recent stories.

CALIFORNIA'S LOST COAST IS AT THE SAME TIME ONE OF THE most desolate and beautiful of shorelines. Northerly winds whip the sand into a dust-devil frenzy; eerie, stationary fogs hang in the trees and distort the driftwood until it resembles the bones of prehistoric mammals; bruised clouds hover above the peaks of the distant King Range, then blow down to sea level and dump icy torrents. But on a fair day the sea and sky show infinite shadings of blue, and the wildflowers are a riot of color. If you wait quietly, you can spot deer, peregrine falcons, foxes, otters, even black bears and mountain lions.

A contradictory and oddly compelling place, this seventy-three-mile stretch of coast southwest of Eureka, where—as with most worthwhile things or people—you must take the bad with the good.

Unfortunately, on my first visit there I was taking mostly the bad. Strong wind pushed my MG all over the steep, narrow road, making its hairpin turns even more perilous. Early October rain cut my visibility to a few yards. After I crossed the swollen Bear River, the road continued to twist and wind, and I began to understand why the natives had dubbed it The Wildcat.

Somewhere ahead, my client had told me, was the hamlet of Petrolia—site of the first oil well drilled in California, he'd irrelevantly added. The man was a conservative politician, a former lumber-company attorney, and given what I knew of his voting record on the environment, I was certain we disagreed on the desirability of that event, as well as any number of similar issues. But the urgency of the current situation dictated that I keep my opinions to myself, so I'd simply written down the directions he gave me—omitting his travelogue-like asides—and gotten under way.

I drove through Petrolia—a handful of new buildings, since the village had been all but leveled in the disastrous earthquake of 1992—and turned toward the sea on an unpaved road. After two miles I began looking for the orange post that marked the dirt track to the client's cabin.

The whole time I was wishing I was back in San Francisco. This wasn't my kind of case; I didn't like the client, Steve Shoemaker; and even though the fee was good, this was the week I'd scheduled to take off a few personal business days from All Souls Legal Cooperative, where I'm chief investigator. But Jack Stuart, our criminal specialist, had asked me to take on the job as a favor to him. Steve Shoemaker was Jack's old friend from college in Southern California, and he'd asked for a referral to a private detective. Jack owed Steve a favor; I owed Jack several, so there was no way I could gracefully refuse.

But I couldn't shake the feeling that something was wrong with this case. And I couldn't help wishing that I'd come to the Lost Coast in summertime, with a backpack and in the company of my lover—instead of on a rainy fall afternoon, with a .38 Special and soon to be in the company of Shoemaker's disagreeable wife, Andrea.

The rain was sheeting down by the time I spotted the orange post. It had turned the hard-packed earth to mud, and my MG's tires sank deep in the ruts, its undercarriage scraping dangerously. I could barely make out the stand of live oaks and sycamores where the track ended; no way to tell if another vehicle had traveled over it recently.

When I reached the end of the track I saw one of those boxy

four-wheel-drive wagons—Bronco? Cherokee?—drawn in under the drooping branches of an oak. Andrea Shoemaker's? I'd neglected to get a description from her husband of what she drove. I got out of the MG, turning the hood of my heavy sweater up against the downpour; the wind promptly blew it off. So much for what the catalog had described as "extra protection on those cold nights." I yanked the hood up again and held it there, went around and took my .38 from the trunk and shoved it into the outside flap of my purse. Then I went over and tried the door of the four-wheel drive. Unlocked. I opened it, slipped into the driver's seat.

Nothing identifying its owner was on the seats or in the side pockets, but in the glove compartment I found a registration in the name of Andrea Shoemaker. I rummaged around, came up with nothing else of interest. Then I got out and walked through the trees, looking for the cabin.

Shoemaker had told me to follow a deer track through the grove. No sign of it in this downpour; no deer, either. Nothing but wind-lashed trees, the oaks pelting me with acorns. I moved slowly through them, swiveling my head from side to side, until I made out a bulky shape tucked beneath the farthest of the sycamores.

As I got closer, I saw the cabin was of plain weathered wood, rudely constructed, with the chimney of a woodstove extending from its composition shingle roof. Small—two or three rooms—and no light showing in its windows. And the door was open, banging against the inside wall . . .

I quickened my pace, taking the gun from my purse. Alongside the door I stopped to listen. Silence. I had a flashlight in my bag; I took it out. Moved to where I could see inside, then turned the flash on and shone it through the door.

All that was visible was rough board walls, an oilcloth-covered table and chairs, an ancient woodstove. I stepped inside, swinging the light around. Unlit oil lamp on the table; flower-cushioned wooden furniture of the sort you always find in vacation cabins; rag rugs; shelves holding an assortment of tattered paperbacks, seashells, and driftwood. I shifted the light again, more slowly.

A chair on the far side of the table was tipped over, and a

woman's purse lay on the edge of the woodstove, its contents spilling out. When I got over there I saw a .32 Iver Johnson revolver lying on the floor.

Andrea Shoemaker owned a .32. She'd told me so the day before.

Two doors opened off the room. Quietly I went to one and tried it. A closet, shelves stocked with staples and canned goods and bottled water. I looked around the room again, listening. No sound but the wail of wind and the pelt of rain on the roof. I stepped to the other door.

A bedroom, almost filled wall-to-wall by a king-sized bed covered with a goosedown comforter and piled with colorful pillows. Old bureau pushed in one corner, another unlit oil lamp on the single nightstand. Small travel bag on the bed.

The bag hadn't been opened. I examined its contents. Jeans, a couple of sweaters, underthings, toilet articles. Package of condoms. Uh-huh. She'd come here, as I'd found out, to meet a man. The affairs usually began with a casual pickup; they were never of long duration; and they all seemed to culminate in a romantic weekend in the isolated cabin.

Dangerous game, particularly in these days when AIDS and the prevalence of disturbed individuals of both sexes threatened. But Andrea Shoemaker had kept her latest date with an even larger threat hanging over her: for the past six weeks, a man with a serious grudge against her husband had been stalking her. For all I knew, he and the date were one and the same.

And where was Andrea now?

■　　■　　■

This case had started on Wednesday, two days ago, when I'd driven up to Eureka, a lumbering and fishing town on Humboldt Bay. After I passed the Humboldt County line I began to see huge logging trucks toiling through the mountain passes, shredded curls of redwood bark trailing in their wakes. Twenty-five miles south of the city itself was the company-owned town of Scotia, mill stacks belching white smoke and filling the air with the scent of freshly cut wood. Yards full of logs waiting to be fed to the mills lined the highway. When I reached Eureka itself, the downtown struck me as curiously quiet; many of the stores were out of business, and the sidewalks were mostly deserted. The recession had hit the lumber industry hard, and the earthquake hadn't helped the area's strapped economy.

I'd arranged to meet Steve Shoemaker at his law offices in Old Town, near the waterfront. It was a picturesque area full of renovated warehouses and interesting shops and restaurants, tricked up for tourists with the inevitable horse-and-carriage rides and T-shirt shops, but still pleasant. Shoemaker's offices were off a cobblestoned courtyard containing a couple of antique shops and a decorator's showroom.

When I gave my card to the secretary, she said Assemblyman Shoemaker was in conference and asked me to wait. The man, I knew, had lost his seat in the state legislature this past election, so the term of address seemed inappropriate. The appointments of the waiting room struck me as a bit much: brass and mahogany and marble and velvet, plenty of it, the furnishings all antiques that tended to the garish. I sat on a red velvet sofa and looked for something to read. *Architectural Digest, National Review, Foreign Affairs*—that was it, take it or leave it. I left it. My idea of waiting-room reading material is *People*; I love it, but I'm too embarrassed to subscribe.

The minutes ticked by: ten, fifteen, twenty. I contemplated the issue of *Architectural Digest*, then opted instead for staring at a fake Rembrandt on the far wall. Twenty-five, thirty. I was getting irritated now. Shoemaker had asked me to be here by three; I'd arrived on the dot. If this was, as he'd claimed, a matter of such urgency and delicacy that he couldn't go into it on the phone, why was he in conference at the appointed time?

Thirty-five minutes. Thirty-seven. The door to the inner sanctum opened and a woman strode out. A tall woman, with long chestnut hair, wearing a raincoat and black leather boots. Her eyes rested on me in passing—a cool gray, hard with anger. Then she went out, slamming the door behind her.

The secretary—a trim blonde in a tailored suit—started as the door slammed. She glanced at me and tried to cover with a smile, but its edge were strained, and her fingertips pressed hard against the desk. The phone at her elbow buzzed; she snatched up the receiver. Spoke into it then said to me, "Ms. McCone, Assemblyman Shoemaker will see you now." As she ushered me inside, she again gave me her frayed-edge smile.

Tense situation in this office, I thought. Brought on by what? The matter Steve Shoemaker wanted me to investigate? The client who had just made her angry exit? Or something else entirely . . . ?

Shoemaker's office was even more pretentious than the waiting room: more brass, mahogany, velvet, and marble; more fake Old Masters in heavy gilt frames; more antiques; more of everything. Shoemaker's demeanor was not as nervous as his secretary's, but when he rose to greet me, I noticed a jerkiness in his movements, as if he was holding himself under tight control. I clasped his outstretched hand and smiled, hoping the familiar social rituals would set him more at ease.

Momentarily they did. He thanked me for coming, apologized for making me wait, and inquired after Jack Stuart. After I was seated in one of the clients' chairs, he offered me a drink; I asked for mineral water. As he went to a wet bar tucked behind a tapestry screen, I took the opportunity to study him.

Shoemaker was handsome: dark hair, with the gray so artfully interwoven that it must have been professionally dyed. Chiseled features; nice well-muscled body, shown off to perfection by an expensive blue suit. When he handed me my drink, his smile revealed white, even teeth that I—having spent the greater part of the previous month in the company of my dentist—recognized as capped. Yes, a very good-looking man, politician handsome. Jack's old friend or not, his appearance and manner called up my gut-level distrust.

My client went around his desk and reclaimed his chair. He held a drink of his own—something dark amber—and he took a deep swallow before speaking. The alcohol replenished his vitality some; he drank again, set the glass on a pewter coaster, and said, "Ms. McCone, I'm glad you could come up here on such short notice."

"You mentioned on the phone that the case is extremely urgent—and delicate."

He ran his hand over his hair—lightly, so as not to disturb its styling "Extremely urgent and delicate," he repeated, seeming to savor the phrase.

"Why don't you tell me about it?"

His eyes strayed to the half-full glass on the coaster. Then they moved to the door through which I'd entered. Returned to me. "You saw the woman who just left?"

I nodded.

"My wife, Andrea."

I waited.

"She's very angry with me for hiring you."

"She did act angry. Why?"

Now he reached for the glass and belted down its contents. Leaned back and rattled the ice cubes as he spoke. "It's a long story. Painful to me. I'm not sure where to begin. I just . . . don't know what to make of the things that are happening."

"That's what you've hired me to do. Begin anywhere. We'll fill in the gaps later." I pulled a small tape recorder from my bag and set it on the edge of his desk. "Do you mind?"

Shoemaker eyed it warily, but shook his head. After a moment's hesitation, he said, "Someone is stalking my wife."

"Following her? Threatening her?"

"Not following, not that I know of. He writes notes, threatening to kill her. He leaves . . . things at the house. At her place of business. Dead things. Birds, rats, one time a cat. Andrea loves cats. She . . ." He shook his head, went to the bar for a refill.

"What else? Phone calls?"

"No. One time, a floral arrangement—suitable for a funeral."

"Does he sign the notes?"

"John. Just John."

"Does Mrs. Shoemaker know anyone named John who has a grudge against her?"

"She says no. And I . . ." He sat down, fresh drink in hand. "I have reason to believe that this John has a grudge against me, is using this harassment of Andrea to get at me personally."

"Why do you think that?"

"The wording of the notes."

"May I see them?"

He looked around, as if he were afraid someone might be listening.

"Later. I keep them elsewhere."

Something, then, I thought, that he didn't want his office staff to see. Something shameful, perhaps even criminal.

"Okay," I said, "how long has this been going on?"

"About six weeks."

"Have you contacted the police?"

"Informally. A man I know on the force, Sergeant Bob Wolfe. But after he started looking into it, I had to ask him to drop it."

"Why?"

"I'm in a sensitive political position."

"Excuse me if I'm mistaken, Mr. Shoemaker, but it's my understanding that you're no longer serving in the state legislature."

"That's correct, but I'm about to announce my candidacy in a special election for a Senate seat that's recently been vacated."

"I see. So after you asked your contact on the police force to back off, you decided to use a private investigator, and Jack recommended me. Why not use someone local?"

"As I said, my position is sensitive. I don't want word of this getting out in the community. That's why Andrea is so angry with me. She claims I value my political career more than her life."

I waited, wondering how he'd attempt to explain that away.

He didn't even try, merely went on, "In our . . . conversation just prior to this, she threatened to leave me. This coming weekend she plans to go to a cabin on the Lost Coast that she inherited from her father to, as she put it, sort things through. Alone. Do you know that part of the coast?"

"I've read some travel pieces on it."

"Then you're aware how remote it is. The cabin's very isolated. I don't want Andrea going there while this John person is on the loose."

"Does she go there often?"

"Fairly often. I don't; it's too rustic for me—no running water, phone, or electricity. But Andrea likes it. Why do you ask?"

"I'm wondering if John—whoever he is—knows about the cabin. Has she been there since the harassment began?"

"No. Initially she agreed that it wouldn't be a good idea. But now . . ." He shrugged.

"I'll need to speak with Mrs. Shoemaker. Maybe I can reason with her, persuade her not to go until we've identified John. Or maybe she'll allow me to go along as her bodyguard."

"You can speak with her if you like, but she's beyond reasoning with. And there's no way you can stop her or force her to allow you to accompany her. My wife is a strong-willed woman; that interior decorating firm across the courtyard is hers, she built it from the ground up. When Andrea decides to do something, she does it. And asks permission from no one."

"Still, I'd like to try reasoning. This trip to the cabin—that's the urgency you mentioned on the phone. Two days to find the man behind the harassment before she goes out there and perhaps makes a target of herself."

"Yes."

"Then I'd better get started. That funeral arrangement—what florist did it come from?"

Shoemaker shook his head. "It arrived at least five weeks ago, before either of us noticed a pattern to the harassment. Andrea just shrugged it off, threw the wrappings and card away."

"Let's go look at the notes, then. They're my only lead."

Vengeance will be mine. The sudden blow. The quick attack. Vengeance is the price of silence.

■   ■   ■

Mute testimony paves the way to an early grave.
The rest is silence.

■   ■   ■

A *freshly turned grave is silent testimony to an old wrong and its avenger.*

■   ■   ■

There was more in the same vein—slightly biblical-flavored and stilted. But chilling to me, even though the safety-deposit booth at Shoemaker's bank was overly warm. If that was my reaction, what had these notes done to Andrea Shoemaker? No wonder she was thinking of leaving a husband who cared more for the electorate's opinion than his wife's life and safety.

The notes had been typed without error on an electric machine that had left no such obvious clues as chipped or skewed keys. The paper and envelopes were plain and cheap, purchasable at any discount store. They had been handled, I was sure, by nothing more than gloved hands. No signature—just the typed name "John."

But the writer had wanted the Shoemakers—one of them, anyway—to know who he was. Thus the theme that ran through them all: silence and revenge.

I said, "I take it your contact at the E.P.D. had their lab go over these?"

"Yes. There was nothing. That's why he wanted to probe fur-ther—something I couldn't permit him to do."

"Because of this revenge-and-silence business. Tell me about it." Shoemaker looked around furtively. My God, did he think bank employees had nothing better to do with their time than to eavesdrop on our conversation?

"We'll go have a drink," he said. "I know a place that's private."

· ■ ·

We went to a restaurant a few blocks away, where Shoemaker had another bourbon and I toyed with a glass of iced tea. After some prodding, he told me his story; it didn't enhance him in my eyes.

Seventeen years ago Shoemaker had been interviewing for a staff attorney's position at a large lumber company. While on a tour of the mills, he witnessed an accident in which a worker named Sam Carding was severely mangled while trying to clear a jam in a bark-stripping machine. Shoemaker, who had worked in the mills summers to pay for his education, knew the accident was due to company negligence, but accepted a handsome job offer in exchange for not testifying for the plaintiff in the ensuing lawsuit. The court ruled against Carding, confined to a wheelchair and in constant pain; a year later, while the case was still under appeal, Carding shot his wife and himself. The couple's three chil-dren were given token settlements in exchange for dropping the suit and then were adopted by relatives in a different part of the country.

"It's not a pretty story, Mr. Shoemaker," I said, "and I can see why the wording of the notes might make you suspect there's a connection between it and this harassment. But who do you think John is?"

"Carding's oldest boy. Carding and his family knew I'd wit-nessed the accident; one of his coworkers saw me watching from the catwalk and told him. Later, when I turned up as a senior counsel . . ." He shrugged.

"But why, after all this time—?"

"Why not? People nurse grudges. John Carding was sixteen at the time of the lawsuit; there were some ugly scenes with him, both at my home and my office at the mill. By now he'd be in his forties. Maybe it's his way of acting out some sort of midlife crisis."

"Well, I'll call my office and have my assistant run a check on all three Carding kids. And I want to speak with Mrs. Shoemaker—preferably in your presence."

He glanced at his watch. "It can't be tonight. She's got a meeting of her professional organization, and I'm dining with my campaign manager."

A potentially psychotic man was threatening Andrea's life, yet they both carried on as usual. Well, who was I to question it? Maybe it was their way of coping.

"Tomorrow, then," I said. "Your home. At the noon hour."

Shoemaker nodded. Then he gave me the address, as well as the names of John Carding's siblings.

I left him on the sidewalk in front of the restaurant: a handsome man whose shoulders now slumped inside his expensive suitcoat, shivering in the brisk wind off Humboldt Bay. As we shook hands, I saw that shame made his gaze unsteady, the set of his mouth less than firm.

I knew that kind of shame. Over the course of my career, I'd committed some dreadful acts that years later woke me in the deep of the night to sudden panic. I'd also *not* committed certain acts—failures that woke me to regret and emptiness. My sins of omission were infinitely worse than those of commission, because I knew that if I'd acted, I could have made a difference. Could even have saved a life.

■   ■   ■

I wasn't able to reach Rae Kelleher, my assistant at All Souls, that evening, and by the time she got back to me the next morning—Thursday—I was definitely annoyed. Still, I tried to keep a lid on my irritation. Rae is young, attractive, and in love; I couldn't expect her to spend her evenings waiting to be of service to her workaholic boss.

I got her started on a computer check on all three Cardings, then took myself to the Eureka P.D. and spoke with Shoemaker's contact, Sergeant Bob Wolfe. Wolfe—a dark-haired, sharp-featured man whose appearance was a good match for his surname—told me he'd had the notes processed by the lab, which had turned up no useful evidence.

"Then I started to probe, you know? When you got a harassment case like this, you look into the victims' private lives."

"And that was when Shoemaker told you to back off."

"Uh-huh."

"When was this?"

"About five weeks ago."

"I wonder why he waited so long to hire me. Did he, by any chance, ask you for a referral to a local investigator?"

Wolfe frowned. "Not this time."

"Then you'd referred him to someone before?"

"Yeah, guy who used to be on the force—Dave Morrison. Last April."

"Did Shoemaker tell you why he needed an investigator?"

"No, and I didn't ask. These politicians, they're always trying to get something on their rivals. I didn't want any part of it."

"Do you have Morrison's address and phone number handy?"

Wolfe reached into his desk drawer, shuffled things, and flipped a business card across the blotter. "Dave gave me a stack of these when he set up shop," he said. "Always glad to help an old pal."

•   •   •

Morrison was out of town, the message on his answering machine said, but would be back tomorrow afternoon. I left a message of my own, asking him to call me at my motel. Then I headed for the Shoemakers' home, hoping I could talk some common sense into Andrea.

But Andrea wasn't having any common sense.

She strode around the parlor of their big Victorian—built by one of the city's lumber barons, her husband told me when I complimented them on it—arguing and waving her arms and making scathing statements punctuated by a good amount of profanity. And knocking back martinis, even though it was only a little past noon.

Yes, she was going to the cabin. No, neither her husband nor I was welcome there. No, she wouldn't postpone the trip; she was sick and tired of being cooped up like some kind of zoo animal because her husband had made a mistake years before she'd met him. All right, she realized this John person was dangerous. But she'd taken self-defense classes and owned a .32 revolver. Of course she knew how to use it. Practiced frequently, too. Women had to be prepared these days, and she was.

But, she added darkly, glaring at her husband, she'd just as soon not have to shoot John. She'd rather send him straight back to Steve and let them settle this score. May the best man win—and she was placing bets on John.

As far as I was concerned, Steve and Andrea Shoemaker deserved each other.

I tried to explain to her that self-defense classes don't fully prepare you for a paralyzing, heart-pounding encounter with an actual violent stranger. I tried to warn her that the ability to shoot well on a firing range doesn't fully prepare you for pumping a bullet into a human being who is advancing swiftly on you.

I wanted to tell her she was being an idiot.

Before I could, she slammed down her glass and stormed out of the house.

Her husband replenished his own drink and said, "Now do you see what I'm up against?"

I didn't respond to that. Instead I said, "I spoke with Sergeant Wolfe earlier."

"And?"

"He told me he referred you to a local private investigator, Dave Morrison, last April."

"So?"

"Why didn't you hire Morrison for this job?"

"As I told you yesterday, my—"

"Sensitive position, yes."

Shoemaker scowled.

Before he could comment, I asked, "What was the job last April?"

"Nothing to do with this matter."

"Something to do with politics?"

"In a way."

"Mr. Shoemaker, hasn't it occurred to you that a political enemy may be using the Carding case as a smoke screen? That a rival's trying to throw you off balance before this special election?"

"It did, and . . . well, it isn't my opponent's style. My God, we're civilized people. But those notes . . . they're the work of a lunatic."

I wasn't so sure he was right—both about the notes being the work of a lunatic and politicians being civilized people—but I merely said, "Okay, you keep working on Mrs. Shoemaker. At least persuade her to let me go to the Lost Coast with her. I'll be in touch." Then I headed for the public library.

■   ■   ■

After a few hours of ruining my eyes at the microfilm machine, I knew little more than before. Newspaper accounts of the Carding accident, lawsuit, and murder-suicide didn't differ substantially from what my client had told me. Their coverage of the Shoemakers' activities was only marginally interesting.

Normally I don't do a great deal of background investigation on clients, but as Sergeant Wolfe had said, in a case like this where one or both of them was a target, a thorough look at careers and lifestyles was mandatory. The papers described Steve as a straightforward, effective assemblyman who took a hard, conservative stance on such issues as welfare and the environment. He was strongly pro-business, particularly the lumber industry. He and his "charming and talented wife" didn't share many interests: Steve hunted and golfed; Andrea was a "generous supporter of the arts" and a "lavish party-giver." An odd couple, I thought, and odd people to be friends of Jack Stuart, a liberal who'd chosen to dedicate his career to representing the underdog.

Back at the motel, I put in a call to Jack. Why, I asked him, had he remained close to a man who was so clearly his opposite?

Jack laughed. "You're trying to say politely that you think he's a pompous, conservative ass."

"Well . . ."

"Okay, I admit it: He is. But back in college, he was a mentor to me. I doubt I would have gone into the law if it hadn't been for Steve. And we shared some good times, too: One summer we took a motorcycle trip around the country, like something out of *Easy Rider* without the tragedy. I guess we stay in touch because of a shared past."

I was trying to imagine Steve Shoemaker on a motorcycle; the picture wouldn't materialize. "Was he always so conservative?" I asked.

"No, not until he moved back to Eureka and went to work for that lumber company. Then . . . I don't know. Everything changed. It was as if something had happened that took all the fight out of him."

What had happened, I thought, was trading another man's life for a prestigious job.

Jack and I chatted for a moment longer, and then I asked him to transfer me to Rae. She hadn't turned up anything on the Cardings yet, but was working on it. In the meantime, she added, she'd taken care of what correspondence had come in, dealt with seven phone calls, entered next week's must-do's in the call-up file she'd created for me, and found a remedy for the blight that was affecting my rubber plant.

With a pang, I realized that the office ran just as well—better, perhaps—when I wasn't there. It would keep functioning smoothly without me for weeks, months, maybe years.

Hell, it would probably keep functioning smoothly even if I were dead.

■   ■   ■

In the morning I opened the Yellow Pages to Florists and began calling each that was listed. While Shoemaker had been vague on the date his wife received the funeral arrangement, surely a customer who wanted one sent to a private home, rather than a mortuary, would stand out in the order-taker's mind. The listing was long, covering a relatively wide area; it wasn't until I reached the R's and my watch showed nearly eleven o'clock that I got lucky.

"I don't remember any order like that in the past six weeks," the clerk at Rainbow Florists said, "but we had one yesterday, was delivered this morning."

I gripped the receiver harder. "Will you pull the order, please?"

"I'm not sure I should—"

"Please. You could help to save a woman's life."

Quick intake of breath, then his voice filled with excitement; he'd become part of a real-life drama. "One minute. I'll check." When he came back on the line, he said, "Thirty-dollar standard condolence arrangement, delivered this morning to Mr. Steven Shoemaker—"

"*Mister?* Not Mrs. or Ms.?"

"Mister, definitely. I took the order myself." He read off the Shoemakers' address.

"Who placed it?"

"A kid. Came in with cash and written instructions."

Standard ploy—hire a kid off the street so nobody can identify you. "Thanks very much."

"Aren't you going to tell me—"

I hung up and dialed Shoemaker's office. His secretary told me he was working at home today. I dialed the home number. Busy. I hung up, and the phone rang immediately. Rae, with information on the Cardings.

She'd traced Sam Carding's daughter and younger son. The daughter lived near Cleveland, Ohio, and Rae had spoken with her on the phone. John, his sister had told her, was a drifter and an addict; she hadn't seen or spoken to him in more than ten years. When Rae reached the younger brother at his office in L.A., he told her the same, adding that he assumed John had died years ago.

I thanked Rae and told her to keep on it. Then I called Shoemaker's home number again. Still busy; time to go over there.

•   •   •

Shoemaker's Lincoln was parked in the drive of the Victorian, a dusty Honda motorcycle beside it. As I rang the doorbell I again tried to picture a younger, free-spirited Steve bumming around the country on a bike with Jack, but the image simply wouldn't come clear. It took Shoemaker a while to answer the door, and when he saw me, his mouth pulled down in displeasure.

"Come in, and be quick about it," he told me. "I'm on an important conference call."

I was quick about it. He rushed down the hallway to what must be a study, and I went into the parlor where we'd talked the day before. Unlike his offices, it was exquisitely decorated, calling up images of the days of the lumber barons. Andrea's work, probably. Had she also done his offices? Perhaps their gaudy decor was her way of getting back at a husband who put his political life ahead of their marriage?

It was at least half an hour before Shoemaker finished with his call. He appeared in the archway leading to the hall, somewhat disheveled, running his fingers through his hair. "Come with me," he said. "I have something to show you."

He led me to a large kitchen at the back of the house. A floral arrangement sat on the granite-topped center island: white lilies with a single red rose. Shoemaker handed me the card: "My sympathy on your wife's passing." It was signed "John."

"Where's Mrs. Shoemaker?" I asked.

"Apparently she went out to the coast last night. I haven't seen her since she walked out on us at the noon hour."

"And you've been home the whole time?"

He nodded. "Mainly on the phone."

"Why didn't you call me when she didn't come home?"

"I didn't realize she hadn't until mid-morning. We have separate bedrooms, and Andrea comes and goes as she pleases. Then this arrangement arrived, and my conference call came through . . ." He shrugged, spreading his hands helplessly.

"All right," I said, "I'm going out there whether she likes it or not. And I think you'd better clear up whatever you're doing here and follow. Maybe your showing up there will convince her you care about her safety, make her listen to reason."

As I spoke, Shoemaker had taken a fifth of Tanqueray gin and a jar of Del Prado Spanish olives from a Lucky sack that sat on the counter. He opened a cupboard, reached for a glass.

"No," I said. "This is no time to have a drink."

He hesitated, then replaced the glass, and began giving me directions to the cabin. His voice was flat, and his curious travelogue-like digressions made me feel as if I were listening to a tape of a *National Geographic* special. Reality, I thought, had finally sunk in, and it had turned him into an automaton.

. ▪ .

I had one stop to make before heading out to the coast, but it was right on my way. Morrison Investigations had its office in what looked to be a former motel on Highway 101, near the outskirts of the city. It was a neighborhood of fast-food restaurants and bars, thrift shops and marginal businesses. Besides the detective agency, the motel's cinder-block units housed an insurance brokerage, a secretarial service, two accountants, and a palm reader. Dave Morrison, who was just arriving as I pulled into the parking area, was a bit of a surprise: in his mid-forties, wearing one small gold earring and a short ponytail. I wondered what Steve Shoemaker had made of him.

Morrison showed me into a two-room suite crowded with computer equipment and file cabinets and furniture that looked as if he might have hauled it down the street from the nearby Thrift Emporium. When he noticed me studying him, he grinned easily. "I know, I don't look like a former cop. I worked undercover Narcotics my last few years on the force. Afterwards I realized I was comfortable with the uniform." His gesture took in his lumberjack's shirt, work-worn jeans, and boots.

I smiled in return, and he cleared some files off a chair so I could sit.

"So you're working for Steve Shoemaker," he said.

"I understand you did, too."

He nodded. "Last April and again around the beginning of August."

"Did he approach you about another job after that?"

He shook his head.

"And the jobs you did for him were—"

"You know better than to ask that."

"I was going to ask, were they completed to his satisfaction?"

"Yes."

"Do you have any idea why Shoemaker would go to the trouble of bringing me up from San Francisco when he had an investigator here whose work satisfied him?"

Headshake.

"Shoemaker told me the first job you did for him had to do with politics."

The corner of his mouth twitched. "In a matter of speaking." He paused, shrewd eyes assessing me. "How come you're investigating your own client?"

"It's that kind of case. And something feels wrong. Did you get that sense about either of the jobs you took on for him?"

"No." Then he hesitated, frowning. "Well, maybe. Why don't you just come out and ask what you want to? If I can, I'll answer."

"Okay—did either of the jobs have to do with a man named John Carding?"

That surprised him. After a moment he asked a question of his own. "He's still trying to trace Carding?"

"Yes."

Morrison got up and moved toward the window, stopped and drummed his fingers on top of a file cabinet. "Well, I can save you further trouble. John Carding is untraceable. I tried every way I know—and that's every way there is. My guess is that he's dead, years dead."

"And when was it you tried to trace him?"

"Most of August."

Weeks before Andrea Shoemaker had begun to receive the notes from "John." Unless the harassment had started earlier? No, I'd seen all the notes, examined their postmarks. Unless she'd thrown away the first ones, as she had the card that came with the funeral arrangement?

"Shoemaker tell you why he wanted to find Carding?" I asked.

"Uh-uh."

"And your investigation last April had nothing to do with Carding?"

At first I thought Morrison hadn't heard the question. He was looking out the window; then he turned, expression thoughtful, and opened one of the drawers of the filing cabinet beside him. "Let me refresh my memory," he said, taking out a couple of folders. I watched as he flipped through them, frowning.

Finally he said, "I'm not gonna ask about your case. If something feels wrong, it could be because of what I turned up last spring—and that I don't want on my conscience." He closed one file, slipped it back in the cabinet, then glanced at his watch. "Damn! I just remembered I've got to make a call." He crossed to the desk, set the open file on it. "I better do it from the other room. You stay here, find something to read."

I waited until he'd left, then went over and picked up the file. Read it with growing interest and began putting things together. Andrea had been discreet about her extramarital activities, but not so discreet that a competent investigator like Morrison couldn't uncover them.

When Morrison returned, I was ready to leave for the Lost Coast.

"Hope you weren't bored," he said.

"No, I'm easily amused. And, Mr. Morrison, I owe you a dinner."

"You know where to find me. I'll look forward to seeing you again."

■ ■ ■

And now that I'd reached the cabin, Andrea had disappeared.
The victim of violence, all signs indicated. But the victim of
whom? John Carding—a man no one had seen or heard from for
over ten years? Another man named John, one of her cast-off lovers? Or . . . ?

What mattered now was to find her.

I retraced my steps, turning up the hood of my sweater again
as I went outside, circled the cabin, peering through the lashing
rain. I could make out a couple of other small structures back
there: outhouse and shed. The outhouse was empty. I crossed to
the shed. Its door was propped open with a log, as if she'd been
getting fuel for the stove.

Inside, next to a neatly stacked cord of wood, I found her.

She lay facedown on the hard-packed dirt floor, blue-jeaned legs
splayed, plaid-jacketed arms flung above her head, chestnut hair
cascading over her back. The little room was silent, the total silence that surrounds the dead. Even my own breath was stilled;
when it came again, it sounded obscenely loud.

I knelt beside her, forced myself to perform all the checks I've
made more times than I could have imagined. No breath, no
pulse, no warmth to the skin. And the rigidity . . .

On the average—although there's a wide variance—rigor mortis
sets in to the upper body five to six hours after death; the whole
body is usually affected within eighteen hours. I backed up and
felt the lower portion of her body. Rigid; rigor was complete. I
straightened, went to stand in the doorway. She'd probably been
dead since midnight. And the cause? I couldn't see any wounds,
couldn't further examine her without disturbing the scene. What
I should be doing was getting in touch with the sheriff's department.

Back to the cabin. Emotions tore at me: anger, regret, and—
yes—guilt that I hadn't prevented this. But I also sensed that I
couldn't have prevented it. I, or someone like me, had been an
integral component from the first.

In the front room I found some kitchen matches and lit the oil
lamp. Then I went around the table and looked down at where
her revolver lay on the floor. More evidence; don't touch it. The
purse and its spilled contents rested near the edge of the stove. I

inventoried the items visually: the usual makeup, brush, comb, spray perfume; wallet, keys, roll of postage stamps; daily planner that had flopped open to show pockets for business cards and receipts. And a loose piece of paper . . .

Lucky Food Center, it said at the top. Perhaps she'd stopped to pick up supplies before leaving Eureka; the date and time on this receipt might indicate how long she'd remained in town before storming out on her husband and me.

I picked it up. At the bottom I found yesterday's date and the time of purchase: 9:14 P.M.

"KY SERV DELI . . . CRABS . . . WINE . . . DEL PRAD OLIVE . . . LG RED DEL . . . ROUGE ET NOIR . . . BAKERY . . . TANQ GIN—"

A sound outside. Footsteps slogging thorough the mud. I stuffed the receipt into my pocket.

Steve Shoemaker came through the open door in a hurry, rain hat pulled low on his forehead, droplets sluicing down his chiseled nose. He stopped when he saw me, looked around. "Where's Andrea?"

I said, "I don't know."

"What do you mean you don't know? Her Bronco's outside. That's her purse on the stove."

"And her weekend bag's on the bed, but she's nowhere to be found."

Shoemaker arranged his face into lines of concern. "There's been a struggle here."

"Appears that way."

"Come on, we'll go look for her. She may be in the outhouse or the shed. She may be hurt—"

"It won't be necessary to look." I had my gun out of my purse now, and I leveled it at him. "I know you killed your wife, Shoemaker."

"What!"

"Her body's where you left it last night. What time did you kill her? How?"

His faked concern shaded into panic. "I didn't—"

"You did."

No reply. His eyes moved from side to side—calculating, looking for a way out.

I added, "You drove her here in the Bronco, with your motor-cycle inside. Arranged things to simulate a struggle, put her in the shed, then drove back to town on the bike. You shouldn't have left the bike outside the house where I could see it. It wasn't muddy out here last night, but it sure was dusty."

"Where are these baseless accusations coming from? John Card-ing—"

"Is untraceable, probably dead, as you know from the check Dave Morrison ran."

"He told you—What about the notes, the flowers, the dead things—"

"Sent by you."

"Why would I do that?"

"To set the scene for getting rid of a chronically unfaithful wife who had potential to become a political embarrassment."

He wasn't cracking, though. "Granted, Andrea had her prob-lems. But why would I rake up the Carding matter?"

"Because it would sound convincing for you to admit what you did all those years ago. God knows it convinced me. And I doubt the police would ever have made the details public. Why destroy a grieving widower and prominent citizen? Particularly when they'd never find Carding or bring him to trial. You've got one problem, though: me. You never should have brought me in to back up your scenario."

He licked his lips, glaring at me. Then he drew himself up, leaned forward aggressively—a posture the attorneys at All Souls jokingly refer to as their "litigator's mode."

"You have no proof of this," he said firmly, jabbing his index finger at me. "No proof whatsoever."

"Deli items, crabs, wine, apples," I recited. "Del Prado Spanish olives, Tanqueray gin."

"What the hell are you talking about?"

"I have Andrea's receipt for the items she bought at Lucky yesterday, before she stopped home to pick up her weekend bag. None of those things is here in the cabin."

"So?"

"I know that at least two of them—the olives and the gin—are at your house in Eureka. I'm willing to bet they all are."

"What if they are? She did some shopping for me yesterday morning—"

"The receipt is dated yesterday *evening*, nine-fourteen P.M. I'll quote you, Shoemaker: 'Apparently she went out to the coast last night. I haven't seen her since she walked out on us at the noon hour.' But you claim you didn't leave home after noon."

That did it; that opened the cracks. He stood for a moment, then half collapsed into one of the chairs and put his head in his hands.

■　■　■

The next summer, after I testified at the trial in which Steve Shoemaker was convicted of the first-degree murder of his wife, I returned to the Lost Coast—with a backpack, without the .38, and in the company of my lover. We walked sand beaches under skies that showed infinite shadings of blue; we made love in fields of wildflowers; we waited quietly for the deer, falcons, and foxes.

I'd already taken the bad from this place; now I could take the good.

NIGHT FREIGHT

Bill Pronzini

Bill Pronzini's "Nameless" detective series is one of the major bodies of work in today's crime fiction.
And his short stories are just as good as his novels.
Here's a bleak, tangled tale redolent of desperate men and rainy nights. And the mourning of a past love.
This is Pronzini country and, as usual, he makes it all his own.

HE CAUGHT THE FREIGHT IN PHALENE, DOWN IN THE CITRUS belt, four days after they gave Joanie the divorce.

He waited in the yards. The northbound came along a few minutes past midnight. He hid in the shadows of the loading platform, watching the cars, and half the train had gone by before he saw the open box, the first one after a string of flats.

He trotted up alongside, hanging on to the big gray-and-white suitcase. There were heavy iron rungs running up the side of the box. He caught on with his right hand and got his left foot through the opening, then laid the suitcase inside and swung through behind it.

It smelled of dust in there, and just a bit of citrus, and he did not like the smell. It caught in his nose and in the back of his throat, and he coughed.

It was very dark, but he could see that the box was empty. He picked up the suitcase and went over and sat down against the far wall.

It was cold too. The wind came whistling in through the open door like a siren as the freight picked up speed. He wrapped his arms around his legs and sat there like that, hugging himself.

He thought about Joanie.

He knew he should not think about her. He knew that. It made things only that much worse when he thought about her. But every time he closed his eyes he could see her face.

He could see her smile, and the way her eyes, those soft brown eyes, would crinkle at the corners when she laughed. He could see the deep, silken brown of her hair, and the way it would turn almost gold when she stood in the sun, and the way that one little strand of hair kept falling straight down across the bridge of her nose, the funny little way it would do that, and how they had both laughed at it in the beginning.

No, he thought. No, I mustn't think about that.

He hugged his legs.

What had happened? he thought. Where did it go wrong?

But he knew what it was. They should never have moved to California.

Yes, that was it. If they had not moved to California, none of it would have happened.

Joanie hadn't wanted to go. She didn't like California. But he had had that job offer. It was a good one, but it meant moving to California and that was what started it all; he was sure of that.

Joanie had tried, he knew that. She had tried hard at first. But she had wanted to go home. He'd promised her he would take her home, he'd promised her that, just as soon as he made some money.

But she had wanted to go right away. There were plenty of good jobs at home, she said. Why did he want to stay in California?

He'd been a fool. He should have taken her home right away, like she'd wanted, and to hell with the job. Then none of it would have happened. Everything would be all right, now.

But he hadn't done that. It had started a lot of fights between them, her wanting to go home and him wanting to stay there in California, and pretty soon they were fighting over a lot of things, just small things, and he had hated those times. He hated to fight with Joanie. It made him sick inside; it got him all mixed up and made his head pound.

He remembered the last fight they had. He remembered it very well. He remembered how he had broken the little china figurine of the palomino stallion. He hadn't wanted to break it. But he had.

Joanie hadn't said much to him after that fight. He'd tried to make it up to her, what he'd done, and had gone out and bought her another figurine and told her he was sorry. But she had gotten very cold and distant then. That was when he knew she didn't love him anymore.

And then he'd come home from work that one night, and Joanie was gone, and there was just a note on the dining room table, three short sentences that said she was leaving him.

He didn't know what to do. He'd tried everywhere he could think of that she might have gone, the few friends they had made, hotels, but she had simply vanished. He thought at first she might have gone home, and made a long-distance call, but she was not there, and no, they didn't know where she was.

A week later her lawyer had come to see him.

He brought papers with him, a copy of the divorce statement, and told him when he was to appear in court. He had tried to make the lawyer tell her whereabouts, so he could see her and talk to her, but the lawyer had refused and said that if he tried to see her there would be a court order issued to restrain him.

He quit his job then, because he didn't care about the money anymore. All he cared about was Joanie. He could remember very little of what happened between then and the time the divorce came up.

He hadn't wanted to go to court. But he knew he had to go, if only just to see her again.

And when Joanie had come in, his heart had caught in his throat. He had stood up and called out her name, but she would not look at him.

Then her lawyer had gotten up and said how he had caused Joanie extreme mental anguish, and threatened her, and caused her to fear for her life. And how he would go off his head and rant and rave like a wild man, and how he should be remanded by the court into psychiatric custody.

He had wanted to shout that it was all a lie, that he had never said anything to cause Joanie to fear for her life, never done any of the things they said, because he loved her, and how could he hurt the one person he truly loved?

But he had sat there and not said anything and listened to the judge grant Joanie the divorce. Then, sitting there, it had come to him why Joanie had left him, and told all those lies to her lawyer, and why she wanted a divorce and didn't love him anymore.

Another man.

It had come to him all of a sudden as he sat there, that this was the answer, and he knew it was true. He did not know who the man could be, but he knew there was a man, knew it with a sudden and certain clarity.

He had turned and run out of the courtroom, and gone home and wept as only a man can in his grief.

The next day he had gone looking for her, through the entire city, block by block. For three days he had searched.

Then he had found her, living alone, in a flat near the river, and he had gone up there and tried to talk to her, to tell her he still loved her, no matter what, and to ask her about the other man. But she would not let him in, told him to go away and would not let him in. He had pounded on the door, pounded. . . .

His head had begun to pound now, thinking about it. His mind whirled and jumbled with the thoughts as he sat there in the empty box.

He lay down on the floor and pulled the suitcase to his body, holding on to it very tightly, and after a time, a long time, he slept.

He awoke to a thin patch of sunlight, shining in through the open door of the boxcar. He stood up and stretched, and his mind was clear now. He went over to the door and put his head outside.

The sun was rising in the sky, warm and bright. He looked around, trying to place where he was. The land was flat, and he could see brown foothills off in the distance, but it was nice and green in the meadows through which the freight was passing. He could smell alfalfa, and apple blooms, and he knew they had gotten up into northern California.

As he stood there, he could feel the train begin to slow. They came around a long bend. Up ahead he could see freight yards. The freight had begun to lose speed rapidly, now.

He could hear the hiss of air brakes and couplings banging together, and the train slid into the yards. There were two men standing in the shade of a shed out there, half-hidden behind it, dressed in khaki trousers and denim shirts, open down the front, and one of them had on a green baseball cap.

They just stood there, watching the freight as it slowed down.

He turned from the door and went over and sat down by the suitcase again. He was very thirsty, but he did not want to get off to go for a drink. He did not want anyone to see him.

He sat there for fifteen minutes; then he heard the whistle from the engine and the couplings banging together again, and the freight pulled out.

But just as it did, there was a scraping over by the door, and he saw two men, the same two who had been out by the shed, come scuttling in through the box door.

The freight picked up speed. The two men sat there, looking out. Then one of them stood and looked around, and saw him sitting there on the floor at the opposite end of the box.

"Well," this one said. He was the one in the green baseball cap. "Looks like we're going to have some company, Lon."

"Sure enough," Lon said, looking around.

They came over to where he was.

"You been riding long?" the one in the baseball cap said.

"Since Phalene," he said. He wished they had not come aboard. He wished they would go and leave him alone.

"Down in the citrus?"

"Yes."

"Where you headed for?"

"What?"

"You're going someplace, ain't you?"

"Yes," he said. "To Ridgemont."

"Where?"

"Ridgemont," he said again.

"Where's that?"

"In Idaho."

"You going all that way on the rails?"

"Yes."

"Well, that's a long pull. You want to watch yourself up there. They don't cotton much to fellows riding the freights."

"All right," he said.

They sat down. The one called Lon said, "Say, now, you

wouldn't happen to have a smoke on you, would you, friend? I just been dying for a smoke."

"Yes," he said.

"Much obliged."

They both took one. They sat there, smoking, watching him. He could tell that they were thinking he did not look like a man who rode the rails. He was not like them. The one in the baseball cap kept looking at his suitcase.

It was very hot in the boxcar, now. The two men gave off a kind of sour odor of dirt and sweat. This, mingled with the heat, made his stomach crawl.

He stood and went over to the door to get some air. He was conscious of their eyes on his back. It made him feel uneasy to have them watching him like that.

The freight moved on at considerable speed. They rode in silence most of the day, but the two men continued to watch him. They talked between themselves at brief intervals, but never to him, except when one of them would ask him for another cigarette.

As the afternoon turned into night, it began to cool down. Very suddenly there was a chill in the air. He could smell the salt then, sharp and fresh.

The one in the baseball cap buttoned his shirt up to his throat. "Getting cool," he said.

"We're running up the coast," the one called Lon said. "Be damn cold tonight."

They kept looking at him, then over at his suitcase. "You know, it sure would be nice if we had something to keep us warm on a cold night like it's going to be," the one in the baseball cap said.

"Sure would," Lon said.

"Say, friend," the one in the baseball cap said. "You wouldn't want to let us have anything in that bag there, would you?"

"What do you mean?" he said.

"Well, it sure going to be chilly tonight. Be real fine if you was to have something in there to keep us warm."

"Like what?"

"Maybe a blanket. Or a coat. Like that."

"No."

"You sure, now?"

"There's nothing in there like that."

"You wouldn't want to be holding out on a couple of fellows, now would you?"

"No."

"Then suppose you just open up that case and let us have a look inside," Lon said.

He put his hand on the case.

"You got no right," he said.

"Well, I say we do," the one in the baseball cap said. "I say we got plenty of right."

"Sure we do," Lon said.

They stood up.

"Come on, friend," the one in the baseball cap said. "Open up that case."

He stood up too.

"No," he said. "Stay away. I'm warning you."

"He's warning us," the one in the baseball cap said. "You get that, Lon?"

"Sure," Lon said. "He's warning us."

They stood there, the two men staring at him. He clutched the suitcase tightly in his right hand. Then, as they stood there, the freight began to slow. They were coming into a siding.

Outside it had begun to get dark. There were long shadows inside the boxcar.

The men watched each other, warily, and then, suddenly, Lon made a grab for the suitcase, and the one in the baseball cap pushed him back up against the wall of the box, and Lon tore the suitcase from his fingers.

He backed up against the wall. He was breathing hard. They shouldn't have done that, he thought. I told them. They shouldn't have done that.

He took out the knife.

Lon stopped pawing at the catch on the suitcase. They were both staring at him.

"Hey!" Lon said. "Hey, now."

"All right," he said to them. "I told you."

"Take it easy," the one in the baseball cap said, staring at the knife.

"Put the suitcase down," he said to Lon.

"Sure," Lon said. "You just take it easy."

"It was just a joke, friend," the one in the baseball cap said. "You know. A couple of fellows having a little game."

"That's it," Lon said. "Just a joke."

"We wasn't going to take nothing," the one in the baseball cap said.

He held the knife straight out in front of him. The blade was flat and wide and very sharp.

"Put it down," he said again.

"Sure," Lon said. He leaned down, never taking his eyes off the knife, and let go of the suitcase. The catch had been loosened in the struggle, and from Lon's pawing, and when it hit the floor of the box, it came open.

He said, "You get off this train. Right now. You just get off this train." He moved the knife in a wide circle and took a step towards them.

The one in the baseball cap said, "Oh, my God!" He took a step backward, and his face was the color of chalk. The freight was at a standstill, now.

"Get off," he said again. His head had begun to hurt.

The one in the baseball cap backed to the door, watching the knife, and caught onto the jamb and then turned and stepped off. Lon ran to the door and jumped off after him.

He put the knife away. He stood there for a time, and his mind whirled, and for a moment, just a moment, he remembered what had happened last night with Joanie—how he had forced his way into her flat, raging with anger, and told her he knew about the other man, and how she had denied it and said she was going to call the police, and how, then, he had hit her, and hit her again, and then he had seen the knife, the knife there on the table in the kitchen, the flat, sharp knife, and then it went black for him again and he could not remember anything.

The freight had begun to pull out of the siding. It was picking up speed. The whistle sounded in the night.

He turned and walked to where the suitcase lay, open on the floor of the box. He knelt down and began to cry.

He said, "It's all right now. We're going home. Going home to Ridgemont. Just like I promised you, Joanie. We're going home for good."

Joanie's head stared up at him from the open suitcase.

CAT'S EYE

Larry Segriff

With three novels and a dozen short stories behind him, Larry Segriff has more than lived up to the excitement created by his excellent story "Seeds of Death."

Here you find Larry working in the suspense genre. He's already a wily professional, stylish, engaging, sly.

He will soon be a major name in both contemporary science fiction and suspense.

I WATCHED THEM AS HE TOOK HER, MY TAIL TWITCHING WITH frustrated anger. He had entered her from the rear—"Cat fashion," I'd thought—and I couldn't tell if the sounds she was making were from pain or pleasure.

Leaping down from the bureau, I landed on the bed and cautiously approached. Closer, now, I could see the hot, silver tears glistening in her eyes and knew that she wasn't enjoying this. *The bastard,* I thought. *Who does he think he is? Marlon Brando?*

Stalking around them, I sniffed delicately at his pumping buttocks and wondered what she saw in him. Certainly his personal hygiene was nothing to write home about.

He noticed me then, though I would have thought he'd be oblivious to everything but his own sensations, and struck at me. I wasn't expecting it, and the blow flung me off the bed and into the wall. I heard her cry out, though whether from my pain or her own I couldn't tell, and I felt a flash of hatred stab through me before the shock sent me reeling back to myself.

. . .

Slowly I raised my head from where it had sagged down onto my chest, and brought shaking hands up to massage my brow. Read-

ing animals was hard enough; controlling them took even more
out of me. I'd be quivering for hours, I knew, but it had been
worth it.

I'd first discovered her only a few days ago. I'd been flying with
a bird, enjoying the freedom of flight and, more importantly, the
freedom from pain, when a small clearing had opened in the
woods beneath us. The bird was a sparrow, not a hawk, so my
eyesight wasn't that great, but I thought I saw something in that
clearing that intrigued me. Exerting my will, I flew down for a
closer look.

I was right. There was a small cabin nestled along one edge of
the clearing with a well-kept lawn and a woman in a lounger. She
was clearly sunbathing, and she was naked. Fluttering down to a
table beside her, I spent some few moments enjoying the view.

It was then that I learned she had a cat.

I never saw it, but I felt something bat at me with incredible
force, knocking me off the table and breaking one of my wings. A
paw fell on me as soon as I hit the ground, snapping my spine,
and a moment later I felt myself seized by a mouth full of needles.

"Percy!" She must have heard the one astonished twitter I'd
managed, or perhaps she'd seen the flurry of murderous activity.
"Bad cat! You drop that bird, Percy, right now!"

Surprisingly, the cat obeyed, but not before sinking his teeth
into my belly and back.

I wished, then, that she hadn't interfered. Her intended kind-
ness had turned into an act of cruelty. I was helpless—more so,
even, than when I was myself—and dying.

She should have let Percy finish me. Even if he'd toyed with
me first, it would have been quicker.

I stayed with the sparrow until the end, and it was a long time
coming. It's a painful, soul-searing thing to share another's death,
but I felt I owed it to the little bird. After all, it would never have
been caught if I hadn't forced it down there.

When the drain opened up, that dark, sucking vortex that at
times seems so inviting, I pulled away from my host. I could have
gone straight into the cat, but I was tired and I'd lost the desire
for sightseeing. Besides, he'd have the taste of my blood in his
mouth, and I just wasn't up to sharing that.

I returned home, instead, to my palsied body and my mechanical bed, but I made a mental note of where this place was. I thought I might want to return, and soon.

I'd worn myself out more than I'd realized, however, and had a rather bad time of it for a while. It was several days before I felt strong enough to return, and when I did, *he* was there.

I had no idea who he was or why he was there, but already I hated him. The way he treated her—hell, the way he treated me—fueled my anger. I spent less time recovering than I should have, and went back there that evening.

■   ■   ■

"Oh, Percival, I'm so sorry."

She held me in her lap, running her fingers lightly along my fur. There was a deep rumble coming from my throat, even though an occasional heavier touch woke flashes of pain in my left side. Broken ribs, I realized, from his blow, and probably bruises on the other side from hitting the wall.

I could hear a shower running. "I don't know what came over him," she said, still gently stroking me. "He's usually so nice, but this afternoon. . . ." Her voice trailed off as the water stopped.

She sighed. "I'd better go see if he wants anything." Setting me carefully on the floor, she eased out of her chair and walked rather stiffly across the living room.

He hurt her, too, I thought, anger flaring to new heights within me. Twitching my tail, I followed her into the bedroom.

He was just coming out of the adjacent bathroom, toweling himself off as he came. He was naked, and I had to admit I was impressed by his physique.

"What's the matter, hon?" he asked as he took the towel away from his hair and noticed her awkward gait.

She was in front of me so I couldn't see her face, but I heard the note of surprise as she repeated. "What's the matter? You were a little rough earlier, Terry, that's what's the matter."

He frowned, and even with my flattened, colorless vision I would have sworn the astonishment on his face was genuine. "I was? But I don't remem—"

He broke off then, right in the middle of a word, and his face changed. The frown fell away, replaced by a sly little smile, and I saw his manhood stir.

"Oh, yeah," he said, and even his voice was different: lower, rougher, and with a hint of mockery in it. "Admit it, Jess, you loved it."

"No," she started, and suddenly his left hand shot out and slapped her once, hard, across the face. Her head snapped back and his hand slipped down toward the front of her floral print dress. I heard a tearing sound, and saw her arms come up instinctively to cover herself, but he was having none of that. Pushing her backwards and onto the bed, he quickly twisted the damp towel into a sort of rope and used it to lash her wrists to the headboard.

Jesus, I thought. *He's like a man possessed.*

She was crying, a bit of blood leaking from her nose. He was sitting on her, fully aroused now, and had his hands on her naked breasts.

"No, stop," she sobbed, but he only grinned wider and squeezed harder.

My last thought hung in my head and understanding slowly dawned. *Like a man possessed.* It was hard for me to accept, although perhaps it shouldn't have been. The thing was, I'd been doing this for seven or eight years, ever since the onset of puberty brought both my gift and my curse, and in that time I'd never seen any indication that others could do this as well.

Until now.

Cautiously, I pulled away from the cat but caused my consciousness to remain. This was hard, almost as taxing as controlling another creature and far more difficult than just riding another's mind, but it was necessary. Slowly, then, and oh so carefully, I brought myself closer to Terry.

I didn't have to enter him to be sure. As I came up against the borders of his self, I could see the dark shadow that lay upon him. More, I could actually glimpse the silvery tether that bound this other telepath with his—I couldn't believe it could be a woman—own body. Worse, though, he sensed me as well.

Terry's head came up, a frown furrowing his brow and his eyes casting around. "What—" he began, and then his gaze fell on the cat. "You!" he said, a malicious grin twisting his lips.

I was no longer attached to Percy, but the cat seemed to know something was wrong. He tried to flee the room, but as he stretched himself into that first long, running stride one of his broken ribs must have shifted within him. He jerked slightly and fell, and in another moment Terry was off the bed and had seized the cat by its neck.

I almost joined with Percy again. The strain of remaining dis-embodied was draining my strength rapidly and, like the sparrow of a few days ago, I felt I owed it to him. I didn't, though. Terry was searching his eyes, looking—I felt sure—for some sign of me. My hope was that, not finding any, he might let the cat go.

My hope was short-lived. Without warning, the muscles along Terry's back and arms bunched. There was a sudden, sickening, snapping sound, and Percy went limp. He was dead, I knew, and Terry flung him into a corner.

Jess cried out, and I knew she'd witnessed the whole thing. My heart went out to her, and so did my self. Without actually willing it, I found myself joined with her.

"Easy, Jess," I murmured within her. I had never done this before, never even known that it was possible, but now that I was doing it I found that it was easy to maintain.

"Who are you?" Fortunately, she only thought the words. Terry was turning back to her, but it was only to resume what he'd started. He didn't seem aware that she had company as well.

"A friend," I replied, knowing that it was a woefully inadequate response. "Listen, Jess, I want you to know that it's not Terry who's doing these things. Another telepath, like me, is using him to do this to you. Do you understand, Jess? He probably won't even remember, later, what his body did."

She couldn't answer me right away. Terry had climbed back on top of her, straddling her stomach, and had just pinched her nip-ples viciously. Twin streaks of agony shot through her, taking all her thoughts and words away.

"Now, Jess," he whispered. "Let's have some fun."

I couldn't let it go on, but neither could I stop it. That one glimpse I'd gotten of the monster within him had showed me that it was stronger than me. Not that that was surprising. My power came from my mind, but the strength to wield it came from my body, and that twisted, painful shell I called home couldn't pro-vide me with much.

He started to really hurt her, and my anger exploded within me. I started to pull out of Jess, but she clung to me with a desperate strength. In that moment, she almost came along, and I found myself wondering whether such a thing was possible. Could I take her, a non-telepath, back to my own body, say? Could I find her a haven while her own physical self was being ravaged?

A wave of weakness hit me and I knew the answer was no. Maybe someone else could have. Maybe the telepath controlling Terry had that kind of strength, but I didn't.

"I'm sorry," I said to her. Her only reply was a wordless cry of anguish and despair. This time, when I pulled away, she didn't cling.

Disembodied once more, I hovered near the edge of that shadow, hunting for another glimpse of his lifeline. When it showed, I seized upon it, knowing that this was the moment of greatest danger.

He had to sense me; he must have felt my touch, but perhaps God was with me. More likely, though, Jess had somehow caught an echo of my half-formed plan. Either way, she moved beneath him just as his head started to come up, drawing his attention to her.

"Hold still, bitch," I heard him say and she cried out. Then I was gone, following his argent umbilical back to his lair.

His strength was awesome. My own line stretched behind me like a gossamer thread, but his was like a rope. It was too bad, really, that I couldn't cut that rope, but it was as immaterial as I was.

A second wave of weariness washed over me as I neared his home and I knew I was rapidly approaching my limits. If I didn't return to my own body soon, I never would. That thought almost sent me fleeing, but I could picture all too easily what was happening at that moment back at the cabin.

"Come on," I urged myself, "you're practically there. Don't give up now."

His house came into view and to my eyes it was a dark, brooding place. Set near some railroad tracks, it was in the seediest neighborhoods around, and this telepath's inner rage was suddenly easier to understand. Poor did not mean evil, I knew, but this part of town bred hopelessness and despair like our sewers bred rats.

He was lying in bed in near-total darkness, but I didn't need any light to see. As I hovered above him, I felt my compassion drain away, overcome by renewed rage. He was older, for one thing, maybe in his fifties or sixties, not the hormone-wracked teenager I'd envisioned. Certainly, he was old enough to be responsible for his actions. More than that, as far as I could tell he was healthy, and that was intolerable. Not that he had it easy, obviously. The room was hardly more than a closet and the whole house little more than a shack, yet I could sense the presence of maybe a dozen other people within its walls. Still, I couldn't help feeling fate had been kinder to him than to me. He got the gift without the curse. In whatever other unkind ways the deck was stacked against him, at least this wasn't his only hope of walking away from it. However slim his chances, he'd had the potential to leave his troubles behind him.

Unlike me.

Yet here he was, not only escaping his own tortured life, but actually inflicting that same pain on others.

Another swell of fatigue, this one with an undertow the other had lacked, surged within me, but I refused to acknowledge it. Instead, I drifted closer and then merged with his empty shell.

The first thing I noticed was the smell, a horrid, fetid miasma of unclassifiable stinks. The second was the sound, a constant, almost physical combination of rats chittering in the dark, the snores and snuffles of too many sleepers in too small a space, and the eerie, haunting hoot of an approaching train. The third thing was the alarm, trilling along his silver lifeline and warning him that something was wrong.

If I was going to do something, it would have to be soon.

Sitting up, I looked around quickly, searching for anything I could use as a weapon. There was nothing. I didn't want to fight him off; that was never even a possibility. What I was trying to do was to find a way to kill his body, but nothing came to mind. Even the windows were useless, all boarded up and free of glass.

It hadn't been much of a plan, I knew, but its failure came as a blow. I tried to cheer myself up with the realization that it hadn't been a total loss. I'd learned where he lived. I could come back some other time, when I was stronger, and try again. Now, though, I had to leave, to get back to my body and recover.

Sorry, Jess.

I could feel him coming, his approach trumpeted along the silver cord, and I started to pull out. In that moment, a tremor passed along my own line and I knew it was too late. I was dying. I could go home if I chose, but I would never be coming back.

Ironically, unexpected strength suddenly poured into me. It was as if my body, aware that all was lost, had opened up the floodgates and given me its last reserves. "Take it," the gesture seemed to say. "Take it and do something."

"I will," I promised. Rising, still clad in this alien body, I fled into the night.

If I'd been stronger, if I'd had more practice with people, I might have tried to move into one of the sleepers. Surely one of them could have strangled this monster, but I didn't even consider it. Instead, I ran for the railroad tracks, and the approaching train.

I didn't make it.

I was still a good ten feet away when he burst upon me. The shock of it drove me to my knees. I tried to struggle against him, but he had too much experience with such things. In a matter of moments he was once more firmly in control of his body, and he had a lock on me as well.

Pain washed over me, then, and for a moment I believed it was simply frustration over my defeat. I thought of Jess, and of Terry, and even of poor little Percival. "I'm sorry," I whispered, aiming it at them like a prayer.

He heard me, though, and misunderstood. "Yeah? Well, sorry ain't good enough, asshole, not by half. No, I think we'll just travel back along that little thread of yours and do to you what you were about to do to me."

The pain doubled and then doubled again, and I felt myself spasm within his grasp.

"Oh, no, you don't," he said, misinterpreting again, and tightened his hold. It was then that I felt the familiar sucking nibbling at the edges of myself and I knew what had just happened.

Smiling, albeit rather grimly, I reached out with the last of my strength. "All right," I answered him. "Let's go."

He still didn't understand, not until we pulled away from his body and he saw that enormous whirlpool waiting to take me. He released his grip on me then and tried to break mine, but like the tether it was not a physical thing. I held on.

A moment later and we were caught. He cried out, once, a long, despairing sound and then, just before the darkness claimed me, I thought I heard the purring of a cat.

THE MIDNIGHT TRAIN

John Lutz

"SFW Seeks Same" is John Lutz's most popular work.
Thanks to the movie.
But Lutz is hardly a one-note author.
A quarter-century into his career, John Lutz has written vir-
tually every kind of popular fiction, and has built a large and
steady following for his books.
Here is a new approach to a somewhat familiar theme, told
in the strong but underplayed style Lutz prefers.

FROM FAR IN FRONT OF ULMAN THE SHRILL, DRAWN-OUT SOUND
of the locomotive's whistle drifted back, long and lonely notes,
like the forlorn wails of a distant siren. Ulman, bracing himself
against a rough plywood wall, in the swaying boxcar, rose slowly.
He could feel the train losing speed already as it slowed for the
unmarked and seldom used crossing just outside of Erebville. It
wouldn't do for him to ride all the way into the Erebville switch-
yard, for he'd been told that the railroad dicks were tough and
eager there, especially this time of year, when the hoboes and
migrant fruit pickers were moving west. Ulman had been told back
east by a knowledgeable one-eyed hobo that the train would slow
for this crossing about midnight, and that was the time to leap.

He made his way across the lurching car to the wide steel door
that was closed all the way to a warped two-by-four, which he'd
jammed in place to keep from getting locked in. He held on to
the edge of the door for a moment, drew a deep breath, then with
all his strength shot it sliding open.

Cool country air rushed in on him as he looked out into moonless darkness. He rubbed his grizzled chin, waiting for just the

right moment. As the train rolled to its slowest point, then began to regain its speed, he leaped.

Ulman got to his feet slowly, slapping the dust off his clothes. His legs felt rubbery after the constant motion and his ears missed the constant roar. He grinned as the roar diminished and he saw the train's lights disappear in the distance. Tomorrow he'd hike to the other side of Erebville and jump the next twelve o'clock train west.

But where to spend the night? That was the problem, but a problem that Ulman had solved hundreds of times before. He stared about him into the darkness, and then he saw the lights. They appeared to be coming from the window of a house about a mile off. It struck Ulman as odd that one of these country families would be up so late, and lucky, for he might be able to negotiate for a bunk in an outbuilding. If not that, at least he'd have a chance for a good feed in the morning. He made sure that nothing had fallen from his pockets, then set off walking.

It turned out to be a small frame farmhouse, and the only outbuildings were a ramshackle barn and a pigpen, neither of which appealed to Ulman as night quarters. He walked quietly toward the porch, noting that the usually present farm dog hadn't barked to reveal his presence. Before stepping up on the porch he decided to peek in one of the shadeless windows.

The inside of the house was dirty and cheaply furnished. The naked bulb in the ceiling fixture cast bright light over a worn carpet, ancient, ready-to-collapse chairs and a ripped sofa. Ulman decided to sleep in the open tonight and approach the house again in the morning for breakfast. He was about to turn away when a woman entered the room.

Her inexpensive flower-print dress matched her surroundings, but the woman didn't. She was about thirty, Ulman guessed, tall and graceful, with fine features, straight brown hair and very large blue eyes. Though the dress she wore was obviously cheap, it couldn't have been designed or worn better to show off her curvaceous figure. The hemline was well above shapely knees, the waist drawn in, the neckline low. She held a white cat cradled in her left arm while she idly stroked it with a graceful right hand. Ulman could tell somehow by her actions that she was alone.

Her beauty caused Ulman to draw in his breath sharply. The remoteness of the situation sent very evil thoughts darting across his mind, thoughts which he quickly dispelled, for Ulman was a poetic if not a literate man, a man who appreciated beauty and was at the same time bound by the peculiar morality of his type.

As he watched, the woman set the cat down and smoothed her dress sensually, seductively, with her slender hands. Ulman backed away from the window, frightened by the lust that was pounding through his veins, knowing to what it could ultimately lead. He turned and made himself walk quietly away. Then he made himself run.

Just after sunrise the next morning, Ulman rose from his cramped position beneath a tree, stretched, brushed off his canvas windbreaker, and began walking toward the farmhouse.

The house appeared more squalid in the daylight than it had the night before. Ulman noted that the fields surrounding it were grown over with weeds. He saw no stock except for a hog near the barn and several chickens in the barren farmyard. Then he noted two more hogs on the other side of the barn, but his eyes were trained on them for only a second. They switched immediately to the woman, still wearing the print dress, hanging a breeze-whipped line of wash.

She was aware of him, Ulman could tell, but she pretended not to notice him as she stretched upward to fasten clothespins as he approached. He stood silently for a moment, taking her in with his eyes, aware of the sharp, scrunching sound of wood and rope on wet cloth as she jammed down the final clothespin to hold a sheet to the line, then turned. There was no surprise or fear in her blue eyes, and this made Ulman even more ill at ease in the face of her beauty.

"Your mister at home?" he asked. He knew the answer to that.

"Ain't no mister here," she said, shifting her weight to one foot and staring frankly at him.

"I, uh, wonder," Ulman said, "if you could spare a bite of breakfast. I'd be willin' to work for it."

She ignored the question. "You hopped off'n that freight went by here last night, didn't you?"

Ulman's heart leaped. Had she seen him at the window? He

decided to play it casually. "Sure did, missy. On my way to a job in California."

"California's a long ways."

"Sure is." Ulman rubbed his chin. "How'd you know I come off that freight?"

"Lots of fellas do," she said. "For some reason they don't want to ride all the way in to Erebville."

"Railroad dicks," Ulman said bitterly. "Always ready to lay a club alongside a man's head."

The woman smiled suddenly. "My name's Cyrila."

Ulman returned the grin, ashamed of his soiled clothes and dirty face. "Lou Ulman."

"Well, Mr. Ulman, you can wash up there at the pump an' I'll fix us some eggs."

Ulman grinned again, his eyes involuntarily running up and down the woman. "I appreciate it, ma'am."

Surprisingly the breakfast of scrambled eggs, bread, fresh-brewed coffee, and a tall glass of orange juice looked delicious. Ulman sat down across from the woman at the table and began to eat with enthusiasm as he discovered the food to be as tasty as it looked. After the first few bites he realized she was staring at him.

"You say you live here alone?" he asked, wiping a corner of his mouth with a forefinger.

Cyrila nodded, her blue eyes still fixed on him intently. "Husband died five years ago."

Ulman took a large bite of bread and talked around it. "Quite a job makin' ends meet for a woman, ain't it? What do you raise?"

"Pigs, mostly. A few chickens."

Ulman nodded. "Them's nice-lookin' pigs. How many you got?"

The woman sipped her coffee. " 'Bout a dozen. Hard to keep more'n that in feed. I sell 'em in the fall when they're fat enough and use some of the money to buy piglets."

"Start all over again then, huh?"

The woman nodded, smiling her beautiful smile. "Toilin' in the fields ain't woman's work," she said with a hint of coyness. "Pigs is about all that's left in these parts. Good profit in 'em if you can afford to feed 'em all summer long."

Ulman finished his eggs and licked the fork appreciatively.

"More, Mr. Ulman?" Her eyelids fluttered exaggeratedly and he suspected she was trying to use her feminine wiles on him, trying to lead him on.

He thought, looking at her, *I ain't that lucky.* "No, no thank you, ma'am. I'm full up."

"If you will, call me Cyrila," she said, toying with her coffee spoon.

Ulman hesitated, then smiled. "Sure will," he said, "Cyrila."

"There's a stack of firewood out behind the barn," she said smiling. "It does need—"

"Now, Cyrila," Ulman interrupted, "I said I'd work for my food an' I meant it. Just show me where the ax is."

After he'd chopped wood for an hour, Ulman found himself scything down the tall weeds behind the house, then mending the crude wire fence that surrounded the pigpen on the other side of the barn. Most of the time he worked he sang to himself, all the time watching for Cyrila as she worked in the house and yard. Now and then she'd smile and wave to him from a window, or turn from getting water at the pump and give him a warm look.

It must get lonely out here without a man, Ulman muttered, wielding the heavy hammer. It must.

It was almost sundown when he finished. He washed up at the pump while she stood gracefully on the porch, watching. He let the still-hot sun dry him briefly, slipped on his shirt, slicked back his hair with wet fingers and walked toward her, following her into the house.

It was cooler inside the house, and dim. The reverberating slam of the rusty screen door rang through the heavy air and left them in silence.

"You surely did a good day's work," she said. Her smile seemed a little forced this time, and she held onto the back of the old sofa as if for support.

He grinned and shrugged. "I guess you need a man around here, is all."

"Don' I know it, now?" She stepped away from the sofa. "I bet you sure worked up a thirst."

"Thirst? Well, yeah. It's close to that ol' bewitchin' hour, though, an' I gotta be on the other side of Erebville to jump that train. But if you got somethin' around . . ."

"I think there's some still in the cupboard," she said, the smile still set on her face. "It'll be old. Jus' use it for guests and medicine."

Ulman followed her into the kitchen. "The older the better."

His eyes roved up her as she stood on her toes to reach the top shelf. There were some cans and three bottles up there, two off-brand whiskeys and a more expensive bourbon bottle half full. She got down the expensive bottle and turned, handing it to him.

Ulman took a long swig, savoring the smoothness and warmth of the bourbon. The woman was watching him. He moved to hand the bottle back to her and her hand closed on his, squeezing the fingers around the neck of the bottle as if she meant for him to keep it. He was surprised to see that she was on the verge of crying.

"You're right, Mr. Ulman," she said, looking up at him. "I surely do need a man around here." She buried her head on his shoulder, sobbing, her body pressed against him. With his right hand Ulman held the bottle, with his left Cyrila's warm back. With his foot he kicked open the bedroom door.

■   ■   ■

It was pitch dark in the farmhouse when Cyrila rose. She stood by the bed, stretching languidly, then walked barefoot into the kitchen. She placed the bourbon bottle back in the cupboard, aside from the other bottles, and slipped into some old coveralls, rolled up at the sleeves.

Then the only sounds in the darkness were a heavy thump in the bedroom and the squeak of the rusty wheelbarrow axle. Some time later, from the area of the barn, came the uneven gnashing of the chicken feed grinder working on something hard, amid the loud, thoroughly satisfied grunting and rooting of the pigs.

An hour later Cyrila was standing on the farmhouse porch. She had on her flower-print dress again, and behind her every light in the house blazed. A far-off wail, like a forlorn siren, rolled through the night. She stood listening to the approaching thunder of the distant train, heard it slow momentarily, then with a blast of new thunder begin to regain its speed. Gradually it left her in silence. She unconsciously smoothed the dress over her hips, sighed, then turned and walked into the house. The midnight train roared westward through the inky darkness—but Ulman wasn't on it.

I'M NOT THAT KIND OF GIRL

Marthayn Pelegrimas

Marthayn Pelegrimas brings a quiet, subtle touch to what could easily be some very noisy stories. Her stuff kind of sneaks up on you. And that's real nice.

Marthayn has worked in several genres but her best work seems to be in the subgenre called "dark suspense." A little darker in theme than the average mystery, yet not quite so horrific as horror.

I READ ONCE THAT LONELINESS IS THE BOND UNITING TWENTIETH century adults. Thousands and thousands of people so desperate for anyone to share a meal with, hold in the night. Don't touch, I warn. Why won't they listen? It's infuriating, predictable and boring.

Men approach me, smug, playing their games, directed by lopsided rules, making private decisions when to disconnect. The pattern is maddening—always the same. Mid-life has left cautious survivors. Wiser, they think naivete was packed away, long ago, with virginity and hope. So vain, so stupid. I warn I'm different. But they've seen it all through myopic, contact lensed eyes. Tyrannical dwarfs ruling the minute kingdom of their diminutive brain.

He watches me, smiles, lifts a half-filled glass: the prelude to a hundred similar scenes. What energizes his gestures? Loneliness or the life weary baggage he lugs from city to city?

He's typical, like all the others: six feet, covered in three pieces of a matching pinstriped suit; he strives to blend in the executive world. Divorced, he's fathered 2.3 children and is now bitter. Love screwed him over, royally. Never again, he's learned that women are bitches, cock-sucking, money-hungry bitches. He's out for a good time now. There's nothing real about him, not even the name he'll introduce. What the hell. He's in Midwest USA for this one evening. He's deodorized, stylized and working on his third scotch and water.

I just want to listen to the band, drink my vodka in the cool dimness. I want to be left alone in a world of desperate joiners, organizers and fanatics. I have no cause, no passion burns inside my heart for inhumanities suffered throughout the world. I crave time to relax, don't want to be cordial, sociable or extend myself.

He smiles again, hoping to snag my attention from his bar stool. I look away. Maybe it's the indifference that attracts. I know him without the benefit of physical contact. He ate dinner alone: a steak, well done, small dinner salad, no roll, no butter, watching his cholesterol count. He lays in the sun, by the pool of his singles apartment on weekends. His eyes never miss a pair of twenty year old breasts bobbing under bikini pouches. His shoes are imitation leather, his watch a genuine Rolex knock-off and the pinkie ring, a six diamond, fourteen karat gold bargain, was purchased through the cousin of a friend.

He comes over to my table. "Mind if I join you?"

"Yes." Not an insult, the truth. "Yes, I do."

He laughs, they always do. His brain long ago deciphered the mysteries of womankind. His father educated that females always mean yes when they scream no. They all want to be raped, son. The American dream.

I look to the stage, concentrating on a red-haired drummer. He beats the skins with vicious force. I feel the man standing at my back, wrestling between anger and dejection. He'll try charm—phase one.

"I didn't mean to offend you. It's just that I saw you sitting here, alone. Has anyone ever told you you're a dead ringer for Grace Kelly?"

"Yes." I don't bother to turn around. Why can't he feel the chill from my cold shoulder? Where's his pride?

"Ahhh, I'm new in town; don't know a soul. Maybe we could have a drink, talk?" His hands go up displaying smooth palms. "I don't bite, honest." Phase two—sympathy.

He won't leave. They never do, even after I warn them. Why

prolong the discomfort of his hovering, shifting from leg to leg? "One drink."

Beaming. His face lights up like it's Christmas, for chrissake. "Look, I meant it. I can tell you're a lady. I just want someone to talk to."

They always say "to" when they mean "at." I can't even pretend interest as he explains the complexities of computers, his hopes for a military contract. He speeds on, his tongue has shifted into third gear. He mistakes my nod for attention.

"I have to warn you . . ." I start. But they always interrupt.

"I know, I know." He touches my hand. "You're not the kind of girl who picks up strange men in bars."

"No, I wasn't going to say that."

"Well, maybe not in so many words, but I can tell. I could see from across the room that you're a lady."

It must be the blond hair. Inside, I'm dark, seething with yearnings never fulfilled. Outside I appear frosted over with calm. "I'm trying to explain . . ."

"Don't worry; I won't hurt you," he assures.

"I wasn't worried."

"Good. I'm one of those old-fashioned, honest type guys. And you're shy, sheltered and trusting. Have to protect yourself. Take it from one who's been around, quite a few times, it's tough out there."

"I know."

"Do you?" he asks, mocking, unbelieving the jade flecks scorching my eyes as anger heats the water filming over.

"Yes."

Phase three: All-Knowing-World-Traveler lectures Sweet-Young-Thing.

He has no hint of my age, wouldn't believe I'm older than the fantasy his hormones dictate to his crotch. He wants me innocent, sees me through his retarded time warp.

The scotch breeds familiarity. Closer, I smell his breath while he snakes an arm across the back of my chair. "You live in a small town."

"I'm not from here, originally."

"Whatever, it's not where you're from, you're alone . . ."

"By my own choosing."

"No. No woman wants to be alone. You want a man, children, a home."

"Who told you this?" Why don't I leave? He'd only follow, apologize, cajole, and patronize.

"Like I said, I've been out there. A woman wants a man, forget all this equality bullshit. Keep 'em barefoot and pregnant. The old timers knew the secret."

"Stop it." No more. I can't handle this another time. I stand, knocking over the low cushioned chair. "I have to go."

"I'm sorry. I didn't mean to cuss. I'm sure you're not accustomed to such language."

Assuming his words offended strictly for their grammatical value, not content, I warn one last time. "You don't know what I'm accustomed to. You don't know anything about me, not one goddamn thing!"

"You're right." He pats me on the head with condescending words. "I don't know you, personally. But I do know women like you, in your position. Look, I didn't mean to come off rude. Can I buy you another drink, please?"

He bends down, sets my chair upright. "Here." Swiveling it around to accept my bottom. "Sit," commanding like an animal trainer. I want to scratch his face.

We're gearing up for phase four—second to the last. He's so desperate, worrying only for his comfort on a long night in a strange town.

"One more drink."

He's shallower than the others. Insincerity is his second skin. I've tried warning him. I am a fair person. And truthful—painfully truthful. But this would be a public service. Maybe I do have a cause, a reason to react.

I sit.

"Come here often?" He begins again.

It's difficult not laughing at his lack of imagination.

"No."

"The band's okay, for a local group."

"How do you know they're local?"

"Playing in a place like this, they'd have to be."

"Oh, I forgot, you've been everywhere. You know all there is to know about women, music . . ."

"Not exactly. I just know about life."

Opps, back step to phase three, another lecture, I intercede. "I don't even know your name and here you are educating me about life. I'm Mary." The name fits his needs, he'll eat it up. I smile at my improvisation.

"I knew it." He nods, lower lip extended in a contemplative gesture. "A sweet name for a sweet lady. Glad to meet you, Mary. I'm Stephen." He offers a hand. Polite. "Steve."

I shake glad-to-meet-you. "Now, you were going to tell me about life."

Wouldn't it be wonderful if Steve What's-His-Last-Name? reflected for a moment, turned and said, "I don't think you need anyone to tell you about life." No, I forgot, he knows my type.

"Oh, right. I don't want to upset you, Mary, but things aren't always what they seem to be."

"Really?" I'm going to rip the mustache off his face.

"Really. People are mean and crazy."

"I know, Steve, for God's sake, do you think I just dropped out of the sky? I do have a life, been around myself, several times."

Phase four—he apologizes, again.

"I'm sorry. I just don't think you grasp my meaning."

"It's not that difficult. You are speaking English. I have excellent hearing. And your I.Q. is certainly not comparable with that of Einstein's. What's not to grasp?" Holding in the majority of my anger, he's only receiving surface irritability.

"I'm saying that people are devious, calculating. I've met more than my share."

"Who hasn't?"

"A girl like you? Pretty, sweet, pampered, used to getting what she wants."

"Some things come easily, others have to be worked for."

"But, someone like you must not have to work too hard and long for what she really wants."

"Ahh, you're so wrong. I want to be left alone and would you believe all the trouble and work I have to extend just for peace?"

"A piece?" He smirks, insulated in the soundproof booth between his ears.

"I'm leaving."

"So soon?"

"Yes, so soon." I'll kill him if I stay another minute, looking into those imbecilic eyes. I stand.

"Can't I walk you to your car, at least?"

"Why?" No more warnings; he's begging for it.

He reaches inside his pocket for bills to pay the tab. "You never know who's out there."

"Yeah, maybe someone waiting to make me barefoot and pregnant." A joke. He doesn't laugh.

"Trust me, the world's crawlin' with freaks and doped-up loonies."

"And we wouldn't want any of them to violate a girl like me."

"No way, sweetheart."

We turn toward the door. Two fraternity brothers take time from chugging their beer as I pass the bar. My dress is cut low in the back; I sense their eyes feeling me up.

"I can find my own car."

"Let a man take care of you, enjoy." He grabs my hand, kisses the tip of each finger.

Phase five.

His touch disgusts me, his sexual, rehearsed nibbling squeezes bile from my stomach into my mouth. He's been warned. I've tried being truthful and honest. He deserves it.

"If it'll make you feel better." Coy now, I'll play the game. "My car's over there."

A smile slimes over his lips, evening wind tries ruffling his hair-sprayed cut as we walk across the black-topped parking lot.

"What a coincidence, we're parked alongside each other." This insignificant detail delights him. "I assume that's your car next to my Mercedes."

My cue to be impressed. "Gee, my old Toyota looks like trash compared to your car." Opening eyes wide, I look up, allow him to gloat.

"Do you have to go right home? I'd like to buy you breakfast."

"I really shouldn't." Act hesitant, that ensures they'll beg.

"Please, just a cup of coffee if you're not hungry."

"Well, I do have work tomorrow."

"Awww." Now it's his turn to stare wide-eyed, con. He's almost as good as I.

"All right. There's a place around the corner."

Opening the passenger door of his red car, he commands, "Hop in."

This is too easy, no challenge, why expend the energy?

"I can take my own car."

Then, he touches again. Nudges me onto the leather seat with his cologned body. "Hey, babe, ride in style. Come on, let Steve take care of you."

The heavy door slams, almost catching my shoe. I vibrate with anger, fury induced by his artificial concern. God, I laugh to myself, this one's too easy.

He lets himself in the driver's side, positioned behind the steering wheel, he leans, kisses me, taking me by surprise. I feel his tongue dart into my mouth. "No."

"I couldn't help myself. You're so beautiful."

Poor, pathetic Steve. He hasn't got a chance at the competition he's entered. I always take first place. I'm the undefeated champion. A song lyric repeats in my head, "pretty girls just seem to find out early, how to open doors with just a smile."

It never surprised me when the butcher gave me candy every time I wore that yellow sundress, tied my hair back in a bow. My first evening gown, realizing I had the boys wrapped around the crook of my pinkie.

In college, professors promised grades for favors. I warned them, I tried telling them, but they were scholars. Dean Chadwell knew all about life, too. Just like good ole Steve. I used to fight against my femininity; now I make it work for me. The intelligence camouflaged under fluffed hair, behind emerald eyes, allows me to manipulate these morons.

"Can we go now? Suddenly, I'm starved."

His eyebrows rise with his hopes. "For what?" He won't give up.

"Breakfast." I play dumb. I'm the champion, remember?

"Whatever your little heart desires." Gallant, he thinks he's scored and is on the field heading for a touchdown.

"First," I insist, "buckle your seatbelt. We don't want anything to happen to you, do we?"

"That's cute." He pats my cheek. "I usually don't bother with the damned thing, messes up the suit. But for you . . . anything."

I purr, "Thank you, Stephen."

Suddenly he whips the silver clasp, striking me along the left temple. "Slut! How much of your shit am I supposed to swallow?"

Don't panic, don't panic. I reach to ease the ache inside my skull. Blood warms a trail toward my ear.

He twists my wrist, pulls me toward him. "Where the hell do you get off thinking you're so goddamn special?" His teeth clamp my lower lip in a vicious kiss. "I'll just have to teach you about the real world, the real threats to your precious little ass."

Not yet, I've been through worse. Hold on, must save myself to win, ensure victory.

Perspiration soaks through his monogrammed shirt; I smell his excitement. He grunts. Shoving me, pulling my legs, he rips off my shoes, throwing them into the back seat. "Now you'll get it. You'll beg for it. Beg. Come on, bitch, start begging."

He's in a frenzy to thrust his hatred inside me. My pantyhose shred as his raging fingers tear through the flimsy material.

I kick, clench my knees together, my purse serves as a weapon. I beat his head with its studded front.

"You're nothing but a goddamn whore. You deserve everything you're gonna get. What kind of lady sits in a bar?"

I struggle as he forces his hand between my legs, turns and wedges his knees inside my thighs while his other hand unzips his pants.

"I knew you were garbage from the first piece of crap outta your mouth." Trying to distract him, I continue to taunt, slapping his face. "Come on, Stud. Think you got what it takes?"

"You'll never forget tonight," he spits.

Crouched over me, his manicured nails scratch into my panties. He looks surprised, they always do—at first. Later on, toward the end, they look stunned. But, at this moment, Steve recoils with a surprised scream that falls from his mouth as my penis unfolds from its black lace binding.

Yanking the blond wig from my head, I scream, "Surprise! Welcome to the REAL world, Stephen, darling."

"Freak!" He presses himself into the driver's seat. "Holy shit!"

I don't realize it's a pen. The cold metal attracts my hand as I claw myself upright. His eyes bulge with the first stab. Bull's-eye! Straight to the heart.

"Oh God!" He looks to verify the pain shooting through his chest.

I'm quick. Five more stabs into his shirt before he can react, much less open the door. The steering wheel pins down his flailing legs.

"You wouldn't leave me alone, would you?"

Stab!

Ten more times. Blood spurts across the dashboard, dribbles down the windshield.

"Dear God!" He doesn't know where to grab first. He's a frantic Dutchboy trying to plug erupting holes with his fingers.

Stab!

He tries wrestling the pen from my hand. Undefeated, I stab again.

"You . . . are . . . so . . . smart." I plunge with each syllable. "You've seen it all. Right, Stephen, baby? Seen any loonies or crazy people lately, huh? ANSWER ME! Seen any whores or blond bitches? SPEAK UP STUD!"

"Please. Why?"

I punch holes along his thigh. Up and down. The car flecks with red dots, his slacks paisley into a bloody maroon. He's quiet, heaving against the seat.

I whisper, "Stephen. Oh, Stephen."

He lunges, revived with terror.

"Good! Man to man—mano a mano—a fair fight." I bend back a little finger until it cracks then gouge his palm.

His hands go to his face, shielding. "What? Jesus Christ! What do you want? Why are you doing this?"

I giggle, digging the sticky pen into his cheek, an unprotected area. "To show you, to make a point." Laughing, I take a Kleenex from my purse, wipe the instrument designed for writing. "Come on, keep up with me." I yell into his ear, jerk his head forward and release it banging into the window.

He whimpers.

Why did I clean the pen? Have to dot my exclamation points.

"I've suffered insulting remarks from bastards like you for too many years. I've tried reason. I've run through years of patience. It's always the same. You won't listen. The whole world is divided by your rules, into two groups: normal and freak. I warned you to leave me alone. I've warned you all.

"But you laughed when I told you to go away. Remember? You, the great sage. Well, I think this is what we call behavior modification."

I stab three short times to his ear. "Can you hear me?"

He's unconscious. Damn. I knew he wouldn't be a challenge. "Stephen," I grab his hair. A flicker of life ripples beneath his eyeballs. "You were right about the world being populated by crazies. One final lesson . . . one last word of advice: Listen. Shut your goddamn mouth long enough to listen."

I stab into his neck. Air hisses through the puncture like a tire pierced with a rusty nail. "Next time, listen when someone warns you. See what a pleasant evening you would've had if only you'd believed me when I told you I'm not *that* kind of girl."

THE MAIN EVENT

Peter Crowther

*Peter Crowther got a late start in writing. Like his country-
man Raymond Chandler, Britisher Crowther was forty before
he began seriously writing and sending out his stories.*

*Peter works in fantasy, science fiction, mystery, and dark
suspense. And works well in them, too. He is one of the most
important of the new wave of European suspense writers.*

Here is a fine example of his work.

"WE GONNA GO BED NOW BABY?" DOLORES TRILLED SLEEPILY AS
she slouched around the table and lifted the Calvados from the
after-dinner wreckage. "Dosie tired."

Vince watched her pour two fingers into a goblet that still held
traces of claret, then he turned around to the window. Listening
to his wife slurp and hiccup, Vince pulled the corner of the curtain
aside and watched the Cadillac's taillights move off down the
drive. The tension in his stomach subsided only when he saw the
car pull out into the street and disappear. The sharp sound of
breaking glass made him spin around in time to see Dolores,
having staggered against the table, picking pieces of cut glass out
of the Roquefort cheese. "Jesus, Dolores!" he snapped.

Dolores straightened up and pouted. "Hey, no need to get spi-
key, honey," she said, slurring the words. "Just a little accident."
She dropped the shards of glass onto a side plate and giggled,
lifting a hand to cover her mouth. Vince saw that she had
smudged her lipstick and he was annoyed to find that it aroused
him. Despite the effects of the alcohol Dolores noticed it, saw it
in his eyes. She leaned against the table and ran her hand through

her hair. "We gonna go up and make Buster warm, huh? We gonna have, you know, the main event now? Are we, honey?"

Buster was Vince's penis. Making Buster warm entailed jamming it inside Dolores as far as it would go. And then some. That was Dolores's main event. Vince sometimes thought that she had some kind of dimensional warp up there, the same way that the inside of Doctor Who's phonebox looked like the Cape Canaveral operations room. Maybe you could ram a broom handle up inside her, right to the bristles, and still not encounter any obstacles, and even if he stared down her throat there would be no trace of the end.

Dolores ran a hand down her camel-colored cashmere rib-knit dress until she reached the outside of her thigh, then she moved it over to her crotch and started to rub between her legs, pushing the material in and out, in and out. Vince moved away from the window and brushed past her. "You're sick, you know that?" he said. "And you said you needed oysters."

"Hey, I di'n't say I *needed* the oysters, honey, I said I *wanted* them. I still can't understand why you wouldn't let me have none." She took another drink of brandy, swallowed hard, and asked, "Why was that, honey? Why di'n't you let me have no oysters? Why'd we haveta have chowder insteada oysters, like Jerry an' Estelle did, huh?"

"There weren't enough." Vince shook a Marlboro out of the packet and tossed it back onto the table, leaned over, and lit the cigarette from the burning candle. "I told you that."

"Yeah, I heard you say there wasn't enough, and that you knew how much they liked oysters so they should just eat and enjoy. 'Eat and enjoy, Jer,' you said." Dolores swept her arm expansively as she mimicked Vince. " 'Cept I know there *was* enough. I saw them when you were preparing them. You threw a whole bunch out with the trash."

Blowing a thick column of smoke across the table, Vince looked at his watch and said, "They were bad. I threw them out because they were bad."

Dolores thought about that for a moment. "How'd you know they was bad?"

Vince looked at her and narrowed his eyes. "I just knew, okay? I know these things. It's what I used to do for a living, remember?"

The truth of the matter was there was nothing wrong with the oysters. None of them. At least, not the ones that Vince had thrown out. He'd just wanted only Jerry and Estelle to eat those he'd saved. Those were the ones with the small capsules inside. Vince couldn't take the chance of his guests getting the wrong ones—the safe ones—if Dolores screwed up the portions. Worse than that, he couldn't take the chance of getting one of the capsules himself. Taken alone, they probably wouldn't do much harm, just an upset stomach, or maybe a bad dose of the runs. But if he and Dolores had eaten them then Jerry and Estelle wouldn't have. And it was important—crucial—that the guests ate all the ingredients.

"Mmm." Dolores plopped onto a chair and hoisted her dress up above the tops of her hose, wafting the pale flesh at the tops of her legs with her free hand. "It was a nice meal though, honey. I meant to tell you that."

Vince nodded.

"Real nice meal."

"So you said," he snapped, glancing at the clock on the wall. "Thanks for the compliment, okay? I appreciate it."

Dolores shook her head and pulled down her dress. "That salad—what was the name of that salad again? Nish-somethin' or other?"

"Niçoise. Salad Niçoise."

"I liked that," Dolores slurred.

"Good," Vince said. He stubbed out his cigarette and adjusted his tie.

"Maybe it was just a little salty, though."

"You just said you liked it."

"I did too like it. All I said was that maybe it was just a little bit salty. That's all." She stood up from the table and walked to the bar and the bourbon.

Vince shook his head as he watched her stagger across the room. "You're drunk."

"I'm getting there," she said, unscrewing the cap. "If we ain't gonna have no main event, then I just might as well have a few drinks." Pouring whiskey into a shot glass, Dolores said, "The cheese tasted the same way."

"Like salad?"

Dolores glared at him. "Like salty," she said. "Salty like the fucking nishwahrs salad."

"Go to bed, will you?"

Dolores shook the liquid in her glass from side to side, watching it climb and fall, climb and fall. "The curry was good."

"You liked the curry. I'm glad. I feel whole again."

She pulled a face. "Smelly, though."

"It was a Korma."

"Not a curry?"

Vince sighed and reached for the Marlboro. "A Korma is a kind of curry, okay? Cream, coconut, lampasander, buttered chicken. Curry. Korma. All the same." He lit a cigarette with a match and shook out the flame.

Dolores looked into her drink some more.

Vince said, "Smelled how?"

"Huh?"

"You said it smelled. You said it was smelly, the Korma. How was it smelly?"

For a moment Dolores looked blank, like someone had reached into her head and turned off the generator. Then she started to laugh.

"What?"

She kept on laughing.

Vince ruffled his hair in frustration and marched across to the window. "Suddenly I'm—what am I? Woody Allen? I ask you—"

"Like a fart," Dolores said amidst chuckles. "It smelled a little like a fart."

Vince turned around and looked at her.

"I'm sorry, hon—"

"Did anybody else think it smelled?"

"Oh, hey, I—"

"Look! I'm fucking asking you if anybody else thought the Korma smelled funny, okay?"

Her smile faded. "Okay," she said. "There's no need—"

"And the answer is? I'm waiting for the answer, Dolores."

She shrugged. "Nobody said nothin'."

He nodded and took a pull on the Marlboro. "Good," he said, around a mouthful of smoke. "That's good."

Silence again.

"He's funny isn't he, you know . . . Jerry."

"How is Jerry funny?"

Dolores drained her glass and reached for the bottle. "His ways, you know."

"He's a very busy, very important man, Dolores."

Dolores laughed as she swallowed, spraying liquor in a fine mist. "He's a crook."

"Look, we been through all this a dozen times. Maybe a hundred times. Jerry is a businessman."

"In a pig's eye." She hiccupped, and then added, disdainfully, "Businessman! Hmph!"

"I'm not going to argue, Dolores, I'm—"

"Why d'you keep looking at your watch?"

Vince lowered his arm and shook it until his shirtsleeve slid down over his wrist. "I'm not looking at my watch."

"You were too. I saw—"

"Okay, I was looking at my watch. I wanted to know what time it was, for crissakes."

Dolores took a slug of bourbon and swallowed hard. "It's about thirty seconds later than it was when you last looked at it," she said.

"What are you? My—" He was going to say "timekeeper" but realized immediately that it sounded stupid. The same with "watchman." Instead, he pulled on his cigarette and shook his head some more. Then he looked out of the window.

"He's a crook, Vinny. You know it and I know it." She swirled the liquor around the glass and then threw it into her mouth. "And you're a crook, too."

Vince looked around at her and smiled. "Hey, we both enjoy the fruits of my labor. I don't see you complaining any about where the money comes from."

She poured some more bourbon into her glass silently.

"He's a businessman. Got a lot of contacts, sees a lot of people, makes a lot of deals. That's how he makes his money. That's how I make my money. I'm not ashamed of it."

"He know a lot of people?"

"A *lot* of people. He knows everybody. And I mean *every*body."

"They all crooks, too?"

"Dolores, not everybody is a crook." Vince pulled one of the chairs away from the table and sat down, loosening his tie. He was starting to feel a little easier. This one was the one. He'd thought about every way he could do it—shooting, knifing, even poison—but each of those methods could have led back to him. But not this way. This way there would be nothing left to lead anyone anywhere. He smiled across the table at his wife, watched her backside stretch the clinging material of her dress, saw the small metal clips of her garters outlined against her thighs.

"He keep all their names in his goddamned book?"

Vince shrugged. "It's his way, okay? He calls it his memory bank." He blew smoke out in small rings and watched them swirl up to the ceiling. "Takes it everywhere he goes. I never seen him without that book. It's like it's attached to him surgically, you know what I'm saying?"

"Yeah, I hear you."

Vince softened his voice. "Hey."

"What?"

"C'm'ere."

"What?"

"I said, c'm'ere." A little harder now.

Dolores stood up and walked across to him. She was trying to look disinterested but the first faint signs of a smile were pulling at her mouth. When Dolores had reached him, Vince patted his knees and shuffled the chair farther from the table. "Siddown."

"I'm fine standing right here," she said petulantly, swaying her body from side to side, legs stretched wide. Vince looked at her, allowing his eyes to travel up and down the curves and bulges. He liked what he saw. Buster liked it, too, uncoiling himself from Vince's Calvin Klein briefs and fighting off the effects of the booze.

He felt good, suddenly. A good evening. He remembered the dessert, remembered thinking it tasted fine and wondering—as he watched Jerry and Estelle gorge themselves on two pieces—if they noticed anything unusually gritty about it. He reached out to trace a finger across Dolores's lower stomach, and said, "Hey, how'd you like the chocolate gateau?"

She stopped swaying and said, "You still wanna talk about the food? I thought we was getting ready for the main event . . . getting ready to warm up li'l Buster, honey."

"We are, we are. I just wondered how you liked the dessert is all."

"I liked it, okay?"

She started swaying again, moving her body closer to him with each pass.

"You didn't think . . . you didn't think that maybe it tasted a little gritty?"

Dolores placed her glass on the table and pulled up her dress, slowly, inch by loving inch, until she exposed the tops of her hose, then the pale flesh of her upper thighs, and then, last but by no means least, the soft blue of her panties. Vince could see thin, spindly hairs curling their way out of the crotch, could see the first faint traces of wet on it, could smell the deodorant she used down there, could smell it wafting across at him. Buster could smell it too, apparently, and he stretched against Vince's trousers wanting to be out. Out and in. "Gritty?" she said. The word came out as a whisper.

Without watching what he was doing, but rather keeping his eyes focused on the endless sky of those briefest of bikini panties, Vince reached out his right hand to lower his glass to the floor beside the large wing chair. As he removed his hand from the glass he heard it topple over with a dull thud. He turned around to see if there was much of a mess on the carpet, and saw the polished black of Jerry's memory bank half-covered by the chair.

At first

takes it everywhere he goes

it didn't register

never seen him without that book

and then

it's like it's attached to him surgically

he looked up at Dolores. She was turning around to look at the window, shuffling her dress back down her legs. "A car, Vinny," she said, simply. "Now who the hell—"

Vince grabbed the book and jumped off his chair. "It's Jerry," he said, "come for his damned book."

"Jesus H. Christ on a fucking bicycle," Dolores snarled, spitting out the words like bad food.

Vince ran into the hall, heading for the door, trying to beat Jerry's having to get out of the car, having to walk up to the house, having to ring the bell, having to waste all that time . . . precious time. As he ran, seeming to take forever, every step like running in slow motion or through water, his life flashed before him. Not his whole life, just the afternoon. One afternoon.

He saw himself working tiny lumps of elemental sodium into small gelatin capsules of oil and then inserting them almost lovingly into the oysters.

He saw himself sprinkling potassium and more sodium onto the anchovies, eggs, and olives. And then more—just to be safe—smeared inside the Roquefort cheese.

He saw himself mixing liberal quantities of sulphur into the buttered chicken.

He saw himself grinding up lumps of charcoal for the chocolate gateau.

Reaching for the key to the front door, he shook his head, trying to convince himself it had all been a stupid idea. It wouldn't work. Why the hell was he panicking?

He saw his arm reach out in front of him, reach out toward the door, the key held in his hand, reaching to the small lock.

He heard the footsteps on the steps, someone coming to the front door. "With you in a second, Jer," he shouted. "Forgot your fucking book, didn't you?"

He heard Jerry laugh.

And then the laugh stopped. Abruptly. Jerry gasped. The sound was a mixture of pain and surprise.

Vince's hand had reached the door, inserted the key. He began to turn his hand and reach for the handle. Then the world turned bright white . . .

The

and somewhere, far off in the distance but getting closer with every millionth of a second . . .

Main

a shuddering growl of thunder sounded, traveling toward him at ten times the speed of light . . .

Event!

traveling with the shards of door and lumps of masonry and a billion tiny spears of glass.

Vince didn't hear the second explosion. Nor did he notice the small pieces of perfumed meat, leather upholstery and blackened metal that rained on the burning ruins of his house.

OBEAH, MY LOVE

Barbara Collins

Barbara Collins has written at least twelve stories that have won her national attention. And several of which have been reprinted in anthologies.

She has a sly, wry sense of humor, and a rather dark take on the subject of humanity.

A BITTERLY COLD CHICAGO WIND CARRYING A MISERABLE MIX-ture of sleet and snow swept across Oak Street, making the simple act of walking almost impossible for a few daring pedestrians.

A woman in a brown mink coat struggled along, clutching its huge fur collar against her face as the blizzard spit into it. The gentleman beside her—his checks as red as if he'd been slapped—grabbed desperately at the plaid Burberry scarf that the wind was mischievously unwrapping from around his neck.

Tanya Green watched them from the window of the espresso-art gallery, *Café et Art*, that she owned with her husband, Joel. Despite the warm temperature inside, she shivered.

Turning away from the window, she crossed the glossy parquet floor and went behind the white marble espresso bar, where she made herself a quadruple grande wholemilk latte with chocolate syrup and extra whipped cream. Then she took the drink to one of the chrome deco tables and sat down. There were no customers in the espresso bar—or the adjoining art gallery, where her husband was working—the storm had seen to that.

She drank the rich, hot beverage, hoping it would lift the mal-aise that had been steadily, stealthily enveloping her, just like the storm out there was doing to the city. Hoping, too, it would quiet the voices in her head.

But the chocolate and caffeine only made things worse.

"How are you feeling?"

Joel's voice, right in her ear, made her jump.

"Oh, honey," he said, apologetically, "I didn't mean to scare you."

Tanya looked up at her husband, a tall man with sandy hair, dark brown eyes and thick eyelashes any woman would envy. He looked so handsome in his gray Armani suit and that silk tie with a Frank Lloyd Wright design she had given him for their second anniversary.

Joel bent down and kissed her.

"I just can't seem to get warm enough," she complained after his lips left hers.

"I can turn up the heat, if you like."

She shook her head, her shoulder-length red hair moving in gentle arcs around her face. "Then it would be too hot for the customers."

Joel smirked. "What customers?" He pulled out a chair at the small table for two and sat next to her. "I've only had *one* all day. . . . A lady who wanted a painting, and she didn't care who by as long as it matched her mauve couch."

Tanya nodded. She knew the type.

"After an hour I suggested she take a picture of the couch and frame *it*," Joel said wryly.

Tanya smiled.

The two fell silent. Outside, the wind rattled the windowpane, trying to get inside.

"Maybe we should say the hell with it, close the store and head for home while we can still get there," Joel suggested.

Tanya didn't respond. She was watching the storm paint abstract designs on the glass with icy fingers.

"Tanya?"

"Huh?"

Joel leaned forward and placed a hand over hers, which had been resting on the table next to the empty coffee mug. His skin was smooth and warm.

"Baby, what's wrong?" he asked softly. "Is it . . . those voices?"

"No!"

"Maybe you should see that psychiatrist again and get some more medication."

"I'm fine!" she snapped, and pulled her hand away. Just the thought of that anti-psychotic drug made her mouth go dry. A wave of nausea spread through her and she felt she might throw up the chocolate coffee, but the moment passed and she composed herself.

"I'm *fine*," she repeated, forcing the hostility out of her voice.

Joel had that hurt puppy-dog-with-big-brown-eyes look again. "I'm just trying to help."

Tanya sighed. "I know you are. It's just that . . ." She started over. "It's just this *damn* weather!"

The truth was she felt if she ever took that medication again she *would* go crazy! Besides making her lethargic and sick, it put a terrible burden on Joel to handle the finances, which was not his forte. And, anyway, the drug never did silence the voices she heard in her head, only blurred the words into gibberish.

Tanya, staring at her hands in her lap, noticed with despair that one of her expensively manicured gold-lacquered nails had broken off. It took every ounce of control she had to keep from bursting into tears.

"Why don't we go on a vacation?" Joel was saying. "Blow this town . . . get away from the weather?"

Tanya looked up from her hands. "Where?"

"Why not Nassau? We had a great time there last year."

"You mean, *you* had a great time."

"What? And you didn't? Shopping? Reading? Sunning on the beach?"

"What else could I do while you were off *gambling*?"

Joel's eyes flared. "Hey, I paid you back, every cent . . . or am I supposed to keep 'paying' for that for the rest of my life?"

Tanya leaned forward. "I'm sorry, Joel," she said quickly. "I don't want to fight. Please forgive me, I'm just not feeling very well."

He nodded, his lips a thin line.

"Maybe you're right," she said. "We should get away from here. But I don't want to go back to Nassau."

"Well, what about one of the other islands?"

"Like what?"

Joel shrugged. "Grand Bahama. Andros. Eleuthera." He paused. "There's one place I heard had the most beautiful beaches in the entire world. Hardly anyone knows about it to even go there. . . . And no gambling casinos." He reached out and ran one finger down her cheek to the corner of her mouth. "We'd practically be by ourselves," he whispered.

Suddenly Tanya's depression lifted. "What's that place called?" she asked excitedly.

"Cat Island."

■ ■ ■

One hundred and thirty miles southeast of Nassau lay Cat Island, a mere fifty miles long. Some believe the island got its name because the shape of the land looked like a cat sitting on its haunches, ready to pounce. Others insist the name came from Arthur Catt, a notorious pirate and cohort of the infamous Blackbeard, who made the island his favorite hideout in the early seventeen hundreds. But regardless of how it got its name, one thing was certain to Tanya as she reread the few pages about the island in the guidebook she'd bought: very little was known about mysterious Cat Island.

On board the MV Seahauler that had left Potter's Cay, Nassau, a little over two hours ago, Tanya looked out from the large cabin of the boat across the endless bluegreen water. They were gliding through the Exuma Sound and the ocean was glass smooth.

Joel, seated next to her on the wooden bench, was engrossed in one of the newsmagazines he'd bought back at the airport; there wouldn't be any available on the island, he'd told her.

The cabin of the Seahauler was full—natives of Cat Island returning home after a visit to Nassau for business or pleasure, their bodies a beautiful brown shade, women in bright cotton dresses and scarves, the men wearing more subdued colors. Tanya tried not to stare at these lucky inhabitants of a world she envied. . . .

A murmur passed through the crowd and Tanya saw a thin line appear on the horizon. She watched the thin line grow larger and larger, until she could make out miles of white, sandy beaches ringed with exotic casuarina trees.

"Joel, look!" Tanya said breathlessly.

He followed her gaze. "Beautiful," he smiled.

"We're going to have such a wonderful time!"

"Knock on wood," he said, and tapped the bench with his knuckles.

At New Bight, the most populated of the villages, all the passengers got off, this being the Seahauler's only Cat Island destination.

Joel retrieved their suitcases, and since there was no taxi service, paid two young island boys, who were waiting for just such an opportunity, three Bahamian dollars apiece to carry the suitcases for them.

Down a sandy-dirt road, about a fourth of a mile along the coast, was Conch Resort, a complex of a dozen rustic cottages built of stone, driftwood and glass nestled among the casuarina trees on the oceanfront known as Fernandez Bay.

Tanya waited outside the main office building with the suitcases while Joel checked in. Above her, whipped cream clouds rowed by in a sky as blue as the ocean, while the sun scattered countless diamonds down into the water.

This was Eden, Tanya thought. Not in a very long time had she felt nearly so happy! She listened. The voices in her head were quiet.

Their cottage, not far from the office, was spacious, with ceiling fans, rattan furniture, a private bath, and a small kitchen. To her delight, there was no phone or television. In several corners hung exotic plants.

"Isn't this a dream?" Tanya exclaimed. "It's better than I'd thought."

"Uh-huh." Joel was putting a suitcase on the bed.

She went over and sat on the mattress that bowed with her weight. "What shall we do now?" she asked impishly.

He stood over her, bent and kissed her, pushing her back on the bed.

"I have an idea," he said.

"What's that?" she smiled.

"Let's go exploring."

"What?" That wasn't what she expected—or wanted to hear.

"Let's check out the island."

"But. . . . I thought we might, you know, check out the bed."

"There'll be time for that, later," he whispered, his lips caressing her ear. "Tonight."

She sighed. "Let's go exploring. . . ."

He helped her up off the bed.

In New Bight Tanya and Joel found a quaint grocery store with fresh fruit and fish, and a supply store that sold souvenirs (Tanya bought a barrette made of shells), a Catholic church and the Commissioner's house. That was the extent of the business district of the village.

At the Commissioner's house was a dirt path and a sign pointing the way to Mt. Alvernia. The sign said Mt. Alvernia was the highest point in all of the Bahamas. In the distance, Tanya could see a stone bell tower on top of the mountain rising toward the heavens.

"I wonder what that is?" she mused.

"I dunno," Joel replied. "Why not find out?"

And he headed up the path.

Tanya followed. The foliage got thicker.

In a small clearing on the slope, they came upon a stone house with a wooden door and thatched roof. Next to the house was a white stone oven, smoke curling gently out of it. Tanya could smell bread baking inside.

Clinking noises drew her attention to a big silk cotton tree behind the oven, its low, gnarled branches reaching out skeletally toward them. Her mouth fell open in surprise.

Hanging from the limbs were mobiles made of bones, and wind-chimes of bottles filled with things that she could not make out from the distance.

"Joel!" she whispered.

He nodded. "*Obeah*," he explained. "It's kind of like . . . Bahamian voodoo."

Then out the wooden door of the hut came a native woman in a long colorful dress. Her age was somewhere between fifty and sixty, Tanya guessed, hair coarse and gray and tied up with strips of cloth and string. Around her neck were more bones, and feathers and shells. At her feet was a big black cat, a red ribbon tied around its neck.

"Good afternoon," she said with a surprisingly slight island lilt. "On your way to the Hermitage?"

Joel answered. "Yes. Can you tell us something about it?"

The woman walked to the oven, where she bent to check to bread. Then she straightened and turned. The cat positioned itself not far from Tanya, staring at her with its yellow eyes.

"Was built by Father Jerome," the Bahamian woman said. "He lived there. Died there, too."

"Then the monastery's empty?" Joel asked.

The woman nodded.

"Excuse me for asking," Tanya said, "but what's all that stuff in the tree?"

The woman smiled, slyly. "Charms."

"Charms?" Tanya asked.

"To keep evil spirits away." And the woman went back to the oven.

Tanya and Joel thanked her, then continued along the path, which grew steeper with every step. Here and there, placed in the undergrowth, were hand carved pictures on wooden plaques. Tanya recognized them as the stations of the cross.

They were nearing the top, the monastery with its tall, stone bell tower looming, when Joel clutched his stomach and doubled over.

Tanya, behind him, rushed to her husband.

"What is it?" she asked, concerned.

"Stomach cramps," he said, out of breath.

He straightened up somewhat, supporting himself with his hands on his knees. "I don't think it's going to go away, if you know what I mean."

"Oh, honey. . . . We'll turn around."

"No. You go ahead."

"But . . . where are you going?"

He laughed hollowly. "Probably into the woods somewhere. I'll see you later at the bottom."

"Well. . . ." she started to say, but he was already heading back down the path. ". . . okay."

"I'll just be a few minutes!" she hollered. After all, how interesting could a monastery be?

But when she reached the top she stood dumbfounded.

The monastery was tiny, like a child's play house!

She approached the stone structure, built precariously on the edge of a cliff, and stood before the bell tower, its entrance coming only to her chin. There was no door so she stuck her head inside, then squeezed her body through.

She was able to stand, but barely, the window at the top of the bell tower she had seen while climbing—and had imagined took hundreds of steps to reach—was at her eye-level.

She couldn't help laughing. Was this some kind of joke? Designed to startle or amuse? Or could Father Jerome have been that diminutive?

Tanya noticed a small door by her feet. Crouching, she reached for the knob, opened it, and like Alice in Wonderland, crawled through to the other side.

In the chapel she had to remain on her knees in a sort of enforced posture of prayer; possibly one, maybe two other adults might also have fit inside. The room was dusty and empty. A half-circle window provided light.

Back outside, in the rear of the monastery, Tanya found what appeared to be the living quarters: three rooms each the size of a small closet. She did not enter them.

A few hundred feet from the living quarters, built into the side of the mountain, she discovered a tomb.

The tomb, however, was not child-size. Over the entrance, where a weather-beaten wooden latticed door hung half off its hinges, was a large cement slab with the inscription, *Blessed Are The Dead Who Die In The Lord.*

She wondered if they had run out of room for the complete verse.

Was there a tiny coffin inside? It would have been easy to slip past the wooden door and enter the tomb—there was evidence others had—but Tanya didn't, whether out of respect or fear, she wasn't certain.

She returned to the bell tower, and stood on the edge of the cliff, gazing one last time at the breathtaking view of the island and the ocean beyond, salty trade winds mussing her hair. She felt oddly at home, like visiting someplace in a dream she'd had.

The voices returned.

Why didn't they leave her alone? What did they want?

"Go away!" she shouted.

And one foot slipped on the cliff's pebbly surface, and she found herself sliding, both hands now clawing at the rock and dirt, trying desperately to hold on. Her slick-bottomed tennis shoes offered no traction and she knew in another moment she'd go tumbling down the mountain.

She shrieked.

A hand reached out, grabbed her arm and pulled her back to safety.

She sat on the edge of the cliff, trembling, too traumatized to speak. She saw a pair of worn sandals, a black burlap robe, a silver cross, then shielding her eyes from the sun setting directly in front of her, she looked at the face: old and world-weary, but with a hint of a once boyish look. He was tall. . . . even from where she was sitting. . . . and the sun shining behind his head sent rays shooting out of his skull like heavenly spears.

But something was wrong with his eyes. Was he blind? Yet he was able to see to help her.

The man spoke, his voice low and gravelly. "Be careful," he warned. "The island is beautiful. But remember, even Eden had its serpent."

Tanya stared up at him. *What a strange thing to say*, she thought.

She tried to stand up, but her right ankle ached, and she was afraid to put any weight on it. So she rolled over onto her knees and using her left leg for support, stood.

The priest or monk or whoever he was had vanished. She seemed alone on the mountaintop.

"Hello!" she called toward the miniature monastery. "Who are you?"

No one answered. Not even the voices in her head.

Panic overtook her. She'd been gone a long time; Joel would be worried!

She hurried toward the path that led downward, her ankle seeming better, and carefully but quickly descended.

As she passed the house with the bizarre hanging bottles the woman—as if waiting for her—stepped out of the doorway, black cat in tow.

"Your husband went back to town," the woman informed her. "He said to tell you he'd see you there."

Tanya approached the woman. "Was he very sick?" she asked anxiously.

The woman raised her eyebrows. "Didn't seem to be."

Tanya, relieved, thanked the woman for giving her the message. Then she asked her curiously, "How small was Father Jerome?"

"Small? Not small. Tall."

"But . . . the monastery. . . ."

"Father Jerome was a very humble man who believed in living that way. He built the monastery to discipline himself."

Tanya wasn't sure she understood.

"He carved the wooden pictures on the path," the woman continued, "and wanted to make more, but couldn't because of his eyes."

"His eyes?"

"Cataracts. Is something wrong?"

"No. No, I have to go."

Tanya, disturbed, left the Bahamian woman and hurried along the path toward town, unaware that the black cat was following her.

■   ■   ■

Niomi Deveaux didn't bother calling the cat back. After all, it wouldn't do any good because the animal was a disobedient creature. Furthermore, as a "witch" it was worthless!

The cat cost her a lot of money—every Bahamian dollar she'd had. She'd bought it in Haiti because—as every *Obeah* practitioner knew—Haiti had the most powerful witches. She wished now she'd gotten the snake, instead. At least snakes didn't eat so much, or demand so much attention.

Niomi went back inside the thatched-roofed hut, which doubled as a small shop. Rice, grits, flour and assorted canned goods were stored in a cupboard to the left. Straight ahead, separating the shop in front from the tiny living quarters behind, was a counter, its top covered with rows of bottles filled with Niomi's own tonics and medicines. Hanging from the ceiling were local bushes and strips of bark, transforming the shop into an indoor jungle.

Niomi passed the counter into the sparse dirt-floored living area and sat in a straw chair, which creaked disagreeably with her weight.

She sighed. She couldn't remember when times were harder.

A descendant of slaves brought over from Africa to Cat Island to work on the cotton plantations, she was born with the gift of necromancy—the art of calling the dead.

As a small child in the 1930s, Niomi could see the spirits sitting in the gnarled branches of the huge silk cotton trees, and wandering listlessly around the Blue Hole, a large marshy pond in the middle of the island. When she grew older, her power grew stronger and a teen-aged Niomi found she could control these "sperrids" and get them to do her bidding. Her favorite was the pirate Arthur Catt, who was always up for some mischief. But one day Catt literally scared someone to death, and Niomi never "called" him after that.

Word of her power spread throughout the islands and Niomi was besieged with clients—and money. For a while she remained on Cat Island, but soon left her simplistic life and backward relatives for Nassau, where she lived in luxury at Greycliff, hobnobbing with royalty and rockstars who stayed there, becoming a sort of occult icon.

If only her powers had extended to the ability to foresee the future, she might not have lost everything: her money, her reputation and eventually the powers themselves. . . .

"Excuse me."

Startled, Niomi glanced toward the counter where the red-haired American woman stood; she was holding Niomi's "witch" in her hands. The cat was affectionately rubbing its head on the woman's breast, something it had never done to Niomi, being coldly indifferent to her.

"He followed me," the woman said, her eyes darting curiously around at this and that.

Niomi rose slowly from the chair because she'd spotted something on the counter in front of the woman that she didn't want her to see. She'd forgotten it was even there. But the mere intensity of her gaze on the object caused the woman's eyes to follow hers.

The red-haired woman dropped the cat to the ground and gasped.

It was too late now for Niomi to do anything but watch the woman's face register bewilderment, then horror.

"Where did you get these . . . these *things?*" the woman demanded. She pointed to the lock of red hair and gold-painted fingernail floating in a small sea of water in a bottle.

Niomi said nothing.

"They *are* mine, aren't they? My hair? My fingernail?"

Niomi nodded.

"But *why?*"

Niomi didn't answer, but instead bent to retrieve a small tin box from a shelf in the back of the counter. She placed the box on the countertop and opened it. Taking out five U.S. hundred-dollar bills, she put them on the counter in front of the woman.

Niomi felt relieved. Relieved to be done with this deception. Relieved to be rid of the money, in spite of how hungry and poor she was . . . because it was the kind of money that had led to her downfall so many years ago. . . .

The red-haired woman looked with puzzlement at the hundred-dollar bills.

"I don't understand," she said.

"Your husband paid me to put a curse on you," Niomi explained with a shrug.

For a moment the red-haired woman said nothing, as the words soaked in. "He . . . he wanted me *dead?*"

"No, no, no . . . just to lose your mind."

The color drained from the woman's face, she moved slowly behind the counter and sank into the straw chair, eyes staring, haunted, an island sperrid herself.

Then she threw her hands to her face and sobbed into them.

Niomi went to her.

"You don't have to worry," Niomi said softly, touching her shaking shoulder. "I've put no curse on you. And even if I had it would do no good."

The woman looked up from hands streaked with tears. "What do you mean 'it would do no good'?"

Niomi sighed. "I was once well known for my powers . . . the most famous sorceress in all the islands. Now children taunt me and throw rocks at my house."

The red-haired woman sniffled. "What happened?"

Niomi looked down at the woman's puffy-red face. How could she explain that white magic must only be used for good? And to delve in the darkness of black magic was a very dangerous business. Had the American even heard of the Bay Street Boys, the Progressive Liberal Party, and the malicious attempt to return whites to supremacy in the islands twenty years ago? Most likely not. So Niomi said simply, "I did work for the Devil and God took my powers away from me."

No more could Niomi call the beloved sperrids, place a spell, or "work witch" (the cat had proven that). Even the voices in her head were gone.

"How do you manage?" the red-haired woman asked. She was wiping her eyes with a corner of her blouse.

"I sell bush medicine," Niomi explained, "which I learned how to make. And once in a while take money from people who haven't heard I've lost my powers. Like your husband."

"And just exactly what were you going to do to me?"

Niomi shrugged. "I still have a few friends who pretend to be spirits if I need them to . . . but never mind about that."

The red-haired woman smirked humorlessly. "Well, I have to admit, your Father Jerome had me going."

Niomi frowned; she didn't know what the woman was talking about.

The red-haired woman stood. "When did Joel contact you?"

"About a year ago, when I was still living in Nassau."

"A *year* ago?" the woman exclaimed. "He'd been planning this for a *whole year*? Telling me he loved me all the while. . . ."

Niomi thought the woman might cry again, but then her face became a cold expressionless mask.

"That bastard," the woman said. And she moved toward the door of the shop.

"Wait!" Niomi said. "Take the money. . . ."

The red-haired woman stopped and stooped and scooped up the cat, which had never left her side.

"Keep it," she said. "I'll take the cat."

"But it doesn't work," Niomi insisted.

The woman smiled nastily. "Joel doesn't know that."

． ▪ ▪

A dozen questions drowned out the chanting in her mind, as Tanya, cat cradled in her arms, hurried along the dirt path toward the village, and Joel.

Had Joel *ever* loved her? Or just her money? Was he planning to commit her to a mental hospital so he would have power of attorney to spend it? Then divorce her after the money was gone?

That sounded like Joel. So calculating, but safe. She would have had more respect for him if he'd just pushed her off the damn cliff!

Dark clouds gathered and the tropical breeze swelled, blowing leaves from the casuarina trees and bending the thorny braceana plants that switched back and forth like dinosaur tails.

By the time she'd reached the cottage, her mood was as black as the sky, and her mounting rage made her body shake.

She yanked open the door and stepped inside.

But Joel was not there.

Tanya backed out of the cottage and walked toward the beach with the cat.

Joel was getting up from a large towel, brushing the sand off the bathing suit she'd bought him at Neiman-Marcus. He cast his eyes skyward at the advancing storm.

A beautiful island girl—in a skimpy bikini Tanya would never have the guts to wear—was moving away from him, down the shoreline. Tanya had the distinct impression they'd been together.

She repeated the strange incantation in her head—ancient words—and Joel turned to look at her.

It was her intention to frighten him—with the odd words and the cat—after all, *he* was the superstitious one, but to her amazement the animal seemed to responded to the words, jumped out of her arms and ran like a panther, leaping into the air and onto Joel's back, its claws drawing blood.

Joel threw the animal off, but it came back again and he fled to the water and safety. He yelled at Tanya, his face contorted with fear, perhaps he said "Stop it!" or "Help me!," she wasn't sure, because the wind carried his voice away.

In disbelief, Tanya watched as the cat pursued Joel into the ocean, swimming like an otter (could cats *do* that?), driving him farther and farther out.

A crowd had gathered on the beach under the blackened sky, partly because of the drama in the water, but mostly because the pretty island girl was screaming hysterically.

A heavyset white female tourist who'd been drawn out of her cottage by the commotion shouted, "Why doesn't someone *do* something?"

" 'Cause he been *witched*," an island man answered her, shaking his head. "Don' mess wid dat. Don' mess wid dat."

It didn't take long before Joel went under; he wasn't a very good swimmer. Hadn't she told him to stick with the lessons at the health club?

Tanya sat down in the soft white sand and waited for the cat, its black head bobbing out on the ocean's surface, making its way back to her. The sky above began to clear.

Others now joined the spectators on the beach. Down by the water's edge was the priest that had warned her on the mountaintop, his head bowed in prayer, hands making the sign of the cross.

Next to the priest stood a craggily handsome man, wearing swashbuckle boots, tattered pants and leather vest. From his waist hung a huge sword. He was laughing, clearly tickled with the chain of events, and he raised one arm and waved at her. But the others on the beach didn't seem to notice him, or the priest, for that matter.

The cat came out of the water, moving lithely, its black fur matted, and settled next to her. The island people gathered around.

Tanya smiled, at peace at last with the voices in her head.

CRACKED REAR VIEW

Jerry Sykes

Jerry Sykes is co-editor of the British crime fiction magazine
A Shot in the Dark *and a regular contributor to* Mystery
Scene. *He is currently editing an anthology of crime stories
based around the millennium for publication later this year.
"Cracked Rear View" is his first of his stories to appear in the
United States.*

FRANK WATCHED THE GUY'S HAND RIDE UP HER THIGH, SURFING
skin still warm and brown from a long summer of lustful rays. The
guy's fingertips found her blue cotton shorts and burrowed under
the hem. Frank saw him lean forward to whisper in her ear. She
lifted her head to the touch of his lips and smiled, listening. Her
movements caused her shorts to tighten across the guy's fingers.
She laughed, eyes crinkling with an easy humour, and glanced
across at Frank.

Stared right at him.

The guy must have said something, thought Frank. Something
about me. He knew he should have looked away, being caught
staring like that, but something made him hold her stare. Maybe
the thought that someone who allowed herself to undergo such a
public mauling deserved to be stared at. He kept on staring.

Her smile widened; her pink tongue appeared and slowly licked
the corners of her mouth, like a lizard caught in a lazy dream. She
angled her face to the ceiling as she ran her fingers through her
long auburn hair. Light caught the specks of dust dancing before
her eyes and melted them into freckles across her face.

Frank was reminded of Alice. He remembered how she had

once told him that as a teenager she had rubbed lemon juice into the freckles that saddled her nose in a vain attempt to rid herself of the devil's scurvy—as a friend's grandmother with a hatred of all things red and human had called them. She had always been led to believe—through years of experience and cruel folklore— that despite nature's attempts to balance the scales—blonde hair, slim figure—she would be forever condemned to the ugly file by the rusty spray across her face. Frank had smiled and told her, "It's just seasoning," and licked her cheeks like a lovestruck puppy.

"Frank?" Mary leaned across the small wooden table and touched her brother gently on the arm. "Frank? You OK?"

Frank looked up at his sister, at the deep sadness in her eyes. There was no clear reason for her sadness, but Frank knew that she would never be happy until the world slipped off its axis. In the meantime she would wring her hands and point a solicitous smile at the petty woes of those around her.

"Sorry. Miles away," he said. He took a sip of beer, lit a cigarette. He noticed that his last cigarette, barely touched, had burned down to a tube of ash in the glass ashtray; the shedded skin of the nicotine snake; a friendly smile that hid a poisonous bite.

"I was just saying, I thought you said Alice had moved up to Manchester."

■   ■   ■

A cold breeze blew off the Heath, rustling the trees that ran in parallel with the railings and bordered the open parkland; leaves tumbled along the pavement. The moon poured a pale light over the scene and Danny's eyes flicked between the shadows that danced for the trees. He followed Paul along the row of parked cars, look-out, a nominal ten feet adrift. A high hedge shielded them from the houses on their right and the rolling darkness of the Heath fell away to their left.

Danny had rubbed some speed into his gums earlier in the night and he could feel it kicking in; a rash of perspiration covered his face and his heart beat to a fast jerky rhythm. He saw Paul quicken his step as he reached the end of the row of cars and suddenly the door of a white Metro was open and Paul in behind the wheel before Danny could focus on what was happening.

Recovering, he glanced over his shoulder to check for traffic and stepped out between a blue Cherokee and a black Escort. He ran toward the Metro, feet slapping the tarmac, and grabbed the passenger door handle. He pushed his face up to the window. Rapid breath fogged the pane and obscured a view of his own wide eyes staring back at him. He rapped on the glass with his knuckles.

"C'mon," he spat through clenched teeth. He tugged at the handle.

No answer.

Danny wiped the window with his sleeve. He cupped his hands around his eyes, fingertips touching, and put his hands up against the window. He held his breath to prevent fogging. In the darkness he could just make out Paul, twisted around in the driver's seat with his head under the dash.

A car passed by, almost brushing Danny's backside. He jerked up and watched taillights disappear down the hill. The wind through the trees had dropped and the dancing shadows had moved on.

Danny peered back into the car. His heart lurched as he saw a shark rise from the deep and reach over and unlock the door for him.

■   ■   ■

Frank blew a plume of smoke out of the side of his mouth and looked across the bar at the girl with the freckles. She was on her own now, swirling the remains of her drink around in the bottom of her glass. Showtime over she looked deflated, all signs of vitality gone from her features. Frank looked away. He thought about what Mary had said, about Manchester. He could vaguely remember saying something, a snarled remark to account for Alice's apparent desertion. He looked up at Mary, a disarming smile, a shrug. "I didn't want you to know that she'd just left me." Another shrug. "You know how you are . . ." he trailed off, knowing he'd said enough.

Mary just smiled in reply: I understand.

"Anyway, that's all in the past," said Frank. He leaned back, put his hands palm down on the table. He looked at his watch. "She should be here soon."

Frank felt the first stirrings of an erection as a cold wave rippled through him.

■   ■   ■

Paul was pushing down on the accelerator, hoping to beat the lights, but at the last moment the guy in the Escort in front panicked and Paul had to jump down hard on the brake.

"Jesus," he spat. "You coulda gotten a whole fucken parade of cars through there, man." He gestured toward the car in front with the palm of his hand. Flecks of spittle bearded his chin.

Beside him, Danny let out a pained sigh. He had had his feet up on the dash when Paul had hit the brakes and his head had jerked forward, bopping his left cheek on his knees.

"Shit, Paul, be careful, will ya?" Danny tenderly touched his fingertips to his cheek, felt a burning amid the cold, clammy skin. He looked at the car in front, back at Paul, frowned.

"What?" Paul raised his arms in a shrug. As he did so the lights changed and the Escort pulled away. He gripped the wheel tightly, arms locked, back straight against the seat and popped the clutch. The Metro jumped into the car in front, bumping it forward. Paul saw the driver's head snap back and his hands come up off the wheel. Paul whipped the car away to the left and sped down the hill.

Danny didn't want to risk putting his feet back on the dash. He found himself opening the glove compartment.

"Anything?" said Paul, glancing across.

Danny fumbled around blindly, nervous tics animating his face. He began flicking things out of the darkness: a half-eaten bar of chocolate, a day parking pass for a garage in Warren Street, a solitary, dry cigarette. A couple of tapes tumbled to the floor. Danny picked them up, read off the titles. From the corner of his eye he noticed that they appeared to be going in the wrong direction. He watched familiar shops pass by, landmarks that belonged to a more peaceful journey.

"Hey, which way you headed? We're supposed . . ."

"Insurance," said Paul flatly, cutting him off. "Just taking out a little insurance." The corners of his mouth twitched.

Danny looked at him for a moment, puzzled, but then the whole of his face broke open into a grin, eyes burning in the darkness. He pulled back his arm and tossed the tapes directly across Paul's line of vision. The window was closed and the tapes bounced off the glass and into Paul's lap.

"Shit!" shouted Paul, glancing down at the tapes. "You want me to crash or something?"

The two of them broke into a deep laughter.

■   ■   ■

The first pains of jealousy had begun naturally enough. Alice was a nurse on the geriatric ward at the Royal Free Hospital and every third week she would have to work the night shift, ten till six. On these nights, after sharing a late supper, Frank would mooch around the flat, unable to settle, unable to sleep. He told himself that it was because he missed her presence in bed; not sex, just the familiar warmth of her closeness.

But as the weeks dragged into months, his fears intensified, fears that he could not always put into words; a raw hollowness spiralled in his chest, beating off all reason.

On a couple of occasions he had even gone so far as to call the hospital and ask to be put through to the nurses' station on the ward:

Take one: No answer—an old guy had croaked and Alice had had to accompany the body down to the cold shelf in the basement; she told him this over breakfast the following morning, unaware that he'd called; he didn't believe her.

Take two: "Hello? Hell-o? Who is this?" He had put the phone down then, hearing his own ragged breathing, and had not heard her final, plaintive, "Frank?"

Alice knew, had known from the outset; those tell-tale signs: the way he would look at the floor and draw shapes in the dust with his toe when she bought fruit from the grocer who always flirted with her; the angry eyes that burned into her own eyes whenever she made a phone call; the times she came home after the late shift and found herself unable to open the front door more than a few inches because Frank was curled up on the door-mat fast asleep.

On one sleepless night, Frank had been looking through a box of Alice's old records—even though they only had a CD player she had insisted on holding on to her records for sentimental reasons, although she had never explained why they were sentimental, much to Frank's annoyance—when he came across a blue envelope containing half a dozen or so photos.

Judging by her appearance they were no more than a couple of years old, but they may have been taken earlier that day for the effect they had on Frank. He felt something break loose in his chest and drift off into an infinite blackness, out of his reach and, eventually, out of his sight, as he shuffled through the prints:

—Alice smiling around a pair of huge sunglasses, the glare of the late afternoon sun broken across the sea behind her, a man in baggy shorts—the photographer—reflected in the lenses.

—Alice sitting on a stool at a beach bar, legs stretching out to the sand, toes barely reaching, a cocktail glass held up in a toast; a second glass on the bar beside her.

—Alice lying face down on a towel, head resting on her arms, bikini strap untied, the pale skin of the side of her breast exposed; beside her, on another towel, the damp after-image of someone else, taller, drying in the sun.

In the last photo the ghost that would haunt Frank appeared in human form.

—Alice leaning into the embrace of a man with his hair whipped by the sea breeze, her hand on his bare chest; a smile crinkling her eyes; a smile that slowed Frank's heart to an imperceptible murmur.

After staring at the photo for what seemed like hours, Frank turned it over, seeking some explanation. Nothing. Who was this man? The name Jack flashed in his mind. Jack. Jack the old guy on Alice's ward who had died the previous week. Jack who kept goosing her. A bit of harmless fun, the guy's eighty-five, said Alice; he got what he deserved, said Frank.

The name became a catalyst for all the jealousy and helplessness and self-pity that festered within Frank. Each time he heard or saw the name—in the newspaper, on TV, in the street—he would feel cold fingers tug on his heart. He went to great lengths to prevent Alice hearing or seeing the name—switching channels mid-programme; throwing out newspapers before she could read them—believing that each sight or sound of the name was another spark that could ignite the old flame.

Everything came to a head during a two-week holiday in Cornwall. After three days of being plunged headfirst into the broiling surf and whacked over the head with the surfboard, Frank had given up attempting to surf and contented himself with lying on the beach watching Alice.

Tears rippled his vision as he began to understand why she had persevered. Not through some primitive desire to tame the waves, but because she was only too aware of the effect the sight of her walking out of the surf, beads of water sparkling on her tan body, bikini moulded to her breasts and buttocks, was having on the pairs of eyes strung along the shoreline.

Unable to bear it, Frank had bundled all her clothes and her purse into the car and driven back to the hotel, leaving Alice to fend for herself. Two hours later she arrived back at the hotel in borrowed shorts and sweatshirt to find that Frank had checked out and returned to London. A chambermaid later found her bag blocking the laundry chute.

The following week Alice was back living in the nurses' home and Frank was telling everyone she had gone to live in Manchester.

But each time he saw the sticker advertising The Surf Shack, St. Ives, in the rear view mirror of his Astra he was reminded of that day in Cornwall and a black cloud would cross his vision.

■   ■   ■

Paul cracked the window and flicked his cigarette butt on to the road. Short blasts of smoke left his nostrils as he silently hummed a distant tune; fingers drummed the wheel to a different rhythm.

Danny was hunkered down in his seat, chewing the cord that ran through the hood of his sweatshirt.

The car was parked down a tree lined side street in a position that afforded them a clear view of the parade of shops that ran along the main road, directly opposite them. A dirty orange street-light cast shadows on the damp tarmac in front of them that looked like fingers trapped under ice.

Danny was watching the activity in the doorway of the Off-licence at the far left of the shops. He wondered what was going on, hoping for violence. A man in shirtsleeves was trying to slip the bolt at the top of one of the doors, but the man outside kept pushing the door open and then pointing to a black Labrador tied to a lamppost in front of the hardware store next door. He appeared to be saying that if he hadn't taken the time to tie his dog up, if the store didn't have that "No dogs allowed" sign on the door, then the store would still be open.

Danny began to laugh quietly to himself, until he realised what the little scene meant—it was now ten P.M. and class would be letting out.

For a long time after Alice's departure, Frank withdrew into himself and brooded on what might have been. He became irritable in the company of others, unable to maintain concentration during even the most banal of conversations. He began to smoke more, just so he could leave the office and go stand out in the street with all the other outcasts in the city. Nights would often find him stumbling home drunk and more often than not bloodied and bruised. But at no time did he consider himself to be at fault. No, it was Alice who had betrayed *him*; it was Alice who continued to darken his thoughts.

One Saturday morning, after flicking through all the TV channels and finding nothing but violent animation—too violent for his hungover eyes—Frank picked up the local weekly paper and almost immediately his eyes settled on an article headed "Surfing UK?" Frank didn't even need to read it to know that he had found the focus for his thoughts.

The article described how a stolen car had been seen hurtling down Heath Road late the previous Sunday night with someone strapped to the bonnet; eyewitnesses said the person tied to the car was "wailing like a banshee." It went on to describe the phenomenon of car-surfing, a craze that had started in, where else, New York, but was almost unheard of in this country. The car had later been found abandoned, rammed through the front window of a Latin American crafts shop at the south end of the Heath.

It was this last piece of information that Frank knew would be the key.

It didn't take him long to find the surfer; he knew that most of the kids in the area hung out around the benches beside the 7-Eleven and that it would just be a matter of time before he showed up. He also knew that he would recognise him immediately; the kids sported the trophies of their crimes like notches on a gun barrel.

On the fourth evening he was just about to head home—his backside was numb and he'd run out of cigarettes—when he saw the kid he'd been looking for. Lurking in a bunch of slack-limbed kids hand-jiving or doing some other tribal shit was a boy of around fifteen. From the rest of his clothes he was indistinguishable from all the other kids, but it was what he was wearing on his head that singled him out: a black felt hat looped with a brightly coloured ribbon, the same style of hat as favoured by Guatemalans.

Frank drove across the road and pulled up outside the 7-Eleven. He wound the window down, leaned on the frame and waited for the kid in the hat to look over. Other kids would occasionally catch his eye, and, holding the gaze, spit on the pavement. When the kid in the hat finally looked his way, Frank raised his chin, gestured for him to come over.

The kid removed something from his pocket and handed it to his friend, pushed the guy into the shadows.

He thinks I'm a cop, thought Frank. Dumb fuck.

The kid strolled over, eyes on the ground.

"I wanna talk to you a minute. Get in the car." Frank jerked his thumb over his shoulder.

"What is it, man?" The kid tilted the hat back on his head, angled his face to look down his nose at Frank. Blackheads peppered his cheeks and nose; his waxen skin glowed red in the neon lights from the store.

"Get in," said Frank again. He looked straight ahead, gripped the wheel.

The kid jumped the fence and got in the car. He leaned against the door with his fingers resting on the handle.

Frank pushed the car forward a few yards, away from the crowd outside the 7-Eleven.

"I know about the surfing," he said, still looking directly ahead. The perspiration on his forehead chilled, tightening the skin.

"But that's just between you and me." Frank tried to look at the kid in the rear view but he had forgotten to adjust the angle. "If you do something for me."

"Hey, man, you ain't no cop!" The kid's face creased. He twisted in his seat and reached for the handle.

Frank turned to him, grabbed his arm. "Did I say I was?"

The kid looked at Frank, shrugged his arm free. Frank could smell the kid's breath: corroded flesh—the kid was a speed freak; he would bite.

All he could hear was the rush of blood in his ears; his legs twitched as he manoevered the pedals, jerking the car forward.

Time had frozen for Danny. All he could see was a wave of blonde hair curling out of a dark hood; the only light in the darkness. He pulled his knees up to his chest and covered his eyes— a child unable to awaken from a nightmare.

Paul jumped on the accelerator. There was a loud screeching before the tyres gripped and the car shot forward.

A scream tore through the car; Danny wasn't sure whether it came from the girl or from inside his own head. He watched in horror as the Astra hit her high on the leg and she was flipped on to the bonnet. Her head spiderwebbed the windscreen and she was rolled over the roof in a rumble of metallic thunder.

Paul hit the brakes and the Astra fishtailed across the road, spinning through 180 degrees, coming to a stop with wheels hugging the kerb.

Through the shattered windscreen Paul saw a kaleidoscopic vision of Alice lying in the road, face down, her right leg at a strange angle to her body. A dark patch grew on her thigh, the colour of fresh blood diminished by the night.

A groan caused him to turn and he saw Danny roll from his seat onto his hands and knees. Paul went over and helped him to his feet. Blood was trickling from his nose and a golf ball with a cross of split skin had appeared above his left eye. He took a few tentative steps, trailing blood along the car with his fingers. His legs buckled under him and he fell to his knees once more.

Paul helped him up again and half-carried, half-dragged him towards the alley that ran along the back of the shops. Before disappearing he took one last look at the scene.

The Astra was blocking his view of the broken and bleeding woman and all he could see of her was her left hand, fingers curled in on themselves, nails piercing the palm. He looked at the car. The back window was splintered where the woman's head had bounced across it. A long crack ran from the point of impact to the bottom right-hand corner, splitting in two a sticker that advertised The Surf Shack, St. Ives.

"There's two hundred in it. Think of all the . . ."

He saw the kid look over his shoulder and a grin break open his mouth to reveal brown peg teeth. Frank turned. Cheeks blistered with acne were bearing down on him.

"My associate," said the kid in the hat.

Frank told them about his five-year-old son . . . the nurse coming off a double shift and falling asleep at the wheel . . . the lenient judge . . .

"A grand," said the kid in the hat, before Frank had even told them what he wanted. "It's gonna cost you a grand. Up front."

Frank looked at his watch: 10:05 P.M. He looked towards the door, as if expecting Alice to walk through at any minute. He looked for the girl with the freckles but she had gone. He lit another cigarette, took a sip of beer. He could feel his erection pushing against the inside of his chinos.

■　■　■

Alice did not recognise the red Astra across the street as she stepped out of the fitness centre after her weekly step aerobics class. The night was chilly, autumn beginning to close in, and she pulled up the hood of her sweatshirt to cover hair still damp from her shower. She took off to her right, walking briskly towards the parade of shops and the road that led to the hospital and the nurses' home.

Paul recognised her immediately. He waited for a break in the traffic and eased the Astra out, drifting towards the central line. He pulled ahead of Alice and signalled right. Round the corner he pulled in behind a green transit van, killed the lights and waited. It was a quiet stretch, a dark cavern between the brick walls of the buildings on either side.

Danny fastened his seat belt. His breathing had become heavy and a nervous sweat slicked his face; he sat on his hands to keep from chewing the fingers down to the bone.

They watched in silence as Alice walked past in slow motion; ten feet, twenty feet.

She drifted to the edge of the pavement and, without breaking her stride, glanced over her shoulder and stepped out into the road.

Paul eased his foot off the clutch and moved slowly from behind the van. Adrenaline coursed through his veins, jangling his nerves

PRETTY EYES

Evan Hunter

Evan Hunter is also Ed McBain and McBain is one of the three or four most important suspense writers of our time. Early in his career, Hunter, who has written a number of best-selling mainstream novels, wrote stories for the "prestige" magazines. This should have been one of them. But oddly enough, it ended up unheralded in one of the lesser periodicals. This is Hunter at his smooth and subtle best.

SHE WAS THIRTY-THREE YEARS OLD.

She was not a pretty woman, and she knew it.

The bellhop who showed her to the room in the Miami Beach hotel whistled all the way up in the elevator, whistled as he unlocked the door and stepped aside for her to enter.

"Nice room," he said. "Best on the floor. Has a balcony overlooking the ocean. Get the cool sea breezes." He grinned. He was no more than nineteen, a redheaded boy with a leering wisdom far beyond his years. "First time in Miami?" he asked.

"No."

"Been here before?"

"Yes," she said. "I come down every year."

"Oh?" The bellhop was still grinning. "First time at this hotel?"

"Yes."

"It's a good hotel." He put the valises on the stand. "You're not married, are you?"

"No," she answered, "I'm not married."

"Must get lonely, a pretty girl traveling all alone."

She looked at his face, and saw the lie sitting in his eyes. She said nothing.

"If you get . . . uh . . . *too* lonely," the bellhop said, his grin widening, "why, just buzz the desk. My name's Johnny. Be happy to . . . uh . . . come up and chat or something."

"Thank you," she said. There were four valises. She had read somewhere that a bellhop's services were worth twenty-five cents per bag. She never tipped more than twenty-five cents per bag and never less. She took a dollar from her purse and handed it to him.

"Thanks," he said briskly, lifting his coat and stuffing the bill into his watch pocket. "Anything I can get you?"

"No, thank you."

"If you hurry, you can still catch a swim and some sun."

"Thank you," she said.

At the door he repeated, "My name's Johnny," and then he left. Alone in the room, she began unpacking. Every year it was like this. The drive to the airport alone. The flight down alone. The cab ride to the hotel—a different one each year—alone. The unpacking. Alone.

A pretty girl traveling all alone.

His lie still rankled. She was not a pretty girl. She had discovered this a long time ago. The discovery had been painful, but she'd adjusted to it. She was not pretty. Her hair was a lusterless brown, and her eyes were a faded gray, and her nose was too long, and her mouth was too thin, and her figure was put together awkwardly. She was not pretty. Nor, she supposed, was she any longer a girl. Thirty-three. And next year thirty-four. And then thirty-five. And forty.

And alone.

The room was silent except for the steady hum of the air conditioner. She unpacked her bags and then went out onto the balcony. She could see the azure of the pool nine stories below, the men and women lounging around it in deck chairs. A muted sound of voices hung over the pool area, washed by the steady roll of the ocean against the beach beyond. She could almost see the bright golden shimmer of heat on the air, could taste the wet ocean salt on her mouth.

She wondered if it would happen this time.

The bellhop suddenly seemed an ill omen. His intentions had been clear, absolutely clear. Nor would he have so obviously spo-

ken his mind had she been a pretty woman. A pretty woman somehow generated fear and respect. A plain woman did not. A plain
woman was a lonely woman, and men sensed this. Oh, not lonely
for the night, no. It was never difficult to find a transitory partner
for the night. She had found many such partners, ever since the
first time when she'd been twenty-six—she could still remember
it clearly, remember the desolation she had felt, the sudden feeling
that life was slipping away too fast and that she would die a dried-
up old maid. And since that time there had been many, and she
knew the approaches now, the pat approaches, the bold, bald
propositions: "What's a pretty girl like you doing all alone on a
night like this?" "Why don't we have a drink in my room?"
"Come on, beautiful, what do you have to lose?" She knew them
all; she had heard them all.

But this time it will be different, she vowed. This time it has to
be different.

Purposefully she changed to her swimsuit and took the elevator
down to the pool.

■　■　■

Sitting alone at the bar that night, she could feel her skin tingling,
and she wondered if she'd taken too much sun that afternoon.
Luckily she did not turn lobster red the way some girls did. She
tanned steadily and graciously, and there had been a time when
she'd thought she was more attractive with a tan, but she no
longer believed this. Still, she was thankful that she tanned rather
than burned, and she wondered now if she had taken too much
sun, wondered if she would spend a sleepless night.

She reached into her purse for a cigarette, put it between her
lips, and was digging into her purse for matches when the lighter
sprang into flame at the cigarette's end.

"Allow me," the man said.

She turned slightly on the stool. "Thank you," she said in cool
aloofness, raising one eyebrow. She sucked at the flame and then
blew out a cloud of smoke and turned away from the man, back
to her whiskey sour.

The man sat on the stool next to hers. He was silent for a
moment and then he said, "Do you like those filter tips?"

"What?"

"The cigarette."

"Oh. Yes, I do."

"I never feel I'm smoking with a filter tip," the man said.

"I don't mind them," she answered. "It's a cleaner smoke, I feel."

"I suppose so," the man said. He ordered scotch on the rocks from the bartender and then turned to her again. "Just check in?" he asked.

"This afternoon," she said.

"First time in Miami?"

"No, no," she said, smiling. "I've been here before."

"Are you with your husband, or is this just a rest?"

"I'm not married," she said.

"No?" he said. He smiled pleasantly. "My name's Jack Bryant," he said, extending his hand.

"Connie Davidson," she told him, and she took his hand. His grip was firm and warm. He released her hand almost instantly.

"Treating yourself to a vacation, is that it?" he asked.

"I come down here every year at this time," she said.

"Where are you from?"

"New York," she answered.

"What part?"

"Are you from New York, too?"

"Yes," he said. "Brooklyn."

"I'm from Manhattan," she said. "Shall I make the Brooklyn jokes?"

He grinned easily. His eyes crinkled at the corners when he grinned. He was a pleasant-looking man in his late thirties, with warm blue eyes set in a tanned, even face. "I'd rather you didn't," he said. "I'm a criminal lawyer. I defend most of the people the jokes are about."

"That must be fascinating work," she said.

"It is. It gets a little tiring, though."

"Are you here on business?" she asked.

"No, no. Just a rest." He sipped at his scotch. "What sort of work do you do?"

"I work for an advertising agency."

"Doing what?"

"I write jingles."

"Really? No! You mean Pepsi-Cola? Like that?"

"Well, not Pepsi-Cola. But like that."

"Well, that's wonderful. You know, you hear the jingles, but you never realize somebody wrote them. It must be fun."

"It is," she said, smiling. "But it can get tiring, too."

He looked at her empty glass. "Would you like another drink?"

"Thank you," she said. "I would."

He ordered for her. They sat silently for a while, and then he said, "Here comes the band. Would you like to dance?"

"Not right now," she said.

"You look like a good dancer."

"I'm fair," she said.

"I'll bet you've taken lessons."

"What makes you say that?"

"I don't know. I just get that feeling."

"I took a few. For the mambo."

"And the cha-cha?"

"No. I stopped before that became the rage."

"There's always a new one," he said, chuckling. "After the cha-cha it'll be the ha-ha or the ho-ho. I think if you know the fox trot, the rhumba, and the waltz, that's all you have to know. Unless you're a fanatic for dancing."

"Well, I like to dance," she said.

"Oh, I do, too. But you can't make it your life's work."

"No, I suppose not."

"How long will you be staying, Connie?" he asked.

"Two weeks."

"Isn't that a coincidence?" he said.

"You'll be here . . ."

"Another two weeks, yes." He paused. "We can have a lot of fun together."

"Well," she said.

"I always wonder how it feels," he said.

"What?"

"You know."

"No, what?"

"A pretty girl like you," he said, "traveling alone."

She looked at him steadily.

"It . . . it feels fine," she answered.

"Must get lonely."

"Not too," she answered.

"Well, it seems to me it must get lonely," he said.

"I . . . I don't mind it," she said.

"Well, we'll have fun," he said, and he covered her hand with his. She did not move her hand for several moments. Then she slid it from his and picked up her drink.

"Think you could teach me the mambo?" he asked.

"Anyone can learn it," she answered.

"It seems so difficult."

"No."

"It seems that way," he said. "I'm always afraid I'll make a fool of myself on the dance floor."

"It's really very simple."

"Just a matter of getting the rhythm, I suppose," he said. "Still, with all those experts on the floor . . ." He shook his head ruefully, embarrassedly.

She knew what was coming next. She could have said the words even before they left his mouth. For a moment she wished desperately that she were wrong, wished that he would not say what she was sure he would say. For a moment she wished that once— just once—a man would look at her and honestly believe she had beautiful hair, or a fine brow, or pretty eyes. Once, just once, and her heart would open like a flower and the warmth would pour from her, the warmth that was stored, ready to burst. Just once, just once . . .

And then he said, "Maybe you could give me private lessons."

She did not answer.

"It's a little stuffy in here anyway, isn't it?" he asked.

"A . . . a little," she said.

"The air conditioner in my room works fine," he said. He smiled pleasantly.

"I . . . I don't know," she answered.

"We could order some drinks up there," he said. "I'd be honored. A pretty girl like you teaching me how to dance. I'd be honored."

"Please," she said.

"Seriously. We could dance a little . . ."

"Please . . ."

". . . and drink a little . . ."

"Please, please . . ."

"You know, have a little fun," he concluded.

She looked at his face soberly. The lie was in his eyes and on his mouth. Blankly she said, "I'm not pretty."

"Sure you are," he answered. "You're one of the prettiest girls in the hotel."

She nodded briefly. Her eyes dropped to the bar. She could see his left hand and the narrow band of white flesh on his third finger, where a ring had belatedly been removed after the skin had tanned.

"You're married?" she asked.

"Yes."

She nodded silently.

"Does it matter?" he asked.

"No," she said. "It doesn't matter. Nothing matters." She rose. "Good night," she said. "Thanks for the drink."

"Hey, what about the private lessons?"

She did not answer. Her eyes were misting as she walked away from the bar.

■　■　■

She checked out that night.

There did not seem to be any sense in staying. There did not seem to be any sense in anything. She wore a white linen suit, and she stood in the hotel corridor with the bellhop, impatiently waiting for the elevator, anxious to get away.

The elevator door slid open. She entered the car, and the bellhop followed with her four valises. A man was standing in one corner of the elevator. He looked at her when she entered. The car dropped leisurely toward the lobby. The man seemed rather nervous, a man of about thirty-five, with solemn brown eyes. He seemed as if he wanted to speak to her, but instead he swallowed repeatedly until the elevator had almost reached the lobby floor.

And then, at last, he very quietly said, "You have pretty eyes. The—" He glanced self-consciously at the bellhop and the elevator operator. "—the prettiest eyes I've ever seen."

She turned to him, naked hatred gleaming on her face. Sharply she whispered, "Stop it! Damn you, damn you, stop it!"

The elevator door slid open.

"Lobby," the operator said.

She stepped out of the car. The man looked at the operator in embarrassment. He waited for the bellhop to leave the car, and then he stepped into the lobby. He watched while she settled her bill. He watched while the bellhop carried her bags out and hailed a cab. He watched as the cab pulled away from the hotel, the girl sitting alone on the back seat. The bellhop returned to the lobby, pocketing a dollar bill.

"Touchy broad, huh?" he said to the man.

The man did not answer for a long while. He kept staring through the wide plate-glass doors at the empty street outside where the girl in the cab had been.

Then he said, "She had pretty eyes. She had very pretty eyes."

He bought a newspaper at the cigar stand in the arcade and sat in the lobby, reading, until midnight.

Alone in his silent room, he went to bed.

GRAVEYARD SHIFT

James Reasoner

As a long-unsung writer of numerous paperback originals, James Reasoner is the kind of person who never gets his due.

In choosing a Reasoner piece for this book, the editor sat down and read twenty Reasoner short stories—and every one of them was virtually without flaw. He can sketch a character in two lines of dialogue, and set a mood in a handful of unpretentious words.

This story is a perfect example.

GRAVEYARD SHIFTS ARE ALL ALIKE. I KNOW TOO WELL THE EMOtions that fill the long nights: boredom and fear. Boredom because nothing different ever happens, fear that sometime it might.

Convenience stores are all alike, too. Boxy little buildings filled with junk food and a few staples like bread and milk. The prices are too high, but where else can you buy things after midnight?

The little KwikStop store wasn't the first one in which I had worked. I've been traveling the country, trying to see some of that I haven't seen, now that I'm a widower and don't have any reason to stay in one place. The convenience stores always need help, and I have experience. Getting a job is no problem.

Neither is the fact that I'm usually assigned the all-night shift. It gives me the days free to do anything I want.

You see the same type of customers, no matter where the store is. Before midnight, you get teenagers buying Cokes and college kids buying beer and potato chips. A lot of young couples come in to buy milk and diapers. Sometimes you get a drunk who wants to buy beer after hours. Sometimes they get nasty when you refuse.

And sometimes you get one like the man who stepped in earlier tonight. That's where the fear comes in.

He was thin and had a pinched, beard-stubbled face, with too-wide eyes that never stopped moving. His clothes were shabby and his hands were pushed deep in the pockets of his windbreaker. I knew the type right away.

I've been working in the little stores long enough that attempted robberies are nothing new to me. Most stores have a policy about robberies that emphasizes cooperation and observation. They tell the clerks to do whatever the robber says. It's supposed to be safer that way.

But as I looked at this guy, I felt an ache in my belly and the palms of my hands began to sweat. This might be one of those times. The hammer of my pulse began to accelerate.

The man picked up a sack of Fritos and came toward the cash register. His other hand was still in his pocket.

The doors opened and two men and a young boy came in, heading for the soft drink case.

The man in the windbreaker looked hard at the newcomers and then dropped a quarter and a penny on the counter to pay for the Fritos. I rang up the sale and began to breathe again as he pushed through the doors on his way out.

It wasn't long afterward that George and Eddie pulled up in their patrol car and came inside for coffee, like they do every night.

"Hello, fellas," I said. "You should have been here a little earlier."

George poured himself a cup of the always-ready coffee and asked, "What happened, Frank?"

"Maybe I'm being paranoid, but there was a guy in here I think was going to rob the place. Some customers came in and he changed his mind."

"Did he pull a gun on you?"

"No, I didn't see a gun. It was just a gut feeling. Like I said, maybe I'm paranoid."

"Gut feelings are the best ones," Eddie said. "What did he look like?"

"Thin, maybe one-forty or fifty, about five-nine, sandy hair, probably about thirty years old. He was wearing blue jeans and a brown windbreaker."

Eddie wrote it all down in his notebook while George asked, "Did you see what he was driving?"

"He walked in. He might've had a car parked out of the lights, but if he did, I didn't see it."

"Okay, we'll keep an eye out for him. He probably won't be back, though, at least not tonight."

Business picked up not long after they left, and I was too busy to worry about the man who had been in earlier. I had quite a few customers in and out until three o'clock, when traffic tapered off. It would be slow now until a little after four, when the early morning workers would start coming in.

It was 3:37 when the man returned. I hadn't even seen a car drive by outside for over ten minutes, and I knew he wouldn't have to back out this time. I nodded to him and tried not to look scared as he stepped up to the counter.

"Pack of Camels," he said shortly. I put the cigarets on the counter between us. "Too late to buy beer?"

"I'm afraid so," I answered. I could feel sweat breaking out on me, dampening the red and white smock all the clerks wore. "Midnight is the latest you can buy it except on Saturdays."

He rocked back on his heels, then forward. His teeth were yellowed and I could see old acne scars on his face. I knew I would never forget the way he looked as he sneered and said, "I guess that'll do it then."

I began to work the cash register. When it popped open, he said, "You come out from behind there. There's a gun in my pocket."

I knew it was silly, but I couldn't help asking, "Is this a hold-up?"

"That's right, jackass. Now you get out from behind that counter like I told you. *Move!*"

I swallowed the huge lump in my throat and began to do like he told me, moving down around the microwave oven and the popcorn machine. The machines shielded me from his view momentarily, and I don't think he even saw my hand go behind my back, under the long smock, to the clip-on holster.

I stepped out, bringing the little pistol up and aiming it at the bridge of his nose. Surprise and fear leaped into his eyes.

The same emotions that must have been on my wife Becky's face when she walked into a little store far away and surprised a man just like this one, a man who had gotten away clean, leaving my world bleeding to death on a dirty tile floor . . .

I pulled the trigger and shattered the expression on his face. He didn't even have time to fire his own gun.

I put the gun on the counter and went to the pay phone to call the police. As I did, I thought about where I would go next. No one would be surprised when I quit this job, not after something like this.

That meant a new town, a new name, a new job. I wouldn't have any trouble finding work.

Like I said, convenience stores are all alike. And I've got plenty of experience.

AMY GDALLA

Jim Combs

Jim Combs is one of the best mystery critics working today. He brings style, grace, wit and real insight to the books under his consideration. He also has the makings of a first-rate fiction writer, as this dark and elegantly wrought little tale demonstrates.

A VAGUE SENSE OF UNEASE DRIFTED THROUGH PHIL. IT WAS HAP-pening rather too often lately. As always, he shivered slightly as if he were coming down with something. It's going around, his mouth mimed absently, *drink plenty of liquids, take two whatever and call me in the morning.* He hated it when his mind went silly on him. After all, this was only the first six months of his year, here as an intern at Eastern Regional Hospital. What is it this time, he mused, as his eyes browsed the horizon. The view from the seventh floor of the hospital was magnificent. The long line of glass swept from one end the of building to the other. An undulating range of dusty brown hills, late autumn leaves thick on the ground, blurred the horizon. He could almost hear the wind stir and rustle. It was a pleasant diversion from the clink, clank and click of the cafeteria behind him. A new batch of green, blue and white-clad employees began to clot up the cashier lanes. He was diverted by the low grinding hiss of trays sliding along the stainless steel counter and almost missed it. There. Slowly moving out of the dark line of pines, two vultures, gliding, catching the updrafts and turning in ever smaller circles. Circles. Loops. He was getting Loops on the brain. He couldn't shake the Loops.

Everywhere he went. Loops. Doctors, stethoscopes looped around their necks. Patients with loops of plastic around their wrists. Nurses, around their necks or wobbling from their ears, loops of jewelry. Traffic, loops of tires. Someone on TV getting drunk. Looped. Even something as esoteric as the mention of Chicago. The Loop.

■   ■   ■

A cloud drifted by and mirrored the window. Phil caught a glimpse of a narrow, horse shaped, pockmarked lunar landscape face, tufts of dirty silver hairs sprouting from Topo Gigio ears. A green name tag with letters nearly spilling over onto the coat: Phil Djemani-kwywcyk. *I'm not only going insane, I'm ugly to boot. My name sucks and no sane woman will ever look at me. I still have the aftereffects of near terminal zits as a teenager and my face looks like the dark side of the moon. Nobody can pronounce my name. Everyone winds up calling me "Jammies." They whisper that I am painfully shy. Is it any wonder? They have no idea how painful "shy" really is. And where would I ever find a sane woman around here? The doctors are worse than the patients and at the rate I'm going I might soon be one. Real soon. If I don't shake the Loops.*

■   ■   ■

The cloud passed and was replaced by a ghostly wavering interior shadow. Phil distractedly turned away from the window and at first couldn't make out the source of the shadow. Then he spotted a small thick man in a white coat pulling out a chair by a table down to his far left. Phil tried to reach out for his coffee cup on the sill and keep his eyes on the man at the same time. He over-reached and tipped the cup. The crash overrode every tinkle and clank in the huge, bustling room. In the silence, all eyes turned to the sound. Phil flushed and bent over quickly and awkwardly towards the broken cup on the tile. He slipped and fell heavily to the floor. *I thrust my nose firmly between his clenched teeth and threw him heavily to the floor, on top of me. Why am I thinking of a line from Mark Twain when every eye in the room is on me? I really, really am losing it. It's all over, Phil. Cash in your chips. Or is that crash in your chips? My mind gone silly on me again.*

■   ■   ■

Are you OK?"

Phil opened his eyes and saw a pair of expensive Italian loafers and followed them up a leg to see the small thick man extending a hand. The room resumed its noisy clatter. He reached for the hand and was pulled smoothly to his feet.

"Sit over here at my table." The man gestured and pulled out a chair opposite his.

"Thanks," Phil mumbled, "I'm so embarrassed."

"Nah, I do it all the time. Been known to trip over a chalk mark on the sidewalk. My name's Bailey, Jerome Bailey, Gynecology." He extended his hand again.

"Phil Djcmanikwywcyk, first year intern, Psychiatry."

Jerome gave Phil's hand a single smoothly powerful shake and sat down.

"Take a load off, sit." Jerome exuded power and authority. Phil sat.

"Shall I get you a new cup?"

"No, thanks, I don't deserve it."

"An odd thing for a psychiatrist-to-be to say."

"Well, yes it is, now that you point it out."

"Well."

"Well, what?" Phil responded in a faintly irritated tone.

"Aren't you going to analyze it?"

"Not really, I already know the answer."

They were silent for a moment. Then they simultaneously blurted, "I'm sorry."

The outburst broke the ice. They chuckled together.

"I'm sorry for being so obtuse," Phil said.

"I'm sorry for being so nosey," Jerome responded.

"You weren't being nosey, just curious."

"And you weren't being obtuse, just private."

They smiled at one another for a moment.

"Now that we are a mutual admiration society, go head, spill it. I've got the time and I've got a shoulder."

■　■　■

Phil eyed Jerome for a second and in that second he knew he was going to tell him about the Loop. A perfect stranger. Maybe that's why people will tell a perfect stranger things they have never told anyone. It's because they are perfect. And a stranger. They won't be critical or as judgmental as a friend and they won't be around as a reminder that they know what no one else does. Besides,

Jerome happened to be one of those immediately likable people, someone you take an instant shine to. *And don't forget that the Loop is all you think about lately and it's about to strangle you if you don't tell someone about it.*

"Are you sure?"

"Shoot. My golf game is called off. The Jag is in repairs. My mistress is in her lunar phase. My insurance is all paid up. My schedule is clear for the afternoon. Do it."

"OK, but this may take a while."

"Like I say, the whole afternoon." Jerome fanned out his hands.

"And your complete confidentiality."

"Absolutely."

"I don't quite know where to start."

"Try the beginning, it's easier that way."

"I think I had better get a new cup of coffee first." Phil scooted back in his chair.

Jerome shot up and held out his hand, palm up like a crossing guard.

"Halt, my treat. Besides, it will give you a chance to find the beginning."

■   ■   ■

A cup of coffee appeared in front of him. He had been sitting there stupefied by his wool gathering all the while.

"Thanks," he murmured.

"Make it so, Number One," Jerome mimicked in perfect Picardese.

"Aye, Captain," Phil returned in passable Riker.

■   ■   ■

Phil sipped his coffee. Enough hesitation. Go.

"Do you know Eleanor Witte?"

"Everybody knows Dr. Eleanor Witte. She's the staff golden boy, as it were, world renowned brain specialist in amnesia. One day she will snag a Nobel, it's just a matter of time. The work she has done on memory is on the cutting edge, as it were." He grinned at his own wit.

"A matter of time . . ." Phil whispered absently.

"Pardon?"

"Ah, nothing. She has an unusual patient in W ward by the name of Hans, Hans Vandermullen."

"Ah, yes, The W for Wacko/Weird ward."

Phil must have signaled a serious look of displeasure for Jerome backpedaled quickly. "Sorry, I really am. Very unprofessional, thoughtless of me. It won't happen again. And I do know a bit about this particular case. Please continue."

"Then you know that he has continued his unbroken, ritual behavior for the past, nearly nine years now?"

"I didn't realize it was that long."

"Have you observed this patient?"

"Yes, once, but that must have been . . . nine years ago. As I recall, they call him the 'screamer.' "

"Then you know his ritual?"

"Vaguely, but it's been a while, refresh me."

"It's a looped behavior. He begins with his arms in front of him, fingers closed and thumbs up. Hands about a foot and a half apart. His arms move up and down parallel to each other. His head keeps turning back and forth to his right. He mumbles a few words. Then he stares fixedly ahead for approximately 2 seconds. His mouth drops for precisely 3 seconds and then he screams for 7 seconds. And then the ritual starts all over again, and again, in an endless loop. For nine years never changing, never varying. Always the same, over and over again like some impossible personal hell. Hans is the most tortured patient I have ever seen. He has his own private level in Dante's Inferno. He's forever frozen in an impossible Hieronymus Bosch vignette. You can't have forgotten the screams."

"No, that I remember, and that's why I never came back to observe him again."

"The screaming is impossible to forget. It is as loud, as powerful and as intense each time. You would think that over the years it would begin to subside. It starts out each day with the exact same decibel level. It subsides during the day as his throat wears out. The only possible relief you can give him is to pour a liquid lozenge down his throat in those three seconds it's open. He has chronic sore throat and sounds like some cheap Hollywood version of the elephant man. His record shows that he was brought in near death from an auto accident and Dr. . . . ."

■　■　■

Jerome interrupted, "You keep stressing exact durations in timing and the exact decibel, how do you know this?"

∎   ∎   ∎

"Because I've recorded it and analyzed it for months. I set up a video camera and watched it over and over. Here are the facts: His ritual loop lasts precisely 12 hours. He sleeps for 12 hours and then loops for 12 hours again. The variable is less than five minutes per 24 hour period. Each behavioral set lasts exactly 47 seconds and each separate action lasts an ordained time. It's incredible. It's as if some dark, supernatural . . . thing has measured out his time here on earth in digitally precise doses of pain and suffering. It kept me awake half the night until I solved it . . . and now I can hardly sleep, hardly carry out my other duties, function, cope . . . my mind gone silly on me. I don't know what I would have done if you hadn't come along when you did. Even so, you will think me quite mad, as well you should."

"It's Hans who is quite mad, not you. Continue."

"Are you sure you want to hear the rest of this?"

"Gads yes, you can't stop now. Go on."

"The breaking clue came early one morning before he became too hoarse. As I taped, I sat next to him. I had accidentally left my ear plugs out. Otherwise you couldn't stand the screaming. I dropped my pencil and was leaning over to pick it up. As my head passed his mouth, I was able to make out what he was saying. He softly but clearly said, 'a me gu doll ah' and after a brief pause, 'please.' He had been saying this all along but so softly it was scarcely audible and, of course, no one wanted to get that close."

"A me gu doll ah, what does that mean? Is it a woman's name, some thing, what?"

"Both. Amygdalla is an obscure part of the brain. And Amy Gdalla is Amy Gdalla Witte, Eleanor's daughter."

"I didn't know her middle name. I knew she died in a car accident about 10 years ago." "A little less than nine years ago. Hans Vandermullen was the driver."

"What? Are you positive?"

"I checked it all out on the microfiche at the library. Hans was full of dope and alcohol according to the blood tests. I had already surmised that his ritual behavior was a reenactment of the accident. He grew up next door to the Wittes. He was literally the boy next door. He and Amy had dated on and off for years. She was engaged to be married to someone else. Because of the 'please' it's likely that he was trying to talk her out of it, pleading with her when the crash occurred. And the kicker is that Dr. Eleanor Witte was on call when they brought Hans in. She operated on him and probably saved his life. According to the paper, Eleanor learned after the operation that the other passenger, the dead girl, was Amy. Amy had gone off with Hans without her purse, which held up the identification process for several hours."

■   ■   ■

"If she had only known what Hans would have to go through, she might have let the knife slip."

Phil laughed. It was the shrill, keening, hollow laugh of the demented. It brought a hush to the late afternoon rush at the cashier lanes. In the ensuing silence, Phil heard his laughter echo off the walls in the cavernous room. It frightened him and he choked back the sound and sputtered to a stop. His face flushed scarlet with effort. He gathered himself for a moment. As Jerome, dumbfound by the outburst, watched him, he saw that somehow the color was draining from Phil's cheeks and into his eyes as they began to glow as if lit by a pure and eloquent madness.

■   ■   ■

"She did let the knife slip, you fool," he screamed.

The scream stopped the flow of noise in the room again. This time people stared at Phil openly without glancing away. He ignored the stares but lowered his voice to a whisper. "She gave the paper the wrong information about the timing, about when she knew that the passenger was her daughter. She gave herself an alibi, and then she used her expertise and her knife to doom Hans to a living hell for the rest of his life. She did it deliberately and with both malice and forethought; because she blamed him for Amy's death, she used her God given talents and looped Hans Vandermullen into the mother of all nightmare déjà vus. He will relive that crash for all eternity. If Hans is not the perfect argument for euthanasia—then there isn't one."

What," Jerome realized that he, too, was whispering, "in the hell are you talking about? You said yourself that she probably saved his life."

"I have proof, unrefutable, undeniable proof of the Loop."

"What Loop, where, how? I take it all back. You are mad, as mad as the March Hare, the Mad Hatter and the whole damn Tea Party to boot."

Jerome's voice had gone up with each word until he was shouting nearly as loud as Phil had laughed. In the crowded room people were now obviously veering away from their section, putting as much distance as possible between themselves and the two men.

.   .   .

A benign calm had descended upon Phil. He realized that he was smirking. Yes, actually smirking at Jerome. So this is what catharsis is really like. *O frabjous day, Callooh, Callay, he chortled in his joy and burbled as he came. 'Twas brillig and my mind gone snicker snack.* Phil was astonished by the weight of the emotional freight that came with the Loop. It was ecstasy to lay that burden down. And it was time for the denouement.

.   .   .

"I wasn't the best hacker in college for nothing. I broke into the hospital data banks and found what I needed to break Witte's code. It was childishly simple. In fact, it was the first password I tried and the longest string possible before Windows 95. It was, of course, 'Amygdalla,' dropping one of the 'l's' to make it fit. I downloaded it all. The how it was done is all there in the rough draft of her new book, *Memory Manipulation*. And you are correct; she will probably win a Nobel for it."

Jerome's jaw clinched and his voice took on a hard edge. "Proof. An unpublished manuscript is proof that a beloved and respected doctor somehow "Looped" as you would have it, one of her own patients into a psychotic limbo?"

.   .   .

"Oh, did I forget to tell you that I also found Witte's notes?" He was feeling much better than he had felt in weeks. He was smiling broadly now. "The notes she made right after the operation. She had recently discovered how to locate, isolate and manipulate traumatic moments in one's life. Their "richest horror," she called it. And she had found out how to construct an "Endless Loop" out of a specific memory. It's all there on my hard drive in my room. I even made a couple of backup disks. It's evidence that will condemn her forever. Maybe not legally. Is Looping a crime? Is there a law against it in the books? Probably not. But it is, at the very least, an ethical crime against humanity, a moral aberration and that alone will drive her out of the profession in complete disgrace." Phil laced his fingers together and stared off into space, a beatific smile on his face.

■   ■   ■

Jerome shot from his chair, leaned forward, and shouted a barrage of words and phrases. Some of them sounded threatening, but Phil wasn't listening. He was far too full of himself and far too happy to care.

■   ■   ■

Suddenly he found himself standing. Standing with his arms pinned to his sides with an impossibly firm grip. Jerome held him with both hands, his face so close to Phil's that his eyes blurred and crossed for a moment. When his eyes focused he was surprised to realize that he was staring at a long bent hair in Jerome's left nostril.

■   ■   ■

In a voice so tightly controlled that it seemed brittle, Jerome spoke as if to a naughty child, "I am. Was. The. fiancé. Amy's. You. Will. Not. Speak. Or Reveal. Anything."

■   ■   ■

Phil found himself sitting. He was aware that he had been "placed" like a chess piece back in his chair. His arms throbbed with a dull ache. He was frightened, confused, and his mind went . . . somewhere . . . When he stirred from his reverie, Jerome was gone and the cafeteria nearly empty.

When Phil took off his white coat and opened the door to his closet that night, a hand reached out and grasped his arm and held him in an impossibly firm grip. He felt the tiny, sharp, unmistakable sting of a hypodermic plunge into his neck and he crumpled into the welcome of a soft, velvet oblivion.

■   ■   ■

A vague sense of unease drifted thought Phil. It was happening a lot these days. It was a curious kind of déjà vu. The view from cafeteria on the seventh floor of the hospital was impressive. The wavy faintly green line of hills was filled with budding trees. A gruff March wind puffed away at the colorful kites several children were attempting to launch. Some were marginally successful and the wind looped them around and around. The kites seemed to be chasing their own tails, looping and looping in ever tighter circles until they crashed and the children shouted out their disappointment.

■   ■   ■

Weary with digging through the avalanche of paperwork, Jerome looked out his office window just as a frisky gust of wind whirled some dry last year's leaves in a counterclockwise swirl. It reminded him of Phil. It was a good thing that Witte had talked him into seeking Phil out and striking up a conversation. Her suspicions were correct. Phil had been up to something and he was right. Witte could and did Loop. Then she learned how to Record. And most of all, how to Erase. Her book was out. It was being hailed as a "giant step forward in the search for a cure for mental illness." Doctors around the globe were reporting astonishing success using the "Witte Manipulation." Patients everywhere reported that the "voices" were finally gone, erased. Phil, at least, had taught him that enough is enough and that he had his own eternal soul to consider. It took some persuasion to convince Witte of hers; but she came around and we did what had to be done, what should have been done a long time ago . . . but nothing could be done for Amy. Amy. Amy. Amy Gdalla. As he thought of her, as he had almost daily for the past nine years, his eyes misted over and a barely perceptible sob bubbled from his lips.

■   ■   ■

A vague sense of unease drifted through Phil. A patient of his had died suddenly. It was definitely for the better. Yet there was something about the case that he couldn't, for the life of him, recall. Things seemed to be . . . missing, like whatever had been in that half gig of hard drive on his computer that was now open. And whatever was in the two backup floppies he thought he had hidden behind his diploma. And those kites . . .

A MATTER OF PRINCIPLE

Max Allan Collins

Max Allan Collins is the new dean of historical mystery novelists. His Nate Heller novels are now the standard against which everything else is judged. Max has lately turned to movies for enjoyment—not watching them, making them, his Mommy *(which he wrote and directed) being a very good thriller indeed. This story will remind his movie fans just how good he is at prose.*

IT HAD BEEN A LONG TIME SINCE I'D HAD ANY TROUBLE SLEEPING. Probably Vietnam, and that was gunfire that kept me awake. I've never been an insomniac. You might think killing people for a living would give you restless nights. Truth is, those that go into that business simply aren't the kind who are bothered by it much.

I was no exception. I hadn't gone into retirement because my conscience was bothering me. I retired because the man I got my contracts through got killed—well, actually I killed him, but that's another story—and I had enough money put away to live comfortably without working, so I did.

The A-frame cottage on Paradise Lake was secluded enough for privacy, but close enough to nearby Lake Geneva to put me in contact with human beings, if I was so inclined, which I rarely was, with the exception of getting laid now and then. I'm human.

There was also a restaurant nearby, called Wilma's Welcome Inn, a rambling two-story affair that included a gas station, modest hotel accommodations, and a convenience store. I'd been toying with the idea of buying the place, which had been slipping since the death of Wilma; I'd been getting a little bored lately and needed something to do. Before I started putting people to sleep,

I worked in a garage as a mechanic, so the gas station angle appealed to me.

Anyway, boredom had started to itch at me, and for the past few nights I'd had trouble sleeping. I sat up all night watching satellite TV and reading paperback westerns; then I'd drag around the next day, maybe drifting to sleep in the afternoon just long enough to fuck up my sleep cycle again that night.

It was getting irritating.

At about three-thirty in the morning on the fourth night of this shit, I decided eating might do the trick. Fill my gut with junk food and the blood could rush down from my head and warm my belly and I'd get the fuck sleepy, finally. I hadn't tried this before because I'd been getting a trifle paunchy since I quit working and since winter kicked in.

In the summer I'd swim in the lake every day and get exercise and keep the spare tire off. But in the winter I'd just let my beard go and belt size, too. Winters made me fat and lazy and, now, fucking sleepless.

The cupboard was bare so I threw on my thermal jacket and headed over to the Welcome Inn. At this time of night the convenience store was the only thing open, that and one self-serve gas pump.

The clerk was a heavyset brunette named Cindy from nearby Twin Lakes. She was maybe twenty years old and a little surly, but she worked all night, so who could blame her.

"Mr. Ryan," she said, flatly, as I came in, the bell over the door jingling.

"Cindy," I said, with a nod, and began prowling the place, three narrow aisles parallel to the front of the building. None of the snacks appealed to me—chips and crackers and Twinkies and other preservative-packed delights—and the frozen food case ran mostly to ice-cream sandwiches and Popsicles. In this weather, that was a joke.

I was giving a box of Chef Boyardee lasagna an intent once-over, like it was a car I was considering buying, when the bell over the door jingled again. I glanced up and saw a heavyset man— heavyset enough to make Cindy look svelte—with a pockmarked face and black-rimmed glasses that fogged up as he stepped in.

He wore an expensive topcoat—tan, a camel's-hair number you

could make payments on for a year and still owe—and his shoes had a bright black city shine, barely flecked with ice and snow. His name was Harry something, and he was from Chicago. I knew him, in another life.

I turned my back. If he saw me, I'd have to kill him, and I was bored, but not that bored.

Predictably, Harry Something went straight for the potato chips; he also rustled around the area where cookies were shelved. I risked a glimpse and saw him, not two minutes after he entered, with his arms full of junk food, heading for the front counter.

"Excuse me, miss," Harry Something said, depositing his groceries before Cindy. His voice was nasal and high-pitched, a funny, childish voice for a man his size. "Could you direct me to the sanitary napkins?"

"You mean Kotex?"

"Whatever."

"The toiletries is just over there."

Now this was curious, and I'll tell you why. I had met Harry Something around ten years before, when I was doing a job for the Outfit boys. I was never a mob guy, mind you, strictly a freelancer, but their money was as good as anybody's. What that job was isn't important, but Harry and his partner Louis were the locals who had fucked up, making my outsider's presence necessary. Harry and Louis had not been friendly toward me. They had threatened me, in fact. They had beaten the hell out of me in my hotel room, when the job was over, for making them look bad.

I had never taken any sort of revenge out on them. I occasionally do take revenge, but at my convenience, and when a score strikes me as worth settling. Harry and Louis had really just pushed me around a little, bloodied my nose, tried to earn back a little self-respect. So I didn't hold a grudge. Not a major grudge. Fuck it.

As to why Harry Something purchasing Kotex in the middle of the night at some backwoods convenience store was curious, well, Harry and Louis were gay. They were queens of crime. Mob muscle who worked as a pair, and played as a pair.

I don't mean to be critical. To each his own. I'd rather cut off my dick than insert it in any orifice of a repulsive fat slob like Harry Something. But that's just me.

And me, I'm naturally curious. I'm not nosy, not even inquisitive. But when a faggot buys Kotex, I have to wonder why.

"Excuse me," Harry Something said, brushing by me.

He hadn't seen my face—he might not recognize me, in any case. Ten years and a beard and twenty pounds later, I wasn't as easy to peg as Harry was, who had changed goddamn little.

Harry, having stocked up on cookies and chips and Kotex, was not buying milk and packaged macaroni and cheese and provisions in general. He was shopping. Stocking up.

And now I knew what he was up to.

I nodded to surly Cindy, who bid me goodbye by flickering her eyelids in casual contempt, and went out to my car, a blue sporty Mazda I'd purchased recently. I wished I'd had the four-wheel-drive, or anything less conspicuous, but I didn't. I sat in the car, scooched down low; I did not turn on the engine. I just sat in the cold car in the cold night and waited.

Harry Something came out with two armloads of groceries—Kotex included, I presumed—and he put them in the front seat of the brown rental Ford. Louis was not waiting for him. Harry was alone.

Which further confirmed my suspicions.

I waited for him to pull out onto the road, waited for him to take the road's curve, then started up my Mazda and glided out after him. He had turned left, toward Twin Lakes and Lake Geneva. That made sense, only I figured he wouldn't wind up either place. I figured he'd be out in the boonies somewhere.

I knew what Harry was up to. I knew he wasn't exactly here to ski. That lardass couldn't stand up on a pair of skis. And he wasn't here to go ice-fishing, either. A city boy like Harry Something had no business in a touristy area like this, in the off-season—unless Harry was hiding out, holing up somewhere.

This would be the perfect area for that.

Only Harry didn't use Kotex.

He turned off on a side road, into a heavily wooded area that wound back toward Paradise Lake. Good. That was very good.

I went on by. I drove a mile, turned into a farmhouse gravel drive and headed back without lights. I slowed as I reached the mouth of the side road, and could see Harry's tail lights wink off.

I knew the cabin at the end of that road. There was only one, and its owner only used it during the summer; Harry was either a renter, or a squatter.

I glided on by and went back home. I left the Mazda next to the deck and walked up the steps and into my A-frame. The nine-millimeter was in the nightstand drawer. The gun hadn't been shot in months—Christ, maybe over a year. But I cleaned and oiled it regularly. It would do fine.

So would my black turtleneck, black jeans, black leather bomber jacket, and this black moonless night. I slipped a .38 revolver in the bomber jacket right side pocket, and clipped a hunting knife to my belt. The knife was razor sharp with a sword point; I sent for it out of the back of one of those dumb-ass ninja magazines—which are worthless except for mail-ordering weapons.

I walked along the edge of the lake, my running shoes crunching the brittle ground, layered as it was with snow and ice and leaves. The only light came from a gentle scattering of stars, a handful of diamonds flung on black velvet; the frozen lake was a dark presence that you could sense but not really see. The surrounding trees were even darker. The occasional cabin or cottage or house I passed was empty. I was one of only a handful of residents on Paradise Lake who lived year-round.

But the lights were on in one cabin. Not many lights, but lights. And its chimney was trailing smoke.

The cabin was small, a traditional log cabin like Abe Lincoln and syrup, only with a satellite dish. Probably two bedrooms, a living room, kitchenette, and a can or two. Only one car—the brown rental Ford.

My footsteps were lighter now; I was staying on the balls of my feet and the crunching under them was faint. I approached with caution and gun in hand and peeked in a window on the right front side.

Harry Something was sitting on the couch, eating barbecue potato chips, giving himself an orange mustache in the process. His feet were up on a coffee table. More food and a sawed-off double-barrel shotgun were on the couch next to him. He wore a colorful Hawaiian shirt; he looked like Don Ho puked on him, actually.

Hovering nervously nearby was Louis, a small, skinny, bald ferret of a man, who wore jeans and a black shirt and a white tie. I couldn't tell whether he was trying for trendy or gangster, and frankly didn't give a shit, either way.

Physically, all the two men had in common was pockmarks and a desire for the other's ugly body.

And neither one of them seemed to need a sanitary napkin, though a towelette would've come in handy for Harry Something. Jesus.

I huddled beneath the window, wondering what I was doing here. Boredom. Curiosity. I shrugged. Time to look in another window or two.

Because they clearly had a captive. That's what they were doing in the boonies. That's why they were stocking up on supplies at a convenience store in the middle of night and nowhere. That's why there were in the market for Kotex. That's what I'd instinctively, immediately known back at the Welcome Inn.

And in a back window, I saw her. She was naked on a bed in the rustic room, naked but for white panties. She was sitting on the edge of the bed and she was crying, a black-haired, creamy-fleshed beauty in her early twenties.

Obviously, Harry and Louis had nothing sexual in mind for this girl; the reason for her nudity was to help prevent her fleeing. The bed was heavy with blankets, and she'd obviously been keeping under the covers, but right now she was sitting and crying. That time of the month.

I stood in the dark in my dark clothes with a gun in my hand and my back to the log cabin and smiled. When I'd come out into the night, armed like this, it wasn't to effect a rescue. Whatever else they were, Harry and Louis were dangerous men. If I was going to spend my sleepless nights satisfying my curiosity and assuaging my boredom by poking into their business, I had to be ready to pay for my thrills.

But the thing was, I recognized this young woman. Like Harry, I spent a lot of hours during cold nights like this with my eyes frozen to a TV screen. And that's where I'd seen her: on the tube.

Not an actress, no—an heiress. The daughter of a Chicago media magnate whose name you'd recognize, a guy who inherited and wheeled-and-dealed his way into more, including one of the satellite superstations I'd been wasting my eyes on lately. The

Windy City's answer to Ted Turner, right down to boating and womanizing.

His daughter was a little wild—seen in the company of rock stars (she had a tattoo of a star—not Mick Jagger, a five-pointed *star* star—on her white left breast, which I could see from the window) and was a Betty Ford clinic dropout. Nonetheless, she was said to be the apple of her daddy's eye, even if that apple was a tad wormy.

So Harry and Louis had put the snatch on the snatch; fair enough. Question was, was it their own idea, or something the Outfit put them up to?

I sat in the cold and dark and decided, finally, that it just didn't matter who or what was behind it. My options were to go home, and forget about it, and try (probably without any luck) to get some sleep; or to rescue this somewhat soiled damsel in distress.

What the hell. I had nothing better to do.

I went to the front door and knocked.

No answer.

Shit, I knew somebody was home, so I knocked again.

Louis cracked open the door and peered out and said, "What is it?" and I shot him in the eye.

There was the harsh, shrill sound of a scream—not Louis, who hadn't had time for that, but the girl in the next room, scared shitless at hearing a gunshot, one would suppose.

I paid no attention to her and pushed the door open—there was no night latch or anything—and stepped over Louis, and pointed the nine-millimeter at Harry, whose orange-ringed mouth was frozen open and whose bag of barbecue potato chips dropped to the floor, much as Louis had.

"Don't, Harry," I said.

I could see in Harry's tiny dark eyes behind his thick black-rimmed glasses that he was thinking about the sawed-off shotgun on the couch next to him.

"Who the fuck . . ."

I walked slowly across the rustic living room toward the couch; in the background, an old colorized movie was playing on their captive's daddy's superstation. I plucked the shotgun off the couch with my left hand and tucked it under my arm.

"Hi, Harry," I said. "Been a while."

His orange-ringed mouth slowly began to work and his eyes began to blink and he said, "Quarry?"

That was the name he'd known me by.

"Taking the girl your idea, or are you still working for the boys?"

"We . . . we retired, couple years ago. God. You killed Louis. Louis. You killed Louis . . ."

"Right. What were you going to put the girl's body in?"

"Huh?"

"She's obviously seen you. You were obviously going to kill her, once you got the money. So. What was the plan?"

Harry wiped off his orange barbecue ring. "Got a roll of plastic in the closet. Gonna roll her up in it and dump her in one of the gravel pits around here."

"I see. Do that number with the plastic right now, for Louis, why don't you? Okay?"

Tears were rolling down Harry's stubbly pockmarked cheeks. I didn't know whether he was crying for Louis or himself or the pair of them, and I wasn't interested enough to ask.

"Okay," he said thickly.

I watched him roll his partner up in the sheet of plastic, using duct tape to secure the package; he sobbed as he did it, but he did it. He got blood on his Hawaiian shirt; it didn't particularly show, though.

"Now I want you to clean up the mess. Go on. You'll find what you need in the kitchen."

Dutifully, Harry shuffled over, got a pan of warm water and some rags, and got on his knees and cleaned up the brains and blood. He wasn't crying anymore. He moved slow but steady, a fat zombie in a colorful shirt.

"Stick the rags in the end of Louis' plastic home, would you? Thank you."

Harry did that, then the big man lumbered to his feet, hands in the air, and said, "Now me, huh?"

"I might let you go, Harry. I got nothing against you."

"Not . . . not how I remember it."

I laughed. "You girls leaned on me once. You think I'd kill a person over something that trivial? What kind of guy do you think I am, Harry?"

Harry had sense enough not to answer.

"Come with me," I said, and with the nine-millimeter's nose to Harry's temple, I walked him to the door of the bedroom.

"Open it," I said.

He did.

We went in, Harry first.

The girl was under the covers, holding the blankets and sheets up around her in a combination of illogical modesty and legitimate fear.

Her expression melted into one of confusion mingled with the beginnings of hope and relief, when she saw me.

"I've already taken care of the skinny one," I said. "Now Harry and me are going for a walk. You stay here. I'm going to get you back to your father."

Her confusion didn't leave, but she began to smile, wide, like a kid Christmas morning seeing her gifts. Her gift to me was dropping the blankets and sheets to her waist.

"Remember," I said. "Stay right there."

I walked Harry out, pulling the bedroom door shut behind me.

"Where are her clothes?"

He nodded to a closet. Same one he'd gotten the plastic out of.

"Good," I said. "Now let's go for a walk. Just you and me and Louis."

"Loo . . . Louis?"

"Better give Louis a hand, Harry."

Harry held the plastic-wrapped corpse in his arms like a B-movie monster carrying a starlet. The plastic was spattered with blood, but on the inside. Harry looked like he was going to cry again.

I still had the sawed-off shotgun under my arm, so it was awkward, getting the front door open, but I managed.

"Out on the lake," I said.

Harry looked at me, his eyes behind the glasses wary, glancing from me to his plastic-wrapped burden and back again.

"We're going to bury Louis at sea," I said.

"Huh?"

"Just walk, Harry. Okay? Just walk."

He walked. I followed behind, nine-millimeter in one hand, sawed-off in the other. Harry in his Hawaiian shirt was an oddly comic sight, but I was too busy to be amused. Our feet crunched slightly on the ice. No danger of falling in. Frozen solid. Kids ice-skated out here. But not right now.

We walked a long way. We said not a word, until I halted him about midway. The black starry sky was our only witness.

"Put him down, Harry," I said. The nine-millimeter was in my waistband; the shotgun was pointed right at him.

He set his cargo gently down. He stood looking gloomily down at the plastic shroud, like a bear contemplating its own foot caught in a trap.

I blasted both barrels of the shotgun; they blew the quiet night apart and echoed across the frozen lake and rattled the world.

Harry looked at me, stunned.

"What the fuck . . . ?"

"Now unroll Louis and toss him in," I said, standing near the gaping hole in the ice. "I'm afraid that plastic might float."

Horrified, the big man did as he was told. Louis slipped down the hole in the ice and into watery nothingness like a turd down the crapper.

"Slick," I said, admiringly.

"Oh Jesus," he said.

"Now you," I said.

"What?"

I had the nine-millimeter out again.

"Jump in," I said. "Water's fine."

"Fuck you!"

I went over quickly and pushed the big son of a bitch in. He was flailing, splashing icy water up on me, as I put six bullets in his head, which came apart in pieces, like a rotten melon.

And then he was gone.

Nothing left but the hole in the ice, the water within it making some frothy reddish waves that would die down soon enough.

I gathered the weapons and the plastic and, folding the plastic sheet as I walked, went back to the cabin.

This was reckless, I knew. I shouldn't be killing people who lived on the same goddamn lake I did. But it was winter, and the bodies wouldn't turn up for a long time, if ever, and the Outfit had used this part of the world to dump its corpses since Capone was just a mean street kid. Very little chance any of this would come back at me.

Nonetheless, I had taken a risk or two. I ought to get something out of it, other than killing a sleepless night.

I got the girl's clothes and went in and gave them to her. A heavy-metal T-shirt and designer jeans and Reeboks.

"Did you kill those men?" she said, breathlessly, her eyes dark and glittering. She had her clothes in her lap.

"That's not important. Get dressed."

"You're wonderful. You're goddamn fucking wonderful."

"I know," I said. "Everybody says the same thing. Get dressed."

She got dressed. I watched her. She was a beautiful piece of ass, no question. The way she was looking at me made it clear she was grateful.

"What can I do for you?" she said, hands on her hips.

"Nothing," I said. "You're on the rag."

That made her laugh. "Other ports in a storm."

"Maybe later," I said, and smiled. She looked like AIDS-bait to me. I could be reckless, but not that reckless.

I put her in my car. I hadn't decided yet whether or not to dump the brown rental Ford. Probably would. I could worry about that later. Right now, I needed to get her to a motel.

She slept in the car. I envied her, and nudged her awake when we reached the motel just inside the Illinois state line.

I'd already checked in. I ushered her in to the shabby little room, its floor space all but taken up by two twin beds, and she sat on the bed and yawned.

"What now?" she said. "You want your reward?"

"Actually, yes," I said, sitting next to her. "What's your father's number?"

"Hey, there's time for that later . . ."

"First things first," I said, and she wrote the number out on the pad by the phone.

I heard the ring, and a male voice said, "Hello?"

I gave her the receiver. "Make sure it's your father, and tell him you're all right."

"Daddy?" she said. She smiled, then she made a face. "I'm fine, I'm fine . . . the man you sent . . . what?"

She covered the receiver, eyes confused again. "He says he didn't send anybody."

I took the phone. "Good evening, sir. I have your daughter. As you can hear, she's just fine. Get together one hundred thousand dollars in unmarked, nonsequential tens, twenties, and fifties, and wait for the next call."

I hung up.

She looked at me with wide eyes and wide-open mouth.

"I'm not going to kill you," I said. "I'm just turning a buck."

"You bastard!"

I put the duct tape over her mouth, taped her wrists behind her, and taped her ankles too, and went over and curled up on the other bed, nine-millimeter in my waistband.

And slept like a baby.

FAMOUS BLUE RAINCOAT

Ed Gorman

Britain's popular culture magazine Million *called Ed Gorman "one of the world's great storytellers."*

Gorman's fiction spans a variety of fields, including mainstream, suspense, and horror. His work has appeared in magazines as diverse as Redbook, Ellery Queen, Penthouse, *and* Poetry Today.

(An interpretation of the Leonard Cohen song "Famous Blue Raincoat")

I SUPPOSE CHAD THOUGHT I'D FORGIVE HIM, THE TIME HE SLEPT with my wife Tish I mean. He had a kind of innocent quality about him. You never quite held him responsible for things. Plus there were his guileless good looks. And that incredible inheritance he'd come into. People were always forgiving Chad something or other.

The spring it happened, I surprised him a little. I didn't forgive him.

It was much easier forgiving Tish. In the second year of our marriage, she'd forgiven me the nurse at the medical clinic where I work—the affair went on the better part of the winter—so I couldn't get too pious about her going to bed with Chad.

And the fact was, I almost couldn't blame her. Our lives were pretty drab and we both knew it. Four years after graduating from college, we found ourselves living in the kind of middle-class housing development that we'd once laughed about, and working at jobs that meant nothing to us. We needed the security and the insurance. We clung to our mediocrity, fearful as supplicants. Instead of my dream of med school, I was a physician's assistant; and instead of a TV anchorwoman, Tish settled for writing advertising copy for a small ad agency.

Tish once joked that Chad was our "human TV." And in a way, he was. We'd known him in college. We'd never been quite sure why he liked us. He spent his life working his way through half the pretty girls on campus. We used to sit with him in one of the student bars and listen to his travails with women. He fell in love easily. The trouble was, he never stayed in love. When a woman treated him badly, his love was almost suffocating. But once she was nice to him, he became bored. Sometimes he had two or three affairs a month. It really was like watching a TV saga with all the ups and downs that only lust can inspire.

Best of all, he asked our advice. It was sort of interactive. He'd come to us with this problem—"Susan's going to see her old boyfriend this weekend, and I'm not sure how to handle it—I mean, should I tell her I'm going to break up with her if she does"?—and we would give him suggestions, which he'd almost always use.

That was the endearing thing about Chad: He had money and looks and poise but he had absolutely no self-confidence. That was our part of the bargain, giving him our wisdom. His part was to keep the great soap opera going—this one needing an abortion, that one starting to bore him, this one (this brand-new one) exciting him so much he just knew she was the woman he'd waited for all his life. So it went, and we could vanquish our griefs and disappointments in it all. No time for fretting over mediocrity when Chad was out there bedding every beauty in sight.

He had his breakdown the summer of our graduation. We went to see him constantly. His parents were both dead and he was not fond of his sister, so we became his stand-in family. Or at least that was how his shrink treated us, anyway. Told us all about Chad's depression, his electroshock treatments, his almost total dependence on how we told him to conduct his life. He spent nine weeks in the sanitarium, lost fifteen pounds, and practically leapt on us every time we went up to see him. Since I had gotten a job that summer, I couldn't visit him as often as Tish could. She went every day. When he got out of the hospital, he rented an apartment next door to ours and had dinner with us every night. He spent more time at our place than his, even during the day with Tish.

Then he decided to see the world. We got letters and faxes from China, Samoa, Paris, Zurich and London asking our advice on how he should handle this or that woman. Chad Atwater had taken the show on the road, as it were. Tish seemed curiously despondent, and no matter what I did or said, she didn't seem to have much interest.

That was when I drifted into my two affairs. I've had some men tell me that cheating on their wives only makes their own bed all the more exciting. Not me. I didn't want to touch Tish. There were days I didn't even want to see her.

Then, five years later, Chad came back to our little midwestern city, bought himself a condo out along the river, and settled back into our lives.

Human TV was once again on the air.

■   ■   ■

The first two women that spring didn't represent any particular obstacles for Chad, and as such were pretty dull. What I'm saying is that Chad knew how to handle them without much advice from us.

Andrea, our favorite of the two, was a high school English teacher with a fetching smile and the somewhat aggravating habit of apologizing for practically every word she said. It was a month before they went to bed—I think she probably sensed that once they began having sex regularly, he'd start looking around for the next one—and ultimately she began using us to plead with him on her behalf. She would make him the perfect wife, she asked us to tell him. She was a nurturer, she said; a nurturer; and that's what he needed, nurturing. We advised against her, of course, when we were alone with him I mean. Nice as she was, she wasn't any fun, not for him, not for us. Human TV required better story lines than hers.

Heather was a bitch but she was entertaining. She was faithless as our Chad himself, at least at first, and it was she who first played the Leonard Cohen song "Famous Blue Raincoat" for us. Cohen tells a story of a somewhat mysterious man who enters the life of a husband and wife and proceeds to tie them up in psychic knots. The narrator of the song, who obviously suspects that his wife had an affair with the man, asks him to come back, along with his famous blue raincoat, because their lives, despite all the pain, just aren't the same without him.

Heather cunningly saw that the song was a reasonable parallel of our situation with Chad. She thought it was funny. After playing it for us in our living room, she laughed and said, "Chad told me all about 'human TV.' I think it's great. I'll try to be as interesting as I can for you people." She was gorgeous and ruthless and we had a lot of hope for her. Unfortunately . . .

Unfortunately, our advice to Chad was a little *too* sage. Just when it looked as if she'd never be faithful to him, we suggested that he seduce her best friend, whom Chad felt had some interest in him. Heather herself had told us that she and her best friend Jane had an agreement—they would never sleep with any man the other friend was going out with.

The night the deed was to be done, Tish came up with a diabolical twist: Chad had the key to Heather's apartment, right? Why not really add insult to injury and make love to Jane in Heather's bed?

Which was exactly what he did.

Heather came over two nights later and wept in our kitchen. Chad had humiliated and debased her and now she realized that she really truly did love him after all.

Chad slept with her a few more times and then, on our advice, said goodbye.

■ ■ ■

A month later Chad slept with Tish.

I came home one rainy afternoon and found Tish curled up on the couch, looking despondent.

"Famous Blue Raincoat" was playing on the CD player.

She had her moods and this seemed to be one of them.

I sat down on the floor next to the couch and put my hand on hers. Her hand was cold and made no effort to respond to my touch. Thunder rumbled. Rain hissed.

"You all right?" I said.

"I slept with him."

I didn't have to ask who "him" was. For years I'd been dreading this moment, and it had come now, and in an odd way I was curious about how I'd react now that it had finally happened.

"This afternoon?"

"Uh-huh."

"That was the only time?"

"Uh-huh."

"Are you sorry?"

"Sorry for me. I don't want to be just one more of his conquests."

"But not sorry for me?"

"You had your little nurse."

"Ah."

"But that wasn't why I slept with him."

"Oh? Then why *did* you sleep with him?"

"Because it was raining."

The thing was, I knew my wife well enough to know that for her this was a complete answer. Rain had a terribly melancholic effect on her, and sometimes lovemaking is the only defense you can put up against the vagaries of the universe.

"You think it'll happen again?" I said.

"No."

"Are you in love with him?"

"I hope not."

"That's not an answer."

"I could be."

"That's not an answer, either."

"I'm afraid I might be."

"That's an answer."

"I wish I was suicidal."

"I'm very angry," I said.

"You don't sound very angry."

"You want me to slap you around or something like that?"

"No."

I stood up. "What I really want to do is slap Chad around."

"That won't change anything. It still will have happened."

"Right now I don't give a shit if it will change things or not," I said, and drove over to Chad's.

As soon as I saw his face in his doorway, I drove my fist into his nose and watched as blood bloomed in both nostrils.

When he'd gotten a cool washcloth for his nose, and a scotch for both of us, and when he took the chair and I took the couch, he said, "I'm sorry I hurt you."

"No, you're not."

"I didn't want it to happen."

"You've been wanting it to happen for a long time. One of the few women you've never taken to bed."

"I'll do anything you want."

"I don't want you to call us or phone us or write us ever again."

He took the washcloth from his nose. "Are you serious?"

"Very."

"But we're sort of a trio."

"Not anymore."

"There's this new woman I met. I wanted to tell you about her. See what you and Tish thought I should do."

"You heard what I said, Chad. No more contact of any kind."

I left.

■   ■   ■

I was impotent for the next three months. Every time I tried to touch my wife, all I could think of was her in bed with Chad. She reminded me that this was how she'd felt after learning about my nurse.

The worst thing was, of course, that she was in love with him. I'd catch her staring at the phone, or looking out the window, or losing attention while we watched TV, and I knew who she was thinking of. One day I came home early and found her sitting in the kitchen, her eyes red from crying. It was raining. They were alike about rain, how it made them so melancholy.

One night, after coming home from the cineplex, we made love in the car, her climbing on top of me in the front seat as we'd done back in college days. I was nice and stiff for her, and then we started making love again a few times a week. I just hoped she didn't close her eyes and imagine I was Chad.

Summer came, and then autumn, and the emptiness was still there. Somehow, we'd never found a life rhythm again after Chad disappeared. There were too many silences, too many nights when we went to bed and lay there silent and isolate, her dreaming of Chad I supposed, me dreaming of the wife she'd once been.

We heard about Chad's car accident through a mutual friend.

Three weeks in the hospital, we were told, and a decided limp for the rest of his life. And depression. Chad had gone back to psychotherapy.

I saw him first. This was on a winter morning, all the downtown display windows rimed with frost, and he was just leaving the medical arcade. He had a limp, all right, and he had the pallor of a sick man.

Before I could turn and hurry away, he saw me and waved. I didn't have a hell of a lot of choice.

"God, it's good to see you," he said.

"I heard about your car accident."

"You know the worst thing about running into that tree?" he said, trying to make it a joke. "I was sober." Then: "I really miss you people. I shouldn't ever have—done what I did. I'm really sorry, and I hope you believe me."

"I accept your apology, Chad. But I still don't want you in my house."

"Not in your house then."

"What?"

"We'll see each other, the three of us, but not in your house. We'll go out. I've got a new woman and I really want you to meet her. I know you won't believe this but I think she's the one."

"That means you haven't broken her heart yet. As soon as you do—"

"No," he said. "While I was healing up, I thought about a lot of things. It's time I settle down. It really is. Her name is Anne."

That was how it started up again, having dinner, the four of us, in a restaurant. Within a few weeks Chad and Anne were dropping by our house, and within a few weeks after that Tish and Anne were having the occasional lunch and the Saturday shopping afternoon. Just as they did "girl" things, Chad got me to do a few "boy" things, helping him pick out a new boat for impending summer, helping him decide which riverside cabin was best to buy.

Human TV didn't start again until he began coming over a night or two a week by himself. He was careful to make sure I was there when he came.

At first, I wasn't sure I wanted to hear any of it but gradually the soap operatics of it all started to draw me in. Anne, quite a stylish if not exactly beautiful woman, had been dumped three times in the past and wasn't sure that she ever wanted to get serious with anybody again. While Chad was wildly serious, she was cautious. She wanted her own life—nights out with her female friends, taking a night school course in fine arts, and keeping separate houses.

Tish's theory was that Anne knew Chad was a heartbreaker and was therefore wary of getting any closer to him. My theory was that she was just what she seemed—a very bright and independent woman who didn't want to move in with Chad. Or marry him.

I didn't realize how serious any of this was until I came home one night to hear Tish screaming from inside.

I ran in the back door to find Chad slumped over the kitchen table. He'd slashed his left wrist with my safety razor. Blood was pooled around his arm.

"You can't let him die," she said, "you can't let him die."

I'd been wondering if Tish had gotten over Chad and now I had my answer. In her hysteria, I saw how much she loved him, how sacred he was to her.

I wrapped a towel around his wrist and carried him to the car and drove through several red lights to reach the nearest hospital.

They stitched him up and gave him three different kinds of white pills.

That night, at Tish's insistence, Chad moved into our guest room. Given his psychiatric history, I supposed it was a humane idea. But I also knew that now I'd never get my wife back again.

Anne changed. His suicide attempt softened her. She no longer seemed quite so sharp-edged or independent. This made me assume that she was going to give in to Chad, and marry him. But no, she wasn't.

"She's all I can think of," Chad said night after night at our dinner table. It was like having a badly depressed son around the house. "I won't ever be able to love anybody else again."

She watched him, Tish did, constantly, love-sick as he was himself. As long as Anne was around, Chad would never love her. I'm sure she realized that.

"What do you think I should do?" he said to me one night as we were having dessert.

"I think you have to break it off," I said.

"That's easy for you to say."

"You asked for my advice, Chad," I said. "So I'm giving it to you."

In the old days, human TV had been such fun.

"What he means," Tish said, "is that you should be with somebody who understands you and loves you and wants to be with you the rest of your life."

She couldn't help herself. She got so emotional during her little speech that she put her hand on his.

Chad looked first at her hand and then at me. He looked afraid that I'd punch him again.

I just sat there.

It became quite a saga, the thing with Anne. They even went to see a counselor together. But Anne wouldn't change her mind. There would be no moving in, no marriage.

He took to sobbing late at night, and Tish took to going in and comforting him. I tried not to think about what was happening in our guest room as the moon waned near dawn, and their voices fell to whispers.

But one night they weren't whispering at all. They were shouting at each other.

I ran in in my pajama bottoms to see what was wrong.

"I won't do it," he said. "That's crazy."

"It's the only way you'll ever be free," she said. "I'm only saying this for your own sake. Look what your life's become because of her. You need to be with somebody who loves you, Chad. Who venerates you the way I do." Then: "Haven't I always given you good advice, Chad?"

I'm not even sure they saw me peek past the dark door I'd just opened, not sure they heard me at all.

I wondered what sort of advice she'd given him. Whatever it was, it had shaken him badly. Just as their shouting had shaken me. I was as hopelessly in love with Tish as Tish was with Chad.

Sixteen nights later, Anne's naked and badly mutilated body was found in a shallow woods. She'd been dead for two days.

Chad was the first and foremost suspect. A homicide detective named Haney was at our house the night following the discovery of the murder.

He took Chad out on the deck and they talked just as sweet spring winds came up from the woods.

Tish found me in the TV room.

"I was just talking with Detective Haney," she said.

I looked at her, leaned close so I could whisper. "He killed her, Tish. Our Chad killed her."

"I told him that Chad didn't leave the house the night she died."

When I heard about Anne's death, my first thought was selfish: Chad will be out of our lives for good now.

"But he did go out," I said. "And he did kill her."

"That doesn't matter."

"It doesn't?" I smiled sadly. "You got what you wanted, didn't you, Tish? Anne's dead, and Chad's all yours. All you had to do was convince him to kill her."

"If you want to stay my husband," she said, "you'll tell the police the same thing I did."

Which I did.

Haney must have dropped in on us ten times over the next few weeks. He didn't believe us, he was angry, he even hinted that he might charge us as accomplices. But he couldn't get us to change our story.

By summer's end, they were making love again, Tish and Chad. At least they were sensitive enough to use the guest room rather than our bedroom. My first impulse was to get angry, of course, and go to the police and tell them that our alibi had been false. But I would lose Tish forever. My second impulse was to confront Chad. But he was so psychologically beleaguered—he talked to himself; he had terrible nightmares; he was constantly asking Tish to check in the closets to make sure monsters weren't hiding in there—that I couldn't say anything without looking like a terrible bully, even to myself.

Not long after that, Chad had his little experience of running down our nice quiet residential street without any clothes on.

He was in the sanitarium for four months this time. He went into deep analysis, he received several experimental drugs for depression, and he took more than two dozen electroshock treatments. His psychiatrist kept the police at bay, allowing them only occasional visits. The detectives still wanted to prove that Chad had murdered Anne.

And then Chad had the sort of luck Chad always had. The police took into custody the serial killer they'd been looking for the past three years. His specialty was women in their mid-twenties. Beautiful women in their mid-twenties. Like Anne. They charged him with eleven homicides, so what was one more? They blamed him for Anne's death, too, and closed the case.

■　■　■

Two weeks before Chad left the sanitarium, he told us about Molly. She was a ballet dancer who'd had a complete breakdown and had been in the asylum for more than four years. He'd fallen in love with her. And she was in love with him. There would be no games this time, on either side. Within a few months, they'd be married. There would be children, and a nice normal life. He was sure of it. But for all he told us about her—that sense of candor he always had—I sensed that there was something about her past he was holding back. Why had she been put in the sanitarium, anyway? Chad never told us.

After his release, Chad moved back in with us. On that first Saturday night, Molly came to dinner at our place for the first time. She was lovely in a delicate, troubled way, all wonderful facial bones and tiny tics of eye and mouth, and she was so wrapped up in Chad it was almost painful to see. Because it was clear, at least to me, that Chad was already losing interest in her. I'd overheard him on the phone the other day, using his best seductive tones. He'd found somebody else to play with on the side.

Tish, too, must have sensed that Chad was already bored. She didn't resent Molly the way she had Anne. She was friendly to the woman in an almost sisterly way.

Molly came around many times, of course. She ate dinner at our place probably three or four times a week. The more she talked about their marriage, the less Chad even bothered to look at her. He'd taken to going out late at night. Obviously he had another woman. And just as obviously, Tish was angry about this other woman. I was awakened one dawn by Tish and Chad arguing bitterly in the living room. When I came out to see what was going on, Tish fled from the room in tears. Chad sat up late in his room playing "Famous Blue Raincoat" again and again.

The next day, I started inquiring about Molly Stevenson. I did it very discreetly, of course, with the help of a friend I had at the credit bureau. They can find out virtually anything about you in a very short period of time.

Spring came, and so I thought it would be nice to have my first lunch with Molly outdoors, at an open air cafe next to the river. She was startled when I called, and not really all that enthusiastic about going, but I hinted that there was something important about Chad we needed to discuss.

We liked each other, and I think she was surprised. I was able to make her laugh a lot and she seemed to appreciate that a great deal. I told her how much I liked her, and I also told her that I didn't want to see her get hurt. And I started giving her little warning hints about Chad. He hadn't, it seems, mentioned most of the women in his background.

There were many more lunches filled with laughter and tics of eye and mouth. She took tranquilizers constantly and sometimes suffered little moments of shuddering, as if she were about to have a seizure of some kind.

A month into these lunches, I told her about Tish and Chad sleeping together. I also told her that I thought it was still going on, and that Chad couldn't even be faithful to Tish. He was also seeing another mystery woman on the side. I emphasized that I wouldn't be telling her any of these things if I didn't care for her so much.

She smashed her wineglass against the edge of the table and then picked up a jagged piece of glass and slashed it down her very lovely cheek. Then she put her head down on the table and wept.

■   ■   ■

The call came two weeks later, late in the night.

Tish, who was still up waiting for Chad no doubt, took the call and then let out a scream. I padded out to the living room and took her into my arms. I'd never heard her sob this way. She seemed to be having convulsions of some kind.

Chad's lawyer asked us to handle all the funeral arrangements and I was happy to.

The District Attorney put Molly back into the hospital, until he could decide if he was going to agree with her lawyer that she wasn't competent to stand trial.

Tish started sleeping with me again. Not making love, you understand. I assumed that was a ways off as yet. The memory of Chad would be too fresh and painful. But she did let me hold her, and I was grateful enough to let her use me as she wished, as father and brother and friend rather than husband and lover.

One night, when the past seemed to aggrieve her particularly, she lay next to me in the moonlight and said, "I just wish Chad had known about her background. God, he never would have gone out with her if he had. I mean, the way she killed her first husband when she found out he'd been unfaithful to her." Then she fell to sobbing again.

You really can find out an awful lot about people from the credit bureau.

I always think about this when I go to visit Molly in the sanitarium. This time, she's up on the third floor where the violent patients are.

The last time I saw her, she said, "I really want to thank you for telling me the truth about him. I really do want to thank you. I was making a fool of myself over him."

Some nights Tish plays "Famous Blue Raincoat" again and again. Those are the hardest nights of all to take because the song is a measure of how distant she still is from me. And every time the song plays, the distance is just that much greater.

A few weeks ago, I had a couple of drinks after work with the nurse I had the affair with.

We ended up late that night out in her car, wrestling around like high schoolers in my back seat.

But when the moment came, I just sat there with my head hung low, and felt nothing. Absolutely nothing at all.

MORNING CALL

Brian Lawrence

This is Brian Lawrence's first story to see print. But certainly many others will follow.

As you'll note immediately, Brian already speaks in his own unmistakable voice. And sees things his own unmistakable way.

He has recently completed his first novel, and is now at work on his second.

"There's only one thing worse than an ex-girlfriend coming back into your life, and that's a psychotic ex-girlfriend." This I said to the cracked, concrete ceiling, as I lay on my back on the hard bunk and stared in fascination at the pieces of peeled, gray paint that hung like little bats from the ceiling of my cell in the Potosi State Prison, one of the finer penal establishments in Missouri.

I rolled onto my side and looked at my cellmate. "How long did you say you've been here?"

"Seven years, four months, and thirteen days. But who's counting?"

Oscar, apparently. I looked around the eight by eight enclosure where I had spent the last nine months, eighteen days, seven hours, and thirty-nine minutes. But who's counting? Two beds, if they could be called beds, one toilet with no lid, a sink next to it and a piece of shiny metal that might be mistaken for a mirror. Oh, and Oscar, my wiry, pockmarked cellmate.

"You going to tell me this story, or what? We've only got one hour before exercise. And you know how I hate to miss my exercise," said Oscar, as he sprawled out on his bed, barely making an impression in the hard, thin mattress.

Exercise? Hardly, that's when Oscar purchases his cocaine. He grew impatient, so I started the story.

.   ■   .

It started with a phone call, about one year ago, as I ate breakfast. Gina, my wife, answered and a woman on the other end asked for me. Gina hesitated but reluctantly gave me the phone. I took the receiver from her and cringed from the nasty look she shot me through her heavily lashed, dark eyes. My wife was a very jealous person. I'll admit, I have a habit of looking at other women. But just looking. She didn't understand. We used to argue endlessly, usually with her accusing me of messing around, me saying I only look and don't touch, and then her accusing me of finding her unattractive. A vicious cycle, but it sustained our marriage for twelve years. Now don't misunderstand, I loved my wife very deeply. She was an emotional, passionate person, normally very bubbly and vibrant. But she had a green streak running through her like a copper vein in the Rockies.

"Hello," I said.

"Bobby, do you know who this is?"

A faint memory stirred in the back of my mind. I thought it was probably an ex-girlfriend, which caused me to blush. My wife, who rarely missed anything, caught the blush. She huffed and stormed out of the room. Surprisingly, she didn't pick up the bedroom extension.

"No, I'm sorry I can't place the voice." Looking back on it there was a very good reason too, but more on that later.

"This is Diana. Diana McCormick. Remember?"

How could I forget? Diana McCormick, a woman I had dated about a year before meeting my wife. The relationship had been stormy, passionate, and brief. It had ended badly. Diana had a habit of sleeping around. Of course, no one bothered telling me until after I found out on my own. We'd been dating about six months when I questioned her about where she'd been the previous night. I'd been stood up. She came right out and said she'd been with another man and did I have a problem with that? Of course I had a problem with that and we argued long and hard.

The neighbors complained. The police came and hauled me away with her screaming if she ever saw me again she'd kill me. Real charming girl. I'd lost track of her; the last I'd heard she had moved far away, to the West Coast, shortly after our breakup.

"Uh, yes, Diana, I remember. I remember you telling me to stay out of your life." To put it mildly.

"That was a long time ago, Bobby. I forgive you. Actually, I forgave you ages ago. I just never had the nerve to call you again."

She forgave me!? Well, she found her nerve all right. But being the soft-spoken, considerate person I am (my wife calls me a wimp), I simply replied, "So, why are you calling me now?"

"I'm in town visiting my sister and wondered if you'd like to get together."

Ah, her sister. The one I always thought would turn out to be the jewel of the family. Dawn was three years younger than Diana, with flaming red hair (Diana's was darker red), a spattering of freckles on her fair skin, and deep green eyes. I remembered Dawn had a tremendous crush on me when I had dated Diana. So much so, that after Diana gave me the old heave-ho, I dated Dawn twice. That didn't last either; she was too young and immature (in other words she wouldn't put out) so I broke it off. I also remembered Dawn had her sister's temper. When I told her I thought we should break it off, she went into a rage, throwing at me everything she could get her hands on. She screamed at me, telling me how much she loved me and how I had used her. Boy, from one extreme to the other with the McCormick girls. The last I had heard, Dawn had moved to New York City, a thousand miles away. It now seemed they'd both returned; be still my aching heart.

"Uh, I don't think that'd be such a great idea. I'm married now, with two kids. It was nice talking to you though." I didn't give her a chance to respond as I hung up the phone. When I turned around my wife had returned. Luckily, she was unarmed or I'd have been dog meat.

"Just who the hell was that?" Her beautiful dark eyes blazed. A cloud hung over her already dark complexion. We were quite the pair, Gina with her jet-black, baby-fine hair, perpetual tan, and dark brown eyes, and me with my blond curly locks, fair skin, and blue eyes.

I wondered if she had caught any of the conversation. If she had at least heard the ending . . . "That was Diana McCormick." A thousand lies flashed through my head, but being the wimp I am I told her the truth. "She was a woman I dated before I met you. Um, she wanted to see me."

Her arm went back and I put up mine to shield my face. She punched me in the gut. Gina was a very reactive person, as she tended to hit first and demand an explanation later. And for someone only five feet tall and weighing around ninety pounds, she packed quite a wallop. While doubled over, clutching my beer belly, I said, "I turned her down and hung up on her."

"Yeah, right. You bastard. How did she get this number?"

"The phone book?"

She walked away and ignored me for the rest of the day and, of course, that night.

I thought that would be the end of it. Gina would settle down with time. But oh, how wrong I turned out to be. The next morning, at about the same time as the previous morning, the phone rang again. Gina leaped up from the kitchen table. The look she shot me said, "Move, asshole and you die." I stayed put.

"Hello . . . No I'm sorry he can't come to the phone . . . I said he can't come to the phone . . . Look, bitch, he's not interested in you so don't bother calling here again." She slammed the receiver down. I chuckled and reminded her the phone had to be switched off. Bad move. Not finding it amusing, she hurled the phone at me.

Luckily, the cord came up short and it clattered to the floor a mere foot from where I sat.

"That was your slut ex-girlfriend." As if she needed to tell me. "Why is she still calling if you told her to go away?"

"I guess I'm just irresistible." I ducked as a bowl whizzed over my head and made a nice impression in the white wall behind me. I have a knack for finding women with short tempers. It must be to counterbalance my sweet, calm personality.

"Look, Gina, the woman's crazy." I told her the story of our breakup. She remained unconvinced, but there was nothing I could do but ride it out.

It turned out to be a rough ride. For the next four days, the phone rang at various times during the morning and evening. My wife always answered it, the caller always hung up. We both knew who called. It got to the point where my wife would not leave the house if I was home, so I had to go everywhere with her, even the beauty parlor.

The phone calls stopped after a week, but the ride got rougher. I came home from work on a Monday and my wife flew at me and thrust a piece of paper in my face. The veins in her neck throbbed. Her mouth moved, but emitted only an unpleasant squeak. She stood in front of me fuming while I read the note. Nothing extraordinary about it, just a request to meet with me and a threat if I didn't. I get them all the time. A threat to me, not Gina. Signed by, who else, but Diana McCormick. I found out, though, the note was the least of the problem.

Gina finally found her voice, a gravelly, restrained voice and said, "Nicky gave me that note. That bitch approached our son. He said this strange, red-haired woman walked up to him at school. Handed him this note. I've called the police." Then she started to cry. Actually, cry is too mild, more like a watershed. Her knees buckled and she sank to the floor. I've never seen my wife so shaken and frightened. And actually, to be perfectly honest, so was I. Diana was unpredictable, and it appeared, dangerous.

The police were their usual helpful selves. They could do nothing. They asked for a description of Diana and I told them what I remembered from fifteen years ago; about five-five, not chunky, but solid, dark red hair, shoulder length, small darting brown eyes, small nose. Then they suggested we transport our children to school (they actually used the word "transport") and keep a close eye on them for a while. The looks they gave us seemed to say they thought we normally let our children run amuck, causing mayhem. They said to let them know if any more incidents should happen.

As shaken up as I felt, I didn't take the threat seriously. I should have. Almost two weeks passed and we heard nothing more from Diana McCormick. But we could feel her presence. It was a gradual realization, one both Gina and I had at the same time. Then, I received a call at work one day, at about four-thirty.

Frantic, Gina said, "There's a car parked on our street. A large four-door. A Buick, I think. I've seen it before. Bobby, there's a woman sitting in it. I know it's her. Please come home, Bobby."

"Just calm down, Gina." Always a good thing to say to a panic-stricken woman. Usually they become incensed. My wife was no exception.

"Don't tell me to calm down, Goddammit. Just get your ass home. I'm calling the police."

She hung up on me and I left immediately. I made some excuse to my boss about my child getting sick and my wife needing help. As I pulled into our subdivision a blue, four-door Buick passed me. It looked familiar. Suddenly, I realized I had seen that car on our street several times over the past couple of weeks. I racked my brain but could not remember seeing it before Diana had first called. When the car passed, I failed to get a good look at the driver, but it was definitely a woman. The angle of the sun blocked out the details of her face, but I saw a flash of red. A chill did a tap dance down my spine as I floored it and prayed to God no children were playing in the street and nothing had happened to Gina. Not in that order, of course. Three corners and three tire squealings later, I pulled into our driveway.

Gina flew out of our ranch style house screaming, "Did you see her? Did you?"

"Yes, Gina. I saw the car. I don't know if it was her or not." I was lying through my teeth. I had no doubt who the driver had been. The hair on the back of my neck standing straight up told me.

"Oh, God, Bobby. What are we going to do?" She clung to me like wet jeans and started crying again. You have to understand, crying was a concept foreign to my wife. She didn't even cry at her father's funeral. We stood in the partly-green-going-to-brown lawn, wrapped in each other's arms, frightened to the core. Actually, thinking back on it, I'd never felt closer to my wife than at that moment.

The police arrived, late as usual. We gave them the description of the car and to no one's surprise they had not seen it coming in. Our small town police are about as useful as a candle in a hurricane. Again, they said they could do nothing. The driver of the car had every right to be on the street. Call them if she makes any more threats.

I never found out why Diana left when she did. She had no way of knowing I'd left work early. I always thought my wife kept something from me, like she had approached the car. She never told me that, but I noticed one of my hunting knives, very large, very sharp, had been shifted in the closet. I let it drop.

The blue car disappeared and life returned to almost normal. Gina continued to look over her shoulder, constantly checking her mirrors when driving and becoming agitated when one of the children wandered out of sight. They were nine and eleven, so it annoyed them to no end to be so closely watched. Other than that, the incident slowly faded into the oblivion of bad memories. But not for long.

The phone calls started again. My wife answered the first one and her face blanched, which is difficult for a dark skinned Italian. She said nothing, just hung up the phone. But this call was different. The phone rang again, not more than a minute after the first one. I answered it.

"Please, don't hang up on me. I have to tell your husband something. It's very important."

"Diana, you sick bitch. Leave us alone." I hung up.

One more time, the phone rang. My wife shoved me out of the way, knocking me into the refrigerator.

"Didn't you hear my husband, you psychotic slut? Leave us alone." Then she became very inventive. I had to laugh, despite the gravity of the situation. "The police have a trace on this line. They're going to find you and haul you away." She slammed the phone down, swore loudly, picked it back up, and turned it off. Then she disconnected it. I thought it wise not to point out we had two other phones in the house. But no more phones rang. Apparently, Diana got the message.

I wish I had talked to Diana the last time she called. It turned out to be a fatal mistake not to. Another week passed and Gina and I were returning from a comedy show at the Westport Plaza in St. Louis. We were driving south on highway 270, Gina at the wheel. She drove everywhere we went because she didn't like my driving and I got tired of hearing about it. Anyway, there's a section of 270 where the highway drops off about twenty feet. At the bottom of the hill are houses and trees. There was no guardrail due to the construction on the highway.

Gina and I were discussing the finer comedy points of the show when she looked up at the rear view mirror and uttered a frightened, "Oh my God."

Turning to look out the rear window, I saw a car coming fast, in the same lane as us. It was too dark to tell the make or color. An extra dose of adrenaline shot through my body. At the last second, the car swerved into the other lane and passed us. It was a dark, four-door, Buick.

I had to grab the wheel to keep us on the road.

"That was her. Oh my God that was her," said Gina, on the verge of hysterics.

Still holding the wheel with one hand, I blared the horn with the other to get Gina's attention. "Calm down. You're going to get us in an accident. It was probably just a car that looked like hers." I hoped Gina had not picked up on how weak my comment sounded.

She shot me a look that even in the dark I could tell contained a lethal mixture of fear and anger. But the other car kept on going and soon disappeared.

We approached the section of highway that has the severest drop-off. Gina drove in the far right lane, staying within the speed limit, still visibly shaken. I looked to my left, out her window, and my heart stopped. "Oh, shit. Gina!"

"What Bobby? What is it?"

I shrieked. The intensity of my voice startled both of us. "Look out. Hit the brake." But it was too late.

The car that passed us only a few minutes earlier came from three lanes over, parallel to us. It slammed into our side. The impact wrenched Gina toward me. Our car left the road and plummeted down the embankment. Images of riding Space Mountain flashed through my mind. Then a deafening crash and I blacked out.

■   ■   ■

When I came to, I lay in a hospital bed. I sat up quickly and lay down just as fast, as dizziness overwhelmed me. A starched white nurse leaned over me and said, "Relax. You're going to be just fine."

"Where's my wife?" I asked.

A frown crossed her face. She fidgeted and shifted from one leg to another.

"Where's my wife, dammit? I need to know." But I already

knew. The nurse confirmed my worst fear. Gina had died in the car accident from a brain lesion.

For the next three weeks I walked around in a haze. Everywhere I went (which wasn't too many places) every dark-haired woman looked like Gina. Utter despondency gripped my heart. Alone, and lonely. My children did their best to cheer me up, but they were devastated as well. Both my mother-in-law and my parents took turns watching the kids. The nightmare had just begun.

One morning, about a month after Gina's death, the phone rang. I knew instantly who slithered on the other end, but I answered anyway.

"Bobby. Hi, it's me, Diana. How are you?"

The lightness of her tone shocked me to the bone. My response came out as a pathetic, "Not good."

"Oh, that's too bad. I know how to cheer you up. Why don't we get together? I'm staying at the Drury Inn, not far from you. I'm in room 257. See you later."

The woman had fallen off her rocker if she thought I'd meet with her. But then an idea took root in a recess of my brain. Maybe I could get her to confess. I ran to the bedroom, threw open the nightstand drawer and rummaged through years of collected garbage. Near the bottom of the drawer, way in the back, I found my mini tape recorder. I clicked it on and it still worked. As I slid the recorder in my back pocket I thought about taking my hunting knife, but then decided if I could get her to talk, I'd best let the police do the rest of the job.

■   ■   ■

Tentatively, I knocked on the door and instantly, there she stood. A smile traced a path clear across her face. Her heavily greased lips spread wide to reveal sparkling teeth. The red in her hair seemed brighter than I had remembered. Her face had some added freckles and her deep green eyes sparkled like fireworks.

"Bobby. I'm so glad to finally see you." She pulled me through the door and wrapped her arms around me. Wasting no time her lips found mine and crushed into my face. I felt her hand go immediately to my rear. I grabbed her hand before it could discover the recorder and broke our embrace. With my other hand I clicked on the device.

"Why did you do it, Diana? Why did you have to kill my wife?"

She just smiled at me and moved to kiss me again. This time I played along and passionately met her mouth with mine. God, it made me sick. Bile welled up in my gut, but I played along.

"Oh, Bobby. I've wanted you for so long. Ever since you left me, I've wanted you. Everyone I dated, I saw you. I've been wandering aimlessly through man after man, searching for someone just like you. Then, when I was offered a job back here, I couldn't stay away. And now that your wife's out of the way, there's nothing to stop us."

Offered a job, wait a minute. Why did that sound wrong? I thought. I narrowed my eyes and looked at her. Something was not right, but I couldn't place it. So I said, "But why kill her?"

I pushed away again.

"Well, geez, Bobby. That's obvious. She wouldn't get out of the way. She was the only thing standing between us." Her attitude was so cool, so casual.

"You could have killed me, too."

"Yeah, well. But see, you survived. That's fate saying you're meant for me."

Again, she moved toward me. But this time, something snapped. The floodgates opened. Use whatever cliché you want but I lost it. I pushed her away and screamed at her. "You murderer. You killed my wife. I'm going to fucking kill you." My blood boiled. I have never felt so angry, so out of control, like taking some type of hallucinogen. Something primal took over and shoved my conscious mind aside. It assumed all control and propelled my body forward, toward her. Fear wrote in script across her face. But she was ready for me. She may have been a crazy bitch, but no one ever accused her of being stupid.

As I closed the gap between us, I found myself face to face with a large kitchen knife. Her intentions were clear, she wanted to carve up this old Butterball. Fortunately, my anger proved to be stronger and quicker than her fear and insanity. She swiped at me with the knife, tracing a line across my stomach. It made only a surface cut, and as her arm passed, I grabbed her wrist with my left hand. Wrenching my hand back toward my left I heard a crack as her thin wrist snapped like dry wood. The knife fell to the floor, point first, where it stuck for an instant and then fell horizontal.

I kicked out with my right leg and caught her in the groin. Not quite the same results as kicking a man there, but painful enough to give me time to retrieve the knife. Without thinking I straightened up and swiped high with my right hand. At the same time she lunged at me, hands out in claw-like fashion. The knife found its mark and cut deeply across her throat. She staggered back, gurgled several times and fell to the floor grasping her neck. Blood sprayed between her fingers onto my shirt. I dispassionately watching her life squirt out from under her hands.

"Oh my God. Bobby, what have you done?"

A woman's voice sounded from behind me; a familiar voice. I whirled, knife ready for another attacker. I came face to face with Diana McCormick. Realization washed over me like a tsunami, driving me to the floor; I just killed her sister, Dawn. But then reality struck home and I straightened back up. Maybe this was Diana's ploy. Maybe . . .

"Oh, God," she said again. She looked past me to her dying sister. Her brown eyes welled up with tears. Of course. I should have noticed that, but in my rage and grief I failed to take in Dawn's green eyes. "I tried to warn you, Bobby. My sister was sick. Very sick. She was obsessed with you. For years she talked about you and then, somehow, she found out where you were. I tried to stop her. I tried to call you, but you and your wife kept hanging up on me." She knelt down by Dawn and cradled her head, blood dripping onto her jeans. "Then yesterday she called me and said you were finally going to be hers. She had killed your wife. Oh, God, Bobby. I'm so sorry."

■   ■   ■

"Man, that was one sick bitch."

"Thanks, Oscar. I wish you could have been at my trial. Fifteen years for second-degree murder. Oh well, just think of all the useful things I can learn while I'm here."

"Yeah, that's for sure. But I don't understand, man."

"Don't understand what?"

"Why you're here, dude. Didn't that Diana woman testify in your behalf? And that tape recording you made?"

"That's the rub, Oscar. She lied at the trial. Said I was the one stalking her sister. Killed my own wife and then went after Dawn.

And the tape recorder . . . the batteries went dead. All it recorded was Dawn kissing me at the door of her hotel."

"Ain't that the shits?"

"It sure is."

THE CASE OF THE LOCKED ROOM NUDE

Maxim Jakubowski

Author, editor, bookstore owner, film critic, London's Maxim Jakubowski is one of mysterie's true dynamos.

Is there ever a convention he doesn't attend? A film festival he doesn't speak at? An anthology he doesn't play at least some role in?

Here is Maxim wearing his author's hat. It's a very comfortable fit.

IT ALL BEGAN WITH A MISTAKE.

Or a bad joke.

Someone had given Chris my name, and recommended me as a person who could help him find his wife. We actually never did meet; it was all transacted over the telephone and I happily went along with the deception. He was a journalist at the BBC, specializing in business and financial matters. I knew what he looked like. Since my affair with Katherine had broken up, I'd somehow become a bit of an insomniac, waking up in the early hours of morning when all you could watch on the box was a succession of pimply young reporters broadcasting live from the car parks of condom factories or some dealing room in the city or pontificating in the studio about the coming of the Information Superhighway and its benefits to the business community. Business journalists? They knew as much about business as a Cambridge history graduate, and wouldn't last a fortnight in the real world of money. I suppose he was one of the worst. He'd done his pretty best to erase his northern accent but still stumbled on words like Vauxhall, Heathrow, or Brighton, a wrong intonation there, a portentous tone of voice here. Anyway, he said that my name had been given to him by a contact in the arts department, a woman he'd come across on a trip to Oslo. He'd probably made a sad pass at her, and she thought it would be funny to put us together.

"They say you're the one person in London who knows most about crime," he said.

"I suppose so," I answered.

"Can you keep matters confidential and discreet?"

This was becoming most interesting. This guy thought I was some kind of private detective. And he wasn't just any old poor deluded guy, but actually Katherine's husband. Believe me when I tell you that when I answered his phone call, my heart began skipping the light fandango for a moment. Had he finally stumbled on my identity?

So I nodded sympathetically, muttered a few uh-uh's over the phone, and he told me his story.

A few months back, he had discovered his wife was having an affair. By then, it was already over, but the thought of the four months of secret assignations, groping in hotel rooms, outright lies, and her defiant and insufficiently apologetic stance afterwards had hurt him badly. Yes, he knew that one day when they were still young he had written to her that he would always stand by her and would even forgive her if she had an affair, but in practice it was different. In some color supplement, there had been an article on adultery with a survey indicating that fifteen percent of cuckolded husbands only would not forgive the errant partner for a one-night stand, but nearly sixty-five percent would not wish to continue the relationship if the affair had lasted over three months. He wanted to forgive her, to be in the minority, but it was so fucking difficult to accept; New Man, my ass!

She seemed sincere in wishing to patch things up. He had been taking her for granted, absorbed by his job and office politics at the corporation; with the other guy it had just been lust, and lust alone. And she'd broken up with him a few days before anyway, as he was becoming too possessive. But she wouldn't reveal his identity. Someone in publishing, he guessed, as that was where she worked.

"Is that why you're contacting me?" I asked, tickled by the prospect of having to investigate myself. Just like a Philip K. Dick novel . . .

"No, I don't think I want to know who the vile bastard is," he answered.

Really, truly, he assured me, he had wanted to forgive her, to forget the whole sad episode, but every time he opened a newspaper, browsed through a magazine, randomly started reading a book, he was reminded of the fact that another man had touched her white skin, ruffled her curly hair, nibbled sensuously on her torn ear, licked her breasts, her sensitive nipples, spread orgasmic flush over the pale flesh of her neck and shoulders, fingered her cunt, entered her repeatedly in the missionary position and from behind, chewed on her labial folds, spent his seed inside the mad pinkness of her innards, as surely he had.

And, yes, I had. A thousand times, a million times, and that wasn't all, was it, I certainly did *not* say to him. I had made love to her slowly on a rickety couch even though she was still having her period and the matted blood smeared all over my cock had seeped, jellified through the dark jungle of my pubic hair; I had colored the pale tips of her small breasts and the lips of her sex with scarlet lipstick salvaged from her handbag and after we had embraced it had been like streaks of blood over my body and the crisp white sheets of the hotel room bed; I had tied her hands together with her silk scarf and attached her to the sofa legs with the belt from my black trousers; I had slapped her rump repeatedly while she rode me to the hilt, her head thrown back and sighs of tortured pleasure escaping from her lips, "more, more" she had whispered as the pain of my palm on her skin turned into joy; I had allowed my outstretched fingers to circle her neck and pressed gently, then harder, feeling the quickening of her pulse coursing through the vein and she said, "I could let you do anything, you know, I trust you so much"; and, another time: "You're the best lover I have ever had." Yes, I had loved her.

All this, Chris had guessed, I knew, from the look of loss in Katherine's dark brown eyes when she admitted to the affair and expressed her contrite regrets and a litany of "never again, never again, Jesus, I swear." But it was too late, he confessed quietly over the phone to me, the new priest in his confessional, the poison had been planted. And poison inevitably spreads. An awkward Christmas holiday divided into visits to sets of parents in Scarborough and Working, an unreliable car that let the rain in to her irritation, the strain of seasonal jollity; later a holiday in Tenerife where he felt awful pangs of jealousy every time a German tourist or a Spanish waiter watched over Katherine lounging in her swimsuit by the pool. This body had been shared by another. Defiled. Once, he was even physically sick.

Their rows became more frequent. It always began with a small thing. She'd forgotten to get salad or tomatoes at the Goodge Street Tesco's during her lunch break and scorned his vegetarianism in the ensuing argument. Or, she'd call to say she'd be home late and he would have to prepare his own meal, she had to see an author who was coming up from Wales after office hours—an excuse she had used often when the affair was in progress. Lack of trust, jealousy. It was eating away at him.

Last week, there had been another argument and she'd walked off.

"So," I interrupted him, "you need me to find her, is that it?"

"Yes," he admitted sheepishly. "I've tried her parents, and a few girlfriends. But nobody knows where she is. I fear she's gone back to this other guy."

I knew she hadn't. My bed was as empty as my life and I couldn't even sleep properly for thinking of her all the bloody time, and longing like a scream for the luminous whiteness of her nudity. Often, to find the solace of dreams, I would close my eyes and jerk off silently, remembering how her long legs moved and the shape of her backside and the taste of her cunt and her heartbreaker of a smile. None of which I could tell him. Or the fact that with several women since Katherine, I couldn't even achieve suitable erections. . . .

"Maybe she has," I told him, thinking all the time that I hated his guts, why does a Christopher shorten his name to Chris, what a silly affectation for God's sake. I hate it when people call me Max. "Maybe, she hasn't." And fuck you, Chris, why did she have to choose you, and who has she gone to now? I thought. "At any rate, it's not the sort of case I can take on. Too trivial, too ordinary, come on, adultery in media circles, what could be more full of clichés? Remember, I'm the one who knows all about crime, and this sure ain't crime by a long stretch, mate. Sorry, find yourself another cheap dick, try the Yellow Pages, there's a firm on Charing Cross Road." I knew that because I'd paid these investigators to find Chris and Katherine's ex-directory number after she split, thinking maybe she'd listen to my pleading, my silly assurances of love eternal, but they couldn't even bribe a telephone company employee for the information and refunded my retainer. "I'm sorry too," said Chris. I put the phone down and left him with his cheap pain, imagining briefly that soon he'd take to the bottle, sink to the gutter in the streets of the lost, just like in a novel by David Goodis.

Maybe it had started as a joke, but having betrayed both of us, where was Katherine now? Of course I had to find out; if she'd moved on to another man, I was already as much of a fool and as insanely jealous as Chris.

I sat back in the reclining black leather chair and pondered. What would Philip Marlowe do?

The evening sky outside was streaked with pink. Already spring, again. My second spring without Katherine's wondrous face. I recalled our night in the Birmingham hotel. She had gone up to do a presentation to library suppliers, and I'd joined her. It must have been two or three in the morning already, we'd somehow made love three times and were drenched in sweat, my cock was aching and I knew it would be on the blink until morning and full powers again. I cuddled up to her, warmed her cold feet, and we stayed there for ages, silent, flesh pressed against flesh, and we were so close I felt like crying, wanting her more than ever. Finally, I asked her as one does, "What are you thinking of?"

In the darkness, she answered "We'll be back in London tomorrow. I'll be taking that train to Charing Cross Station and the office, and looking at the faces of all the people, all so sad, feeling mediocre like them. Surely, there must be more to life than this."

I didn't quite know what to say in response.

I held her even tighter against me.

"Wouldn't you just like to run away, take a train, take a plane, and just go?"

"Yeah."

"One day, we'll go off together."

"No, we won't."

"Yes, we will," I said insistently. "Where would you go?"

"When I was younger, I often thought of pissing off to India. But it would be too hot and dirty. You can't drink the water. You mentioned how much you liked New Orleans when you went to that convention there. Yes, New Orleans. That's where I'll disappear to."

And she fell asleep in my arms.

How the hell was I to know it was to be the last time?

.   .   .

My friend O'Neil had worked on the New Orleans police force. He picked me up from Moisan airport and gave me a quick tour of the Crescent City before dropping me off at my hotel in the French Quarter. He suggested we talk over a meal. I insisted we visit the Pearl just off Canal Street where the oysters are just so juicy and pungent and cheap and they have framed pages of James Lee Burke novels by the window, in which the restaurant is mentioned. I'd always promised myself that I'd get the Pearl into a story someday too. And the bowl of gumbo was no disappointment either.

O'Neil gave me some useful names, as I had no damn idea where to even begin my search for a tall, dark-eyed blonde in this city of dreams and sudden rains.

On my first night, I had a series of nightmares, a sleeping prisoner in a Cornell Woolrich story where coincidences and the implacable finger of fate kept on evoking the faces of all the women I had known and loved. I waited for Nicole by a train station clock and a policeman came to announce her death and the fact I was a suspect. I awoke, or thought I did, and there was Lois watching me, dressed in Lüsa's clothes, and when she opened her mouth, her voice was that of Marie-Jo. The clock ticked away, and I guessed that somehow my time was running out and that I had to find a woman by daybreak or my whole world would come tumbling down, or worse. But I didn't know which woman I was supposed to find. I thought of the dimple in Lois's chin, the mole on Pamela's neck, the scar on Katherine's cheek, the gap between Nicole's front teeth, the smile of Julie Christie in *Billy Liar*, Jasmine's round glasses and Julianne Moore's orange pubic thatch in *Short Cuts*. Still the minutes kept on ticking by, and I was tied to the bed, Sharon Stone's opulent shape straddling me with a knife in her hand, but her face was now that of Katherine. And I missed them all, and loved them all, I wanted to shout, but no sound would come from my lips. Tick. Tock. Tick. Tock.

Struggling with my past. With images of women long gone or unattainable.

Faces. Bodies. Breasts. Legs. Lips.

Save me, please, from the memories that hurt so much.

Forgive me for the lies, the betrayals, I didn't know what I was doing.

And somewhere inside me on that endless Dauphine Street night, the voice of reason kept on saying that the damned don't die, they just have nightmares that never end.

At last, New Orleans morning and deliverance from the devils. I ventured out. Municipal workers were cleaning Jackson Square shoveling the deadbeats' detritus from the previous night into black plastic bags. I had a coffee at Tujague's and collected my thoughts. If Katherine had never been here before, what would she do? Well, I didn't have a clue. What a lousy private eye I was!

If she'd left their south London home in a hurry, I assumed she wouldn't have taken much in the way of reading matter. Maybe a few paperbacks at the airport. She would soon run out of things to read. I remembered the way she would cram two or three books into her bag even when we'd gone away for the weekend, although she knew there would be little time to read, and we'd spend all our time fucking, talking, and fucking. I knew, I was the same and never went anywhere without a few days reading just in case, you know. We had so much in common. I phoned Reage, the cop O'Neil had recommended and obtained a list of the town's main bookshops, both new and second-hand. As I expected, there weren't that many. New Orleans wasn't that sort of city.

I spent a couple of days describing Katherine, the way her curls flowed down over her shoulders, the sort of clothes she would usually wear, her distinctive way of walking, hunched slightly forward, how her lips curled, the irregular teeth. Surely there could not be more than one British woman answering her description in New Orleans right now, and she was bound to visit a bookshop along the way.

I was almost ready to give up when, in the last shop on my list, a dusty emporium on Chartres with a cache of book club editions of Rex Stout and Dell Shannon mystery novels, a customer who'd heard my forlorn enquiries came over to me and said he had seen a woman answering to my description coming out of a bar on Bourbon Street the previous evening.

"I thought she did look English, you know," the old guy said. "But you can't be sure, can you . . . and that place she'd been in, not very respectable, you know. No, sir, not a place for a decent woman, you understand?"

Full moon over Bourbon Street. The drunks roll up and down the noisy arcade holding their plastic glasses of beer in precarious hands, while up there on the forged iron balconies revelers laugh aloud at the sinners beneath and black kids tap dance on the pavement to the rhythm of beat boxes.

TOPLESS. BOTTOMLESS. ALL NUDE. MALE. FEMALE. THE ORGY ROOM. OLD-TIME BURLESQUE. ONE $1 BEER.

At the door, a tall Hispanic guy urged me forward.

"Best pussy in town, sir. Come on in, entrance is free, drinks are only five bucks a go."

I enquired after Katherine.

"Tall, blonde, small tits, biggish ass. Yeah, man, we can supply that. We've got 'em in all colors, shapes, and sizes."

Inside.

There was a stripper dancing to a dirge of a Leonard Cohen song. Her movements were slow and languorous. She moved with deliberation across the small stage like a swimmer through water or an astronaut in space. She was a small brunette, Italian-looking, couldn't have been much over five feet tall, her dark hair was bunched in a chignon, a few strands escaping from its clutch and reaching her shoulders. She removed her spangled bra and revealed an absolutely perfect pair of breasts, delicately rounded spheres, dark areolae pointing gently upwards, firm, creamy-skinned like the rest of her body. By the bar, there was a piece of cardboard on which someone had scrawled MONIA in thick red felt pen. This must be her name.

A brassy barmaid served me my Coke, no ice. Five bucks, the same as beer.

The song ended.

A strong beat rushed through the club and a louder song roared its way through the industrial speakers. The Walkabouts singing Townes Van Zandt's "Snake Mountain Blues."

Monia began to squirm to the accelerated beat, her legs dancing up and down the length of the miniature stage. She thrust her backside at some of the punters. Squatted on her haunches, projected her crotch forward, stretching the thin fabric of her G-string. Customers slipped dollar bills into the elastic holding up the small square inch of material. When she moved toward me, her body still twitching in spasms to the music, she smiled at me as she opened her legs indecently wide just a few inches away, but all I could see was the dead zone that surrounded her eyes. When I did not proffer a green bill, she moved away, stood up and twirled her slight body around the central pole that anchored the stage, the smooth contours of the wood pressing between her perfect breasts, molding her sex. The song came to an abrupt end, and Monia walked away offstage into an area of darkness.

"That's the one thing about Noo' Orleenz I don't like," a fat Texan still wearing a ridiculous cowboy hat and sitting on my right said. "The law don't allow them to take off their panties and show us some real pussy, like in Vegas or L.A."

A new stripper took the stage. She had a tattoo of a rose on her right shoulder and another, of a snake, circling her left wrist. I sipped my Coke, thinking who could I ask about Katherine without giving the wrong impression. Monia reappeared, wearing a silk dressing gown over her stripping apparel. She tapped my shoulder and flashed that all-purpose smile again.

"One to one?" she inquired. "There's a room at the back. I'm sure we can agree on a price." She had a strong European accent. I nodded back. Maybe in private, she might be willing to answer my questions.

The back room walls were plastered with movie posters, some new, some old. RESERVOIR DOGS, CHOOSE ME, VERTIGO, LA JETEE. Monia slipped the dressing gown off. She was only wearing the thin G-string. On her own, like this, she really appeared tiny.

"Wanna fuck? Blow job? You can come over my tits."

I handed her a fifty buck note and described Katherine.

"Why didn't you say so before, that you wanted the English woman?" Monia said.

"Is she here?" I asked her, a tightening in my gut, a twinge of fear and expectation in my heart.

"Well, she wasn't very good at dancing, was she?" the small

stripper said. "Hernandez gave her a tryout, but she had no sense of rhythm, you know, couldn't move her butt to the beat, and she spooked the customers, reading at the bar all the time between sets."

"Where is she?" I asked.

"Hernandez has got this private joint off Toulouse, very private, where they go all the way. You know, live shows. Your blonde Englishwoman, he says she's pretty good at cocksucking, but doesn't shake enough when the men fuck her, says all she can whisper is 'Jesus, Jesus' as they pound her meat, y' know, they want noise, a few screams, makes it sound real, but she can't even manage that."

"Enough, tell me where to go."

"Not so easy, man."

I slipped a couple of green bills into her outstretched hand. "Please."

"You wait here. I'll bring her round. Hernandez doesn't like new faces at the other place."

She moved toward the door.

"Wait," I said. "What if . . ."

"Trust me," said Monia of the perfect breasts.

. . .

I imagine dark clouds occluding the full moon outside. The sounds of Bourbon Street reach me, quieter now, filtered through the buffer of my fear.

Katherine is in the room. Her makeup is clumsy, the gash of red over her lips isn't straight, there is a lattice of needle holes across her forearm, there are holes in her stockings.

"You?"

"Yes."

"How did you know, how did you find me here?"

"I did. Why?"

"I had to get away. I had so badly betrayed the two of you. I hated myself. Felt guilty. Ashamed I had given in to lust and spoilt everything. Absolutely everything."

"But this, Katherine, how could you? It's too much like a bad pulp novel. X-rated Willeford. Surely there were other alternatives?"

"Maybe. But what's the point? My heart has grown cold so I've given myself over to lust. Perhaps I should have recognized the fact earlier, understood the nature of it. I try to forget, you, Chris, London! I take the cocks of strange men into my mouth and caress their purple crowns with the tip of my tongue and feel them grow larger and larger inside me to the point that sometimes I almost choke. None taste the way you did, though. For the right amount of cash they can fuck me, and if the money's good enough I'll take two at the same time. It doesn't make much difference, does it? And others can watch, can touch, can stretch me, tear at my orifices. It's nothing, it doesn't matter."

"But, Katherine . . ."

"You know, it's true what they say of black men, a lot of them here do have these huge cocks. But I can take it. The pain helps keep me awake. Look . . ."

She slips out of the cheap calico dress she had been wearing, unclips the garter belt, and rolls down the black stockings. She's not been wearing anything else.

"My skin is so very white. They like this here."

There's a network of bruises over her thighs. Her pubic curls have been trimmed to a thin band above the lips of her bare sex.

"Is this what you remember?" she asks me.

I see the nakedness of her desire and absurdly realize that we never went dancing and know that we shall not grow old together.

"Come," I beckon her. "Let me hold you."

I have locked the door from the inside. Her nude body moves across the purple carpet where so many have fucked before. I open my arms; she is cold, her hair needs a wash, her curls are impossibly tangled, I recognize the particular smell of her breath as she presses her face against my shoulder. We stay like that for what feels like an eternity. Finally, my fingers move to her throat, hold her firmly, then press hard against her carotid. Katherine does not resist. A nervous impulse races through her and a pale nipple quickly brushes against my elbow. I keep on pressing. She closes her eyes, keeps on leaning against me. She dies. A small trickle of urine splashes my feet as her whole body at last relaxes.

It began as a joke and ends as a locked-room mystery. Just the way I always liked my John Dickson Carr stories. Soon, Monia or someone else will knock at the door to tell me my time is up.

I unthread the belt from my trousers and attach it to a steel hook protruding from the room's ceiling. Why was it there? SM games? I find a chair, which I climb onto. One end of the belt around my neck, I tighten it by a few notches.

On the floor, Katherine's body lies in repose, her splendid nudity for my eyes only.

When they batter the door down later, it'll be a perfect mystery.

I jump off the chair.

THAT SUMMER AT QUICHIQUOIS

Dorothy B. Hughes

Dorothy Hughes was one of the most important suspense writers of her generation. She was also, arguably, its most important critic.

Things are never what they seem in Dorothy's stories, as is certainly the case here, in this long and gripping tale of thwarted love.

TIME AND PLACE DO NOT MATTER. THEY ARE HAPPENINGS. SIMPLY happenings.

There are other happenings. Some you don't or won't remember. Some you will. Deliberately. It is not that you remember the important and don't remember the unimportant. Often it's the other way around. Like dancing with Voss.

Sometimes I think of Voss and I cry. Tears. Wet tears. I don't cry easily. I don't make myself cry. It's just a happening.

I didn't actually know him. He was just someone I danced with. When I was fourteen years old. By the accident of him being there and me being there when the music changed. Does anyone remember the "Paul Jones"? Sort of like a grand march only gentlemen going one way and ladies another. Touching hands but not clasping, touching in passing. Until the music changes. Without warning. Like in "Going to Jerusalem." Musical chairs.

And that happening was when the music changed. I was right beside Voss. So I danced with Voss. Close tight, chest to chest, feeling him surrounding me. Engulfing me. Almost as if I were an integral part of his body. For those few moments.

I was nothing to him. Not a happening to him. It was simply

the way he danced. To him that was the happening. To dance. As if dancing were created by him, for him.

Except Elektra. When he danced with Elektra they were one person. Not two dancing. One. Transformed. Two become one. Tightly together. Never again one and one. Two melded. Like by flame. The flame of movement and music.

My cousin Katty was sixteen going on seventeen. She and her very best friends—four or five of them—would have none of Voss. He wasn't privileged. Their cant word of the summer. He worked in a *butcher shop*! Henschel's Butcher Shop. His uncle Gus. Underprivileged. As if Voss had blood spattered all over his clothes. Like Uncle Gus had on his white apron when he waited on my aunt Georgie. In those days in a small town, meat didn't come prepackaged and iced by Armour or Swift. It came from a nearby farm. The farmer butchered and brought the haunch to the butcher shop. It was hung in an icebox room out back. The butcher cut from the haunch what the customer wanted. Sometimes blood would spatter on his white apron.

Voss worked mostly at the front counter. By the cash register. By the big front window.

But the girls shrieked "underprivileged" when I asked about him. The girls accepted only the privileged. Like Katty's choice for the summer, Roddy Rockefeller. No, not the rich Rockefellers with the wizened old golfer who gave a dime-a-day tip to his caddy. Rockefeller is a common name in upstate New York.

"What's Claude?" I asked them. Deliberately to provoke them. Claude had to be privileged. He was a Clark. Founders of Clarksvale back in Revolutionary days. His father was owner and president of the bank. The one where Aunt Georgie used to work and now owned a big piece of.

Of course they shouted with laughter at my question. "Whey-face?" I did not ever understand "Whey-face." He had a round doughy face. Something about curds and whey.

They added their other names for him. "Toady." "Cipher." And one daring friend of Katty's who considered herself sophisticated, "Faggotty."

Voss let Claude hang around. That was about all. Voss was a loner. He didn't have friends. Didn't want them.

We went back to the village every other summer. We—my

mother, the children—my eight-year-old brother and six-year-old sister, and me. My father wanted us to know his people. He didn't come with us. He had his business as excuse. He had had enough of villages before he walked away from them to make his mark in the city. And did, all the way to California.

Every other summer we took the train—there were trains in those days—from California to New York, upstate New York. Change at Chicago to the N.Y. Central. Disembark at Albany. But not for the local train. Met there by Aunt Georgie and her chauffeur Fred. He was one of the garage men in a chauffeur cap. We stayed with Aunt Priscilla. George was the younger sister by two years. She was the businesswoman. She owned half the town by now. Aunt Priscilla was the stay-at-home who took care of her kinfolk's children.

Katherine—Katty—had always lived with Aunt Pris. Her mother died in childbirth and her father was in the air corps, a captain or something. He wasn't on land very often.

This summer Aunt Pris also had the Tompkin boys. Their father, a nephew, was an archaeology professor at one of the universities, and so was his wife. They were off to some big dig deep in South America. No place to take little boys. The boys were around my brother's age.

I shared Katty's room in summer and we didn't see much of the children. Not if we could help it.

The village itself was a happening. For a girl born and raised in a big city, it was like a storybook holiday. Walking around town. No traffic. No streetcars. No buses. A post office with its walls of neat little golden boxes. An ice-cream parlor with tables and chairs.

And every Saturday night there was dancing on the pavilion in the town park. Which was how a fourteen-year-old came to dance with an older young man. That summer at Quichiquois. That summer of Elektra.

An open pavilion up a flight of steps to raise it above the park benches and the paths below. The pavilion was also the bandstand. The band played there in summer every night. Except Saturday. On Saturday night there was an orchestra, a real orchestra. Live music, it is called today. Miss Estelle had for some twenty-five years taught classical piano to all the children of the village whose parents were music minded, but on Saturday night in summer she played mean jazz. Deacon Raven of some local church played violin for the service. For dancing at the pavilion, he played a jazz fiddle. The drummer was the owner of the local hay-and-feed store. He was in the National Guard band. On special occasions, the city fathers would enlist a clarinet player, a young farmer up the road a piece who played in his college band. Musicians who aren't professionals have a certain spirit. They play for the love of it, certainly not for the pittance they are paid.

Everyone danced. Little children capered with one another. Or now and again politely waltzed with their mums or dads. Even the grampaws and gramaws sashayed around the floor.

And I danced with Voss. A happening only that once. Although after that night the older girls taught me how to lag. Without appearing to lag. No one would know you were looking for one specific partner. When you saw him you would lag a step here or there until he was almost beside you. Katty and I would practice it at night in her bedroom. But I never had a chance to try it out for real.

Because Aunt George decided. She made all the decisions in the family. Aunt Priscilla acquiesced or did not. If she did not, it was the end of that happening. Aunt Pris was a woman of few words. Quietly spoken. Aunt Georgie was the talker. Emphatic. Accurate. Almost always. A businesswoman, accustomed to dealing with men. With yea and nay. No palavering.

She decided that the children should have three weeks at Lake Quichiquois. There are myriad small lakes all through the Berkshires. This was nearest to Clarksvale, about twenty miles. No resort. Just summer cottages. Friends of Aunt George offered theirs as they were going north to visit family for several weeks. The cottages were in the woods above the lake. Each was surrounded by woods, land was not costly, everyone had privacy. Just comfortably set far enough apart.

Aunt Priscilla acquiesced. My mother, being company, had no yea or nay. My mother preferred the busiest city street to the beauties of the woods. Not to the beauty but to the creatures that came with it, flies and spiders and bees and creepy crawlers. But my mother was company. Polite. Company was expected to acquiesce.

Of course, Aunt Georgie wasn't going. Shut up for three weeks surrounded by children? Like my father, she had business excuses.

After her decision, Aunt Georgie said, "I have a hired girl to go along. No sense of you and Elizabeth [my mother] turning your holiday into a wash and iron and cook for six children."

Aunt Priscilla was wary. "Who is the hired girl?"

"I hired Elektra." Aunt Georgie slid the name off her tongue as if she just recalled it.

A look. From one to another of the aunts. And returned the other to the one. Aunt Pris decided, half-reluctantly, "Well, she's as good as we could hope for this late in the summer."

Imperceptible. Aunt George had been apprehensive. Priscilla could have said no. She hadn't. Now Aunt Georgie could resume her position as head of the family. In name. She paid the bills.

"She's strong," Aunt George said. "Remember how she took up all your rugs last spring—beat them like a man would, the air was grimy."

"And laid them all again," Aunt Priscilla mentioned. "And she would carry the whole laundry in one load up the stairs."

There were twenty-three steps up from the living room to the second floor. I had counted them. I always count steps. Another eighteen up to the attic bedrooms where the boys slept, and live-in help when Aunt Priscilla tolerated it.

I don't know how many steps to the basement. I didn't go to the basement. The furnace was there and the storage. Years of the *Saturday Evening Post* and the *Geographic,* and old trunks filled with old clothes.

Elektra was strong. Elektra didn't matter. She was scrub clean. The aunts ticked off her good points. Nothing said of the bad. Of the cause for apprehension one to the other. Somehow I didn't want to ask Katty. Katty had a way of embroidering words to make a bland story an exciting one. If not exactly a true one.

I'd seen Elektra, of course. Someone must have said, "There's Elektra." Walking on Main Street. Or going into the post office. Or sitting at a soda table at the soda fountain. "There's Elektra." I could describe her as if I'd seen a snapshot of her. Tall. Man tall. Lean. Man lean. Straight black hair, held back by a barrette. Hanging to her waist. Not when she was working. Then piled in

braids or in loops. High ruddy cheekbones. Straight nose. Like on
an Iroquois.

I'd seen her. She delivered the ironing that Aunt Priscilla sent
to Gammer Goodwife. Gammer lived in that big square yellow
rooming house on the terrace you passed walking to town. The
townsfolk called it the "Poor House." Elektra lived there too. She
was kin to Gammer.

I'd seen Elektra. Dancing with Voss.

I couldn't but wonder if Katty had put the idea of Lake Quichiquois into Aunt Georgie's head. Linda, her best friend, was
going up there for the rest of the summer. Her family owned a
summer cottage there. There was a boys' camp across the lake.
For little boys, but the counselors were privileged!

And so we went to Lake Quichiquois. Aunt George's chauffeur,
Fred in the chauffeur's cap, drove us up there in the seven-seater.
The ladies in the backseat. My younger sister squeezed in by my
mother. Katty and I on the jump seats. The three little boys in
front with Fred.

Elektra would be up the next day. Fred was borrowing a pickup
truck from the garage to carry our trunks. The aunts always took
trunks, even for a short stay. Elektra would ride with Fred in the
cab of the pickup.

Time goes quickly by the water. Too quickly. We are water
people. Quichiquois was a dream happening. Elektra would have
the breakfast cooked and served before eight o'clock every morning. She'd rev up the kitchen while we waited out the dictum:
"Do not go in the water until one hour after eating." We
wouldn't. But we would go down to our dock before the hour was
up and the children would splash through the shore water. Elektra
would get our rowboat turned over, ready to row out for anyone
in trouble. Elektra was a strong swimmer. She cleaved the water
as beautifully as a dolphin.

Dover Camp, a long established one, was just across the lake.
The little boys and our boys could and did exchange taunts across
the water.

And of the three counselors, two were already in college,
lordly sophomores the coming year. The other was a senior in
prep school. Katty and Linda were in rhapsodies. New boys—or

as they called them, men—and these girls were practiced at
making boyfriends. The boys were at Brown, and the girls' college was just across the Massachusetts line. The talk became all
about football games and weekend soirees. And house parties in
the spring.

Across the lake was also Mr. Gruen's general store and soda
fountain. The meeting place for all lakers. He had a year ago built
on a room for the soda fountain. He had old-fashioned tables and
chairs in there during the week, but they were moved out on
Saturday and there was dancing to a juke box. No Paul Jones.

The Dover Camp boys only had to walk downhill a short way
to the soda fountain. On our side it was a quarter-mile walk, after
we reached the lane from the cottage, down to the bend that led
to the store. It was much shorter to get into the rowboat and row
right across to the store dock. If you knew how to row. We didn't.
Elektra did. She tried to teach us. It isn't easy to learn to row.
The boat goes around and around in circles. Unless you have a
very strong arm. Muscles. Like Elektra. The children, Katty, and
I were allowed to go with Elektra in the boat on Saturdays. My
mother and Aunt Pris would walk over later to fetch the little
children home early. Katty and I were allowed to stay until the
eleven-fifteen closing. With Elektra.

Until our first Saturday evening, I had not known Voss was also
working at the camp. Three afternoons a week. Instructing the
young campers on the fine points of sailing.

And I couldn't help but wonder which one of them had decided
to find a job up at the lake, when the other had been already
hired.

The cottagers danced. Katty and Linda and the counselors
danced. The little boys and girls tried to dance. Voss and Elektra
danced together. I watched from the sidelines. So did Whey-face.

I never did find out why he was called Whey-face. The girls
would simply explode into "curds and whey" when I asked. He
was sort of doughlike, not fat but a bit puffy; he would always be
a little off side. No matter how fine an education he would have.
No matter that when he grew up he would take over the president's chair at the bank and his father would retire to chairman
of the board.

Both Claude and I just sat on the bench in the corner and

watched the dancers. Sometimes I'd get him up on his feet and would try to show him how to move to the music. But he never understood rhythm or timing or movement. Two left feet. He always came out to the lake on dance nights to drive Voss back to town. On weeknights Voss hopped a ride to Clarksvale with workers at the camp.

Once—just once at Quichiquois—I danced again with Voss. He walked over to where Claude and I were sitting to ask Claude something or other. I think he recognized how my feet were in rhythm even while sitting down there on the bench. He would understand because he was a dancer. Not a professional, but bred in the bone, roiling in the blood. Without warning, he took my hand and pulled me up from the bench, said, "Come on," and we danced out onto the floor. Entirely different from the Paul Jones. A jazz jazzy. Exhilarating.

When Elektra came back from powdering her nose or whatever, Voss sat me down. He winked at me as they went off. But ours had been the best jazzy of the evening. It even led to my having some dances with Katty's older boys. Yes, I too have dance in my blood and bones.

It was that same night that I asked Claude how Voss could know so much about sailing to be able to teach the boys. Claude looked at me aghast. How could I know Voss and not know that? I tried to explain that I didn't know Voss. It was our hired girl who knew Voss. I'd just happened to dance with him once in the Paul Jones at the pavilion.

So Claude told me, "He's going to join the coast guard. He's been studying all this year to pass their tests or whatever you have to do to get in. He used to sail when he was a boy and lived up the coast. His father was a sailor. On a cargo boat. His father sailed all the way to China." It could be so. Or a sailor's yarn to a small hero-worshiping boy. It didn't matter. Voss would be a sailor if that was what he wanted.

I remember so well everything about that last dance night. It was getting on to eleven thirty, and I didn't see Elektra anywhere. I excused myself to Claude and walked across to where Katty was whooping it up with her current favorite boyfriend. Katty didn't shoo me away. Maybe I looked that worried. "Where's Elektra?" I asked her.

She surveyed the dancers on the floor. "She's probably down at the boathouse," she said.

"What's she doing down there?" I asked. Innocence. Too young. For a beat Katty and her friends just looked at me. And Linda started laughing. Katty joined in. The boys were politely inexpressive. They were sophisticates.

After she'd stopped laughing, Linda said, as if everyone knew that, "It's where couples go."

Katty added, "When they want to be alone."

"Smooching," Linda said.

I caught on. I wasn't that innocent. Necking, they called it at my school.

"She'll be here after the music stops," Katty said. "She wouldn't dare not," she explained to her friends. "She knows Aunt Priscilla is waiting up."

Truly true. Aunt Priscilla wasn't as sharp-tongued as Aunt George. But you could bully Aunt George by a temper tantrum. Katty explained it to me early in the summer. Aunt Priscilla was immovable.

When Mr. Gruen dimmed the colored lights and set the juke box for the last dance, always "Three O'Clock in the Morning," I saw them. Elektra and Voss. Dancing. Two become one. I watched through the whole record. Daydreaming. Why call it "day" when it's at night? Someday I'd grow up and have a boyfriend who danced like Voss.

Voss and Claude said good night and walked off. Elektra rowed us home. Aunt Pris glanced at her watch. "It will be midnight before you get to sleep." This was a nudge to go to bed, not stay up talking. "And we have to start packing up tomorrow. Aunt George and Fred will be here Monday morning."

Katty and I didn't talk much. Too tired. Too much, each of us, to remember. From the beginning of summer through this our final night of the boys' farewell across the water. "Good Night, Ladies . . ."

We had to miss Sunday morning church when at the lake. The nearest was in Clarksvale, too far to walk. Aunt Priscilla read her Bible. The children were kept quiet, and Katty and I usually slept until noon. In the afternoon we were allowed to swim and splash by our dock.

This Sunday was different. I woke—it wasn't eight o'clock—to the children gabbling in loud voices. Loud voices. Like on a weekday. My mother and Aunt Pris were ahead of me to the kitchen. Mother with her hair still in kid curlers, Aunt Pris with her gray hair in a plait down her back. Both in their nightgowns and robes. Aunt Pris was asking, "Whatever is the matter?" and my mother saying to her two, "Quiet. Quiet now. What's wrong?"

The children all talked at once. Emerged, one question. "Where's Elektra?"

Aunt Pris was dubious. "She isn't here?"

"No. She isn't here," all talking again at once. Almost shouting. "She's not here. There's no breakfast."

"Perhaps she overslept," Aunt Pris said. She hesitated. Then made her way to the back of the house, past my room, sleepy-eyed Katty just emerging, saying, "What's wrong?"

On to Elektra's bedroom beyond. Aunt Priscilla proper. Knocking on the door. Calling gently, careful not to startle a sleeper. "Elektra . . . Elektra . . . it's Miss Priscilla."

No response. She tried it again, a bit louder. Again no response. Aunt Priscilla took hold of the doorknob. Reluctantly. It was against all the principles of good manners. To open another's bedroom door. Even a servant's. But with no sound within, she did open the door, one small slant. Enough to peep inside. Then wider. And she said, "She isn't here."

"She must be around someplace." Katty and I had followed into the room. Katty said, "She can't have left. She hasn't taken her things." The hairbrush was on the bureau. The box of powder and the puff also there. Her nightdress still folded neatly over the back of a chair. The bed already made up. Or was it used last night?

"She'll be back," Aunt Priscilla decided. "I'll dress and then I'll cook breakfast."

Mother said, "I'll give the children some cornflakes and milk to tide them over." She had already put the kettle on for Aunt Priscilla's morning tea.

Aunt George came up in the afternoon. She said the same as Aunt Priscilla. "She'll be back." Her reasoning was different. "I owe her five dollars. For last week. She won't leave without her pay."

But she didn't come back. Not that day.

Not the next day. My small suitcase was packed. All else was confusion. Katty trying to curl her hair before closing her suitcase. Aunt Priscilla had packed all of Elektra's belongings into her own trunk. There wasn't much. The skirt and shirt she wore to work in, the few cosmetics, even her toothbrush and toothpaste had been left behind, and her undergarments (one to wear, one to wash, one to dry), her bedroom slippers, and an old night-robe that Aunt Pris had given her. Of course she'd taken her purse with her; the one she carried last night wasn't in the room. There'd be a comb and lipstick and powder compact in it.

Aunt Priscilla was trying to get everything shipshape, as it had been when we arrived. Mother was trying to get her children ready to leave. Aunt George arrived and added to the confusion while insisting, "Of course Elektra's gone back to Clarksvale. For reasons of her own." She finally took the Tompkin boys out to Fred, let him keep them busy out by the truck.

I managed to slip out the side door at a propitious moment when all the others were in the house or in front by the cars. I skulked rapidly through the trees until I was on the path that led to High Peak. It wasn't a real path. Just bumpy earth, pebbles and rocks, bits of green that wasn't weeds or wild grass, just green stuff. I zigzagged up the path to the promontory at the top. High above the shore. Elektra's special place. One afternoon when Katty and Linda were being exceptionally boy-crazies, Elektra had let me go with her to the peak. This was her time off from children and chores—why would she take me with her? Maybe because Voss danced with me once in the Paul Jones.

She didn't talk about him. She didn't talk when we were there. She just stood on the promontory and looked at the sky or down at the water. Under the promontory but still high on the slope there was a shelf. Not far below the peak. No way to get to it except by zigzagging down the slope and stooping your way under the protruding upper slope. She didn't take me there. She didn't go there either. Just pointed it out to me as we leaned over the tip. Scary.

I didn't want to go there now. She wasn't there. But she had been here last night. With Voss? A farewell? In each other's arms. Two into one. "Stop dreaming," Katty would say. Or my mother. Or anyone if I spoke of it. But I knew. Before I saw the bead, the red glass bead on the green stuff scattered on the earth. She wore those beads to the dance last night. She always wore them with her summer dress, her white dress with the little roses sprinkled across the pattern. The beads almost looked like crystals. Not really. They were pretend, cut like crystals, but made of glass. They were a little handful of beauty to her. She must have searched for them when the strand was broken. Caught on a tree branch, or the button on a man's jacket. Too dark to find all of them. I looked. There was one out on the tip, but I didn't go there. I scruffed through the green and found another. And another, with leaf mold patterning it. No more. I hadn't time to search for more. I ran until the cottage was in sight. Then I just hurried, the beads tight in my left fist. Fred was loading the last of the suitcases.

My mother came to me with, "Emmy, where have you been?" and as she looked into my face, softly, "Saying good-bye?"

She understood the need to say good-bye. To the woods and the water. To some of summer memories. In some secret place you had marked as your own.

■   ■   ■

Another week and the end of August. Of summer. My mother and the children off for California and school days again. Long good-byes until Christmas. Behind the scenes it had been decided that I would enter Mount Academy this year, the school where the women of my father's family had all attended to be finished. Katty had graduated there this spring. My mother approved though as a Californian she had been finished there. I would stay on with Aunt Priscilla until school started. Aunt George had assured me that with a diploma from Mount Academy I could attend any college of my choice. Such was its academic standing. Even Cambridge? Yes, even Cambridge. I doubted. Cambridge wasn't exclusively female, and Aunt Georgie with all her modern ideas and bold business maneuvers did not hold with coeducation. It was all right for primary students. Although better for the girls to go to Miss Mastersons and the boys to Albany Cadet. No hanky-panky.

It was one of those last nights before Katty would depart for college. Aunt Pris, Katty, and I had had early supper and cleanup and were relaxing in the living room. Until Aunt Georgie came by. She was again all het up about Elektra. She'd been at some

meeting and none of the women knew anything about the dis-
appearance of Elektra. No one had seen her since she went to the
lake with us. They seemed to think Aunt Priscilla and Aunt
George were to blame.

Aunt Priscilla said, "Stop worrying your head about the five
dollars. I was going to have to let her go anyway. She was beginning to show."

They exchanged a few of their wise looks and dropped the subject.

Later when Katty and I went up to our room, I asked her.
"What did Aunt Pris mean? Beginning to show."

Katty just looked at me. Stared. Finally she said, "You know."

"I don't know. If I knew, why would I ask you? 'Beginning to
show'? Do you know?"

"Of course I do. Everybody knows. That she's going to have a
baby. That's what it means."

"She's married!" I could not believe it. But if she and Voss were
married . . .

"No. She's not married," Katty stated.

But if she's not married, how can she—I didn't ask that question
out loud. Some people did. We just didn't know people who did.
I sighed to Katty. "How do you know all these things?"

"Emmy," she told me, "you find out a lot living with the aunts.
You keep quiet and listen and they forget you're there. And you
learn a lot."

I figured for myself. In a small town you learned things that
city girls didn't know about. Small towns were evolved from farm
country. Where life and death were the beginning and end, and
in between were all manner of happenings.

Another week of flurry and then we drove with Katty to Albany
to put her on the train for New York. Three of her friends were
also going to the college on the Hudson. Linda, of course, and
Willa and Maleen. The college proctors would meet the train with
the school bus.

When we returned to the house late that afternoon, we collapsed into chairs, even Aunt Georgie. I would be the next to go.
But only as far as Hudson, where I'd be met by the school bus.

I'd stopped listening to the aunts long before they were talked
out. It became tiresome listening to all the memories of Aunt A

and Uncle B and Cousins C, D, E, etc. When I didn't know any of them. They were reminiscing to each other, remembering their own college days.

Finally Aunt Georgie gathered her gloves and string bag and high-stepped to the front door. She'd sent Fred and the car home; she'd be walking. Of course she carried her umbrella as always, to ward off sun or rain.

She said to me, "You be ready in the morning, Emmy. I'll come by for you about ten o'clock."

Aunt Priscilla showed mild surprise. "You're taking Emmy along?"

"I certainly am." Evidently I'd missed something in their long conversation. "She's the last to see Elektra."

"I saw her," Aunt Pris corrected.

"You weren't with her all evening. Or in the boat."

I could have told them I knew no more than Aunt Pris. Elektra never talked. She spoke necessary words, but she never talked. Not even phrases like "Is my lipstick on straight?" "Does my petticoat show?" Things all females say to each other.

Instead I asked, "Where are we going?"

"We're going looking for Elektra. Find out where she is. Find out why she hasn't been around for her five dollars. You think of some questions yourself, Emmy. We'll both ask questions."

I reacted in my veins. In my bones. I was to be a Miss Paul Pry. I could ask a dozen questions. I could ask Voss: "Where did she spend the night? How did she get back to Clarksvale? How did she break her strand of red glass beads?" But I wouldn't. It was none of my business. Just the same, I carried the three red glass beads along in my party handkerchief deep in my little purse, where I had tucked them away while we were still at the cottage. While no one was looking at me. Before I got into the car and shared a jump seat with Katty.

I was ready for Aunt George when she arrived next morning. She had walked over. "No sense in taking the car. More trouble than it's worth." She was thinking out loud. "We have to prowl."

We prowled along Town Street, which carried you into Main Street. But we stopped before then. We stopped at the big yellow boardinghouse where Elektra had lived. A flight of wooden steps led up to the porch. Aunt George didn't ring or knock on the

door, she opened it. She knew her way around here. I followed
her. She walked past the staircase that mounted to a second floor,
and strode down the uncarpeted corridor, all the way to a door
near the back of the house. She knocked a ratatat on that door.
And again, stronger. From within now came a voice shouting,
"Who's that come knocking at my door?" Aunt George shouted
back, "Just Aunt George, Gammer, that's who." Everyone in town
called her Aunt George or Georgie.

Came another shout: "George Fanshawe?"

"What other George do you know, Gammer?"

Sometime along the years I'd heard, just like an aside from
someone in the family, that Aunt George had been married once
on a time. Not for long. That's why she wasn't a Davenport like
Aunt Priscilla and my father and his family.

"Well, don't stand out there yammering, Georgie. Come on
inside."

My aunt opened the unlocked door and went in, me following
behind her.

"Gammer," she said, "this is my niece Emmy."

I managed to stammer a "How d'you do" to the diminutive old
woman in the big rocker with varnish peeling from it. This was
Gammer Goodwife, supposed to be kin of Elektra. Half-toothless,
a browned corncob pipe clutched by the few remaining teeth. A
squawky voice like something was caught in her throat. The ironing woman. Hard to believe that those rheumatic cramped fingers
could iron ruffles until they rippled. Could iron linen napkins
down to the very edge of the hand hem. Could iron lace as delicately as if she'd spun it. She took one look at me out of her
spiteful black eyes and dismissed me as without interest.

She had three different ironing boards set up in her large untidy
room. One, oversize, for sheets, tablecloths and such; a middle-
size one for the usual clothes wash, and a baby one, a sleeve board
it was called. Probably for the ruffles and laces. A screen closed
off a corner of the room. Behind it, Aunt Georgie told me later,
was the bed and washbasin. An old-fashioned rooming house with
the bathroom down the hall.

"I don't have your laundry done," Gammer spat.

"I didn't come for my laundry," Aunt George informed her. "I
didn't bring any this week."

"Then what you doing here?"

"I'm looking for Elektra."

"Well, you can see she an't here." Gammer set the rocker rocking hard again. "She's up at the lake with your sister."

"She isn't up at the lake. We've all left the lake."

"Did you bring her back here?"

"We couldn't," stated Aunt George. "She left before we packed out."

"Why did she leave?"

"That's what I want to know. I want to ask her."

"Well, she an't here."

"Where's her room?"

"She an't in her room."

"How do you know she isn't up in her room?"

Gammer cackled. A cackle laugh. I'd read of them. But I didn't know there was really such a sound.

She dug her fist into a voluminous pocket in her skirt. "Because I got her key." She unreeled a long chain attached inside the pocket. On the end of it was a large ring of keys. "She leaves it with me when she's out of town. So nobody gets into her things." She beetled suspiciously at Aunt George.

"You haven't seen her since she came back? You haven't had any message from her?"

Gammer kept humming "Nnnnoooo" and rocking harder. Like little boys do to make it go faster.

"Then where is she?" Aunt George said. Not exactly to Gammer. At her own frustration.

But Gammer responded. "She's a Canuck. I told you that before. A Canuck witch." She restarted the rocker. "She flew away—up high—way up high . . ."

"On your broomstick," Aunt George bristled. She'd had enough of Gammer's antics. She stood up and brushed the dust off her skirt, although the chair she'd sat on had been brushed by her handkerchief before she sat down on it. "If you do see her or hear from her," Aunt George instructed, "tell her I'm looking for her. To pay her the money I owe her."

The rocking stopped like that. "You can pay me. I'll give it to her."

"I'll pay her. No one else."

"You think I'd spend it on myself."

"I pay what I owe to the one I owe." With that she stalked out while Gammer was still embroidering her role as a caretaker of Electra's money as well as her room. I sidled out beside Aunt George. I didn't want to be left alone in that room with Gammer.

All the way to Main Street Aunt George kept talking to herself, not to me, about the perfidious Gammer and her grandniece. I managed to keep up with her fast walk by saving my breath. Only three blocks to Main Street.

Waiting to cross the street, I could ask, "Now where do we go?"

"We'll go to Gus Henschel's. I understand his nephew, Voss, and that girl were what we used to call an item."

"Did everybody know?" Somehow I'd thought it was a private affair, known only to Katty and her friends who saw them dancing together.

"It's the talk of this town the way she went after him." She was opening the door of the butcher shop before I could think of some excuse to keep from going in there. I didn't want Voss to see me and think I'd talked about him and Elektra.

Voss wasn't up front today. His uncle was. He was arranging steaks for his display case. "Morning, Miss Georgie," he said, but it was a glum morning from his expression. "What can I do for you today?"

"You can let me talk to that nephew of yours."

"Voss?"

"I understand that is the name."

He peered over the counter at me. I was too young to be a friend of Voss so he dismissed me from his answer. To Aunt George he growled, "I'd like to talk to him myself. That javel never come back from the lake. That camp has been calling and calling him. He hasn't been around there either."

Aunt George was only temporarily speechless. "You haven't seen Elektra?"

"That the pawky girl been hanging around him all summer?"

"She hasn't been around lately?"

"Not since she went up to the lake with your sister. Leastways that was what she told him."

Both of them gone. Together. But she wouldn't go without taking her belongings. Yes, she might. If he was in a hurry. He'd have some money with two jobs. He'd buy her a new hairbrush and nightgown.

"Good riddance to bad rubbish," Uncle Gus was saying. "But he'll be around once he runs out of money. I paid him before he went off to the lake that Saturday. He'll be back."

"I owe Elektra some money. I don't like to owe money. If either of them turns up, you let me know. Right off. Hear?"

"I ain't deaf, Aunt George. I hear."

And she stomped away, me trailing. Again talking to herself. "They'll turn up when they want money."

I could have told her they weren't coming back. They had each other. But she wouldn't have believed me.

II

Ten years ago. Eleven come summer. High school and college over and done. Two years assistant women's editor on a medium-small-town newspaper. You want to know what an assistant women's club editor covers? Women's club meetings. Women's club social teas. Women's club holiday occasions. Washington's birthday cardboard hatchets. Cotton Easter bunnies in straw bonnets. Fourth of July crepe paper firecrackers. September, miniature grandmothers' school slates. October, take your pick, witches, brooms, jack-o'-lanterns. November, yarn turkeys. No need to illustrate December and January. How often can you write that the decorations were so charming, unique, attractive, amusing—add your own adjectives.

I couldn't get out of the groove. The editor wanted me where I was. I could spell.

On a September morning, I read on the AP tape, DATELINE CLARKSVALE. HUMAN BONES FOUND AT LAKE QUICHIQUOIS.

I didn't have to read on. I knew exactly where, and, without knowing, I knew who. And a chance to break from my shackles. I knocked on Editor Briar's door. His office is a square of window glass, but we observed the courtesy of a knock. He was chewing his pencil. Obviously working on his weekend editorial. Yes, he uses a pencil. A yellow wooden pencil with very black lead.

"Mr. Briar," I said, "I'd like to leave now. My page has gone to press."

"Who's going to read proof?"

"You are," I told him. "Or one of those callow youths you call reporters." I'd known Mr. Briar a long time. Since I was subeditor on the college paper. I knew how to give him just enough information to whet his news appetite. "I have a story that takes investigative reporting, and I want to get at it ahead of the pack."

He stuttered and glowered and called anathema on my head. A hot story was for callow Quentin, the one he was training to be a star metropolitan reporter. Like he'd always wanted to be.

He was wasting my time. I interrupted him. "It just came over AP. Finding bones upstate. Human bones."

His pink face glistened. "I'll send Quent—"

"Indeed you won't," I countered. "I have the inside track. I was there." Stress on there. "When that girl disappeared. I can beat the city slickers. They'll be coming around. But I know these folks. See you Monday."

With which I was out the door, leaving him to his blood pressure.

I retrieved my car from our parking lot and took off for Clarksvale. Ninety miles upstate. I didn't stop to pack up anything. I could buy a toothbrush. Borrow everything else from Aunt Priscilla or Aunt George.

I stopped at Aunt Priscilla's house—it was on the way into town. After ejaculations of surprise, I told her, "I'm here to cover the big story. Finding human bones at Quichiquois."

"I'll call George. She'll want to hear about this."

Aunt George was over to Aunt Priscilla's in a trice. She must be well in her sixties now and just as spry and as domineering as ever. As that summer of Elektra.

"You think it's Elektra," she said after I'd given her a rundown on the news story.

I did think so. I'd always thought that she had never left the lake. But couldn't let myself say it back then. Didn't want it to be so.

"Aunt George, you come uptown with me," I invited. "You know all these local officials. In case they try to freeze me out. I want the story."

"You'll get it." She did not doubt. She was too accustomed to getting what she wanted from the town fathers.

As we came out on Aunt Priscilla's porch she asked, "Is that your car?" nodding to where it stood in the driveway.

"We'll walk," she told me, just as she always said ten, almost eleven, years ago. "Easier than trying to park. Talk to more people anyhow."

And there were plenty of people out on Main Street. Gossiping. Gawking. And there was Claude, near the bank, his father's bank. Also Aunt Georgie's.

He greeted us Claude-like. "Good morning, Aunt George. Hello, Emmy. You haven't been to Clarksvale for a long time." He was still a whey-face, but he had some assurance now. He had been appointed an attorney with the county. Aunt Priscilla had kept me informed of all Clarksvale news. She wrote me every week.

Claude and I shook hands. As visitors do.

Aunt Georgie said to us, "I'm going on down to the court-house." Where she could gather information.

Claude said, "You're here about the bones."

I showed him my newspaper card. "It was on the AP wire this morning."

"We sent the bones to the lab in Albany. Two weeks ago. They're on the way back here now. With the report."

I was reluctant but I asked. "Do you know . . ."

"Yes." He said almost to himself, "The director informed me. I inquired . . ." It took a moment or so before he could continue. But he said it without inflection. "They are male bones. The bones of a young man probably in his twenties. The skull has been bashed."

I only half asked. "They were found under the promontory, the one called High Peak."

"There is a ledge, an open cave. The bones were there. Nothing left of clothing."

"No leather? A belt? A wallet?"

"Not after ten years. Pumas take refuge there if a winter storm interrupts their hunting. Sometimes there are bears."

I didn't want to say it but I had to. "She killed him."

"We don't know that."

"She loved him. He was going away. She couldn't let him go."

"If she did, we will never know," Claude said. "She cannot be brought back to trial. Not without evidence. Even if she is found."

"She was carrying his child. He was leaving her and their child."

Somewhere there is a little girl, near ten years old. Straight as a lance. Long dark hair hanging down her back. Or a sandy little boy. Agile. Scrawny but muscular. Strong.

"She loved him." I kept repeating it. Not for Claude. For myself.

Claude said, "I don't think she planned it. I don't think she intended it. I think it was by accident."

In a rage, she struck him. There were some sizable rocks on the promontory. There would be some in the cave. And kept striking him until he was gone. Before she knew what she was doing.

He broke the strand of beads trying to get away from her. She must have had a rock. He was stronger. If it had been possible to get away from her, he could have stopped her.

"I hope you won't mention her in your story. Why torment her further? She'll always live with this. An agony of loss."

He had loved Voss. The way he'd never love anyone else. Nothing homosexual about it. A teenage boy's hero-worship of his hero.

"I won't. There may be gossip but it will come to nothing. There aren't many who really knew her." And I hesitated. "Gammer . . ."

"Everyone knows Gammer makes up tall tales."

We were left with a pause of silence, each in his own thoughts. Then Claude said, "Shall we go down to the courthouse? It's time for them to get here with the report. You can call your paper from my office."

Together we walked the half block. On the way he said, "I'm going to be married this spring. To Willa. Do you remember Willa?"

"She was one of Katty's very best friends."

"We'll have a church wedding. Bridesmaids, attendants. All the frills. Willa wants it. We'll send you an invitation. I hope you'll be able to come. Katty's coming from Maryland."

Katty's husband is in government.

It occurred to him. "You're not married?"

"Not yet. I'm a career woman. I'm younger than Katty and her friends."

"That's right," he recalled. "You were just a little girl. You sat on the bench with me and we watched Voss."

"That's right," I echoed. I closed my eyes and I could see him. "He was a wonderful dancer."

Maybe to keep from tears, he laughed. "You tried to teach me to dance."

I laughed for the same reason. "You had two left feet."

So we went into the courthouse to hear the full report on the bones. Just another happening.

But I did not tell Claude that I would give up the story. I wouldn't mention Elektra. Not unless someone else did. But I would try to find her. I'm an investigative reporter. I have to know the entire story.

ALAS, MY LOVE

Ron Goulart

Ron Goulart's writing teacher was the late and esteemed mystery critic/author Anthony Boucher. This is easy to see in Goulart's writing, which honors all the Boucherian verities— precision, color, surprise, and a rueful look at this vale of tears we all share together. Ron works in a variety of fields but his best work is his detective stories.

LEE COULDN'T THINK OF MUCH TO SAY TO THE POLICE. BECAUSE by the time they grabbed him, he was pretty certain he'd killed the wrong person. That made it difficult to claim what he'd done was justifiable homicide.

So he kept quiet and let them book him for murder. Maybe he and his attorney can work out something for him to say.

Meantime, all sorts of stories and rumors have started circulating, some of them even more interesting than the truth. Not that I'm completely certain myself what the truth is in this case. I know as much, or maybe a bit more, than poor Lee Branner did. But even if I knew everything, I'm not going to get involved in this mess. Lee really did commit a murder after all.

■ ■ ■

When he first mentioned *Alas, My Love* to me, he was feeling completely positive about the book, nearly euphoric.

We were jogging side by side along an early-morning stretch of Southern California beach and I'd remarked on the new maroon running suit he was decked out in.

"What?" He was a tall, lanky man, sunbrowned and nearly

thirty-six. "I didn't catch your remark over that godawful wheeze of yours."

"Warmup suit," I gasped. "Yours. New?" I'd only started daily running earlier in the month and after a half mile I did sometimes develop a mild wheeze.

"You're wondering," said Lee, grinning and breathing evenly, "how a washed-up TV hack writer like me can afford underwear, let alone a three-hundred-dollar—"

"You got," I inquired, "a new writing assignment?"

"Seems incredible to you, doesn't it? Lee Branner, six-time Emmy runner-up. Head writer on such dramatic hits of past seasons as *Hula Cops*, *Wuthering Heights Revisited*, and many more. You were sure I was on the skids for good."

"Never thought one way or the other. Noted sweatpants no longer full of holes. Congratulations."

"Through it all," he said, never once breaking his easy sandpounding stride, "only one person stuck by me and continued to believe in me. That was Emily, the most loyal wife a man could—"

"What's the assignment?" I rasped.

"You sound godawful, sport." He slowed, halted beside a large sprawled hunk of driftwood. "Better rest for a spell, huh?"

"Doctor says—" I shook my head "—do mile morning before work."

I'd stopped next to him, panting. "Good for heart."

"But cardiac arrest won't be good for your heart at all." Lee nodded at the log. "Sit a spell and I'll fill you in on how I'm going to zoom right back up the ladder."

"Get cramps if sit down too soon after running."

"Suit yourself." He gazed out at the hazy blue Pacific, laughing.

"Emily knew I'd make it back, even after seventeen long months without a writing assignment. She's been a constant source of inspiration to me, through thick and thin." He turned and gestured up at the hillside. "Even when it looked as though we might have to give up our five-hundred-thousand house up there, she— Damn, did you see that?"

I was sucking in air. "See what?"

Frowning, Lee pointed up at his impressive red-tile and Moorish stone mansion and at the thick foliage that separated it from its neighbors. "I thought I spotted a flash of something, as though someone was watching me through binoculars." He frowned and turned back toward the morning ocean again. "Might be my imagination. Might be some pinhead trying to spy on celebrities. They still remember Emily, you know, even though it's been three seasons since she quit TV's top-rated nighttime soap, *Heavy Breathing*, to devote herself full time to our marriage."

"What's the new job?"

"This isn't the first time I've thought I was being—aw, you've got to watch out for Hollywood paranoia." He rubbed his hands together. "I'm not just making a comeback, I'm bringing off a *triumphant* comeback. I'm going to do a miniseries."

"Great. That'll pay—"

"Top dollar. Enough to pay off our debts, or most of them, anyway. It was really rough going there for a while. We came damn close to losing both the Mercedes. Emily didn't complain once, but sometimes I could see in her eyes that—Hi, Tag."

Tag Marlo, with a silky golden spaniel on a leash, was approaching from behind. "How you doing, Lee?" He grinned, waved, as the dog tugged him forward.

"Was that grin at all sheepish?" Lee asked me after the incredibly handsome young actor had passed.

"Didn't appear to be."

"He's heard. He knows I'm on the way back up," said Lee, nodding. "When he was doing Heathcliff in *Wuthering Heights Revisited*, we were great buddies. He and that dippy folk-rock singer he was living with dropped in on Emily and me all the time. The past year or so, though, it's been averted gazes and sheepish smirks. And he only lives a half mile down the damn beach from us."

"He's heard, you've heard," I said, checking my watch. "I'd like to hear before I hasten off to my ad agency."

"Sure, Tag Marlo'd like the lead in *Alas, My Love*," reflected Lee, watching the actor recede. "Who wouldn't? And he's aware that Bosco Cheever, hottest young producer in Hollywood, has hired me to do the damn script."

"*Alas, My Love*," I said. "That's a book, isn't it?"

"Is it a *book!*" He took a step back on the yellow sand, spreading his arms wide. "*Alas, My Love* is the blockbuster novel of the year, cuz. Been on every bestseller list from coast to coast for forty-seven weeks or more. Paperback rights sold for nine hundred thousand, which ain't bad in tight times like these. It's outselling books about cats, Jewish American Princesses, and how to reduce the size of your backside. It's a fantastic hit and I'm going to be turning it into a five-part miniseries."

"Have you read it yet?"

He shook his head. "I'm going to pick up a copy this afternoon. Two copies in fact, one to read and one to mark up. I imagine it's just one more fat romance, but I know I can turn it into a first-class miniseries. Tag might not be bad for one of the leads at that. I hear it's about a triangle situation."

My breathing was nearly normal. "Nobody seems to know much about the author."

"What a pen name he's got! Jason Renfrew, Junior." He laughed. "Probably a little-old-lady librarian living in Oxnard."

"Well, I'm glad to hear you're working again," I told him. "I got to be heading for work."

"Let's have lunch later in the week," he suggested. "My treat."

"I'm free Thursday."

"Thursday it is. I'll phone you about the place," he said. "That's another great thing about being in the chips again. They won't be disconnecting my phone for a while yet. I think I'll do another couple of miles before getting to the old typewriter." He went running with ease off along the bright morning beach.

■   ■   ■

Lee wasn't smiling when he came into Señor Legumbre's VegMex Restaurant that Thursday. He was wearing a new sport coat, new slacks, and new Italian shoes, but he looked pale under his tan. His walk reminded you of a kid coming in after school to write something a hundred times on the blackboard. Tucked under his arm was a fat hardcover copy of *Alas, My Love.*

"What's that godawful smell?" he inquired as he sat opposite me on the sunlit patio section of the place.

I obligingly sniffed the air. "Chili powder?"

"No, no—something vile."

"Guacamole?"

When he set the novel down on the glass tabletop, I noticed

his hands were trembling slightly. The dozens of tiny yellow paper bookmarks fluttered like leaves in the wind. "Are you wearing a new aftershave?" he said.

"Matter of fact, yes. One of our advertising clients just intro—"

"Smells like a lumberjack's armpit."

"It's supposed to. What happened to your euphoria of the other day?"

He glanced around at the scatter of other lunch customers. "How many people have to buy a damn book to put it on the bestseller list?"

I shrugged. "I don't know. A hundred thousand?"

"More than that probably." Lee sighed. "And there are hordes of others taking it out of libraries. That's dreadful to contemplate."

"Isn't the novel any good?"

"In less than three weeks the paperback edition'll hit the stands. Paperback book critics no doubt have review copies already." He took another look around. "Some of the pinheads right in this room have read *Alas, My Love*."

"Possibly. But what does that—"

"It's about—" He leaned toward me, his voice dropping low. "You haven't read it?"

"Nope. I read mostly nonfict—"

"The godawful thing is about *me!*" he said in an anguished whisper. "About me and Emily!"

I scratched at my nose. "You mean about a couple sort of like you two. A television writer married to an actress who—"

"Don't I get paid handsome sums for expressing ideas clearly and concisely?" he asked. "No, I don't mean the damn thing is about a couple with a few similarities. I mean, cuz, the book is about me and Emily!"

"What they call a roman à clef?"

"What I call a knife in the back, a rug pulled out from under my life, a scaffold trap sprung beneath my hopes and—"

"That's right," I realized. "It's about adultery, isn't it?"

"*Alas, My Love*, old chum," he said, teeth on the verge of grinding, "is about how Emily has an affair behind my back. Emily, who I've always believed was one of the few supportive and trustworthy women in this entire godawful town. My other wife, you know, was a—"

"But this is fiction," I reminded him, reaching across to tap the book's bright dust jacket. "Even if you noticed a superficial resemblance to you and—"

"Superficial? Do you think I'd be on the verge of a total collapse if the halfwit resemblances were merely superficial?" Sighing again, he gazed at the high adobe wall around the restaurant patio. "Things had been going so well, too. The whole town knows Bosco Cheever gave me the nod for this miniseries. The trades are even hinting they'll get somebody like Richard Chamberlain for one of the leads. I'm hot again. MSG called me yesterday about working on a new series pilot for them. *Us, People, TV Life,* and *Mammon* have all called, begging for interviews. Even that pinhead Jess Rawlins wants to do a story for *The National Intruder.* Two years ago he was underfoot all the time, when I was writing *Passion* for CBS. Lately, though, it's sheepish grins and furtive nods from across the room." He folded his hands to keep them from quivering. "Then I had to go and read this damn book."

"You had to if you're going to adapt it."

"The horns of a dilemma," he said. "I don't have the heart to continue on this project, yet I need the damn dough and the credit."

"So do it," I advised.

"They'll all laugh at me," Lee said forlornly. " 'The poor cuckold, scripting his own humiliation.' "

"Most of the people in your circle probably don't know what cuckold means, so—"

"They sure as hell know the principle involved."

"Tell you what, I'll read the book. Maybe you're imagining these parallels between you—"

"This isn't the result of a deranged mind at the end of its tether," he assured me, his voice rising as he snatched *Alas, My Love* up off the table. "Bosco Cheever doesn't offer nearly twice scale to a scriptwriter who's on the verge of going bonkers—" He paused, grew thoughtful. "I wonder if Bosco *knows.* He did give me a rather sheepish look once when my agent and I were in negot—"

"Say, you airheads, this ain't a literary tearoom." The stocky moustached proprietor had come stalking over to our table. "You want to read books, hire a—Oops! Sorry, Mr. Branner."

"That's okay, Lyle."

"I know you're on the rise again," apologized the owner. "I just didn't recognize you from the back. It's my steadfast policy never to insult people unless they're on the way down." He glanced over at me appraisingly.

"My chum's neither on the rise or the decline," explained Lee. "He's an advertising account exec and has remained on a successful dead level for untold eons."

"I got some great ideas for ads," confided Lyle to me.

"We'll order shortly," Lee said.

"Sure, take your time." He strode off, pausing to snarl at the patrons of another table.

"See? My status has improved," said Lee. "When I was in here last month, Lyle kicked me in the slats." He opened the novel to the place marked by the first of the dozens of slips of yellow paper.

I noticed that nearly half the left-hand page had been marked with a pale-yellow highlighting pen. "Maybe we ought to order pretty soon. I've got a client meeting at—"

"Listen to this." Lee cleared his throat. " 'She stood poised upon the precipitous diving board above the liquid turquoise of the sun drenched opulent swimming pool. Her petite figure was exquisite, a nubile statue of frozen poetry capped by her desirable auburn hair, which was the color of burnished brass forged in the smithy of idolatry. Jacques Rambeau's manhood was aroused as he drank in the ravishing radiance of her lithe—' Well?"

"Vivid writer."

"The prose is godawful. But don't you recognize my wife when you hear her described?"

I shook my head. "Lots of women are small and have red hair."

"So thought I." He ran his finger along the underscored paragraph. " 'On the lush inner portion of her maddening left thigh was a delicate scar in the shape of a crescent moon.' See?"

"Does Emily have a scar the shape of a crescent moon on her thigh?"

"Surely you've noticed it, all the times you've been poolside at our place."

"We were only there once, Lee, four years ago. Tell you the truth, when I swim I take off my glasses and I can't see a—"

"Well, she does and this Renfrew bastard describes it exactly. Along with many other intimate details of her structure." He slammed the book shut. "He also recounts, as best he can in his halting prose, her speech patterns, attitudes, likes and dislikes. He even knows that her favorite after-sex snack is popcorn with garlic salt smeared on it."

"Emily's a well-known actress. Lots of magazine articles might have—"

"No, this guy knows her, cuz." He flipped *Alas, My Love* open again. "How about this passage? 'He was tall and reed-slim, a Lincolnesque sapling of a man with a foursquare face and hands like slabs of raw lumber.' That's me—called Lance Bengal in this book."

"That could be a young Gregory Peck or dozens of other guys."

"Okay, I grant you some of this could be coincidence," Lee admitted, commencing to leaf through the pages. "But as Renfrew goes on and describes this disgusting and steamy affair between Emilia Bengal and Jacques Rambeau behind the noble and unsuspecting back of Lance Bengal, he—"

"Is Bengal a writer like you?"

"No, that's switched around. Emilia's the writer, her husband's a fading movie actor, and Rambeau is a hotshot TV director."

"Which isn't very close to your—"

"Allow me to continue," he requested while turning to another marked passage. "Every time Emily and—every time Emilia and Jacques meet to perpetuate their filthy relationship, all the dates match."

"What dates?"

"If Lance Bengal is out of town or stuck late at the studio the dates given in the damn book match exactly with the dates that I myself, in real life, was out of town or delayed at the studios over the past four, five years. Every damn one!"

"How can you be certain of that?"

"Because I keep a journal. I went back, once I realized what I was reading here, and double-checked," he said. "I'm going to leave all my notes and journals to the University of—"

"You're really convinced this novel is a fictionalized account of an affair between Renfrew and your wife?"

"Yes, there's no other answer." He closed the book once more. "It's tearing me apart."

"But if Emily'd been having an affair for years, you'd have suspected some—"

"Has your wife ever fooled around?"

"No, she doesn't go in for—"

"How can you be sure?"

"I just am."

"You go out of town on godawful assignments for your nitwit agency all the time. There's no way you can be absolutely certain she—"

"I trust her."

"Ah, I trusted Emily, too." He held up the thick novel. "And look."

I said, "What does Emily say?"

"I haven't mentioned it to her."

"Why not? If you're brooding about whether or not it's true, you—"

"I'm not brooding about that. I know this godawful book is true, a thinly veiled account of my trusted wife's infidelity."

"Maybe, though, she could suggest another explanation for how—"

"I don't intend to bring the subject up with her," he said firmly. "I have a certain pride and I'll be damned if I'll go sniveling to her over this."

After a few seconds I suggested, "Maybe this Jason Renfrew, Junior, could offer some explan—"

"Oh, I'll find *him*," he said, turning the back of the book toward me. "He's a mystery man right now, but I'll track him to his lair."

The author's photo on the dust jacket was a shadowy thing, showing only the back of a man wearing a trenchcoat with the collar turned up and a sport-car cap. You couldn't get any real idea what he looked like.

"It might be better to forget all about it," I said. "Just do the script, collect your money, and—"

"*Forget?* Forget about the one man in the world who's made a mockery of my life? Emily has been my main source of inspiration all these happy years and— No, I'll find Renfrew, whoever he may be, and wherever he is on the face of this earth."

"If he's really writing about you and Emily, he's got to be in Greater Los Angeles somewhere."

"I'll find him and teach him a lesson."

"Hey, what do you mean? Doing any violence to him'll only cause you more—"

"Once I confront the man, I'll decide exactly how to handle him," he said. "There are certain unwritten laws that apply to situations such as this."

"My advice," I said, "is to—"

"This has gone beyond advice."

■   ■   ■

Two days later, I had to fly to Iola, Wisconsin, and so I wasn't around while Lee Branner carried out most of his investigation to find out who the mysterious Jason Renfrew, Junior, really was. We did talk by phone once or twice, so I know what he was up to. One of our clients, Mother Zooker's Cookies, has its main offices back in Iola. You've no doubt seen pictures of the famous two-story-high giant cookie jar that houses the company's offices there. We've used, at the insistence of the company, the cookie-jar offices in quite a few of our print ads. Millions of people associate that quaint jug-shaped building with Mother Zooker's Cookies and the slogan "Nearly As Good As Homemade!"

The problem we had in Iola was that three members of a radical terrorist group called the Skid Row Commandos had waylaid and robbed a Kropfhauser Armored Car, stolen $420,000, and were, due to a complex and highly unlikely string of circumstances, holed up in the cookie jar. They'd been there for twenty hours when I was sent to Wisconsin, and by that time television-news viewers all across the country had seen the famous cookie-jar offices surrounded by armed police.

It was publicity certainly, yet we were afraid a certain percentage of people would start associating our cookies, all 26 Goodness-to-Gracious Varieties, with crime and violence. My job was to come up with a quick radio campaign that would cash in on the media attention while at the same time disassociating us from these wild-eyed, bearded terrorists.

The assignment kept me in Iola for close to two weeks. The armored-car robbers held out in there for seven and a half days and by the time they surrendered and came out, the cookie jar was riddled with bullet holes. I had to work out some print ads to minimize that, too, and also convince the client to patch the thing up as soon as possible. Certain members of the Mother Zooker board wanted to flaunt the holes and launch a campaign about their cookies being made while the bakeries were under siege and so on. I talked them out of that, pointing out that gunshots and cookies make for poor fusion. But it took a full three days of meetings and conferences.

■　■　■

All the while, Lee was on the trail of Jason Renfrew, Jr. It is possible that originally he intended only to confront the guy. As the pursuit dragged on, however, his anger and outrage increased. Having written several police shows over the years, he knew how to go about his search in a methodical way. Even though he was dead sure Renfrew was a pen name, he patiently searched through all the local phonebooks and city directories. He even used his contacts with the motor-vehicle people and the phone company. There was no listing anywhere. Not even an unlisted phone for anyone named Jason Renfrew, Jr.

Next, feigning casualness, he called the producer of the miniseries.

Bosco Cheever had a thin nasal voice and a terse style of speech. "So?" was his greeting when Lee phoned him at his Burbank offices.

"I've been reading *Alas, My Love*," began Lee. "It's a—a great book, Bosco. I really appreciate the opportunity to turn it into television, it's going to be—"

"Okay, okay."

"The thing is, Bosco, I—what's that gurgling sound?"

"Toilet flushing."

"You're in the john? You're taking this call on that phone of yours in there?"

"Yep."

"Far be it from me to criticize—you're a man of culture and sensibility, Bosco—but flushing the toilet while talking business lacks dignity."

"I don't do it with everybody. What's up?"

"I think it'd be a good idea for Renfrew and I to talk over a few things. Minor character problems and—"

"Who's Renfrew?"

"The fellow who wrote the book."

"Oh, him. Impossible."

"Why?"

"Who can figure writers? It's in his contract. No direct contact with us."

"Wouldn't he make an exception if—"

"Nope. That all?"

"Who's his agent?"

"Ugh. That Lena Kapp bimbo."

"Thanks. I'll have the treatment in to you by no later than—"

"So long."

Lee heard water running as the phone was being hung up.

■   ■   ■

He tried to charm fat Lena Kapp. "You're looking well, Lena. Trim and fit."

She sat, immense in a flowered caftan, behind her small blond desk. "Horse crap," she replied. "I look like a sack of lard. Who's your agent these days?"

"Lowell Swinefort."

"Lowell Swinefort." She chuckled. "I thought he'd died."

"He's alive and doing very—"

"Sure, like I'm trim and fit."

He looked beyond her. Out the windows of her tower office he saw a private plane go drifting by through the haze. "The reason I—"

"I'm not taking on any new clients."

"No, no, I'm happy with Lowell. The reason—"

"How can you be happy with a pinhead who's coked out of his nut ninety-nine percent of the time and hasn't gotten you work in two years?"

"I was only out of work seventeen months. And I've just signed to do the *Alas, My Love* miniseries."

"I know. That was Renfrew's idea. Sounded suicidal to me, getting a washed-out hack to take a—"

"Wait now." He stiffened in the low chair. "Renfrew suggested me for this scripting job?"

"It sure as heck wasn't my idea. Renfrew had enough clout with Cheever to convince him you were the one."

"Then Renfrew and Bosco have met?"

She shrugged, her massive body jiggling. "Who knows? Renfrew is too damned independent for me, but the book's already earned almost two million five so I don't kvetch too much."

"Lena, I'd like to meet Renfrew. Talk the book over with him, explain how I want to approach it for television."

"No." She stood and the floor shook. "Jason Renfrew, Junior, is a very private man. He grants no interviews, won't see anyone. It's fouled up the chance to get him extra publicity, but—"

"Since he knows my work, Lena, he'd make an exception in—"

"Listen, schmuck, he won't even see *Life* magazine. You think he's going to talk to you?" She rumbled toward the door. "See you around campus."

Lee stood, remaining next to his chair. "A letter? Can you forward him a letter in which I'll outline my questions and feelings and—"

"He doesn't want to hear anything from anybody." She jerked her office door open wide. "I don't send him anything but money."

"You've seen him, haven't you?"

Her tiny eyes avoided meeting his. "Haven't so far, no," she answered. "He's a recluse."

"Don't you even talk to him on the phone?"

"He doesn't have a phone."

"Renfrew is a pen name, isn't it?"

"Is it?" She nodded at the open doorway. "Scram now, Branner."

■　　■　　■

Lee didn't do any writing on the television treatment of *Alas, My Love* over the next few days. He'd sit in his studio, gazing out at the calm Pacific far below, with the novel resting in his lap.

Every time he started to try to work on adapting it, he'd become distracted by one of the passages he'd marked earlier.

"You know what my mother used to fix me when I came trudging home from school?" inquired Emilia as she reposed in silken but sparsely clad luxury upon the languid bed in their Beverly Glen hideaway. "Ketchup sandwiches. Yes, just ketchup spread on cheap white bread. We were disgustingly poor in my youth, dearest Jacques . . ."

"Ketchup sandwiches," he muttered. "That's what Emily's half-wit mother fixed her. She's always telling me that sad story. Even on our honeymoon, she— Hey!"

He leaped up, book thumping to the floor, and ran to the side window of his studio. Scowling, he scanned the distant trees and scrub on the nearest hillside. He'd sensed the brief flash of sunlight hitting the lenses of binoculars.

Even though he remained at the window for several minutes, he couldn't make out anything.

Finally, book tucked under his arm, he left. He drove his Mercedes over into the Beverly Glen canyon, searching for the lovers' hideaway cottage as described in the book. He had no luck, and one suspicious old lady who was out pruning her flowers wrote down his license number.

■   ■   ■

Four more uneasy days went by. He hadn't found Renfrew and he hadn't written a word. When Bosco called, Lee lied, told him he was turning out pages of the treatment each and every day and would have it finished by the following week.

That evening, as dusk settled over the beach, he decided to talk to his wife about the whole business.

"Must you bring that thing to the dinner table?" she asked when he plumped *Alas, My Love* down next to his plate.

She was a slim auburn-haired woman, and as attractive and bright as Renfrew had described her.

"It's my work," he said.

"You know how much I dote on you and what you write, Lee," Emily said, passing him the salad bowl. "Still, you've been a real grump ever since you got this damn assignment."

"Can you," he inquired, watching her intently, "guess why?"

"I suppose it's because you haven't done a day's work in two and a half years and you feel rusty. That's understandable. But—"

"Seventeen months. I was only without an assignment for seventeen months. Emily, I've read this damn book from cover to cover. Twice."

"I hear it isn't very well written."

"Oh, so? You haven't read it?"

"You know I read mostly anthropology and—"

"It's about us!" He'd lost control, was shouting. "About you and me and—this Renfrew bastard!" He slapped the cryptic photo of the author. "Its six hundred and forty-two godawful pages deal in minute detail with the affair this lout had with you over the past five years or so. And about how I, fool that I am, never suspected a blinking thing. Never even guessed I was being cuckolded."

"Being what?"

"Ah, that's perfect. I knew you'd pull that, avoid the major issue and pick at my language."

"Have you stopped taking those pills Dr. Hedley gave you?"

"What the hell has that got to do—"

"You're getting all purplish in the face and froth is forming on your pale lips," she pointed out. "I think you ought to take something to calm you down."

"You deny it?" he was on his feet now, waving the novel in the air.

"That I had an affair with—Renfrew, is it?"

"Here I looked up to you as the ideal wife, a constant source of inspiration for me. Now—" His shoulders slumped, the book dropped to his side.

She rose gracefully to her feet. "Our relationship is better than this, Lee," she said quietly. "I won't have you accusing me of—"

"Did you or didn't you?"

"I'll be sleeping in the guest room tonight." She left him there at the dinner table with the cooling food.

■   ■   ■

The next morning at dawn, while running along the grey beach alone, Lee suddenly halted. "Lena sends him royalty checks," he said, snapping his fingers.

That afternoon he went into the building on Wilshire where Lena Kapp had her offices. By hiding in a deserted conference room that had once been used by a now defunct cable-television service, he was able to linger in the building until it was locked up for the night. Then he went sneaking up two flights to Lena's suite and, after determining the agent and her staff were long gone, let himself in.

On the address wheel on her desk he found Jason Renfrew, Jr.'s, address given as 232 Otramar Road, San Amaro Beach, California.

Lee slipped free of the building by way of a service door, hurried to his Mercedes, and went driving down the night coast to the nearby beach town.

.   .   .

There was a prickly fog that night. Lee spent twenty minutes finding Otramar Road and nearly ten more spotting 232, which for some reason was situated between 242 and 248. Renfrew lived in a cottage that sat on the downside of the twisting road, its back hanging out over the dark beach and propped up on stilts.

He parked his car up the road from the place, sat in it for a few minutes. He discovered he was breathing openmouthed, nearly panting. Pressing his lips together, he opened the glove compartment and yanked out the .32 revolver he kept there.

He tucked that into the waistband of his trousers and climbed free of the car. Striding, he hurried down to the front door of the cottage.

Lights were on and he heard an electric typewriter going, along with a hi-fi playing Beethoven.

Lee didn't knock. He just turned the knob of the door, found it wasn't locked, and shoved his way into the cottage.

Seated at a woebegone old desk, facing the doorway, was a small sandy-haired man of thirty-one. He lifted his glasses up, resting them atop his head, and stared at Lee.

"You, huh?" Lee crossed the threadbare matt rug. "Jess Rawlins, a hack reporter for that godawful *National Intruder.*"

"What brings you to my—"

"This is terrible. It's bad enough she makes a cuckold of me, but to do it with a schlub like—"

"Makes you a what?"

"It's disenchanting," muttered Lee, edging nearer to the staring Rawlins. "She, the woman who, up until now, inspired me to my greatest creative heights has a shabby affair with you. Then, you slime, you turn it all into a sleazy novel and to top it off tell them to hire me to do the TV adaptation."

"Lee, listen." Rawlins rose carefully out of his chair. "I admit I wrote the book."

"Of course you did." He tugged out the revolver and pointed it at him. "You defile my wife, brag about it in print, make me the butt of Lord knows how many cruel jokes. Now I'll get even with you for that!"

"Lee, you know I'm just a hack—a writer for hire."

Lee fired twice.

"Just the front." Both slugs caught Rawlins in the chest. He cried out and went stumbling back until he smacked into the window behind him. "I only ghosted the book for your wife. She wanted to make some extra money so—" He slumped, fell dead.

Lee lowered the gun. Then he realized what Rawlins had been trying to tell him.

FIRETRAP

Greg Cox

As a major New York editor, Greg Cox can't always spend as much time writing as he'd like.

But even given his time limitations, Greg has managed to publish a substantial body of work known for the spareness of its style, the deft touches with its characters, and the surprising turns of its story lines. He is a fine writer.

Here we see Greg borrowing elements from at least two other genres to fashion a truly spellbinding take on the theme of love killing.

MOVING NIGHT, AND THE HOUSE SQUATTED BEFORE THEM LIKE an empty wooden crate waiting to be filled. The chartreuse paint job was mercifully muted by the fading light so that it had merely the sick green look of a possessed child's vomit. Although there were two other homes in the cul-de-sac, one on either side, its location at the end, as well as the wedge-shaped empty spaces between the houses, made theirs seem deceptively alone and apart.

If this is the future, Gordon thought glumly, let's get it over with.

For starters, the doorknob came off in his hand. "Terrific," he muttered as he pocketed the chipped glass knob and pushed the front door open with his foot. Carla and Mick squeezed past him into this, their new communal home. Gordon glanced backward; from the front porch, which was badly in need of repainting, he could see the lights of the campus, less than a mile up the hill. His fingers explored the circular hole where the doorknob had rested all too loosely. For this, he thought, I gave up my cozy room in the dorm? Hell, for this I moved away from home?

The door refused to close behind him, so Gordon left it hanging ajar. Later, after they'd finishing moving their boxes in, maybe he could prop it shut with a rock or something. He found his housemates in the ground-floor living room, which was unfurnished, uncarpeted, and dusty. The floor consisted of worn hardwood planks, separated by as much as half an inch of a dry, black, gummy substance. The bare white walls were whitest in those patches where large holes had obviously been plastered over. The landlord, he recalled, had said something about a rugby team living here before.

Blue eyes beaming, Carla danced around the room as though she'd never seen it before. "Well," she said, throwing out her arms theatrically, "welcome to Altered Estates!"

"Otherwise known as the Amityville Horror, Part Six," Gordon replied.

By any name, their new address was a two-story residence located in the middle of Bellingham's "student slums," within walking distance of the university. The age of the house was given away by its antiquated heating system: a coal-eating furnace in the basement that still needed to be regularly de-ashed by hand and shovel. So, Gordon thought, on top of everything else, we can also look forward to black lung disease.

"Have you seen the bathtub?" Mick asked. "There's enough dirt along the bottom that it could pass for a terrarium." He shrugged his high, stocky shoulders. "Then again, I suppose we can always grow our own food in a pinch."

Carla assumed a threatening pose, elbows out, fists on her hips. Gordon thought she looked like some red-haired Irish Amazon out of an old John Ford movie—even if she was from Hawaii. "That's enough, both of you. This is *our* house now—for just three hundred dollars a month, mind you—and all it needs is a little work to make it perfect. Don't tell me you want to go back to dorm food, not to mention all those stupid regulations."

"It'll look better," Mick conceded, "once we get all our stuff unpacked, I guess."

The eternal stoic, Gordon thought. What admirable unflappability in the face of disaster. Or maybe Mick simply didn't realize yet what a dreadful mistake this was.

"I want you both to remember that this wasn't my idea."

"No," said Carla, grinning, "but you agreed to it quick enough."

Under false pretenses, Gordon almost shot back, but caught himself in time. True, when Carla had first called him up over Christmas break to tell him about this wonderful old house she'd discovered, he had thought that she was talking about the two of them, well, living together; only after five or six glorious minutes had he realized that she was proposing instead a more innocent three-way arrangement involving Mick as well. He had covered himself hastily, but still wasn't sure if Carla had picked up on his initial misconception.

God, that would be embarrassing.

Unwilling to meet Carla's eyes at this particular moment, Gordon leaned casually against the lower pane of the window facing their weed-infested front yard. Almost immediately, the wooden ledge gave way beneath his elbow, and he found himself sprawling on the floor. His glasses skated across the floor, coming to rest in the crack between two planks. His throbbing funny bone pulsed in rhythm to the fervent chorus in his head: This is a terrible, terrible, terrible mistake.

Mick and Carla laughed as he scrambled to his feet and wiped the dust and tar off his hands. Probably got splinters too, he guessed. "That's right, gang up on me, see if I care. I know what's going on here: You two and the house are in cahoots to kill me."

"I'm sorry," Carla said. She still looked like she was watching an unusually funny sketch on Monty Python. "Are you all right, Gordon?"

His injured elbow was already forgetting the fall. "I seem to be intact, despite the best efforts of this residential death trap."

I suppose, he thought, I should be glad that Mick and Carla get along so well. My best friend and sort-of girlfriend. He remembered the first time he'd brought Carla back to the dorm to meet his roommate, after a marathon study session at the college library; for a while he'd been afraid that Carla would take Mick's dour silence as some sort of snub, even if that was the way he always was. Not to worry. Pretty soon, Carla had practically moved in with them, and was suggesting they make the household official. Granted, the fact that she hated her own roommate didn't hurt.

They were so different, though. Carla: ebullient, moody, temperamental. Unable to pick out any one major or field of study, but the self-appointed cheerleader and social director of their own little troika. The Irish Amazon from Honolulu. And Mick, who *was* Irish but acted as though he'd stepped out of one of Ingmar Bergman's slower-moving pictures; Gordon half expected to find him playing chess with Death one day. Even when Mick was drunk (which Gordon had seen more than once), he still made Norman Bates look like Buster Keaton. The only difference between Mick sober and Mick plastered was the shit-eating grin that spread across his wide, jaw-heavy face as he slowly faded into oblivion. Carla and Mick. Fire and earth. Dorothy and the Tin Man (sans heart). The only thing they had in common, as far as Gordon could see, was that they both kept their hidden depths hidden.

And where did he, the ever-fluid Scarecrow, fit into this cosmology? Witty, sardonic, the future whiz-kid of American film studies? Well, self-analysis was best left to the vain and idle. He had more important things to worry about.

Like this wreck of a house, for instance.

■ ■ ■

The first part of moving in, carrying their boxes and sleeping bags in from Mick's van, went easily enough. Gordon estimated they had unloaded two dozen cartons of books alone, but at least the night sky, although cloudy, had declined to snow. By nine o'clock, they were already in the kitchen, washing the newsprint off cups and plates that, mere moments before, had been protectively swaddled in back issues of *The Bellingham Herald*. Then Carla plugged in the toaster, and all the lights went out.

The kitchen was totally black. Gordon heard a plate or something shatter against the floor, followed by Mick's muttered curse, but he couldn't see a thing. Great, he thought. Suddenly we've gone from a visual medium to starring in an old-time radio show. *Inner Sanctum*, probably, or *Lights Out*.

■ ■ ■

GORDON: Who knows what evil lurks in the hearts of men . . . ?

MICK: Must have blown a fuse.

GORDON: Just by plugging in one appliance? Boy, cooking is going to be an adventure in this place.

CARLA: Careful. I think there's broken glass on the floor.

MICK: Sorry about that.

GORDON: No problem. But now what are we going to do?

MICK: The fuse box is in the basement, I think. I'm not sure how we're going to find it in the dark, though.

CARLA: Anybody pack a flashlight? Wait, hang on a second. . . .

▪ ▪ ▪

A match flared to life a few feet away from Gordon, and for once he was glad Carla was a smoker. She held the match up in front of her so that it cast a dim orange glow over her face. The flame, and the shadows it threw beneath her nose and brow, made her look like a jack-o'-lantern's bride. Behind her, Mick was visible only as a looming gray shadow.

"Gordon, look in that box over by the cupboard. No, the other one. There should be some candles in there, with the rest of my decorations." The match sputtered dangerously close to her fingertips, and Carla flicked it into the sink, where the light drowned instantly in soapy water. Gordon groped through ribbons and greeting cards until he grabbed onto something round and waxy. Carla lighted another match; the something turned out to be a large yellow skull. Or rather, judging from the wick in the cranium, a candle shaped like a skull.

"Leftover from Halloween," she said, lighting the skull, then blowing out the match. "There should be a Santa in there too."

Gordon found the jolly red candle and handed it to Mick. The kitchen still looked creepy in the flickering candlelight, but at least they could navigate again. "Let's try the basement," Mick said.

The door to the basement was at the far end of the kitchen, next to the fridge. Gordon unbolted the door and looked down a steep set of stairs into darkness. "Careful with the candle going down the steps," Carla warned. "We don't want to burn the place down on our first night here."

"Only if we're lucky."

"What?"

"Never mind."

Mick led the way down the stairs, from the bottom of which their candles revealed all but the farthest corners of the cavelike basement. The ceiling was braced with wooden beams, and was low enough that Mick, the tallest of them, had to stoop slightly as he stepped past the narrow archway at the foot of the steps. Their coal-eating dragon, already christened "Smog," chugged noisily just beyond intersecting rings of candlelight. Wispy cob-webs hung from the beams and brushed against their faces, much to the annoyance of Mick, who hated spiders with a passion he seldom displayed over anything else.

"Jesus Christ," Gordon whispered as he looked around.

They had been here before, of course. In the daylight. With the landlord. That had been some weeks ago though and things had obviously changed since then. A tattered mattress occupied the center of the basement floor, surrounded by garbage: bottles, pop cans, candy wrappers, newspapers, cereal boxes, and bones. A small window located just above eye-level was conspicuously bro-ken; the missing glass piled in a heap by Gordon's feet. The base-ment smelled of urine and recent habitation.

"Someone's been living here."

"Obviously," Gordon said, then regretted it. Carla looked upset enough. To be honest, he wasn't exactly thrilled with this devel-opment himself.

"Who do you think it is?" Carla wondered aloud.

"Just a vagrant," Mick said. "Nobody we'd know." Gordon kicked the scattered debris aside. "I don't know," he said. "Re-member that weirdo who used to hang out on campus? The one who claimed to be a 'professor of black magic'?"

"You mean Dmitri the Dark?"

"Yeah. That's the one."

"I never figured out how Geraldo missed him," Mick com-mented. "What a flake."

"Creepy, though," Carla said. "I remember, once, he crashed a party at Higginson, back when it was an all-girls dorm, and started showing off this Nazi dagger of his, which he told us he had—get this—'sanctified in a ceremony of blood and sperm.' Ugh!" Her pale face grimaced, as though she were digesting a rancid memory. "Gordon, you don't really think this is him?"

He examined the trash with an imaginary magnifying glass. "It's a possibility. He used to sleep in the library until Security finally ran him off campus." Should I go on? Gordon wondered. Why was he trying to spook everybody like this anyway? Then again, when you're standing in the dark holding a burning skull, what else are you supposed to do? "I heard he attacked someone."

"That was just a rumor," Mick said. "Besides, Dmitri was hardly the only transient in town."

"Or the only psycho," observed Carla, obviously getting into the spirit of the thing. "There was that guy who used to perch on the roof of the dining hall, pretending to be a gargoyle."

"Only during finals," Mick said. "He was just a harmless, stressed-out chem major."

Party pooper, Gordon thought. "Don't forget the Hillside Strangler. He eventually ended up in Bellingham."

"And the Green River Killer . . . damn, now you've got me doing it!" Mick's large fingers sank into the warm wax Santa in his fist. Claws into Claus. He trudged into the web-strewn shadows, searching for the fuse box. "What are you trying to do, Gordon? Fill us full of nightmares?"

There are three possible answers, Gordon thought. One. I'm putting on a hell of a show for my own amusement, and maybe Carla's. Two, I'm getting totally paranoid in my old age. Three, there really is a homicidal maniac living here, and we'll all be dead by morning.

■　■　■

The circuit breakers proving inscrutable and intractable, the three sophomores decided to call it quits for the night. Electrical repairs and further unpacking seemed better suited to daylight, so they carefully navigated the stairs to the second floor, where—oh, un-collegiate luxury!—they each had a bedroom of their own. Gordon's was at the end of the hall, farthest from the stairs: a bare, rectangular chamber, about one-fourth as spacious as the basement, lacking both furnishings and light. The uncurtained window opposite the bedroom door offered a dim view of the evergreens in the empty lot behind the house, along with the meager comfort of knowing that very few chain-saw cannibals were likely to come smashing through that particular window, not when an interior stairway was so much more convenient.

As he unrolled his sleeping bag in the middle of the floor, Gordon was not looking forward to the first night in his new room. This house is a stranger, he thought. And if everyone knew that you shouldn't talk to a stranger, how much more foolhardy it must be to actually go and *live* in one.

Still, he blew out the skull before undressing and crawling into
the sleeping bag like a skinny pink hermit crab retreating into a
padded, polyester shell. The best he could hope for, he knew, was
an instant descent into dreamless sleep, hopefully to rise again
with the dawn. No such luck. For an uncertain, insomniac interval
he lay on his back, looking past the foot of the bag at the rustling
pines outside his window. A hint of moonlight suffused the cloudy
sky beyond, and the trees were silhouetted against a purple background like monster triffids with dozens of vibrating, venomous
spikes. He wondered how the campus gargoyle had made it to his
rooftop perch, and realized that the would-be Quasimodo must
have climbed trees much like these. Harmless, Mick had said? A
likely story. Gordon rolled over in his hundredth futile attempt to
physically shift himself into unconsciousness. How in the world
had he been talked into this? It was all Carla's fault.

His face buried in the bag's insulation, unable to see the twisting trees or empty room, Gordon was betrayed by his ears. Noises,
vague and unidentifiable, swirled around his blinded awareness;
he "saw" them in his mind as a shifting cloud of ghostly insects—
not fireflies, *whisperflies*. Christmas is definitely over, he thought,
for this was sure no Silent Night. Noises from outside his window.
Noises from above. Noises from the other side of the wall on his
right . . .

Wait. Carla was on the other side of that wall. He concentrated
on the sounds coming from that direction, pushing the other whispers out of the way so that he could listen more closely to what
he now distinctly recognized as the sound of someone moving in
the room next door. Not footsteps; the sounds were too irregular
for that. Someone crawling, perhaps, or struggling. Could Carla
be doing sit-ups at this hour? Or having a bad dream?

Slowly, trying hard not to make any noises of his own, Gordon
sat up in his sleeping bag, listening. The cool air chilled his exposed neck and shoulders. Dammit, why couldn't he hear more
clearly? Carla could be in trouble. In the dark, he pulled on a ratty
pair of jeans and tiptoed to the not-quite soundproof wall between
his room and Carla's. Just as he placed his ear against the rough
(and surprisingly cold) surface of the wall, Carla suddenly cried
out. He heard an unmistakable gasp, then silence.

Jesus Christ, he thought, scrambling for the skull-candle on the floor, searching his pockets for a match. She's being strangled! With shaky fingers he found the wick and lighted it. The skull glowed: a miniature campfire in the icy blackness of the room. Lifting the skull to the level of his chin, Gordon quietly crept into the hallway outside the door. Insanely he found himself afraid to make even the littlest noise necessary to breathe. This is crazy, he thought. If there is a madman in her room, why aren't I charging to the rescue? And if there isn't, who am I afraid will hear me?

If. That was the problem, wasn't it? That was why he wasn't calling to Mick for help. What if he was wrong? Standing outside Carla's door, the hot wax flowing off the skull so that he constantly had to adjust his grip to avoid being burned by the viscous yellow rivulets, Gordon found himself paralyzed by uncertainty. In the slippery light of the candle, it seemed too easy to dismiss what moments before had been a clear, high-resolution image of Carla, and then the rest of them, being stabbed or strangled or smothered in their sleep by Dmitri the Dark or someone even more malignant. By the invader who had taken possession of what was supposed to be their home.

He stood outside her door, listening but hearing nothing.

Either Carla has rolled over and gone back to sleep, he thought, or there's someone else in there, listening to me listening for him. I should knock on the door, get this over with one way or another, but what if I'm wrong? How am I going to explain this to Carla? Against his will, Gordon remembered that other night, a few months back when, fired up by too many beers and a steamy movie on TV, he had called her up in the middle of the night, waking her from what was no doubt a sound sleep, and then babbled incoherently about how much he wanted to come over right that minute and . . . God, how he'd made a fool of himself! Humiliating was not a strong enough word, and the worst part had been having to face her the next morning at breakfast.

He'd rather meet a psychotic killer than go through that again. Almost.

He leaned toward her door, straining to hear. The old cliché was true: it was quiet, too quiet. Even if Carla was sleeping peacefully, she should be making more noise than this. There was something terribly *deliberate* about this unnatural, prolonged silence.

The basement, Gordon thought. He would have come from the

basement. Had they left the door to the basement unlatched after they'd climbed back up the stairs to the kitchen? Gordon couldn't remember. He was pretty sure he hadn't, but less so about Mick and Carla. It had been really dark in the kitchen, even with the candles.

There was only one way to be sure—about all of it. Stepping cautiously upon the old timber floor, he turned away from Carla's door and headed for the stairs. Scanning the shadows, holding on to the burning skull with one hand and the railing with the other, he descended to the first floor. The empty living room seemed unusually cavernous now that midnight was past. He was afraid to glance at the tall, uncovered windows on his left; it was too easy to imagine that heart-stopping moment when he saw a crazed, wild-eyed figure looking back at him from the other side of the glass. He could see the whole scene in his mind, feel his breath catching in anticipation.

No question about it. He had definitely seen too many slasher movies.

By contrast with the bleak vastness of the living room, the kitchen, with its counters and cupboards and stove, was reassuringly cozy. The light of the candle exposed almost the entire room; there were not as many black corners from which an attacker could come charging. What was he most afraid of, Gordon asked himself, the monsters in shadows, who couldn't be seen, or the monsters in the windows, who could?

From where he was standing, just inside the kitchen, the door to the basement appeared to be closed. But was it locked? It was too dark to tell.

All things considered, he thought, I'd rather not see the monsters.

Still, sliding his feet softly against the spillproof tile floor, he approached the basement door. He held his candle far in front of him, in hopes of being able to spot something before he got too close. He was glad that the kitchen floor was tiled, for surely his shuffling pace would have filled his bare feet with painful slivers on any of the rougher wooden floors in the house. Finally he was near enough to the door to cast the heart of the candle's glow upon it.

Not only was the door unlatched, it was open by a crack.

Oh God. Gordon expelled a long, slow breath. He experienced a sudden urge to run, to shout, to wake up Mick and (hopefully) Carla, if only just to share this anxiety with someone else. Instead, he pulled the door open and started down the steps.

Descent after descent, he thought. Just like What's-her-name in *Psycho*—the one who stayed out of the shower—when she went down into the fruit cellar to find Norman's mother, even though everyone in the audience is screaming at her to run the other way. Why did she keep going? Gordon understood now. Momentum. The urge to completion, to see things through to the end, maybe even to wreak a little mayhem of your own instead of staying perpetually on the defensive. Who is least likely to survive: the hero or the monster? Neither, he realized. It's the born victims who get chewed to death every time. The extras, the cannon fodder, the romantic lead's best friend . . .

His shadow followed Gordon down the creaky basement steps, whose peeling paint scratched his feet and lodged between his toes. Cobwebs fell in strands from the sloping ceiling above, too thin and insubstantial to cast shadows of their own but solid enough to sizzle dangerously whenever the candle drew too near. The basement was noticeably cooler than the rest of the house; Gordon could feel the temperature drop a few microdegrees with each step that took him farther down toward the trash-littered lair of their unwanted visitor. It was the architectural layout, though, that was really sadistic. The stairway was flanked by a partial interior wall, so that there was no way to see the rest of what was down there until you actually reached the bottom (just like this), turned to the right (just like this), took a deep breath, and saw . . .

At first, nothing. Just the cramped clutter of mattress and garbage, wooden beams and heaps of burned-out coal and ash. And the shadows, of course, who alone knew what evil lurked, et cetera. Gordon enjoyed a few frantic heartbeats of relief—until the furnace came noisily to life with an unexpected clank, startling him and yanking his attention to the most distant, blackest corner of the basement, where, outlined by the red glow that escaped the furnace gratings, a dim but definite figure rose up from behind sloping dunes of discarded ash.

Yes! It wasn't his imagination. He could *see* it.

Gordon screamed, an incomprehensible outpouring of rough, senseless, throat-tearing noises. He stumbled backward, almost falling. The figure lurched toward him, its face lost in darkness, its arms reaching for Gordon, about to touch him. No, he thought, stop it! A newspaper headline flashed through his head: STUDENT MURDERED IN HOME.

"Wait . . ." he began; then the figure slammed violently into him, and the back of Gordon's head collided with the wall. The force and speed of the attack left him stunned and breathless. The smell of dirty hair and skin, like the dry and dusty musk of baked blacktop, filled his nostrils and mouth. A numbing ache spread from a sharp, bright nova of pain at the base of his skull, and his glasses tumbled from his nose as a clenched and bony fist struck his stomach like a missile.

It wasn't like the movies, he discovered. Real violence wasn't something visual, something choreographed and carefully lighted. It was a force that tore at your flesh, smashed into your bones, and reduced you to a mere solid object buffeted by other objects, harder and more relentless.

Shoved against the basement wall, his world a blur of shadows and sudden shocks, Gordon didn't even notice the burning skull slip from his fingers.

Then the figure, the opposing force, went away, and he collapsed forward onto his hands and knees. My glasses, he thought. I have to find my glasses so I can see who it is, Dmitri or the gargoyle. First though, he needed just a minute, please, to recover, to let his head stop hurting, to spit the blood and saliva from his mouth and try to breathe again. Just a couple more minutes . . . He shut his eyes. He smelled smoke.

"Jesus, Gordon, the place is on fire!"

He looked up to see Carla standing over him, Mick running past. "My glasses," he whispered, and moments later felt the plastic frames placed in his hand. As his vision came back into focus, so too did he gradually become aware again of where he was and what was happening.

His candle had landed amid a mess of grocery sacks and old newspapers. Not all the trash had ignited yet, but already a small fire was consuming the scattered candy wrappers and cereal boxes and sending red-hot flakes of burning paper adrift on the air. Wearing only a dark blue bathrobe, Mick beat down the flames with an old, skeletal rake; an orange and yellow gout of fire erupted out of an empty paint can only a foot away from his bare leg. "Shit!" he cried, jumping backward. Thick white smoke poured out of much of the soggier trash, transforming the basement into a foggy hell worthy of Jack the Ripper or the Werewolf of London. His head throbbing, Gordon looked for his attacker and saw only his housemates. There are three possibilities, he realized. One, the invader had run off before Mick and Carla arrived. Two, he *became* Mick and Carla. Three, he was still here . . . somewhere.

"Gordon, are you all right?" Carla asked. She crouched beside him, wearing only a nightgown and fog.

"Get some water!" Mick shouted at them. "Hurry, we're going to need some water!"

Gordon stared into the spreading flames. All that from one little skull . . . ?

"Will *somebody* get me some fucking water?"

That snapped him out of it, finally. Lurching to his feet, he followed Carla up the stairs to the kitchen sink.

■   ■   ■

Bellingham is a damp and moldy town. In the end, it took only four trips, seven pots of tap water, and a pitcher of sacrificed pink lemonade to extinguish the blaze. The bottom half of the wall beneath the broken window was somewhat blackened, but otherwise the structural integrity of Altered Estates had been preserved; ditto for Gordon, whom Carla, in her best Florence Nightingale mode, determined to have received a bump and not a concussion. By dawn, there was even time for explanations.

"Are you sure you saw somebody?" Mick asked.

"No, I hit myself on the back of the head . . . of course I saw somebody!"

"Well, technically," Carla pointed out, "the only thing that hit your head was a wall. And that was a stationary object."

"And Dmitri, or whoever, shoved me into the wall. Same difference."

"I know," she said soothingly, checking once more the bandage behind his ears. In the absence of any other furniture, they were seated in a circle atop the vagrant's abandoned mattress. Carla had draped a frayed yellow quilt over the stained surface of the mattress so they wouldn't be too grossed out. At the same time, she had retrieved a bathrobe of her own from one of the boxes upstairs, presumably not, Gordon assumed, for fearing of grossing out the rest of them. That would be impossible, especially where he was concerned.

"We found the front door open when we came downstairs," she continued, "and somebody made a lot of noise down here, even after you screamed."

"I screamed?"

"You screamed like a gorilla with a rhino up his ass," Mick said, with a grin so wide that Gordon wondered if he'd been drinking.

"Well, it worked for Tarzan. . . ."

"The bum probably just panicked, then decided to get the hell out of here."

"Yeah, you can be pretty terrifying in the dark, Gordo." Carla reached out and ran her finger along one of his ribs. "Probably got one look at that skinny bod of yours and decided the Living Dead had come to get him."

Gordon wasn't sure if he was being insulted or flirted with, but he laughed anyway. They all did, even Mick.

It was moments like this, Gordon decided, that would make this whole "Altered Estates" venture worthwhile.

Maybe.

They boarded up the basement window right away, then put another bolt on the door in the kitchen. By midterms, a few weeks later, the house was filled with secondhand furniture, what Gordon termed "Early American garage sale." He had to admit that there were advantages to living off-campus, like relief from blaring stereos and biweekly fire alarms, and even though he still woke up sometimes in the middle of the night, he wasn't hearing strange noises anymore, from either below or the room next door. In time, he even got up the nerve to ask Carla about the gasps and commotion he'd thought he'd heard that first night.

"Dreams," she said.

"About what?"

She smiled slyly. "I'm not telling."

Ah, Carla! So tantalizing and bewildering. He still didn't know exactly where he stood with her, not that there was much chance to find out with Mick perpetually hanging about. A great housemate, and easy to get along with, but it was undeniably awkward living with the archetypal "third wheel." If only Mick would fall for some alluring coed who lived on the other side of town; these late-night threesomes in front of *David Letterman* were idyllic as such things go, but a night alone with Carla, just the two of them . . . well, if nothing else, the suspense was killing him.

Nor were things always idyllic, for that matter. Despite their proven compatibility, trouble sometimes surfaced in paradise, like the time Gordon came home from a long night at the library to discover that Mick and Carla had fixed themselves an elaborate steak dinner, complete with veggies and dessert, and not even saved him any leftovers!

"We just felt in a cooking sort of mood, Gordo."

"Yeah, and we had no idea when or if you were coming home. I mean, it's not like we have any designated dinnertime."

"Might as well be back in the dorm," Carla said.

"Fine. Sure. I understand. But I am paying a third of the grocery bill around here, you know."

"If it really bothers you, Gordon, we can deduct the cost of the steaks from your share of the rent next month."

"No, don't bother." Gordon realized he sounded like a crabby old man; he felt a headache coming on. "That way madness lies. We don't want to end up rationing the beers and counting our Rice Crispies."

In the end, peace was restored, but he went to bed that night with a belly full of Top Ramen and undigested resentment. He understood now how so many happy marriages had run aground on household bills and budgets.

And then, of course, there was the Great Unicorn Incident. . . .

■   ■   ■

Gordon was upstairs typing an essay on Brian DePalma when he heard the front door swing shut. He briefly considered calling out to see which of his absent housemates had returned, but, no, he wasn't quite ready to call it quits on this paper yet. Maybe after a few more pages he could wander down and socialize.

Then Carla shouted from the foot of the stairs, "Gordon! Get down here!"

She sounded upset—and a little bit angry. Gordon had no idea what was up, but already he didn't like it. Uninvited, images of Dmitri the Dark astride a burning skull, brandishing a cum-stained knife, played in the multiplex of his mind. "What's the matter?" he asked as he bounced off the bottom step and skidded to a halt beside Carla.

"What happened to my unicorn?"

"Huh?" He looked across the living room, whose gummy black floor was now covered by an ersatz Arabian rug, at the small end table where, as recently as lunchtime, a foot-high crystal unicorn had posed with its glittering hooves raised up to paw the air. Now those hooves, along with the rest of the figurine, lay in pieces beneath the table. Gordon spotted a spiral horn, curiously unbroken, amid the other chips and fragments.

"At least you could have cleaned up the mess afterward," Carla said. "Not that there's any chance of putting it back together. You really did a number on it."

"It was fine the last time I saw it!" Gordon was genuinely appalled at the accusation. "Why the hell would I want to break it? I gave you that unicorn!"

"I'm not saying you did it on purpose, Gordon."

"I didn't do it at all!"

"You were the only person here this afternoon, weren't you? You must have at least heard something. That crystal looks like it's been dropped *and* stomped on.

She had a point, but since when had Carla become such a demon prosecutor? And of him, no less. "Maybe I was flushing the toilet when it happened."

"When what happened? Even if you didn't hear anything, that still begs the question: How did it get broken?" Carla's tone softened somewhat, and she sat down on the couch beside the unicorn's former perch. "Hey, if it was an accident, that's fine. I'm just trying to figure this thing out."

Gordon barely heard her. The logic of Carla's argument grabbed onto his aching brain and dragged it toward the only possible answer: Someone else, someone destructive, had been in the house today, and maybe still was.

Flames in the basement. A dark figure reaching out . . .

He dashed into the kitchen, cutting off Carla in the middle of a conciliatory sentence. Puzzled and momentarily speechless, she followed him and found Gordon staring at the door to the basement, tugging on the knob.

Both bolts were in place. The door wouldn't budge.

He must have got in some other way, Gordon decided. He turned to face Carla. "Dmitri . . . I mean, the man in the basement. He's back."

"Are you serious?"

"Who else could have broken it? You weren't here, Mick wasn't here, I didn't do it . . . who else could it be? It had to be him, right?" he challenged her. "Right?"

"I suppose," she said finally, but there was a doubt, a wariness, in her eyes that Gordon had never seen there before. He saw the same doubt in Mick's eyes later on when their other third came home that evening. Very well, he thought, don't believe me. I guess it's up to me to protect the both of you, whether you like it or not.

The very next day, Gordon bought a gun.

■   ■   ■

The newly acquired curtains over the windows made the kitchen and living room even darker than before. Flashlight in hand, Gordon stalked noiselessly through the sleeping house; his other hand held tightly onto the heavy gray pistol thrust deep into the pocket of his sweatshirt. The flashlight's beam patrolled before him, darting over the walls and furniture, scouting out the shadows where who-knows-what may hide. So far, Gordon had surprised nothing more than a small army of ghostly white silverfish who put on a convincing simulation of Brownian motion before disappearing back into the cracks along the kitchen counter. Still, he felt ready for anything.

Except maybe the sound, a few yards behind him, of floorboards creaking beneath a heavy tread.

His throat dried so fast he thought he was choking. The cold that raced over him, freezing him from inside out, shocked him in its intensity; he would have thrown up if he had had the strength or the time. Executing a graceless half-turn, he banged his elbow on the kitchen doorframe, barked an incoherent command at the approaching footsteps, and raised up the flashlight instead of the gun.

The beam caught Mick directly in the face. "Hey, watch the light, will you," he whispered, raising a hand against the glare. "And keep it down. Carla's been sound asleep for hours."

"Jesus Christ!" Gordon said hoarsely. His hand jerked away from the gun in his pocket. Mick would never know how close he came to being blown away. "You scared me to death. When you came up behind me . . . my heart is still racing!" And not just from the shock of Mick's sudden appearance. *God, what would I have done if I had shot him?*

Thankfully neither Mick nor Carla knew about the gun.

"I heard noises downstairs and thought I'd check them out," Mick said. "Tell you the truth, for a while there I even thought it might be that bogeyman of yours, Dmitri."

Since when did Dmitri become exclusively *my* bogeyman? Gordon wondered. Now that the panic and adrenaline were wearing off, he felt a little annoyed by Mick's attitude. Hey, there were lots of things he'd rather be doing than worrying about protecting the house from Dmitri. He was doing this for Mick, and Carla too.

"What are you doing down here anyway, Gordon? An attack of the midnight munchies?"

If I'm smart, he thought, I'll let it go at that. Instead, he held the flashlight between them so he could look Mick in the eye and said, "What am I doing? I'm doing the hard work of making sure that Dmitri, or whoever it is that is sharing this house with us, doesn't get away with anything too terrible while the rest of you are getting a good night's sleep."

"You're joking, right? Since when did we need a security guard around here?"

"Remember the unicorn?"

"That was over a week ago. Anyway, it was just some dumb accident. I know why I'm standing here in the middle of the night. I heard a strange noise, which turned out to be you. Have you heard anything . . . besides me?"

"Not yet. I mean, not really. But that doesn't mean we don't have a major problem here. I didn't make up that lair in the cellar. I was there when that weirdo attacked me!"

"Ssshh, keep it down." Mick adopted a more sympathetic tone. "That was a shitty thing to happen to you on our first night here,

but you can't let it make you crazy. We've checked out the basement several times since then without finding a trace of him. The
bum's probably selling his blood in Spokane now, or hiding out
in somebody else's basement."

"The unicorn . . ."

Mick peered at Gordon over the glowing, upturned lens of the
flashlight. Feeling unaccountably exposed, Gordon was tempted
to flick off the light. "How long have you been doing this nightly
patrol shtick?"

"Since last Friday. On and off."

"Mostly on, I'll bet. You look like hell, Gordon."

"Thanks a lot."

"No, I'm serious. You're shaking, you've got bags under your
eyes . . . look, did I ever tell you about my brother?"

"What about him?"

Mick leaned against the nearest wall; Gordon hoped this wasn't
going to be a long story. His head was starting to hurt again.

"My older brother, James, drives trucks for a living. Long-
distance hauls. Sometimes he'll drive for days at a time on little
or no sleep. After a while, he told me, on the really long trips, he
starts to hallucinate behind the wheel. He says he sees people,
mostly friends and family, standing in the center of the road. He
runs them down, too."

"Wonderful." Gordon yawned. "But aside from giving me serious second thoughts about driving on the highway, at least when
your brother's on the road, I'm not sure what this has to do with
the Dmitri situation."

"The moral is," Mick said, with too much emphasis, "sleep
deprivation is a terrible thing."

So is getting murdered in your bed, Gordon thought.

The next day in class though, he had to admit he was feeling
the strain. He felt dull, logy; his eyes burned with the effort it
took to keep them open, but whenever he closed them, just for a
second, he seemed to lose minutes at a time. That today's "lab"
consisted of sitting in the dark during a screening of the old, silent
version of *The Phantom of the Opera*, minus musical accompani-
ment, did not make it any easier to stay awake. When he dozed
off during the Masque of the Red Death (his favorite part!) and
then snapped to attention to discover the Phantom dead, the lov-

ers reunited, and the lights in the lecture hall coming up, he decided to call it a day.

Too bad he couldn't sleep through the walk home. With spring only weeks away, Bellingham remained cold and uncomfortable. The noxious smell of the paper plant down by the harbor permeated the air, leaving a bad taste in Gordon's mouth. His right eye began to throb, a sure sign of a migraine on the way. Hands tucked within the sleeves of his jacket, he staggered downhill to Altered Estates. The run-down house, with its yard full of brown, dying weeds, had seldom seemed so inviting.

Be it ever so desolate, he thought, there's no place like home.

Fatigue made him clumsy, and he dropped his keys three times before finally getting the front door open. He pushed it quietly shut behind him, too exhausted to close it with any more noise or enthusiasm. I will be unconscious, he promised, within five seconds of hitting the bed. First, however, a couple of aspirin.

Procuring tablets in the bathroom, he wandered slowly into the kitchen for a glass of water. When he spotted the basement door, his aching, reddened eyes grew wider than they had been all day.

The door to Dmitri's den was unlocked and propped open with a brick.

Oh God, he thought. Not again. He considered calling out, but, no, there was no reason to alert the intruder until he, Gordon, was good and ready.

Slipping off his shoes, he tiptoed upstairs as quickly as he could and retrieved the pistol from a shoe box at the bottom of his closet. Then he checked both Mick and Carla's rooms. They weren't home. Probably just as well, he concluded.

Gordon returned to the kitchen and approached the half-opened door. Gently he eased it open the rest of the way, until he could look down the entire length of the stairs ahead. The basement lights were dark, but a red, flickering glow came from the interior of the cellar, just out of sight.

Flames. Fire. Fists, and falls, and pain.

Gordon started down the steps. Partway down, he heard a series of harsh, breathy moans. Like a nonsilent phantom, he thought. Or a housemate in distress. Holy rerun, Batman; here we go again. This time, however, he was armed and dangerous.

The gun in his hand was the center of his being, as if he were holding on to his heart and not a loaded weapon. He placed a finger against his temple and felt the veins pulsing under the skin. The angry pounding within his skull beat over and over until he felt sick to his stomach. Trembling despite the comfort of the pistol, he stealthily rounded the corner at the foot of the stairs and gazed at the tableau before him.

The dim, dancing light came from Carla's other holiday candle: a miniature wax Santa Claus poised atop a stack of wooden cartons at the far end of the basement. Candlelight shone down upon the fresh black sheets that now covered Dmitri's mattress. Gordon noticed an empty bottle of disinfectant lying abandoned in a corner.

Mick was lying on his back upon the mattress, his head pointed toward the furnace against the opposite wall. He was nude except for the silky black blindfold over his eyes. His arms were tucked under him, almost hidden from view, as though they were tied (handcuffed?) together behind his back. Carla sat astride his legs, her back to Gordon, her lush red hair falling over her shoulders, as white and bare and delectably smooth as her back and buttocks. Her fingers stroked Mick's straining erection and coyly ambled across his stocky chest, around his nipples, across his ribs, and down to tangle themselves in the wiry brown hair above his testicles.

The veins in Mick's biceps and neck stood out as he rocked and groaned beneath her.

I knew it, Gordon thought. No, that's not true. I didn't know anything. . . .

Carla's unclothed body was even more stunning than he had imagined. She held Mick's torso down with both hands and laughed in a way that both tortured and provoked.

"At last, good sir, I have you in my power! How fare you, gentle knight, in this, my Dungeon of Delight?"

"Fuck, Carla, enough with the games already," Mick pleaded. Sweat ran from his forehead to soak the blindfold beneath.

"What's that, milord? Do you yield already to my dark designs?" She spit upon her palm and rubbed the moistened flesh over the red, engorged head of Mick's penis.

"I yield! I yield!" Mick struggled visibly to free his hands. "For Chrissakes, Carla, hurry up before I come!"

"Very well, then. I shall grant you your last request."

Carla shifted forward, and Gordon had a glimpse of her breasts, taut and oh-so-touchable, before she lowered herself onto his best friend and onetime roommate. The impassioned gasp that escaped her lips was all the worse for being unmistakably out of character.

He had to look away, at the incongruous Christmas candle, at the wavering fingertip of flame above Santa's cap, of anything but the sight of Carla and Mick screwing away on those freshly purchased ebony sheets. And so *tacky*, he tried to tell himself: junior league S & M by way of D & D. A couple of college kids playing at decadence. It was embarrassing, really.

Oh Jesus, he thought, his eyes tearing. Why him? Why not me?

He stared at the candle flame. He wouldn't, couldn't, look at them, but he could still hear them: breathing hard, whispering I-love-you's and indecent requests. The sound of sticky, sweaty bodies pulling apart and coming together again. His head felt as if it were going to explode. He almost wished it would. Where, he wondered, is Dmitri now that I need him? The cold metal gun hung heavy in his hand.

The burning Santa filled his vision, bright and beautiful and inescapable. He knows if you've been bad or good, Gordon remembered. He knows what evil lurks in the hearts of men.

Flames. Shadows. Candlelight. Fire.

Gordon raised the gun. He thought he heard footsteps on the steps behind him. He felt Dmitri take hold of his hand.

Fire.

■   ■   ■

"No, I'm sorry. You have the wrong number. Mick and Carla don't live here anymore."

Gordon hung up the phone. When were people going to get the message? Carla and Mick were gone. They had eloped to Alaska. That's what he had told everyone. That's what had happened.

He had new housemates now. Like Dmitri over there on the couch, polishing his Hitlerian blade and singing Christmas carols in April. And the gargoyle, bounding about on the roof or swinging in the trees outside Gordon's window every night. Even the Phantom, who he had thought was dead but who was looking much better now that he had finally had the last laugh on those smug, selfish, deceitful lovers.

This wasn't such a bad house, Gordon realized. True, as the weather grew warmer, there was an increasingly unpleasant smell coming from the basement, but that was okay. Nobody ever went down there. Nobody must ever go down there.

There were still three possibilities, he thought. One, he could move on someday and leave all this behind him, but wait, that wouldn't work. Other people would move in then. New tenants would unlock the basement door. Two, he could try to explain to someone about Dmitri and what he had done, but the only person who understood about Dmitri was Dmitri. Three, he could find another housemate, maybe a woman, to move in with them. Except . . .

There were no more possibilities. He had to like it here.

These were his housemates, and Altered Estates was his home. From now on.

THE CALCULATOR

Joe Hensley

Joe Hensley was a federal judge for many years, thus giving his Roback series a lawyerly authenticity. Joe has produced some very fine fiction in virtually every one of the genres. But his real fortre is the suspense novel. He has quietly amassed an important body of work, and will someday have all the readers he so richly deserves.

THAT WAS THE YEAR CYRIL RATCHFORD ABANDONED PRACTICING law until Hysell hired him for a dollar. It was a year that began badly, with Judge Evans granting a guardianship of the person on Ratchford. Ratchford felt no anger at Evans, who was an old friend. He even admitted during the judge's hearing that he had been drinking heavily since Connie had died, that his legs had recently given out, and that he'd not been eating properly—or hardly at all, for that matter.

Judge Evans appointed one of the young partners in Ratchford's law firm as guardian, and together they plotted and sent Ratchford to the Sunset Years Nursing Home. There he began to mend—or mend as much as can be expected of a seventy-year-old man with a bad liver and a problem heart.

Sunset Years was all right with Ratchford. The food was good and plentiful and his appetite returned. The attendants were friendly, although Ratchford quickly learned one didn't leave items worth stealing in view. His legs came back a little so that soon, with two stout canes and much effort, he could slowly get around.

The nursing home was full of old people and problem people, many of them forgotten or abandoned. Once Ratchford was well he soon got to know most of them and found they were people who'd lived uninteresting lives and were awaiting routine deaths. Ratchford, who'd spent his own life in deadly combat in court-rooms, found they mostly bored him.

There were minor exceptions. Down the hall there was a large old man who hit at people. He hit at attendants, nurses, doctors, and other patients—he was impartial about it. He liked to lie in wait and spring out from behind things, laughing and striking mean little blows.

The second time he did it to Ratchford, Ratchford thumped him with one of the canes. The large old man cried a little and seemed confused and hurt about it, and refused to lie in wait for Ratchford thereafter.

There was also a lady who had something growing inside her head and could no longer communicate. She talked but none of the words associated or made sense. Now and then she would stumble into Ratchford's room, fall into the lone chair, and blather away, very bewildered and earnest about it.

Ratchford found himself, more and more as time wound down for him, enmeshed in a vague ennui. He resisted attempts to get him back to the office. When he was asked if he wanted to move elsewhere he recoiled from the idea. Sunset Years was home.

He did have his guardian instruct the nursing home manage-ment that he should be allowed to wander outside by himself.

Outside was where he remet John Hysell.

■　■　■

Sunset Years had once been a resort hotel-motel until cooler win-ters and newer motels had forced it into receivership. It had then been picked up by the nursing home chain which now operated it. Ratchford thought his firm might have handled some of the transactions.

Across the road from the rambling main nursing home building he found a path that led down between huge beach houses to the sea. Partway down the path, leading from the largest mansion— now in disrepair and seemingly abandoned—someone had built a new boardwalk continuing to the beach and terminating in a roofed lookout complete with a weathered picnic table. The lookout was open from floor to roof, but the breeze was pleasant there and the roof kept the sun from being too fierce.

So during the days, to escape the talker and to avoid the accusing eyes of the bully man, Ratchford would take a book and walk laboriously to the lookout. Sometimes he'd read, other times he sat watching the birds and the waves and the passing boats, sharing the luck of occasional fishermen and observing the beach walkers who passed.

The third time he was there John Hysell came. He came from the huge, half-ruined house, and Ratchford didn't know him at first. He rode in an electric wheelchair fabricated of shiny aluminum, and he operated it smartly. He wheeled into the lookout and smiled at Ratchford. He was carrying an ornate box on his blanket-covered lap. In one shirt pocket Ratchford spied a thin battery-powered calculator.

"You play checkers?" he asked.

Ratchford saw that Hysell's legs were useless under the thin lap blanket. His left arm was also affected. But the right arm still worked some and, above the neck, he seemed all right—smiling and waiting for an answer.

"I play checkers, chess, cribbage, gin rummy, and anything else you can think of." Connie had been a game fanatic.

Hysell's face tilted. "Don't I know you?"

"Cyril Ratchford. I am—or was—a lawyer."

Hysell nodded. "You did some work for me years back. And I built you a house. I'm John Hysell."

Ratchford remembered. Hysell had been a young, intent engineer-builder. Ratchford had later heard Hysell had made a fortune in construction and acquired a reputation as a man who did things right. He had built Connie's dream house when Ratchford could barely afford dreams, and it had continued to be her dream house until she died. In Florida, where anything built could be sold, Ratchford had been grateful.

"I've been watching you from what the last hurricane left of the balcony," Hysell said, pointing up. "I like the way you swing down here on those canes—like it was an effort but worth it. I'm not allowed out by my sweet new wife, Miss Two-Ton, but today she went to a bingo party and by now she's probably stuffed herself full of ice cream and cake. It was easy to sneak past the maid. She takes a nap every time Miss T-T goes out."

"Your wife doesn't understand you," Ratchford said, smiling.

"Very perceptive," Hysell said, smiling in return. He appraised Ratchford—the expensive clothes, the white hair. "She'd like *you*," he said.

"Is that good?"

"No, not really," Hysell said. "She has a history of not picking her males for permanence." He thought for a minute, looking away so that Ratchford could no longer see his face. "Can I hire you?"

"Perhaps. I'm still a lawyer, although I've been inactive."

Hysell found a worn dollar in one of his pockets. He handed it up. "Consider yourself retained."

"For what?"

"What I really need is someone to help me kill my wife. Would you do that? No?" He shook his head. "I shouldn't have asked. I can read the shock in your eyes."

"I'm only a lawyer," Ratchford said. He looked down at the troubled man. "I can be hired only for that kind of work." He hesitated and then put the dollar in his pocket. "Have been hired," he amended.

Hysell sighed. "I've never really understood your profession. I suppose that now if anything happened to her you'd report me, wouldn't you?"

"No, I wouldn't. Some lawyers would. It's a technical point of ethics. I'm going to treat what you told me as a privileged communication."

Hysell nodded. "Well, if you won't help and you won't tell, that puts us back into the checkers area." He handed over the lap box. Ratchford opened it and found an exquisite folding checkerboard.

"The checkers are in that little drawer. We turn them over for kings." He smiled. "I shouldn't stay too long. Next time I'll sneak away as soon as she goes. But she doesn't go often. She's the meanest, most calculating woman I've ever known. My third wife." He lost the smile.

"I see."

"I remember when we were younger you did a lot of criminal work, Mr. Ratchford. Did you ever defend anyone accused of killing his wife?"

Ratchford nodded. "Many times."

Hysell shook his head. "It's such a problem. She's big and strong. I bumped her once accidentally with my chair and she stopped me cold. I put some stuff in her wine, some corrosive cleaner, but she spit it out. She watches me all the time so I can't go out and buy a gun." He shook his head. "I used to be a good engineer. Now I can't do anything but operate this infernal chair and play with my calculator. It lowers the possibilities. So I suppose she'll just sit and wait for me to die." He shook his head. "She won't even let me live someplace decent." He looked up at the old wind-damaged house. "She inherited that from her last husband."

"Divorce her," Ratchford said.

"She told me if I try to divorce her she'll hold it up and maybe get me committed. Probably to a place like your Sunset Years. Could she do that?"

"Perhaps." Ratchford considered the ruined man before him. "Maybe even probably." He remembered the frustrating years in practice, the slowness, the frequent futility. "Getting a divorce can take a while, but Sunset Years is all right."

"I wouldn't mind that much, but I don't want her to realize it. Not too long ago some policemen came looking for her and questioned her about one of her husbands who died. I think she knows she has to treat me carefully." He looked out at the sea, a long look. "When we were married she talked me into putting a lot of things into joint title. When I die my two kids will get next to nothing.

"She put on almost a hundred pounds after I had my stroke. She can let me die, but I think right now she's afraid to do more. So she'll outwait me, if she doesn't eat herself to death. She went on a diet when I first met her. That was when I imagined she loved me. Now she picks and punishes and argues, trying to hasten me along. And she eats and eats." He shook his head, sick and bewildered. "How did a smart engineer wind up in a mess like this?"

"Why not make her mad enough to put you in Sunset Years?"

Hysell nodded and smiled craftily. "I'll bet that's where she'd put me. She's too smart to let me get far out of sight, too fat and lazy to want to travel far to see me dying. Sunset Years would be convenient." He gave Ratchford an odd, calculating look. "She'd see you there too. While she's involved in that maybe I could . . ."

All of it meant nothing to Ratchford, but Hysell had been a joy to Connie in building her house. He owed him semi-free advice and counsel for that.

"You can try," he said.

■   ■   ■

A few days later Ratchford found Hysell as the newest resident of Sunset Years, ensconced in a double room with a man named Schmidt who continually muttered terrible things about his family. Ratchford had thought Schmidt pitiful and had avoided the man's room. Schmidt's family were all dead.

Hysell smiled up at him from a bed. "She took my wheelchair away when we first started arguing, but I'll get it back. She's got some tax papers I have to sign and she's afraid to forge my signature." He nodded. "Look in my nightstand drawer."

Ratchford did. Inside was a deck of plastic playing cards and a fancy cribbage board.

"You're better at checkers than I am, but I'm going to beat you to death playing cribbage," Hysell announced. He punched some numbers on the ever-present calculator. "The odds are two to one."

■   ■   ■

They were playing that afternoon when Mella Hysell came visiting.

"Who are you?" she asked Ratchford from the door. Her face was all arched eyebrows and full cheeks, but Ratchford could see she was a handsome woman. Even far overweight she'd never be ugly—blimpish, but very pretty. She looked thirty years younger than Hysell.

Ratchford stood up haltingly. She watched him with eyes that seemed sympathetic.

"My name's Cyril Ratchford. Your husband was instructing me in a game called cribbage." He smiled at her. He'd been charming juries all his life.

"And you live here?" she asked, smiling back.

"Temporarily," Ratchford said.

She fussed around Hysell's bed, fluffing the pillows, straightening the sheets, all the time watching Ratchford.

"I brought those papers," she told Hysell in a low, intent voice. "Sign them now and I'll bring over your wheelchair."

"Bring my chair and *then* I'll sign," Hysell answered.

She nodded, still watching Ratchford, who was beginning to feel like a snake being eyed by a mongoose. "I started my diet today," she said to both men.

Hysell laughed. "I'll bet."

She gave him a baleful look. "Well, I did. And you know when I make my mind up to it I can do anything." She calculated him and the room. "Be nice and I'll bring you home."

"It's more restful here," Hysell demurred. "Or it will be when I get my chair."

"You'll get your chair when you come home."

Hysell smiled. "I'll sign the papers then too."

She smiled. "Whatever will Mr. Ratchford think of us—quarreling in front of him." She nodded at Ratchford. "He argues with me sometimes, but he knows what Momma says is best."

Ratchford smiled politely.

■   ■   ■

After she'd gone, Hysell seemed unwilling to go back to the cribbage game. He was pensive.

"Cyril," he said, "you must know some criminals. Couldn't you contact someone for me to hire? I know I can't last a lot longer."

Ratchford shook his head. "Let's suppose I did. If you made a deal, in law, I could be as guilty as you. Besides, your wife doesn't seem so bad. I think you're exaggerating."

Hysell gave him a penetrating glance. "She was interested in you, just as I predicted. By the time she sees you again she'll have checked you out. She took one look at your white hair and decided she was going to lose weight." He nodded. "She did that for me too. She was married then, to a man with a bad heart. He died shortly after I met her."

"You keep saying things like that. You talk about police and such. Are you saying she killed her last husband?"

"All I'm telling you are my suspicions. When we were married, for example, she admitted to two previous marriages. From what she's let slip and from what I've deduced since then, I've got to be at least number five or six. Those earlier husbands had to pass out of the picture somehow." He shook his head. "She's a creature for our time, Cyril. Florida abounds with old people. Mella's especially apt at caging the males of the species. She becomes impatient when she's not hunting. So I must watch myself and plan." He smiled. "One thing's for sure—she'll lose weight now."

"Many people diet."

Hysell shook his head. "Mella loves to eat. She'll lose now for one reason only. She means to impress you."

"I quite probably don't have as much time left on this earth as you do," Ratchford protested.

"She wouldn't be interested in you if you had a lot of time left," Hysell replied. "I wish you'd help me. Just a name and a telephone number would do for starts."

"I'm a lawyer, not an assassin."

"Fair enough. I'll just ask for one thing then—one favor. Show some interest in her."

Ratchford hesitated, then nodded, intrigued.

■   ■   ■

Ratchford found Mella Hysell the most direct and forward woman he'd ever known. It was as if she knew she could say whatever she wanted and that he was too much of a gentleman to argue or disagree.

Like the hitting man, she lay in wait for him, stalking him. Hysell took to sleeping away the long afternoons. That meant Ratchford must either spend the afternoons in his own room, lost in the agonies of daytime television, or go outside and cripple his way to the lookout area.

When he knew she waited for him he tried to find another alternative, but he was unsuccessful. Other than the path to the sea there was little of interest, and there was no other way to get to the beach within reasonable distance. To the north there were scores of tiny tract houses, most of them occupied by pensioners from the North. To the south there were more large homes, most of them damaged and unoccupied, then a bait store, then a boat place. Neither was a place to spend the long afternoons, although he tried, wandering north, then south.

So he went back to the lookout.

She waited for him on the unrailed balcony. At first she wore long concealing dresses. Later, as her weight diminished, she went to daring things—no bra, and finally bikinis.

Ratchford was alarmed, flattered, intrigued, and half a dozen other things all at once. She was perceptive to this, playing on his moods like a skilled harpist. If he seemed alarmed at the speed or direction of the ersatz affair, she soothed him. If he asked about her past life, she lied well. If he foresaw a dismal future, she always pictured them together in it.

"John isn't well," she told him. "He hates me because of that. He can't last much longer, his doctors say. And I need someone, Cyril. Someone like you—experienced, urbane." She'd accompany these speeches with a melting look that became more and more effective as her excess flesh vanished. Ratchford estimated her weight loss after eight weeks at almost forty pounds. It went more slowly thereafter, but she continued to lose. It was as if, knowing the strength of her web, she knew it would support only a lean spider.

Hysell watched and, after a while, laughed at Ratchford, but it was a laugh which understood and sympathized.

"Now you know," he said.

Ratchford shook his head, not knowing.

"In your practice how many divorces did you obtain for women?"

"Hundreds, perhaps thousands," Ratchford said.

"Didn't any of those women try to latch onto you?"

Ratchford nodded. Some had, and it had been an agony for him to treat them nicely. Connie was alive then and she was the only woman for him. There had been divorcees who clutched and cried and promised multitudes of delights. Some had been beautiful. All had been interested in matrimony, a replacement of the one shed in court. But none of them, not even the best schemer he remembered, had been as good at intrigue as Mella Hysell. He found himself enjoying the performance, and uncertain as to whether he was moved by it or not.

．　．　．

There was a sane Ratchford who stood in the shadows watching all.

What would you do with her? the sane Ratchford asked. *I mean, what good would she be to you?*

But he could dream and he was intrigued. It was as if, in what he knew to be the last of life, he was to be allowed once again to engage in a "first affair."

"How much weight do you figure she's lost by now?" Hysell constantly asked, using his good hand to doodle on his calculator. "Does she still wait for you on the balcony?"

"She's your wife," Ratchford told him. "This is embarrassing me. I think you should come with me."

Hysell shook his head. "She has my chair. She's using it to get me to come home, and I think it'll be time soon." He doodled some more with the calculator, cleared it, and snapped it off. "Not quite yet though. Tell me what you see in her."

Ratchford shook his head. "She's young. She's ardent. She has definite ideas about things. And she's vivid and handsome. Sometimes I feel as if I'm in distress and she's a knight riding to my rescue. She reverses the roles of romance."

Hysell smiled. "Those were my feelings exactly."

"But not now?" Ratchford said.

"Mella is interested mainly in the chase and the capture, not the afterwards. She'll pursue you as she chased me. Sooner or later you'll become the pursuer. Then she will temporize, demand plans, ask various conditions to prove your love. When you accede she'll marry you." He smiled. "By that time I'll be dead and you'll be the heir apparent."

Ratchford, realizing that Mella had already forced things between them close to the temporizing stage, said nothing.

"I tell her I hate you when I see her alone," Hysell confided. "She tells me to come home and look after my business. She understands jealousy." He smiled. "I'm not jealous. I'm only trying to figure some neat way to do her in before she does me in, but ideas that seem workable are hard to come up with. For her it would be easy. Too much or too little medicine, perhaps a pillow over the face or a fall down the steps—" He smiled again, more interested than afraid. "She's a lot stronger than either of us, Cyril. With your help, I might kill her more easily." He gave Ratchford an inquiring look.

Ratchford shook his head.

"Remember, when I go you'll be next."

"What if I'm not interested in her?"

"But you are," Hysell explained.

■   ■   ■

A few days later Hysell was gone. A nurse told Ratchford that Mella had taken him home. Ratchford waited for him at the lookout, but only Mella came.

"Where's John?" he asked, careful not to show too much interest.

"He's not feeling well," she said quickly. "He's failing, I'm afraid. Soon to be with me no more." She shook her head and Ratchford was unsurprised at the tears in her eyes. "Then I'll be alone."

He waited.

"It's been the story of my life. I've fallen in love with mature men. First John, then you. Now John will die and leave me." She eyed him warmly.

Ratchford, fascinated but wary, had a problem holding himself back from offering the wanted substitute.

"I'd like to see John," he said.

She inclined her head. "I know he's told you stories. I hope you don't believe them. I'll bring him out onto the balcony tomorrow so you can see him." The tears became profuse, and it was hard to disbelieve them. "It may be for the last time."

She groped for his hand and held it.

■   ■   ■

The next day he went early to the lookout and waited. After a time he was rewarded. John and Mella came onto the balcony. They waved to him, Mella enthusiastically, John feebly. Ratchford hobbled up the boardwalk to be closer, to call out to them.

Suddenly, without Ratchford seeing why, Mella flew down, screaming, to join him, her black-and-white-print dress fluttering in the sea breeze as she fell. By the time he got to her she was dead, her eyes unseeing, her now thin body lying broken on the flagstones.

After a while John appeared on the boardwalk. He rolled down to Ratchford in his aluminum chair.

"She stopped my medicine," he said. "I think she was sure that would do it. I acted as if it was about to, but I feel all right." He looked down at her and did one more calculation on his calculator. "She'd lost a lot of weight. Just enough."

Ratchford nodded. "Have you ever told anyone else the things you told me?"

"Regrettably, yes."

"Well, tell no one else. And somehow you've picked up a bit of black-and-white cloth on the front of the arm to your chair."

Hysell nodded, his color better than Ratchford had ever seen it.

"Are you sure you're all right?" Ratchford asked.

"I'm fine."

"Certainly there's no way you could feel well enough to talk with the police about this tragic fall. When they arrive, you'll answer no questions. After all, your wife is dead." He looked at Hysell, whose good right hand was working at the nooks and crannies of the arm of his chair.

"Every thread," Ratchford ordered.

A SODA FOR SUSAN

Richard Deming

Richard Deming was one of the last of the pulp pros. The trouble was, his career began about two years before the pulps folded in the early fifties. He then shifted to paperback books, where he did a lot of novelizations and other for-hire projects. Most of his material died with its era. But he did some extraordinary pieces in his time, and this is certainly one of them.

THOUGH SHE WAS NEARLY FIFTEEN, THE GIRL WAS SO SMALL AND thin-boned, she looked no more than twelve. The man was somewhere in his mid-forties.

There was something furtive about the man which made him oddly repellent in spite of his neat appearance. His thin, too-white hand gripped the girl's with a possessiveness which didn't seem quite normal.

The girl's face was set in placid lines as she trudged along by his side eating the candy bar he had given her. Looking up into the man's face, she noted the strange urgency in it, but it didn't seem either to puzzle or disturb her.

St. Louis' Forest Park is dotted with refreshment stands but the girl had paid no attention to the several they had passed up to that moment. Now, as they started to pass the last stand before the entrance to the bridle path toward which they were headed, she suddenly hung back against the man's grip. Obviously the enticements of the stand motivated her, however, and not reluctance to go on with the man.

He attempted to drag her past, but stopped abruptly and forced a thin smile when the child spoke in a piping voice which clearly carried to every customer at the stand.

"I'm thirsty, mister," she said. "Can I have a soda, please?"

More than twenty customers clustered about the refreshment stand, a mixture of couples of all ages, young girls in giggling groups, groups of young men who speculatively eyed the gigglers, plus a few people who seemed to be alone. A number turned to glance at the man and girl when the girl spoke.

One was a powerfully built sailor in his late teens, a clean-looking youngster with his cap jauntily riding the back of his crew-cut head. He looked from the small girl to the man with a frown.

His face frozen into its smile, the man said in a voice so low it was audible only to the girl, "Later. After a while I'll buy you all the soda you want. Come on now."

"But I'm thirsty, mister," the girl piped.

Several people were now frowning at the man, and dead silence fell over the group about the stand. The sailor's expression became an undecided scowl.

The man avoided looking at anyone but the girl. "Wait here," he said in a unnerved voice, released her hand and walked over to the counter.

"Bottle of soda," he said, laying down a dime.

The attendant had been too busy serving customers to notice either the man and child or the sudden unnatural silence of his patrons. In a harried voice he asked, "What kind?"

"Any kind," the man said.

Shrugging, the counterman uncapped a bottle of orange, set it down and picked up the dime. The man quickly carried the bottle to the girl.

"Come on now," he said, starting once again to move toward the entrance to the bridle path.

"You didn't get me a straw," the child said loudly.

The man stared at her as though he would enjoy boxing her ears, but he forced another thin smile. His gaze avoiding the numerous eyes now studying him with indecisive hostility, he returned to the counter, plucked a straw from a glass container and carried it to the girl.

"Thanks, mister," she said in a clear voice, sticking the straw in the bottle and trustingly holding her free hand out to him again.

The man grasped it convulsively and moved off toward the bridle path at such a rapid pace, the girl's thin legs almost had to run to keep up. Every eye at the refreshment stand stared after them.

The teen-age sailor's indecisive scowl suddenly became an expression of determination. Straightening away from the counter, he announced generally, "That kid doesn't know that guy from a hole in the wall. You people can stand here and think about it all day, if you want, but I'm going to check up on this."

He strode off after the man and child. Almost instantly a group of three young men followed, then another lone man, and then the entire group was trailing after the sailor.

Casting a worried look back over his shoulder, the man saw the crowd of more than twenty people streaming toward him, and halted in sudden terror. He attempted to jerk his hand from the girl's, but the move surprised her into tightening her grip, so that he couldn't run without dragging her along with him. Frenziedly he slapped at her wrist, belatedly causing her to turn loose, but by then the sailor was upon them.

The man backed to a tree, both hands raised defensively and his face forming what he meant to be a placating smile. It came out as a grimace of fear.

Now that he had his quarry cornered, the sailor wasn't sure how to proceed. Stopping directly in front of the cringing man, he clenched his fists but said nothing. Both were still standing in silence, the man attempting an appeasing smile and the sailor glaring at him, when the rest of the crowd arrived and formed a semicircle about them.

A middle-aged woman with a lantern jaw, trailed by a meek-looking man her own age, took the initiative from the sailor.

In a demanding voice she asked the girl, "Do you know this man, dear?"

The child had been staring around interestedly at the crowd so suddenly formed about her and her companion. She didn't seem in the least disturbed by the phenomenon. At the question she focused her attention on the lantern-jawed woman.

"No, ma'am," she said politely. "He's just a nice man who bought me candy."

The woman's nostrils flared as she looked at the man. Then her attention returned to the girl and she summoned a smile designed to get the child's confidence.

"You just met this man today, honey?"

"Yes, ma'am. Just outside the rest room over at the pavilion."

The woman turned to the man, her expression approaching ferocity. "You were hanging around the woman's rest room, were you? Waiting for some innocent child too young to know she shouldn't talk to strangers. Where were you taking her? Off in the bushes?"

"Listen," the man said feebly. "I ain't done nothing. What's eating all you people?"

"Where were you taking her?" the woman repeated in a voice of doom. "There's nothing up this bridle path but a lot of deserted spots."

"We was just taking a walk," the man said in a semi-whine. "There's no law against giving kids candy. I just like kids."

"That I believe," the woman spat at him.

The man's eyes darted around the circle of hostile faces without much hope. He gulped twice before he could manage words that bordered on hysteria, "You people got no right to question me. I ain't done nothing."

His tone, his expression and his whole manner were so obviously guilty that his mild opposition only further incensed the crowd. It was enough to finally trigger the rage of the young sailor, who all this time had been standing before the man and had never unclenched his fists.

"You damned kid raper!" he said, and smashed the man back against the tree with an uppercut.

The man made a feeble effort to defend himself, but he didn't have a chance against the powerful youngster. Deliberately, with almost emotionless calculation, the sailor beat him until his face was a bloody pulp and his body a quivering mass of bruises. When the man tried to end the one-sided fight by huddling on the ground with his arms protectively around his head, the sailor jerked him to his feet, held him erect against the tree with one hand and smashed blow after blow into his face and body.

The crowd watched silently with a mass look of grim approval, not a semblance of horror on any face.

The girl watched too, her placid expression evaporating with the first blow and a peculiar intentness replacing it. As the sailor warmed to his task, her expression became more and more excited until her eyes seemed to glow feverishly.

When the sailor finally began to tire, the girl's excitement simultaneously began to fade. Unobtrusively she backed through the crowd, which was too intent on the beating to notice her, and drifted away toward the refreshment stand. By the time the sailor let his unconscious victim slump to the ground, the girl was well beyond the stand and had quickened her pace to a near trot.

An hour later, when she entered her house, she found her father asleep on the front-room sofa and her mother reading the Sunday society column.

As the girl came in the front door, her mother looked up casually and said, "Back already, Susan? Have a nice time at the park?"

"Yes, ma'am," Susan said politely.

"What do you find to do there?" her mother asked. "I should think that after a few Sundays you'd exhaust the facilities. You haven't missed a Sunday this summer, have you?"

But the question was only an idle attempt to show parental interest, and she didn't expect an answer. She had returned to her paper before her daughter could even reply.

■　　■　　■

The following Sunday Susan arrived at the pavilion promptly at two P.M. as usual. Seating herself on a bench against the wall just outside the men's rest room, she waited quietly.

Though she was an intelligent girl and unusually well read for her age, it was knowledge born of experience rather than from books that made her pick this particular spot. Any text on abnormal psychology could have told her that public rest rooms are a favorite hunting ground for sexual deviates. She hadn't any books on abnormal psychology or sexual deviates, but she did know that if she sat on this particular bench long enough, the type of person necessary to her Sunday-afternoon game would inevitably appear.

She had developed an instinct for spotting the type, and she dismissed most of the men who passed in and out of the door with a glance. Once she smiled tentatively at a nervous-looking man in his sixties, but he only gave her a pleased smile in return, said, "Hi there, young lady," and walked on.

It was nearly three-thirty before she found the man she wanted. He was a slovenly dressed, red-faced man of about fifty-five, with little red-rimmed eyes which constantly shifted from side to side. He glanced at her as he started to pass on his way to the rest room, then stopped abruptly when she gave him a radiant smile.

He smiled back, not in the way most adults smile at children, but in an appraising manner, running his eyes slowly over her thin form. "Waiting for your daddy, honey?" he asked hopefully.

"No," she said. "Just resting. I'm not with anybody."

The red-faced man looked gratified. He glanced around in a vaguely furtive manner. "Like to go over to the zoo and look at the bears?"

"I saw them," she said. "I'd rather have a bar of candy."

The man took another cautious look around, seemed satisfied that no one was paying any attention to them, and asked, "Now why should I buy a little girl candy? What would that get me?"

"Whatever you want," she said placidly, looking straight at him.

The man looked surprised. He examined the girl again and a faintly glazed expression appeared in his eyes.

"How do you mean, whatever I want?"

"Well, you know. Buy me some candy and we'll play whatever game you want. I'll go look at the bears with you, or take a walk somewhere, or whatever you want."

He licked his lips. "Take a walk with me where?"

"Anywhere. I know a bridle path where nobody ever goes, hardly."

The man's expression became a mixture of hope and amazement. "You know pretty much for such a young one, don't you? How old are you?"

"Twelve," she lied.

He ran his eyes over her thin body again. "You been to this bridle path with men before?"

"Sure," she said. "When they buy me candy."

Again the man glanced all around, an increasing furtiveness in his manner.

"They sell candy right there," Susan said, pointing to the refreshment stand in the center of the pavilion. "I want a chocolate bar with nuts."

"All right," he said. "You wait here."

Hurrying over to the stand, he returned with a candy bar and gave it to her. She said, "Thank you," in a polite tone and rose from the bench. Familiarly she slipped her hand into his.

"This bridle path is pretty far," she said. "Halfway across the park. I'll show you where."

Bridle paths snaked over a good portion of Forest Park, and the girl led her companion in a direction exactly opposite to the one she had taken with her companion of the previous Sunday. They walked nearly a half mile, passing two refreshment stands en route, before they came in sight of their destination.

Here, as in the location she had chosen the previous Sunday, a refreshment stand was situated only a short distance from the place the bridle path came out on the road. The usual mixed crowd ringed the stand, men and women of all ages, plus a few children. As she and the man neared it, she scanned the faces of the customers, her attention settling on a young soldier in uniform whose wide shoulders strained the material of his suntan shirt.

Directly alongside the soldier Susan suddenly hung back from her companion's grip.

"I'm thirsty, mister," she said in a clear voice. "Can I have a soda, please?"

The man halted, his red face growing even redder and his gaze anxiously studying nearby reaction to the girl's words. The serviceman turned slowly and looked from Susan to the man with a frown. Other eyes centered on the man and the little girl with him.

Dropping Susan's hand, the red-faced man self-consciously began to fumble in his pocket for a coin. Susan's face was placid as she looked up at him, but its placidity concealed growing excitement at what she knew would shortly begin to happen. Excitement mixed with the hate she felt for all men who bought little girls candy.

There wasn't a suggestion of the vengefulness flowing from her small breast in such concentrated venom as she raised her piping voice again:

"Please, mister. Can't I have a soda?"

HOT EYES, COLD EYES

Lawrence Block

After a quarter decade, the general reading public is discovering what mystery readers have known all along—that Lawrence Block is one of the most reader-friendly writers in the world.

Whether it's the light comedy of his Bernie Rhodenbarr novels, or the brooding noir of the Matt Scudder books, Block is always great company.

Here he gives us a nasty slice of a very dark life.

SOME DAYS WERE EASY. SHE WOULD GO TO WORK AND RETURN home without once feeling the invasion of men's eyes. She might take her lunch and eat it in the park. She might stop on the way home at the library for a book, at the deli for a barbequed chicken, at the cleaner's, at the drugstore. On those days she could move coolly and crisply through space and time, untouched by the stares of men.

Doubtless they looked at her on those days, as on the more difficult days. She was the sort men looked at, and she had learned that early on—when her legs first began to lengthen and take shape, when her breasts began to bud. Later, as the legs grew longer and the breasts fuller, and as her face lost its youthful plumpness and was sculpted by time into beauty, the stares increased. She was attractive, she was beautiful, she was—curious phrase—easy on the eyes. So men looked at her, and on the easy days she didn't seem to notice, didn't let their rude stares penetrate the invisible shield that guarded her.

But this was not one of those days.

It started in the morning. She was waiting for the bus when she first felt the heat of a man's eyes upon her. At first she willed herself to ignore the feeling, wished the bus would come and whisk her away from it, but the bus did not come and she could not ignore what she felt and, inevitably, she turned from the street to look at the source of the feeling.

There was a man leaning against a red brick building not twenty yards from her. He was perhaps thirty-five, unshaven, and his clothes looked as though he'd slept in them. When she turned to glance at him his lips curled slightly, and his eyes, red-rimmed and glassy, moved first to her face, then drifted insolently the length of her body. She could feel their heat; it leaped from the eyes to her breasts and loins like an electric charge bridging a gap.

He placed his hand deliberately upon his crotch and rubbed himself. His smile widened.

She turned from him, drew a breath, let it out, wished the bus would come. Even now, with her back to him, she could feel the embrace of his eyes. They were like hot hands upon her buttocks and the backs of her thighs.

The bus came, neither early nor late, and she mounted the steps and dropped her fare in the box. The usual driver, a middle-aged fatherly type, gave her his usual smile and wished her the usual good morning. His eyes were an innocent watery blue behind thick-lensed spectacles.

Was it only her imagination that his eyes swept her body all the while? But she could feel them on her breasts, could feel too her own nipples hardening in response to their palpable touch.

She walked the length of the aisle to the first available seat. Male eyes tracked her every step of the way.

■　　■　　■

The day went on like that. This did not surprise her, although she had hoped it would be otherwise, had prayed during the bus ride that eyes would cease to bother her when she left the bus. She had learned, though, that once a day began in this fashion its pattern was set, unchangeable.

Was it something she did? Did she invite their hungry stares? She certainly didn't do anything with the intention of provoking male lust. Her dress was conservative enough, her makeup subtle and unremarkable. Did she swing her hips when she walked? Did she wet her lips and pout like a sullen sexpot? She was positive she did nothing of the sort, and it often seemed to her that she could cloak herself in a nun's habit and the results would be the same. Men's eyes would lift the black skirts and strip away the veil.

At the office building where she worked, the elevator starter glanced at her legs, then favored her with a knowing, wet-lipped smile. One of the office boys, a rabbity youth with unfortunate skin, stared at her breasts, then flushed scarlet when she caught him at it. Two older men gazed at her from the water cooler. One leaned over to murmur something to the other. They both chuckled and went on looking at her.

She went to her desk and tried to concentrate on her work. It was difficult, because intermittently she felt eyes brushing her body, moving across her like searchlight beams scanning the yard in a prison movie. There were moments when she wanted to scream, moments when she wanted to spin around in her chair and hurl something. But she remained in control of herself and did none of these things. She had survived days of this sort often enough in the past. She would survive this one as well.

The weather was good, but today she spent her lunch hour at her desk rather than risk the park. Several times during the afternoon the sensation of being watched was unbearable and she retreated to the ladies' room. She endured the final hours a minute at a time, and finally it was five o'clock and she straightened her desk and left.

The descent on the elevator was unbearable. She bore it. The bus ride home, the walk from the bus stop to her apartment building, were unendurable. She endured them.

In her apartment, with the door locked and bolted, she stripped off her clothes and hurled them into a corner of the room as if they were unclean, as if the day had irrevocably soiled them. She stayed a long while under the shower, washed her hair, blow-dried it, then returned to her bedroom and stood nude before the full-length mirror on the closet door. She studied herself at some length, and intermittently her hands would move to cup a breast or trace the swell of a thigh, not to arouse but to assess, to chart the dimensions of her physical self.

And now? A meal alone? A few hours with a book? A lazy night in front of the television set?

She closed her eyes, and at once she felt other eyes upon her, felt them as she had been feeling them all day. She knew that she was alone, that now no one was watching her, but this knowledge did nothing to dispel the feeling.

She sighed.

She would not, could not, stay home tonight.

■   ■   ■

When she left the building, stepping out into the cool of dusk, her appearance was very different. Her tawny hair, which she'd worn pinned up earlier, hung free. Her makeup was overdone, with an excess of mascara and a deep blush of rouge in the hollows of her cheeks. During the day she'd worn no scent beyond a touch of Jean Naté applied after her morning shower; now she'd dashed on an abundance of the perfume she wore only on nights like this one, a strident scent redolent of musk. Her dress was close-fitting and revealing, the skirt slit oriental-fashion high on one thigh, the neckline low to display her décolletage. She strode purposefully on her high-heeled shoes, her buttocks swaying as she walked.

She looked sluttish and she knew it, and gloried in the knowledge. She'd checked the mirror carefully before leaving the apartment and she had liked what she saw. Now, walking down the street with her handbag bouncing against her swinging hip, she could feel the heat building up within her flesh. She could also feel the eyes of the men she passed, men who sat on stoops or loitered in doorways, men walking with purpose who stopped for a glance in her direction. But there was a difference. Now she relished those glances. She fed on the heat in those eyes, and the fire within herself burned hotter in response.

A car slowed. The driver leaned across the seat, called to her. She missed the words but felt the touch of his eyes. A pulse throbbed insistently throughout her entire body now. She was frightened—of her own feelings, of the real dangers she faced—but at the same time she was alive, gloriously alive, as she had not been in far too long. Before she had walked through the day. Now the blood was singing in her veins.

She passed several bars before finding the cocktail lounge she wanted. The interior was dimly lit, the floor soft with carpeting. An overactive air conditioner had lowered the temperature to an almost uncomfortable level. She walked bravely into the room. There were several empty tables along the wall but she passed them by, walking her swivel-hipped walk to the bar and taking a stool at the far end.

The cold air was stimulating against her warm skin. The bartender gave her a minute, then ambled over and leaned against the bar in front of her. He looked at once knowing and disinterested, his heavy lids shading his dark brown eyes and giving them a sleepy look.

"Stinger," she said.

While he was building the drink she drew her handbag into her lap and groped within it for her billfold. She found a ten and set it on top of the bar, then fumbled reflexively within her bag for another moment, checking its contents. The bartender placed the drink on the bar in front of her, took her money, returned with her change. She looked at her drink, then at her reflection in the back bar mirror.

Men were watching her.

She could tell, she could always tell. Their gazes fell on her and warmed the skin where they touched her. Odd, she thought, how the same sensation that had been so disturbing and unpleasant all day long was so desirable and exciting now.

She raised her glass, sipped her drink. The combined flavor of cognac and crème de menthe was at once warm and cold upon her lips and tongue. She swallowed, sipped again.

"That a stinger?"

He was at her elbow and she flicked her eyes in his direction while continuing to face forward. A small man, stockily built, balding, tanned, with a dusting of freckles across his high forehead. He wore a navy blue Quiana shirt open at the throat, and his dark chest hair was beginning to go gray.

"Drink up," he suggested. "Let me buy you another."

She turned now, looked levelly at him. He had small eyes. Their whites showed a tracery of blue veins at their outer corners. The irises were a very dark brown, an unreadable color, and the black pupils, hugely dilated in the bar's dim interior, covered most of the irises.

"I haven't seen you here," he said, hoisting himself onto the seat beside her. "I usually drop in around this time, have a couple, see my friends. Not new in the neighborhood, are you?"

Calculating eyes, she thought. Curiously passionless eyes, for all

their cool intensity. Worst of all, they were small eyes, almost
beady eyes.

"I don't want company," she said.

"Hey, how do you know you don't like me if you don't give me
a chance?" He was grinning, but there was no humor in it. "You
don't even know my name, lady. How can you despise a total
stranger?"

"Please leave me alone."

"What are you, Greta Garbo?" He got up from his stool, took
a half step away from her, gave her a glare and a curled lip. "You
want to drink alone," he said, "why don't you just buy a bottle
and take it home with you? You can take it to bed and suck on
it, honey."

■   ■   ■

He had ruined the bar for her. She scooped up her change, left
her drink unfinished. Two blocks down and one block over she
found a second cocktail lounge virtually indistinguishable from the
first one. Perhaps the lighting was a little softer, the background
music the slightest bit lower in pitch. Again she passed up the
row of tables and seated herself at the bar. Again she ordered a
stinger and let it rest on the bar top for a moment before taking
the first exquisite sip.

Again she felt male eyes upon her, and again they gave her the
same hot-cold sensation as the combination of brandy and crème
de menthe.

This time when a man approached her she sensed his presence
for a long moment before he spoke. She studied him out of the
corner of her eye. He was tall and lean, she noted, and there was
a self-contained air about him, a sense of considerable self-
assurance. She wanted to turn, to look directly into his eyes, but
instead she raised her glass to her lips and waited for him to make
a move.

"You're a few minutes late," he said.

She turned, looked at him. There was a weathered, rawboned
look to him that matched the western-style clothes he wore—the
faded chambray shirt, the skin-tight denim jeans. Without glancing down she knew he'd be wearing boots and that they would be
good ones.

"I'm late?"

He nodded. "I've been waiting for you for close to an hour. Of course it wasn't until you walked in that I knew it was you I was waiting for, but one look was all it took. My name's Harley."

She made up a name. He seemed satisfied with it, using it when he asked her if he could buy her a drink.

"I'm not done with this one yet," she said.

"Then why don't you just finish it and come for a walk in the moonlight?"

"Where would we walk?"

"My apartment's just a block and a half from here."

"You don't waste time."

"I told you I waited close to an hour for you. I figure the rest of the evening's too precious to waste."

She had been unwilling to look directly into his eyes but she did so now and she was not disappointed. His eyes were large and well-spaced, blue in color, a light blue of a shade that often struck her as cold and forbidding. But his eyes were anything but cold. On the contrary, they burned with passionate intensity.

She knew, looking into them, that he was a dangerous man. He was strong, he was direct and he was dangerous. She could tell all this in a few seconds, merely by meeting his relentless gaze.

Well, that was fine. Danger, after all, was an inextricable part of it.

She pushed her glass aside, scooped up her change. "I don't really want the rest of this," she said.

"I didn't think you did. I think I know what you really want."

"I think you probably do."

He took her arm, tucked it under his own. They left the lounge, and on the way out she could feel other eyes on her, envious eyes. She drew closer to him and swung her hips so that her buttocks bumped into his lean flank. Her purse slapped against her other hip. Then they were out the door and heading down the street.

She felt excitement mixed with fear, an emotional combination not unlike her stinger. The fear, like the danger, was part of it.

．　■　■

His apartment consisted of two sparsely furnished rooms three flights up from street level. They walked wordlessly to the bedroom and undressed. She laid her clothes across a wooden chair, set her handbag on the floor at the side of the platform bed. She got onto the bed and he joined her and they embraced. He smelled faintly of leather and tobacco and male perspiration, and even with her eyes shut she could see his blue eyes burning in the darkness.

She wasn't surprised when his hands gripped her shoulders and eased her downward on the bed. She had been expecting this and welcomed it. She swung her head, letting her long hair brush across his flat abdomen, and then she moved to accept him. He tangled his fingers in her hair, hurting her in a not unpleasant way. She inhaled his musk as her mouth embraced him, and in her own fashion she matched his strength with strength of her own, teasing, taunting, heightening his passion and then cooling it down just short of culmination. His breathing grew ragged and muscles worked in his legs and abdomen.

At length he let go of her hair. She moved upward on the bed to join him and he rolled her over onto her back and covered her, his mouth seeking hers, his flesh burying itself in her flesh. She locked her thighs around his hips. He pounded at her loins, hammering her, hurting her with the brute force of his masculinity.

How strong he was, and how insistent. Once again she thought what a dangerous man he was, and what a dangerous game she was playing. The thought served only to spur her own passion on, to build her fire higher and hotter.

She felt her body preparing itself for orgasm, felt the urge growing to abandon herself, to lose control utterly. But a portion of herself remained remote, aloof, and she let her arm hang over the side of the bed and reached for her purse, groped within it.

And found the knife.

Now she could relax, now she could give up, now she could surrender to what she felt. She opened her eyes, stared upward. His own eyes were closed as he thrust furiously at her. *Open your eyes*, she urged him silently. *Open them, open them, look at me—*

And it seemed that his eyes did open to meet hers, even as they climaxed together, even as she centered the knife over his back and plunged it unerringly into his heart.

■ ■ ■

Afterward, in her own apartment, she put his eyes in the box with the others.

HE LOVED HER SO MUCH

Sandra Scoppettone

Sandra Scoppettone has a voice and style all her own. She writes about big cities and their effects on vulnerable but very competent middle-aged females.

In a matter of a few pages, she can be violent, tender, funny, and poignant—without ever letting the narrative lag.

This story has the feel of journalism—stark black and white with no room for grays.

WHEN KAREN BRADLEY SAID YES TO JEFF HARK'S INVITATION, HE couldn't believe it. The first semester at the university he hadn't even been able to look her way as she passed him on campus, and it was deep into the second semester before he'd screwed up enough courage to sit across from her in the library.

Karen was blond and wore her hair loose and wavy. She had eyes the color of his favorite faded work shirt, and her mouth made him think about mangos and kiwi fruit. But he was sure she was out of his reach, unattainable. And then she smiled at him.

■　■　■

Karen Bradley never noticed Jeff Hark before the day he sat across from her in the library. She thought he was cute and particularly liked the way his dusky hair slooped down over his forehead and covered one of his brown eyes. She smiled at him and he smiled back, not trying to act cool or anything, and she liked that. Most guys tried to be so cool, they just seemed sappy to her. The book he had in front of him was on anthropology. She was reading about Henry James.

"Hi," he said softly.

"Hi."

"Henry James, huh?"

"Yeah." She said it as noncommittally as possible because, for all she knew, this guy loved James. Or maybe hated him. "You're into anthropology?"

"Yeah."

She couldn't tell if he liked it or not, so she nodded.

They looked at each other and Karen felt nervous. She didn't know who he was or what crowd he hung around with. Not that it made much difference. Unlike her parents, she didn't judge people by those kinds of standards. And the truth was, she felt surprisingly attracted to him. There were lots of guys she went out with, but none of them was very important or meaningful to her.

They told each other their names, and when he asked her if she'd like to go to dinner and a movie on Friday night, she said yes. She would break the date she already had.

•   •   •

The first date was nearly a total disaster. Jeff couldn't believe he was actually out with Karen. It was almost more unreal to be with her than to have her in his thoughts. He was clumsy and kept bumping into her as they walked through the campus to the bus stop. And he wasn't good at making small talk. But she was, thank Christ. Even so, he found himself giving her monosyllabic answers, worried he'd say the wrong thing, something that might turn her off.

At dinner he couldn't eat. That appeared to bother her. She kept asking him why he wasn't eating, and the only answer he could come up with was that he felt a bit sick. And that turned out to be the dumbest thing he could've said, because she suggested they call it a night. Fearful of losing her, he forced himself to eat half of his pasta. Karen ate the rest and he marveled at her appetite as she was so slim. It also made him wonder about her feelings for him. How could she eat if she dug him the way he dug her?

Although he hated them, after dinner he suggested a French film thinking it was the kind of movie she'd like. But she said she despised foreign films. He felt like an asshole.

Then Karen said, "We could see the new Spielberg movie."

He hated Spielberg's films but agreed enthusiastically.

"How about going for a drink," he asked when they came out of the theater.

"Neat," she said.

"The Hobbit?" he asked.

She wrinkled her nose in distaste. "I go there a lot. How about Danzinger's?"

Danzinger's was a little more exclusive than the Hobbit, and Jeff prayed he had enough money. Also, he couldn't help wondering if she'd nixed the Hobbit because she didn't want to be seen with him.

By the time they got to the bar, he was feeling like shit.

■ ■ ■

By the time they got to the bar Karen was feeling like shit. She was sure he didn't like her. It had been dumb to say no to the French film. Ditto the Hobbit. But if they'd gone there, everybody she knew would have joined them, and she wanted to be alone with Jeff, get to know him.

Danzinger's was fairly crowded but they got a table for two in the back. Even though Jeff was the shiest guy she'd ever gone out with, the evening turned around when they both ordered Coors beers at the same time. It was then that she discovered how much they had in common.

When he took her back to her apartment, he didn't even try to kiss her good night. At first she felt lousy about it, believing he didn't like her at all, but when he called the next day, asking to see her that night, she realized his behavior had been a compliment. Jeff was the only guy she'd ever known who didn't try to hit on her on the first date.

■ ■ ■

They saw each other every night for a week before they slept together. It wasn't that Jeff didn't want to before that, but he was scared. In the past, with the two other women he'd been with, sex hadn't gone well. And Karen meant so much to him that he wanted it to be perfect. When they finally got to it, it wasn't awful but it wasn't good.

"Don't worry about it," Karen said. "We have to get to know each other."

She calmed him down, made him feel better, but later he wondered just how many guys she'd been with before. How did she
know it was not so hot because they had to get to know each
other? Thinking about her with other guys made him angry, and
for a moment, he imagined himself twisting her arm, forcing her
to tell him who they were. Then the fantasy vanished as quickly
as it had appeared.

Karen had been right. Sex did get better. And better. For the
first time Jeff felt manly. And adored. He couldn't believe that
someone like Karen really cared for him. Even though he knew it
bugged her, he asked her a lot if she really loved him. She said
she did. Still, it was hard to believe, and even harder to believe
things were going so great. Then at Easter she took him home to
meet her parents and as they pulled up in front of the big Colonial
house, he started to feel like shit.

■   ■   ■

Karen knew it wasn't going to be easy. Jeff wasn't exactly her
father's idea of the perfect boy for her to date. And her mother
wasn't going to be overjoyed either. But, hell, it was her life, and
she thought it was time they met him. She knew Jeff was going
to be very important in her life.

Her parents were polite to Jeff, as Karen knew they would be.
Then, while Jeff was taking a walk, her father called her into his
study and started grilling her about Jeff.

Finally Karen said, "Look, Dad, he's very shy. It takes a while
to get to know him and see how neat he is."

Larry Bradley, who was a large and imposing man with a per-
ennial tan, said, "He's not right for you, Karen."

"Why not? How can you say that when you don't even know
Jeff?"

"I know him," he insisted.

"What's that supposed to mean?"

"It means he's a hustler. I know his type. I've seen hundreds of
Jeff Harks in my life, believe me. He knows a good thing when he
sees one."

"For your information, Dad, Jeff didn't know a damn thing
about me when we met. Like if you're talking about money, Jeff
couldn't care less about money. He's going to school on a full
scholarship, you know."

"Why?"

"Because he's so smart."

"And because his family doesn't have a pot to piss in, right?"

Karen felt furious. "So what? Is that a crime?"

"No. But if he comes from a poor family, believe me, Karen, money means plenty to him."

"I think your attitude is disgusting," Karen said.

"Maybe so. But I don't like what I see. I know I can't control you; you're grown and living away from home. Still, I'm telling you that this bozo isn't for you. He gives me the creeps."

Karen was taking psychology as a minor and was sure that her father was feeling threatened because he could see that Jeff meant more to her than any other guy she'd ever brought home. She thought about telling him this but knew he wouldn't understand. Instead she said, "I love Jeff."

Larry closed his eyes for a second, as if he'd been punched. "There's nothing I can do about that, but please don't ever bring him here again."

"I can't believe this," she said. "I can't believe what you're saying to me."

Her father said nothing, just looked at her with his cold blue eyes.

Karen slammed out of the study.

■   ■   ■

Jeff didn't know how to tell Karen that he never wanted to go to her parents' house again, but it didn't come up before the semester ended.

He thought he would die being away from her for three months. There was no way he was going to her place, and definitely no way he was inviting her to his home. His parents were divorced and his mother lived with a man Jeff hated.

Anyway, Jeff had to work in a gas station all summer, so he tried to content himself with letters and occasional phone calls. But they didn't help, and often made things worse. Most of the calls ended with one or the other of them hanging up, furious. He accused her of seeing other guys. She swore she wasn't, but he found it hard to believe. After these fights she always called him back, and for a while he was soothed. Then the doubts would creep back, and he'd make another call to her, starting the whole thing over again.

When school began in the fall, he saw right away that he'd been stupid. She loved him more than she ever had.

·   ·   ·

As the months flew by, Karen felt closer to Jeff than she'd ever felt to another person. Her parents' attitude toward him hadn't changed, so she didn't go home for Thanksgiving and only stayed home for three days over the Christmas holiday, choosing to come back to school to be with Jeff, who hadn't bothered to go home at all.

In January he moved into her apartment. Karen continued paying because, although Jeff worked two jobs, he couldn't afford to contribute. He said he felt lousy about the arrangement, but she assured him it was fine. Secretly Karen enjoyed the idea of her father unknowingly supporting Jeff.

When she told Jeff she was going home for the Easter holiday, he became livid. He accused her of wanting to see some other guy, calling her horrendous names. And he slapped her.

On the plane ride home she reviewed what had happened. Of course, he'd been remorseful and had begged her forgiveness, promising never to hit her again. Still, something nagged at her. But when she got home and saw her father's stern face, her mother's long-suffering one, and they grilled her again about Jeff, she buried her doubts about him and extolled his good points, refusing to give him up. And when her father threatened to cut her off, she retaliated with a threat of her own: She'd marry Jeff if they didn't stop harassing her.

·   ·   ·

The second summer apart was much harder for Jeff than the first one. Karen was touring Europe with her best friend. The letters were fewer and took longer to arrive, and the rare phone calls were even more unsatisfying than they'd been the year before. This time, if they fought and he hung up on her, she didn't call back.

When they returned for their junior year, Jeff was convinced Karen had met someone else, and nothing she said could reassure him. It wasn't until the beginning of November that he felt good about things again. But when she said she was going home for Thanksgiving, he had a fit.

"You didn't go last year. What the hell's this about?"

"My father's insisting, Jeff. I mean, he *is* paying my bills, you know. Sometimes I have to do what he says."

"Like a whore," he accused, and saw the hurt in her eyes. Still, he couldn't stop, and continued badgering her even while he felt she was slipping away from him. And then he started again on the summer before, insisting she'd had an affair.

Finally she broke down and admitted that she had met someone, that they'd gone out a few times, but nothing had happened because she loved Jeff and wasn't about to cheat on him. He slapped her twice, knocking her to the ground.

Of course he'd apologized as they stood at the airport, waiting for the plane that would take her home for Thanksgiving. She said it would be all right, but he knew it would never be the same. How would he ever believe her now? He should break off with her. She was untrustworthy, just as he'd always thought. But he loved her so much. They would have to have some serious discussions when she got back.

■   ■   ■

Between Thanksgiving and Christmas, Karen tried many times to tell Jeff it was over. But she couldn't go through with it, because if she even hinted that something was wrong, he'd either become so angry she felt frightened or he'd cry, touching her in a way that made her feel he'd die without her. Still, she was anxious to go home again for the holidays, anxious to get away from him.

During Christmas vacation they had their usual, awful phone calls, and finally Karen decided that, cowardly as it was, she would tell him on the phone.

"Jeff, I need to tell you something," she said the day before New Year's Eve.

"I don't see why you can't come back so we can be together tomorrow night," he said, not hearing her.

She tried again. "I want to tell you something, Jeff. It's over."

"What is?"

"Us."

There was a long silence.

"Did you hear me, Jeff?"

"Who is he? Is it the guy you met last summer?"

"There's nobody," she answered truthfully.

"Then why?"

"Because I just can't take it anymore. Your possessiveness and jealousy."

"Don't give me that shit, Karen. I know there's someone else."

"No," she said simply. "It's you."

"You said you loved me," he yelled into the phone.

Holding the receiver away from her ear, she was glad she wasn't in the same room with him.

Again she said, "I did love you, but I don't anymore."

He swore at her, and when he stopped, she told him that she would expect him to move out of the apartment by the time she returned to school.

For the rest of the vacation he phoned three or four times a day until Karen had her father answer. He made it clear that if Jeff called again, he would have the police intervene.

Jeff didn't call again, but Karen knew there was no way he wouldn't confront her when she got back. Still, she was shocked when she returned to the apartment to find that he was waiting for her and hadn't moved out any of his belongings.

"What the hell is this, Jeff? I told you to move."

"I'm not going anywhere until you tell me the truth," he said, and walked toward her, his hands in fists at his sides.

Karen felt incredibly frightened and turned to leave. He caught her by the sleeve of her jacket.

■   ■   ■

He'd never been so angry. He pulled her around so that his back was to the door, blocking her exit. Everything inside him was shaking. Jeff couldn't believe this bitch was really going to dump him. He hadn't taken her seriously when she'd told him to move out. And then when her father threatened him, he figured that Karen was forced to say things she didn't mean. Now he knew for sure that she was seeing someone else.

"Who is he?" he asked once more.

"Oh, Christ, don't start that shit again," she said.

"Tell me who he is, Karen."

"There's nobody, Jeff. I just don't want to be with you anymore. I told you, I don't love you."

He heard the words, and suddenly he believed them. It was over. They'd been together eighteen months, meant everything to each other, and now, just like that, she didn't love him. The room turned many colors, as if he were on acid. A rage came up from his toes, filling his gut, bursting through the top of his head.

And then he saw her, eyes bulging, face a shade of blue. His hands were around her throat, his thumbs pressed deep into her pink flesh. She was limp. Gently he laid her down on the floor.

Standing over her, looking down, he couldn't believe that she was dead. But it wasn't his fault. Still, how was he going to describe what had transpired? Who could comprehend what he'd done? If only she hadn't smiled at him that day in the library. She was all he'd ever had and she'd wanted to leave him. So maybe when he told them, maybe when he explained that he loved her so much he had to kill her, maybe they'd understand, after all.

MIDNIGHT PROMISES

Richard T. Chizmar

> *It's always nice to discover a major new voice in crime fiction.*
> *Richard Chizmar has been publishing stories for the past four or five years but it's only been in the past two years that his stories have been receiving the acclaim due them.*
> *The following is pure Chizmar, a sad and startling tale with an unforgettable sting on the end.*

SHE PEEKS AROUND THE EDGE OF THE DOOR. TIPTOES INSIDE THE room and kisses him good morning. A soft peck on the cheek.

He doesn't stir.

She walks over to the window and pulls open the curtains. It's June and the sky is rainbow blue with lazy white clouds swimming by. The view is a pretty one—distant trees swaying in the breeze, a bed of flowers blooming in the foreground—and she wishes, as she does every morning, that she could open the window just a crack.

She places her bag at the foot of the bed, takes off her windbreaker, and sits down in the chair. She gently takes his right hand and begins stroking each of his fingers.

Later, when he wakes up, she'll move over to his left side so that he'll be able to see outside the window.

But for now she sits with her back bathed in golden sunlight.

■　■　■

The cancer is taking him away—inch by inch.

Every day, a little more of him disappears.

And she sits and watches.

Always she watches.

She leaves at night now but only because they make her.

"You need your rest, Mrs. Collins."

"We'll take good care of him."

"I promise that we'll call if your husband needs you for anything."

"You remember what happened last time, Mrs. Collins. We don't want a repeat of that, now do we?"

So now she goes home each night. Precisely at ten o'clock with the other visitors.

A silent elevator ride to the lobby. A slow walk to the parking lot. And the lonely drive home.

Home . . . where there is nothing left for her.

Just a quiet, cold house. A mug of hot cocoa in the dark kitchen. The day's mail. And an empty bed.

Home is like a stranger to her now. Or perhaps *she* is the stranger. She can remember a time when this house smiled at her each time she walked through the door. Whispered in her ear as she crossed the foyer that everything was safe and sound and wonderful.

Now there is only silence.

Not even a whisper of life there: no lights or television or radio. No laughter or idle conversation. Nothing.

Just the same damn thing, night after night after night.

Hot cocoa. Mail. Bed.

And, of course, the nightmares.

They come more often now.

Sometimes—very, very rarely—she dreams happy thoughts: *A close-up of his smile. The sound of his laughter. The feel of his lips on hers. The touch of his hand as they walk barefoot on a moonlit beach.*

But most nights she dreams darker thoughts: *an x-ray view of his torso . . . showing nothing. Absolutely nothing inside—just a hollowed-out husk of a man. Surviving on nothing but air.*

Or her standing alone in a cold, driving rain. Standing above his open grave. Dropping a single red rose onto the shiny black casket . . .

Or the apple dream. This one is the worst of all—sheer terror. *She sees the two of them sitting in front of a large desk of dark, polished wood. Holding hands. Listening to a doctor. The doctor's face is grim. His lip is trembling. He tells them that the first reports were wrong, that the cancer has spread and he holds up an x-ray . . . and the image is that of an apple tree. Tumors everywhere, hanging there like fat, ripe apples. Dozens of them. Dark and moist and plump. Waiting to be picked . . .*

Thank God, this dream doesn't come very often.

Because when it does, she almost always wakes up screaming.

■   ■   ■

It's lunchtime and the hallway is buzzing with activity.

She gets up and closes the door.

He's sleeping again, but she isn't worried about the noise disturbing him. It's the smell—he can't stand the smell of the hospital food. It makes him nauseous.

A lot of things do that to him. Food. Flowers. Perfume. Even some liquids. They all smell funny now. One of the drugs is responsible, but she can't remember which one.

He doesn't eat the food, anyway. Not anymore. They use a tube for that now. A shiny, little clear thing that snakes right into his stomach.

She remembers that as a particularly bad time—the week he stopped eating.

But even worse was when he stopped talking.

It's been thirteen days now. And barely a whisper in all that time. Too weak, the doctors explain. Too many drugs.

So, most days, they just sit there and hold hands and stare into each other's eyes. Sometimes they smile and make silly faces, sometimes they just sit there and cry.

With the door closed, the room is very quiet except for the constant beeping of the I.V. She turns the volume down a notch—she knows the machines as well as any nurse on the floor—and starts to read again from a letter she'd written him just before they were married. Her voice cracks several times and there are tears in her eyes, but still she keeps reading. She has a stack of letters in her bag, tightly bound with a thick rubber band, and she is determined to get through them all.

■   ■   ■

The mornings are no kinder than the nights. Same routine every day—up by six-thirty, out the door by seven-thirty.

She starts each morning with a long, hot shower and she always tries her hardest to think of something nice, something cheerful to start the day with. But she never can.

She forces herself to eat a good breakfast most of the time. Toast. Fruit. Juice. For energy. She knows this was the reason she'd gotten sick last month and needed to see the doctor—not because she was sleeping in his hospital room every night! Not because she was overtired, for goodness sake!

She had simply forgotten to eat. For three or four days. She can't remember which.

So now she takes the time to eat most mornings. And when she's done, she washes the dishes and wipes down the countertop. Then she grabs her keys from the foyer and locks the door behind her. She gets into her car and pulls away from the curb. And never once looks back.

■　■　■

Dinner is served at quarter to six.

She closes the door as soon as she hears the familiar squeaking of the tray-cart working its way down the hallway.

He's awake now and they are looking at photos.

High school. College. Summers at the beach. Even pictures of the wedding. She brought them all.

He smiles at most of the pictures. Points and grins and raises what's left of his eyebrows. It's the most animated—and alert—he's been in weeks, and it does her heart wonders to see him this way.

When she gets to one particular photo, he really surprises her. His face lights up like a child's and he takes it from her with trembling fingers.

It's an old photo. From the very first summer they spent together. A narrow strip of three small black-and-whites from one of those cheap little booths you sit inside. In the first two, their faces are pressed together cheek-to-cheek and they're grinning like goofy kids. In the last one, they're kissing.

He lifts the photo to his face and tries to kiss it. But the tubes get in the way.

So she takes it from him and kisses it herself, then lays it on the sheet atop his chest.

He smiles at her and closes his eyes.

She does the same and moments later when she hears the whisper—"*thank you*"—she thinks she must be dreaming . . .

Until she opens her eyes and sees his stare and the tears streaming down his cheeks.

And at that exact moment, she knows with complete certainty that she is doing the right thing—the letters, the photos . . .

In her heart, she knows . . .

Just after eight o'clock, he falls asleep again and she returns the photos to her bag. Except for his favorite one—she leaves that right where it is.

She holds his hand and watches him sleep until ten. Just like so many times before.

Then she kisses him goodnight and heads for the elevator.

■   ■   ■

Sometimes, when she's away from the hospital, she tries to convince herself that he's improving. That he's looking better. And that she'll walk through the door the next morning and he'll be sitting up and talking and maybe eating some scrambled eggs. And she'll bounce over to the bed and say, "Hey, kiddo, I *thought* you had some color in those cheeks last night—"

But she knows none of this is true. She knows what's really happening.

Fourteen hours a day is enough to convince anyone.

He'd lost his hair during the second cycle of chemo.

By the end of the third, he was thirty pounds lighter.

A month later—halfway into the final cycle—they knew it wasn't working.

So they'd switched to different drugs and a different program.

And it had worked for a while, too. For a few weeks, at least, he seemed to stabilize. His energy crept up a few notches, his weight maintained.

But then, as if the whole thing was just some sort of cruel joke, it all went downhill and fast.

He stopped eating.

His skin turned a sick combination of yellow and green.

He started to sweat so much and the smell . . . oh God the smell . . .

And then, almost overnight, the pain doubled. Then tripled.

And then it got so bad that he started to cry—something she had never seen before. Not when his mother died, not when they first learned about the cancer. Never.

So they'd immediately injected him with the heavy stuff . . .

. . . and most of the pain had gone away . . .

. . . almost overnight, just as fast as it had come, it had gone away . . .

. . . and her husband had gone away with it.

Now he sleeps most of the time.

And when he *is* awake—well, it isn't much different than when he's still sleeping. Or at least it seems that way to her. His eyes are so milky and unfocused, he barely moves a finger, he doesn't talk . . .

She feels miserably guilty for thinking this way. Of course, she's glad he no longer feels the pain. Of course, she's grateful to the doctors for making him so much more comfortable.

But God, she can't help it—she misses his voice, his laugh, his charm; she misses the way he once looked at her.

Without those things, she is not only afraid, she is all alone.

■　■　■

She slides the ring onto his finger and closes his hand into a fist. His fingers are skinny and gnarled—like an old man's—and she's worried that the ring will fall off. Tumble down to the floor and no one will find it.

She lets go of his hand and stares at it for a long moment, then walks over to the window.

It's almost midnight and a full moon is shining far away in the distance, coating the trees with a silver luster, making everything look wet and slick like just after a rainfall.

She parts the curtains slightly and a sliver of moonbeam enters the room.

She looks at her bag on the floor. Thinks about the letters and the photos inside. Wonders why she didn't leave the bag back in the car.

She knows she's stalling, but she can't help it.

She turns and looks into the shadows: at the blinking machines and the tangle of tubes and the clear, dripping bag with the big red sticker that reads: *CHEMO: Do Not Handle Without Protective Gloves.*

She stares at the man she loves so dearly, the only man she has *ever* loved.

Thirty-four years of life and he's been there over half of them, she thinks.

Just you and me against the world, kiddo . . .

She puts her hand inside her jacket pocket.

Walks to his bedside and leans over.

Kisses his sweaty forehead.

Closes her eyes and whispers: "I'll forever love you, my darling."

And her words will live in this room forever.

She places the gun to his forehead and makes good on her promise.

There's a sudden explosion of sound and light and she falls hard to the floor.

She looks up involuntarily and shudders.

And then, for the first time in all their years together, she breaks her word to him. She opens her mouth wide, slides the cold barrel inside and pulls the trigger.

A promise kept.

A promise broken.

And the unending silence of night.

THE NEW GIRL FRIEND

Ruth Rendell

There is no better psychological novelist working in the world today. She is imitated, to be sure, but no other writer has shown Ruth Rendell's skill at charting the fever dreams of all the insular, frightened and despairing people who inhabit this nowhere little planet of ours.

That she constantly brings wit, surprise and even shock to her work is testament to her skills as a journalist of the heart. She goes where none has gone before, and brings back her particular truth.

"YOU KNOW WHAT WE DID LAST TIME?" HE SAID.

She had waited for this for weeks. "Yes?"

"I wondered if you'd like to do it again."

She longed to but she didn't want to sound too keen. "Why not?"

"How about Friday afternoon, then? I've got the day off and Angie always goes to her sister's on Friday."

"Not *always*, David." She giggled.

He also laughed a little. "She will this week. Do you think we could use your car? Angie'll take ours."

"Of course. I'll come for you about two, shall I?"

"I'll open the garage doors and you can drive straight in. Oh, and Chris, could you fix it to get back a bit later? I'd love it if we could have the whole evening together."

"I'll try," she said, and then, "I'm sure I can fix it. I'll tell Graham I'm going out with my new girl friend."

He said goodbye and that he would see her on Friday. Christine put the receiver back. She had almost given up expecting a call from him. But there must have been a grain of hope still, for she had never left the receiver off the way she used to.

The last time she had done that was on a Thursday three weeks before, the day she had gone round to Angie's and found David there alone. Christine had got into the habit of taking the phone off the hook during the middle part of the day to avoid getting calls for the Midland Bank. Her number and the Midland Bank's differed by only one digit. Most days she took the receiver off at nine-thirty and put it back at three-thirty. On Thursday afternoons she nearly always went round to see Angie and never bothered to phone first.

Christine knew Angie's husband quite well. If she stayed a bit later on Thursdays she saw him when he came home from work. Sometimes she and Graham and Angie and David went out together as a foursome. She knew that David, like Graham, was a salesman or sales executive, as Graham always described himself, and she guessed from her friend's life style that David was rather more successful at it. She had never found him particularly attractive, for, although he was quite tall, he had something of a girlish look and very fair wavy hair.

Graham was a heavily built, very dark man with a swarthy skin. He had to shave twice a day. Christine had started going out with him when she was fifteen and they had got married on her eighteenth birthday. She had never really known any other men at all intimately and now if she ever found herself alone with a man she felt awkward and apprehensive. The truth was that she was afraid a man might make an advance to her and the thought of that frightened her very much. For a long while she carried a penknife in her handbag in case she should need to defend herself. One evening, after they had been out with a colleague of Graham's and had had a few drinks, she told Graham about this fear of hers.

He said she was silly but he seemed rather pleased.

"When you went off to talk to those people and I was left with John I felt like that. I felt terribly nervous. I didn't know how to talk to him."

Graham roared with laughter. "You don't mean you thought old John was going to make a pass at you in the middle of a crowded restaurant?"

"I don't know," Christine said. "I never know what they'll do."

"So long as you're not afraid of what I'll do," said Graham, beginning to kiss her, "that's all that matters."

There was no point in telling him now, ten years too late, that she was afraid of what he did and always had been. Of course she had got used to it, she wasn't actually terrified, she was resigned and sometimes even quite cheerful about it. David was the only man she had ever been alone with when it felt all right.

That first time, that Thursday when Angie had gone to her sister's and hadn't been able to get through on the phone and tell Christine not to come, that time it had been fine. And afterwards she had felt happy and carefree, though what had happened with David took on the colouring of a dream next day. It wasn't really believable. Early on he had said:

"Will you tell Angie?"

"Not if you don't want me to."

"I think it would upset her, Chris. It might even wreck our marriage. You see . . . " He had hesitated. "You see, that was the first time I—I mean, anyone ever . . . " And he had looked into her eyes. "Thank God it was you."

The following Thursday she had gone round to see Angie as usual. In the meantime there had been no word from David. She stayed late in order to see him, beginning to feel a little sick with apprehension, her heart beating hard when he came in.

He looked quite different from how he had when she had found him sitting at the table reading, the radio on. He was wearing a grey flannel suit and a grey striped tie. When Angie went out of the room and for a minute she was alone with him, she felt a flicker of that old wariness that was the forerunner of her fear. He was getting her a drink. She looked up and met his eyes and it was all right again. He gave her a conspiratorial smile, laying a finger on his lips.

"I'll give you a ring," he had whispered.

She had to wait two more weeks. During that time she went twice to Angie's and twice Angie came to her. She and Graham and Angie and David went out as a foursome and while Graham was fetching drinks and Angie was in the ladies', David looked at her and smiled and lightly touched her foot with his foot under the table.

"I'll phone you. I haven't forgotten."

It was a Wednesday when he finally did phone. Next day Christine told Graham she had made a new friend, a girl she had met at work. She would be going out somewhere with this new friend on Friday and she wouldn't be back till eleven. She was desperately afraid he would want the car—it was *his* car or his firm's—but it so happened he would be in the office that day and would go by train. Telling him these lies didn't make her feel guilty. It wasn't as if this were some sordid affair, it was quite different.

When Friday came she dressed with great care. Normally, to go round to Angie's, she would have worn jeans and a tee shirt with a sweater over it. That was what she had on the first time she found herself alone with David. She put on a skirt and blouse and her black velvet jacket. She took the heated rollers out of her hair and brushed it into curls down on her shoulders. There was never much money to spend on clothes. The mortgage on the house took up a third of what Graham earned and half what she earned at her part-time job. But she could run to a pair of sheer black tights to go with the highest heeled shoes she'd got, her black pumps.

The doors of Angie and David's garage were wide open and their car was gone. Christine turned into their driveway, drove into the garage and closed the doors behind her. A door at the back of the garage led into the yard and garden. The kitchen door was unlocked as it had been that Thursday three weeks before and always was on Thursday afternoons. She opened the door and walked in.

"Is that you, Chris?"

The voice sounded very male. She needed to be reassured by the sight of him. She went into the hall as he came down the stairs.

"You look lovely," he said.

"So do you."

He was wearing a suit. It was of navy silk with a pattern of pink and white flowers. The skirt was very short, the jacket clinched into his waist with a wide navy patent belt. The long golden hair fell to his shoulders, he was heavily made up and this time he had painted his fingernails. He looked far more beautiful than he had that first time.

.   .   .

Then, three weeks before, the sound of her entry drowned in loud music from the radio, she had come upon this girl sitting at the table reading *Vogue*. For a moment she had thought it must be

David's sister. She had forgotten Angie had said David was an only child. The girl had long fair hair and was wearing a red summer dress with white spots on it, white sandals and around her neck a string of white beads. When Christine saw that it was not a girl but David himself she didn't know what to do.

He stared at her in silence and without moving and then he switched off the radio. Christine said the silliest and least relevant thing.

"What are you doing home at this time?"

That made him smile. "I'd finished so I took the rest of the day off. I should have locked the back door. Now you're here you may as well sit down."

She sat down. She couldn't take her eyes off him. He didn't look like a man dressed up as a girl, he looked like a girl and a much prettier one than she or Angie. "Does Angie know?"

He shook his head.

"But why do you do it?" she burst out and she looked about the room, Angie's small, rather untidy living room, at the radio, the *Vogue* magazine. "What do you get out of it?" Something came back to her from an article she had read. "Did your mother dress you as a girl when you were little?"

"I don't know," he said. "Maybe. I don't remember. I don't want to *be* a girl. I just want to dress up as one sometimes."

The first shock of it was past and she began to feel easier with him. It wasn't as if there was anything grotesque about the way he looked. The very last thing he reminded her of was one of those female impersonators. A curious thought came into her head, that it was *nicer*, somehow more civilized, to be a woman and that if only all men were more like women . . . That was silly, of course, it couldn't be.

"And it's enough for you just to dress up and be here on your own?"

He was silent for a moment. Then, "Since you ask, what I'd really like would be to go out like this and . . . " He paused, looking at her, "and be seen by lots of people, that's what I'd like. I've never had the nerve for that."

The bold idea expressed itself without her having to give it a moment's thought. She wanted to do it. She was beginning to tremble with excitement.

"Let's go out then, you and I. Let's go out now. I'll put my car in your garage and you can get into it so the people next door don't see and then we'll go somewhere. Let's do that, David, shall we?"

She wondered afterwards why she had enjoyed it so much. What had it been, after all, as far as anyone else knew but two girls walking on Hampstead Heath? If Angie had suggested that the two of them do it she would have thought it a poor way of spending the afternoon. But with David . . . She hadn't even minded that of the two of them he was infinitely the better dressed, taller, better-looking, more graceful. She didn't mind now as he came down the stairs and stood in front of her.

"Where shall we go?"

"Not the Heath this time," he said. "Let's go shopping."

He bought a blouse in one of the big stores. Christine went into the changing room with him when he tried it on. They walked about in Hyde Park. Later on they had dinner and Christine noted that they were the only two women in the restaurant dining together.

"I'm grateful to you," David said. He put his hand over hers on the table.

"I enjoy it," she said. "It's so—crazy. I really love it. You'd better not do that, had you? There's a man over there giving us a funny look."

"Women hold hands," he said.

"Only *those* sort of women. David, we could do this every Friday you don't have to work."

"Why not?" he said.

There was nothing to feel guilty about. She wasn't harming Angie and she wasn't being disloyal to Graham. All she was doing was going on innocent outings with another girl. Graham wasn't interested in her new friend, he didn't even ask her name. Christine came to long for Fridays, especially for the moment when she let herself into Angie's house and saw David coming down the stairs and for the moment when they stepped out of the car in some public place and the first eyes were turned on him. They went to Holland Park, they went to the zoo, to Kew Gardens. They went to the cinema and a man sitting next to David put his hand on his knee. David loved that, it was a triumph for him, but Christine whispered they must change their seats and they did.

When they parted at the end of an evening he kissed her gently on the lips. He smelled of Alliage or Je Reviens or Opium. During the afternoon they usually went into one of the big stores and sprayed themselves out of the tester bottles.

■ ■ ■

Angie's mother lived in the north of England. When she had to convalesce after an operation Angie went up there to look after her. She expected to be away two weeks and the second weekend of her absence Graham had to go to Brussels with the sales manager.

"We could go away somewhere for the weekend," David said.

"Graham's sure to phone," Christine said.

"One night then. Just for the Saturday night. You can tell him you're going out with your new girl friend and you're going to be late."

"All right."

It worried her that she had no nice clothes to wear. David had a small but exquisite wardrobe of suits and dresses, shoes and scarves and beautiful underclothes. He kept them in a cupboard in his office to which only he had a key and he secreted items home and back again in his briefcase. Christine hated the idea of going away for the night in her grey flannel skirt and white silk blouse and that velvet jacket while David wore his Zandra Rhodes dress. In a burst of recklessness she spent all of two weeks' wages on a linen suit.

They went in David's car. He had made the arrangements and Christine had expected they would be going to a motel twenty miles outside London. She hadn't thought it would matter much to David where they went. But he surprised her by his choice of an hotel that was a three-hundred-year-old house on the Suffolk coast.

"If we're going to do it," he said, "we may as well do it in style."

She felt very comfortable with him, very happy. She tried to imagine what it would have felt like going to spend a night in an hotel with a man, a lover. If the person sitting next to her were dressed, not in a black and white printed silk dress and scarlet jacket but in a man's suit with shirt and tie. If the face it gave her so much pleasure to look at were not powdered and rouged and mascara'd but rough and already showing beard growth. She couldn't imagine it. Or, rather, she could only think how in that case she would have jumped out of the car at the first red traffic lights.

They had single rooms next door to each other. The rooms were very small but Christine could see that a double might have been awkward for David who must at some point—though she didn't care to think of this—have to shave and strip down to being what he really was. He came in and sat on her bed while she unpacked her nightdress and spare pair of shoes.

"This is fun, isn't it?"

She nodded, squinting into the mirror, working on her eyelids with a little brush. David always did his eyes beautifully. She turned round and smiled at him.

"Let's go down and have a drink."

The dining room, the bar, the lounge were all low-ceilinged timbered rooms with carved wood on the walls David said was called linenfold panelling. There were old maps and pictures of men hunting in gilt frames and copper bowls full of roses. Long windows were thrown open on to a terrace. The sun was still high in the sky and it was very warm. While Christine sat on the terrace in the sunshine David went off to get their drinks. When he came back to their table he had a man with him, a thickset paunchy man of about forty who was carrying a tray with four glasses on it.

"This is Ted," David said.

"Delighted to meet you," Ted said. "I've asked my friend to join us. I hope you don't mind."

She had to say she didn't. David looked at her and from his look she could tell he had deliberately picked Ted up.

"But why did you?" she said to him afterwards. "Why did you want to? You told me you didn't really like it when that man put his hand on you in the cinema."

"That was so physical. This is just a laugh. You don't suppose I'd let them touch me, do you?"

Ted and Peter had the next table to theirs at dinner. Christine was silent and standoffish but David flirted with them. Ted kept leaning across and whispering to him and David giggled and smiled. You could see he was enjoying himself tremendously. Christine knew they would ask her and David to go out with them after dinner and she began to be afraid. Suppose David got carried away by the excitement of it, the "fun," and went off somewhere with Ted, leaving her and Peter alone together? Peter had a red face and a black moustache and beard and a wart with black hairs growing out of it on his left cheek. She and David were eating steak and the waiter had brought them sharp pointed steak knives. She hadn't used hers. The steak was very tender. When no one was looking she slipped the steak knife into her bag.

Ted and Peter were still drinking coffee and brandies when David got up quite abruptly and said, "Coming?" to Christine.

"I suppose you've arranged to meet them later?" Christine said as soon as they were out of the dining room.

David looked at her. His scarlet-painted lips parted into a wide smile. He laughed.

"I turned them down."

"Did you *really*?"

"I could tell you hated the idea. Besides, we want to be alone, don't we? I know I want to be alone with you."

She nearly shouted his name so that everyone could hear, the relief was so great. She controlled herself but she was trembling. "Of course I want to be alone with you," she said.

She put her arm in his. It wasn't uncommon, after all, for girls to walk along with linked arms. Men turned to look at David and one of them whistled. She knew it must be David the whistle was directed at because he looked so beautiful with his long golden hair and high-heeled red sandals. They walked along the sea front, along the little low promenade. It was too warm even at eight-thirty to wear a coat. There were a lot of people about but not crowds for the place was too select to attract crowds. They walked to the end of the pier. They had a drink in the Ship Inn and another in the Fishermen's Arms. A man tried to pick David up in the Fishermen's Arms but this time he was cold and distant.

"I'd like to put my arm round you," he said as they were walking back, "but I suppose that wouldn't do, though it is dark."

"Better not," said Christine. She said suddenly, "This has been the best evening of my life."

He looked at her. "You really mean that?"

She nodded. "Absolutely the best."

They came into the hotel. "I'm going to get them to send us up a couple of drinks. To my room. Is that OK?"

She sat on the bed. David went into the bathroom. To do his face, she thought, maybe to shave before he let the man with the drinks see him. There was a knock at the door and a waiter came in with a tray on which were two long glasses of something or other with fruit and leaves floating in it, two pink table napkins, two olives on sticks and two peppermint creams wrapped up in green paper.

Christine tasted one of the drinks. She ate an olive. She opened her handbag and took out a mirror and a lipstick and painted her lips. David came out of the bathroom. He had taken off the golden wig and washed his face. He hadn't shaved, there was a pale stubble showing on his chin and cheeks. His legs and feet were bare and he was wearing a very masculine robe made of navy blue towelling. She tried to hide her disappointment.

"You've changed," she said brightly.

He shrugged. "There are limits."

He raised his glass and she raised her glass and he said:

"To us!"

The beginnings of a feeling of panic came over her. Suddenly he was so evidently a man. She edged a little way along the mattress.

"I wish we had the whole weekend."

She nodded nervously. She was aware her body had started a faint trembling. He had noticed it too. Sometimes before he had noticed how emotion made her tremble.

"Chris," he said.

She sat passive and afraid.

"I'm not really like a woman, Chris. I just play at that sometimes for fun. You know that, don't you?" The hand that touched her smelt of nail varnish remover. There were hairs on the wrist she had never noticed before. "I'm falling in love with you," he said. "And you feel the same, don't you?"

She couldn't speak. He took her by the shoulders. He brought his mouth up to hers and put his arms round her and began kissing her. His skin felt abrasive and a smell as male as Graham's came off his body. She shook and shuddered. He pushed her down on the bed and his hands began undressing her, his mouth still on hers and his body heavy on top of her.

She felt behind her, put her hand into the open handbag and pulled out the knife. Because she could feel his heart beating steadily against her right breast she knew where to stab and she stabbed again and again. The bright red heart's blood spurted over her clothes and the bed and the two peppermint creams on the tray.

THE QUIET ROOM

Jonathan Craig

Jonathan Craig wrote a number of very good paperback originals in the fifties and sixties, and then disappeared from the racks, much of his work, alas, forgotten.

Here is one of the most remarkable stories of the 1950s, one that Simenon would undoubtedly have been proud to have written.

DETECTIVE SERGEANT CARL STREETER'S HOME ON ASHLAND AVenue was modest. So were the dark gray suits he always wore, and the four-year-old Plymouth he drove. But in various lock boxes around the city he had accumulated nearly fifty thousand dollars.

He was thinking about the money now as he watched his daughter Jeannie clear away the dinner dishes. He never tired of watching her. She had just turned sixteen, but she was already beautiful, and lately she had begun to develop the infinitely feminine movements and mannerisms he had once found so irresistible in her mother.

The thought of his wife soured the moment, and he frowned. It had been wonderful, having Barbara away for a few weeks. But she'd be back from the seashore next Monday, and then the nagging and bickering and general unpleasantness would start up again. It didn't seem possible, he reminded himself for probably the ten thousandth time, that anyone who had once been almost as slim and lovely as Jeannie could have grown into two hundred pounds of shapeless, complaining blubber.

"More coffee, Dad?" Jeannie asked.

He pushed his chair back from the table and got up. "No," he said. "I guess I'd better get going if I want to get down to the precinct by seven."

"Seven? But I thought your shift didn't start till eight."

"It doesn't. There are a couple things I want to take care of down there, though."

"When will you be home?"

Depends. Not until three or four, anyhow. We're a little short-handed."

"You put in too many hours, Dad."

"Maybe," he said. He grinned at her and walked out to the front hall to get his hat. Just another few months, he thought. Six months at the outside, and I'll have enough to put Jeannie in a damned good college, ditch Barbara and her lard, and tell the Chief to go to hell.

Sally Creighton was waiting for him in the Inferno Bar. She pushed a folded piece of paper across the table as he sat down facing her.

"How's the Eighteenth Precinct's one and only policewoman?" Streeter asked.

Sally looked at him narrowly. "Never mind the amenities. Here's the list we got off that girl last night."

He put the list into his pocket without looking at it. "Did you check them?"

"Don't I always? Only two of them might be good for any money. I marked them. One's a dentist, and the other guy runs a bar and grill over on Summit." She lifted her beer and sipped at it, studying him over the rim of the glass. "There've been a few changes made, Carl." Her bony, angular face was set in hard lines.

"Like what?"

"From now on I'm getting fifty percent."

"We've been over that before."

"And this is the last time. Fifty percent, Carl. Starting as of now."

He laughed shortly. "I do the dirty work, and take the chances—and you come in for half, eh?"

"Either that, or I cut out." She put a quarter next to her glass and stood up. "Think it over, Sergeant. You aren't the only bruiser around the Eighteenth that can shake a guy down. Start making with the fifty percent, or I'll find another partner." She moved toward the door with a long, almost mannish stride.

Streeter spread his fingers flat against the tabletop, fighting back the anger that he knew would get him nowhere. For almost a full minute he stared at the broken, scarred knuckles of his hands. By God, he thought, if it's the last thing I ever do I'll knock about ten of that woman's yellow teeth down into her belly.

Hell, he'd taught her the racket in the first place. He'd shown her how to scare hell out of those underage chippies until they thought they were going to spend the rest of their lives in jail if they didn't play ball. Why, he'd even had to educate Sally in the ways of keeping those girls away from the juvenile authorities until she'd had a chance to drain them.

He closed his right fist and clenched it until the knuckles stood up like serrated knobs of solid white bone. Damn that Sally, any-how; she was getting too greedy. Fifty percent!

He got up slowly and moved toward the door.

■   ■   ■

Twenty minutes later, after he had checked in at the precinct and been assigned a cruiser, he pulled up in a No Parking zone and took out the list Sally had given him. His anger had subsided a little now. Actually, he realized, no cop had ever been in a better spot. His first real break with the Department had been when they had organized the Morals Squad and assigned him to it as a roving detective. The second break had occurred when Sally Creighton was transferred to the Eighteenth. He hadn't talked to her more than ten minutes that first day before he'd realized that he had found the right person to work into his ideas.

In three years, working alone every night as he did, he had loaded his safe deposit boxes with almost fifty thousand dollars.

He lit a cigarette and glanced at the list. Of the two names Sally had marked, the man who owned the bar and grill was the best bet. The other, the dentist, lived on the far side of town; and besides, Streeter had found it was always best to brace a man at his place of business. There was a tremendous psychological factor working on his side when he did that, and especially if the guy happened to be a professional man. He memorized the address of the bar and grill and eased the cruiser away from the curb.

It was too late for the short-order dinner crowd and too early for the beer drinkers, and Streeter had the long bar entirely to himself.

The bartender came up, a thin blond man in his middle thirties.

Streeter ordered beer, and when the blond man brought it to him he said, "I'm looking for Johnny Cabe."

The bartender smiled. "That's me. What can I do for you?"

"Quite a bit, maybe," Streeter said. "It all depends."

Some of the bartender's smile went away. "I don't follow you."

"You will," Streeter said. He took out his wallet and showed the other man his gold badge.

"What's the trouble?" Cabe asked.

"Well, now," Streeter said, "there really doesn't have to *be* any." He took a swallow of beer and leaned a little closer to Cabe. "You had quite a time for yourself last night, they tell me."

Cabe's eyes grew thoughtful. "Last night? You kidding? All I did was have a few beers over at Ed Riley's place, and—"

"Yeah," Streeter said. "And then you picked up somebody."

"What if I did?"

"Then you took her over to your room."

"So what? They don't put guys in jail for—"

"The hell they don't," Streeter said. "Raping a girl can put you away damned near forever, boy."

"Rape? You're crazy! Hell, she wanted to go. She suggested it."

"Next you're going to tell me she charged you for it."

"Sure, she did. Twenty bucks."

"That's a damn shame," Streeter said. "Because it's still rape, and you're in one hell of a jam."

Cabe moved his lips as if to speak, but there was no sound.

"That girl you took home with you was only fifteen years old," Streeter said. "She—"

"Fifteen! She told me she was nineteen! She *looked* nineteen!"

"You should have looked twice. She's fifteen. That makes it statutory rape, and it doesn't make one damn bit of difference what you thought, or whether she was willing, or if she charged you for it, or anything else." He smiled. "It's statutory rape, brother, and that means you've had it."

Cabe moistened his lips. "I can't believe it."

"Get your hat," Streeter said.

"You're arresting me?"

"I didn't come in here just for the beer. Hurry it up."

"God," the blond man said. "God, officer, I—"

"Kind of hard to get used to the idea, isn't it?" Streeter asked softly.

Cabe's forehead glistened with sweat. "Listen, officer, I got a wife. Best kid on earth, see. I don't know what came over me last night. I just got tight, I guess, and . . . God, I—"

Streeter shook his head slowly. "Good thing you haven't got any children," he said.

"But I have! Two of them. Seven and nine. And my wife, she's—she's going to have another baby pretty soon. That's why— I mean that's how come I was kind of anxious for a woman last night. I—" He broke off, biting at his lower lip.

"Tough," Streeter said. "Real tough. But it's that kind of world, friend. I've got a kid myself, so I know how it is. But—" he shrugged—"there isn't a hell of a lot I can do about it." He shook his head sadly. "When little guys—guys like you and me—get in a jam, it's just plain tough. But guys with dough . . . well, sometimes they can buy their way out."

Cabe looked at him a long moment. "How much dough?"

"Quite a bit," Streeter said. "More than you've got, Johnny. Better get your hat."

"Let's cut out this crap," Cabe said. "I asked you how much dough."

"We got to think of your wife and kids," Streeter said. "So we'll have to go easy. Let's say a grand."

"I ain't got it."

"You can get it. A little at a time, maybe, but you can get it." He took another swallow of his beer. "How much you got in the cash register?"

"About three hundred. I got to pay the help tonight, or there wouldn't be that much."

"Too bad about the help," Streeter said. "Let's have the three hundred. In a couple weeks I'll be back. By that time you'll have the other seven hundred, eh, Johnny-boy?"

Cabe went to the cash register, took out the money, and came back. "Here," he said. Then, softly beneath his breath he added: "You bastard!"

Streeter put the money in his pocket and stood up. "Thanks, Johnny," he said. "Thanks a lot. You reckon I ought to give you a receipt? A little reminder to get up that other seven hundred bucks?"

"I'll remember," Cabe said.

"I'm afraid you might not," Streeter said, smiling. "So here's your receipt." He leaned across the bar and slammed his fist flush against the blond man's mouth.

Johnny Cabe crashed into the back-bar, blood trickling from the corners of his mouth.

"Thanks again, Johnny," Streeter said. "You serve a good glass of beer." He turned and went outside to the cruiser.

He spent the next four hours making routine check-ups and trying to think of improvements in the system he had worked out with Sally Creighton. The system had been working nicely, but it was a long way from foolproof. Most of the cops on the force were honest, and for them Streeter had nothing but contempt. But there were a few like himself, and those were the ones who worried him. He'd had reason lately to suspect that a couple of them were getting on to him. If they did, then his racket was over. They could politic around until they got him busted off the Morals Squad. Then they'd take over themselves. And, he reflected, they wouldn't even have to go that far. They could simply cut themselves in on a good thing.

And that Sally . . . He'd have to start splitting down the middle with her, he knew. Maybe she was even worth it. One thing was sure: she'd learned how to terrify young girls better than anyone else he could have teamed up with. He'd seen her work on just one girl, but it had been enough to convince him. Sally had wrapped her arms around a fourteen-year-old girl's throat in such a way that the girl was helpless. Then, with a hand towel soaked with water, she had beaten the girl across the stomach until she was almost dead. When the girl had recovered slightly, she had been only too willing to tell Sally every man she'd picked up during the last six months.

That particular list of names, Streeter recalled, had been worth a little over ten thousand in shake-down money.

He came to a drug store and braked the cruiser at the curb.

In the phone booth, he dialed Sally's number, humming tunelessly to himself. He felt much better now, with Johnny Cabe's three hundred dollars in his pocket.

When Sally answered, he said, "Streeter. Anything doing?"

"I got one in here now," Sally said. "A real tough baby. I picked her up at Andy's trying to promote a drunk at the bar."

"She talking?" he asked.

"Not a damn word. I got her back in the Quiet room."

"What's her name?"

"Don't know. All she had in her bag was a lipstick and a few bucks." She paused. "Like I said, she's tough. She won't even give us the time of day."

"Listen," Streeter said. "Things are slow tonight. See if you can get her talking. Maybe I can collect a bill here and there."

"That's an idea."

"You haven't lost your technique, have you?"

"No."

"All right. So turn it on. Give her that towel across the belly. That ought to make her talkative."

For the first time he could remember, he heard Sally laugh.

"You know," she said, "I'm just in the mood for something like that. Maybe I will."

"Sure," Streeter said. "The sooner you get me some names, the sooner I get us some dough."

"Don't forget, Carl—it's fifty percent now."

"Sure."

He hung up and went back out to the cruiser.

After another slow hour of routine checks, he decided to see how Sally was making out with the tough pick-up. He stopped at a diner and called her.

"God," she said, as soon as he had identified himself, "we're really in it now, Carl." Her voice was ragged, and there was panic in it.

"What do you mean?"

"I mean I went too far. I was doing what you said, and—"

"For God's sake, Sally! What's happened?"

"I—I think I broke her neck . . ."

"You think! Don't you know?"

There was a pause. "Yes. I broke her neck, Carl. I didn't mean to, but she was fighting, and all at once I heard something snap and . . ."

The thin film of perspiration along his back and shoulders was suddenly like a sheath of ice.

"When, Sally? When did it happen?"

"J-just now. Just a minute ago."

"You sure she's dead?"

"Dead or dying. There was a pulse a few seconds ago, but—"

"But her neck! You're positive it's broken? That it just isn't dislocated, or something?"

"It's broken. This is it, Carl. For both of us. God . . ."

"Listen, damn it!" he said. "Was she wearing stockings? Long ones?"

"Yes. What—"

"Take one of them off her and hang her up with it."

She seemed to have trouble breathing. "But I—I can't do that. I—"

"You've got to! Do you hear? It's the only way out. Tie one end of the stocking around her neck. Then put a chair beneath that steam pipe that runs across the ceiling. Haul her up on the chair with you and tie the other end around the pipe. Leave her hanging and kick the chair away, just like she'd done it herself."

He waited, breathing heavily.

"All right," Sally said. "I'll try."

"You'd better. And hurry. Get her up there and then leave the room for a few minutes. When you go back to see your prisoner, she's hanged herself. See? They'll give you hell for leaving her alone with stockings on, but that's all they can do. She panicked and hanged herself; that's all."

"But, Carl, I—"

"No buts! Get busy!"

■   ■   ■

He opened up the siren and kept it open all the way back to the Eighteenth. He ran up the station steps, through the corridors. He was breathing quickly. When he arrived at the second floor he was soaked with perspiration.

He forced himself to walk leisurely through the large room that housed the detective headquarters, back toward the short corridor that led to the Quiet room. The Quiet room was a small, sound-proof detention cell where they sometimes put the screamers and howlers until they calmed down enough for questioning. It had been designed to provide some degree of quiet for the men out in the headquarters room, and not as a torture chamber.

But it had served Streeter and Sally Creighton well and often.

Streeter paused at the door to the corridor and drew a paper cup of water from the cooler. Where in hell was Sally? he wondered. She should be out here by now, killing time before she went back to discover that her prisoner had hanged herself.

He glanced about him. There were only two other detectives in the room, and both were busy with paperwork. A man in a T-shirt and blue jeans sat dozing in a chair, one wrist handcuffed to a chair arm.

Then he heard footsteps behind him, and Sally's voice said, "Thank God you're here."

He turned to look at her. Her face was gray and her forehead was sheened with sweat.

"Where've you been?" he asked.

"To the john. I don't know . . . something about this made me sick in the stomach."

"Yeah. Well, let's go down there and get it over with."

He led the way down the corridor to the Quiet room and threw the heavy bolt. The goddamned little chippie, he thought. So she'd thought she was tough . . . Well, she'd asked for it, hadn't she? She'd asked for it, and she'd damn well got it.

He jerked the door open and looked up at the girl hanging from the steam pipe. Her body was moving, very slowly, a few inches to the right and then back again.

He stared at her while the floor seemed to tilt beneath his feet and something raw and sickening filled his stomach.

He took a faltering step forward, and then another, his eyes straining and misted. It was difficult for him to see clearly. Absently, he brushed at his eyes with his sleeve. The hanging figure before him sprang into sudden, terrifying focus.

The girl's body was as slim and graceful looking in death as it had been a few hours ago when he had watched her clearing away the dinner dishes. But not the face, not the horribly swollen face.

"Jeannie," he whispered. "Jeannie, Jeannie . . ."

MY HEART CRIES FOR YOU

Bill Crider

*Bill Crider has written mysteries, horror novels and westerns.
What his books have in common is their great characters, and
the way the world makes them struggle to survive.*

*Over the past few years, Crider has been getting long overdue
critical attention, especially for his fine, dark suspense novel*
Blood Marks.

I MET ETHEL ANN ADAMS ON VALENTINE'S DAY AND WE MET
cute, just like in the movies. I was in the flower department at
Kroger, thinking I might buy some flowers to send to the woman
who'd just ditched me two days before for a man who drove a
BMW. I thought maybe she'd feel sorry for me and give me another chance. I don't know. Anyway, I was standing there looking
at the roses when Ethel Ann ran into me with her grocery cart.

She didn't knock me far, not more than a foot, and I figured
the bruises would go away in a week or two, so I told her not to
worry about it. To forget it. I was fine.

If she'd been good-looking, it might've been a different story,
but she wasn't the kind of woman I was interested in at all. She
was short and chunky, about five-three and 140 pounds. Solid.
She had black hair like wires—curly wires, the kind inside a sofa
cushion. Those were on her head. Her mustache was black, too,
but the hairs weren't curly. They were too short.

She wouldn't leave me alone, though. She acted like she'd done
me irreparable harm and it was her duty to make it all right.

"Here, let me help ya," she said. She had a voice like a steve-
dore. "I'll pick up ya packages."

She scuttled around like a crab with Saint Vitus's Dance and picked up the cereal box and the granola bars and the Hamburger Helper, then stuffed them back on top of my basket.

"Ya okay now?" she said.

"I'm fine," I said, always the gentleman. "I'll be just fine, thanks."

"Good, good. I'm glad. Ya buying some posies for your chick?"

She really said things like that: Posies. Chick.

"No," I said. "I was thinking of sending some to my mother." My mother had been dead for ten years, but how do you say you were thinking of sending flowers to someone who'd just dumped you?

"Ya got a chick?"

"I beg your pardon?"

"Ya got a chick? A babe? A hotsie-totsie?"

She really said that. Hotsie-totsie.

"No," I said, rather coldly I'm afraid.

"A nice-looking hunk like you? All alone on the most romantic day of the year? I can't believe it."

I am rather nice-looking, I have to admit. A slight natural wave in my hair, a nice smile (thanks to extensive orthodontic work in my youth), and a trim body (thanks to a three-times-a-week jog of up to three miles).

"Ya got cute buns too."

Buns. I ask you.

"I betcha wouldn't believe I don't have a fella myself."

"Uh . . ."

"Yeah, I know. Hard to believe. But true." She tried to look wistful, but instead looked only dyspeptic. She had on a horrible pair of knit stretch pants that did nothing to help the effect.

"Look," she said. "Why don't you and me get together? I mean, it's a real shame, two hot numbers like us, all alone on the most important romantic day of the year."

She stood there and looked up at me with her black eyes way back in her head under the heavy ridges of her brows. The brows were black and straight, like her mustache. I had heard of the supermarket as being one of the hot places to meet dates nowadays, but this was too much. Hot numbers. I mean, give me a break.

Still, there I was. Ditched not two days before by the light of my life, who said she thought I lacked ambition and "charisma." I had told *her* that I liked selling shoes, and that you didn't need charisma to do that. She had laughed at me and said she could tell I'd never amount to anything and that she was going to start dating somebody named Chris. "He drives a BMW," she said. "Not a tacky old Subaru." I told her that Subarus had even better repair records than BMWs, but it didn't do any good.

So call it temporary insanity. Call me irresponsible. Or call me a masochist, which is probably more like it. I was punishing myself for losing somebody who liked a car better than she liked me. Anyway, for whatever reason, I looked into Ethel Ann's pitchy black eyes and said, "Why not?"

She told me her name then, and I told her mine, which is Wayne G. (for Garfield, but I never tell anyone that, not since that cat in the comic pages) Cook, and we agreed that she would come by and pick me up later at my apartment.

"I got a nice car," she said. "You'll like it. Plus I like to drive. We'll have a few drinks, tell a few jokes, see what develops."

Then she leered at me, a truly frightening sight, and icy fingers ran up and down my spine. Not the Old Black Magic kind. The kind that you get when you're reading Stephen King on a dark and stormy night, except that she was even scarier. . . .

But I'd given my word and that was that. I finished my shopping, without buying any roses, checked out, and went home to get ready.

She arrived right on time, wearing a red skirt with a white blouse that just sort of hung on her flat chest. She had a white envelope in her hand. "Here," she said, sticking the envelope at me. "I got ya a valentine."

I hadn't gotten her one, of course. The thought never even entered my mind, and if it had I would have rejected it instantly. I took the envelope.

"Aren't ya gonna ask me in?" she said.

I opened the door a little wider and she walked through. My living room is nothing to brag about, not being much larger than most people's second bedroom, but it is at least tidy.

She walked over and sat down on the couch while I tore at the envelope. When I got it open, I pulled out the card. It was in the shape of a heart (not a real one, of course, but a valentine one, which has absolutely no relationship to the human heart that I can see) with eyes and a mouth drawn on it. The mouth was turned down in a frown, and there were tiny tears in the corners of the eyes.

I opened the card. Inside it was written in red letters, *My heart cries for you.*

"Cute, huh?" Ethel Ann said.

"Very," I said. I put the card down on my coffee table.

"So where ya wanta go?" she said. "Find a nice spot, hoist a few brewskis?"

Brewskis. Of course.

"I was thinking more along the lines of a movie," I said. The idea of what Ethel Ann might be like after a couple of "brewskis" frankly terrified me.

"Aww ri-i-i-i-ght!" she said. "There's this new one out I've been wanting to see over at the Plaza Town Eight."

"Fine," I said. "What is it?"

"It's a new one for Valentine's Day. I EAT YOUR HEART. It's about these teenagers, see, who have this Valentine's party and this maniac or something—"

"I can't wait," I said.

.   .   .

She was right about one thing, at least. I loved her car. It was a perfectly restored 1957 Chevrolet.

"Original factory paint," she said. "It was a bitch to find the purple, too, believe me."

"I can imagine."

"The white for the top was easy, though. I wanted to go with red, but the guy who did the work wouldn't go for it. Some people got no taste at all."

"Too right," I said.

The movie was worse than I'd thought it might be. It wasn't so much the actual movie, though the sight of entrails and brains and exploding teenage skulls didn't really do much for me. No, the worst thing was the way Ethel Ann behaved.

She belched.

I suppose that could be my fault. After all, I did ask if she wanted something to drink to go with her popcorn (two large tubs, buttered), and carbonated water does that to some people.

She didn't have to do it so often, however. I think some of it must have been deliberate.

Also, she laughed raucously every time some semi-innocent victim lost one of his or her vital body parts or got skewered with a tree limb, broken boat paddle, lug wrench, or whatever.

Everyone else cringed, gagged, or simply looked away. Not Ethel Ann. She brayed like a mule. Or is it donkeys that bray? Well, you get the idea.

And then she . . . there's simply no delicate way to put this, really. She . . . broke wind.

Loudly.

At a time when the audience sat in absolute silence as the maniac crept quietly up on yet another teenage beauty who had thoughtlessly rejected him and who in fact had laughed when he sent her a valentine.

Just as he raised his arms high, prepared to bring the jagged mop handle down into her chest as she lay sleeping on a sofa, just as the quiet in the theater had grown almost unbearable, Ethel Ann broke wind.

It was like a gunshot, but more drawn out, if you understand what I mean.

Heads turned.

Giggles began.

Ethel Ann joined in the giggles, looked at me, and pointed her finger, shaking her head sadly as if to say, "He does that all the time."

The giggles turned to laughter as I tried, without much luck, to melt through the bottom of my seat.

It was, beyond any doubt, the worst evening of my life. I can't recall ever being more repelled or disgusted. People were still giving me surreptitious glances as we left the theater. Then they would look away quickly and laugh, sometimes putting their hands over their mouths as if they didn't want me to see.

Ethel Ann wasn't bothered in the least. "That was great, huh? I don't know when I've seen so much guts on the screen."

I didn't say anything. I just wanted to get home, lock my door,

and get away from her. Thank God, I would never have to see her
again.

                                        .   .   .

Exactly three months later, Ethel Ann Adams and I were united
in what is loosely referred to as holy matrimony.

It was a lovely service, and the bride wore white. She hadn't
lost any weight over the intervening months, and she looked a
little like a sow stuffed into a wedding gown. Her little piggy eyes
watched me from under her veil as we repeated our vows.

I managed not to throw up as I kissed her. The hairs of her
little mustache pricked me under my nose.

It all came about because of her brother.

The day after Valentine's, he'd come by my apartment. It was
late afternoon, and I'd just gotten in from a hard day of trying to
make women's feet fit into shoes that were generally ill made and
about a size too small for the feet that were being forced into
them.

I wasn't in a good mood, and Ethel Ann's brother didn't cheer
me up.

He stood there in my doorway wearing a lavender silk shirt and
a pair of jeans so tight that you could see the outlines of certain
personal portions of his anatomy. The jeans were bell bottoms, so
when he told me that he was Ethel Ann's brother, I wasn't surprised. He didn't mention that he had chosen what we call these
days an "alternate life-style," but then, he didn't have to. I could
just tell.

His name was Raymond, and I asked him to come in. I didn't
know what else to do with him.

"This is such a *sweet* little place," he said, pirouetting around
to get a good look at it. "Ethel Ann said that you were charming
and handsome, and she certainly didn't exaggerate. She has a ten-
dency to do that, you know." He posed there with one hand on
his hip and another in the air. "Is it all right if I sit?"

"Look," I said. "I just got in from work, and I'm not feeling
too well. I'm not sure what you want, but if it's about your sister,
well, I'm sorry, but I don't really think I want to see her again."

I hoped that was all it was. I hoped that Ethel Ann wasn't a
recruiting service for her brother. I didn't feel like fighting him
off. I really didn't.

"Oh, my dear boy," he said. "It's not at all what you think, I'm sure. Not at all. Why, you wouldn't be able to guess in a million, trillion years what I want. I'm *sure* you wouldn't."

"Why don't you tell me, then," I said.

"All right, I will, if you insist on rushing me into it. I had hoped that we might discuss the matter in a civilized manner, you know. Not rushing into it like a pair of primitives."

"I'm sorry," I said. "I'm tired, and I need my rest. If you have something to say, please say it."

"Very well. It's simple, really." He waved the hand that was in the air. "I want you to marry Ethel Ann. And then to kill her."

I just looked at him for a second or two. Then I asked him to sit down.

■ ■ ■

It was all very simple, really. I hadn't realized that Ethel Ann's father was Ronald H. Adams, the richest man in town, an oil millionaire from one of the big booms of the twenties. He was quite old now, and, according to Raymond, on his last legs.

"The old dear is going to kick off any day now," is the way Raymond put it.

As far as Raymond was concerned, that was just fine, since there was no love lost between the two of them, and that was just the problem: Raymond was cut out of the will.

"Almost, dear boy. *Almost*. Should my sweet, ingenuous sister die first, predecease me as they say in the legal offices, then the money goes to me. Not that there is much of a chance of that in the natural order of things. Ethel Ann is as healthy as a horse." He sighed. "Still, there are ways."

"Why me?" I said. "I'm just a shoe salesman. There are professionals for that kind of thing." It wasn't that I had anything against the idea. If ever anyone deserved to go, it was Ethel Ann Adams.

"Oh, *please*," he said. "Are you suggesting that I get some sort of *hit*man? That is so *common*."

Common. Well, he was probably right. I wondered how he and his sister got to be so different. Ethel Ann would have gone to a hitman in a minute. Less, probably.

"Besides, dear boy, don't you read the newspapers? Every single hitman in this city is a policeman working undercover. The last three people who have hired hitmen around here have wound up in prison."

"That's right," I said. "Not a nice place. You could get raped in there."

"I didn't say it didn't have its attractive side," he said. "It's just that I don't want to spend my *life* there."

"What about *my* life?"

"It would have to look like an accident, of course. There could be no question of your involvement. No hint of scandal could ever touch you."

"If that were possible, which I don't for a minute say it is, what's in it for me?"

"Why, money, of course; money, dear boy."

Of course.

It turned out that Raymond had managed to find out a good deal about me in the course of the day. As soon as he discovered that his sister had managed to find an actual *date*, he got the name and started to work. The idea had been in his head for weeks.

And I was the ideal subject, as it turned out. A man who had been recently rejected by a woman and who had a history of such rejection.

"How did you find that out?" I said.

"It was easy," he said, but he wouldn't elaborate. I didn't argue. It was true. The latest was just one of a continuing series. All of them for more or less the same reasons.

"And that's the problem we can solve," Raymond said. "You can show them that they were all wrong. You can show them that you are virtually *filled* with drive and ambition. That you can marry the richest woman in town and obtain a great deal of money in the process."

"If they can stop laughing," I said.

Raymond smiled. "People seldom laugh at rich people very long." He sounded as if he knew whereof he spoke.

"How much?" I said.

He told me. It was more than I'd ever dreamed of.

"And my share?"

"Let's say . . . half."

"Let's say sixty percent."

"Done," he said, and stuck out a soft pink hand.

"I don't suppose we could put this in writing," I said.

He tittered. I don't think I'd ever heard anyone titter before, but that was what he did. There's no other way to describe it. "I don't suppose we could," he said. "You'll just have to trust me, dear heart."

"I'll think about it," I said, and I did.

It took a lot of thought. I'd never even thought of killing anyone before, and it took some getting used to. On the other hand, I'd never had the chance to become a millionaire before. And, let's face it, there was never anyone on the face of the earth that I could more cheerfully kill than Ethel Ann Adams.

Raymond had given me his number. I called him back two days later. "I'll do it," I told him. "For sixty-five percent."

"Greedy, greedy," he simpered. "But all right. Sixty-five percent."

"I may need a little help."

"We'll talk about it. After the marriage."

"I've been thinking about that part. Why do I have to marry her?"

"Opportunity, of course," he said. "You'll be close to her at all times. Who knows what might come up? She might climb a ladder. Slip in the bath. And you'll be right there."

"We'll talk later," I said.

After I hung up, I called Ethel Ann and, God help me, asked her for a date.

■ ■ ■

I won't try to tell you what the marriage was like. If you have the nasty habit of imagining the bedroom scenes played out in other people's lives, then feel free to go ahead, but such events are far beyond my own poor powers of description. Suffice it to say that those scenes were as horrible as I had anticipated they might be, and in some ways even worse. I'd prefer not to think about it.

I called Raymond after a month. He said the time was "not ripe as yet, dear boy," and that his father still had a while to live. There was no rush.

I called after another month had dragged its way past, and after that I called every week. Raymond didn't seem in a great hurry. "Remember," he said, "if anything happens too soon after the wedding, there are bound to be nasty rumors and suspicions. Caesar's wife, dear boy. Caesar's wife."

I wasn't worried about Caesar's wife. I was worried about mine. She snored like a riveter. She ate like a horse. She wallowed in the bed like a wounded rhino.

She couldn't cook, and she refused to allow me to do so, though I am fairly competent in the kitchen. "It wouldn't be right to let ya do it," she said. "I'll take care of the meals."

So we subsisted on a diet of Budget Gourmet frozen dinners, along with occasional treats such as Mrs. Paul's fish sticks and Pepperidge Farms croissant pizza.

And she was a far worse housekeeper than cook. If she used a tissue, she left it in the chair or couch. Or she tossed it aside on the rug. She never dusted, and she was too lazy even to put such dishes as we used in the dishwasher. Powder covered the washstand in the bathroom. Mildew grew rampant in the shower and in the pile of towels that began to accumulate in a corner by the shower stall.

My formerly tidy apartment into which we had moved was becoming a slum area. It was almost unrecognizable.

I tried to avoid taking her out in public. She looked far worse than when we first met. As she put it, "Now that I got ya, I can afford to let myself go."

And go she did. Up by twenty or more pounds. She quit using makeup. "Too much trouble, sweetie. Bring me another brewski."

Ah, yes, the beer. Four six-packs a day at the very least. She guzzled the stuff.

Still, her father doted on her. We visited him twice a week, every week. He was a frail old man with a pink scalp and a few strands of white hair. Hands like claws.

After every visit, I called Raymond.

"Now, now," he said. "Don't be in a rush. If you're so eager for the money, just let the old man die. Then your wife will have it all."

"I don't want her to have it. I want her out of the way. Besides, if she dies then, I'll be suspected for sure. No one knows how I can stand her anyway."

"Just smile mysteriously if they ask," he said. "And don't worry."

I did worry, though, and finally I couldn't take it anymore. It was just after Ethel Ann threw up on the carpet—"Too many brewskis, I guess, honey"—and then passed out on the couch, leaving me to clean up the mess.

I called Raymond. "This is it," I told him. "Now, tonight."

"Wait—" he said.

I hung up the phone.

Looking at Ethel Ann there on the couch, her mouth open, the snoring rattling the windows in the apartment, I knew I could do it. Oddly enough, I'd worried about that earlier. When it came right down to it, could I actually kill another person?

The answer was yes if the person was Ethel Ann.

I didn't think much about how to do it. I concocted some wild story about rapists and killers and went to the kitchen for a knife. I didn't have a gun, or I would have used that.

I'd slit her throat, then leave. Go to a movie. Make sure I was noticed. Then come home and find her dead. I would be the grieving husband. No one would ever know.

In my current state, it even sounded logical.

I got out the knife and tested the edge with the ball of my thumb, a stupid error, since I always kept my knives sharp.

I cut a deep gash in my thumb.

Blood was running everywhere. I got a towel from under the sink and wrapped my thumb. The bitch was going to pay for this. I rarely use foul language, but that was the way I thought of her then. The bitch.

Even then I might have done it if I hadn't stepped in the vomit. I should have cleaned it up first, I know, but I forgot. In my haste, I forgot, and I put my foot right in the middle of it.

What a vile feeling that is, knowing what you've stepped in even though at the same time you're surprised. I brought one hand up and the other hand down. The sharp blade of the knife just missed the towel and sliced neatly into the palm of my hand. Neatly and fairly deeply. I hardly felt it at first.

Later, I felt it, of course.

I managed to get the towel around my hand and stop the blood. I knew the cut was bad. Somehow I didn't think the police would buy my story about the movies now. I left Ethel Ann lying there and went to the Emergency Room instead.

I said I'd been chopping lettuce, but no one really cared.

I bled a little on the seat covers of Ethel Ann's '57 Chevy. That was the only satisfaction I got.

■ ■ ■

The next time I vowed to be much more careful. And to plan better.

I waited until just the right moment, after she had drunk her daily allotment of brewskis—*beers*; after her daily allotment of beers. Then I offered to take her to the movies.

"Ya mean it? We don't hardly go out much no more."

"I mean it," I said. *"Nightmare on Elm Street V."*

"Aww ri-i-i-i-ght!"

She got ready in mere moments, ready to see Freddy.

"Where's the car?" she said as we got to the street. "Has the car been stole?"

"No, no," I said. "I just had to park across the street. It's right over there." I pointed, and sure enough the car was there, right where I'd parked it. "Just a minute, before we cross," I said. "My shoelace is untied." I knew it was untied because I'd never tied it. I bent down.

My plan was simple. We lived on a fairly busy street. We were standing between two parked cars. I would wait until I heard a car coming, rise up fast, and bump Ethel Ann in her gigantic rear end.

She, in turn, would stumble in front of the oncoming car and be crushed to jelly.

It should have worked, but what happened was rather different.

Apparently, she moved. So, when I made my move, she wasn't where she should have been. That, in itself, wouldn't have been so bad.

The bad thing was that, while pretending to tie my shoe, I had actually done so. But in trying to keep an eye out for the oncoming car, tie the shoe, and judge Ethel Ann's position, I had managed to tie my shoelaces together.

I raised up, took a half step, which was all the step I could take with my shoes tied to one another, and pitched forward into the street.

I have to give the driver full credit. He was much more alert than I would have thought he might be.

He almost managed to stop.

One of the doctors in the Emergency Room asked if I had been in before. He thought I looked familiar.

I didn't answer him. I just lay there and suffered.

Three cracked ribs. Numerous contusions and abrasions, most of them coming from skidding along the concrete street. Several gashes that required stitches.

Aside from that, I was just fine. Ethel Ann couldn't wait to get me home.

"Oh, he is my ittle itsy boogums," she said. "I take care wuv itsy boogums."

Itsy boogums. Good God.

She kept me in bed and fed me Budget Gourmet, potato chips, ice cream, and brewskis—*beers*.

She kept the television set on all the time: *The Love Connection. The New Hollywood Squares. Divorce Court. The People's Court. Superior Court.* A few more weeks of convalescing, and I might have been able to pass the bar in most states. *The New Newlywed Game* was the worst. The only thing the announcer didn't ask the contestants—if indeed they should be dignified by that word—was whether they liked to grease their mates with salad oil before they "made whoopie." (I was beginning to learn where Ethel Ann picked up her expressions.) Of course, he might have asked them that on an earlier show.

"I wonder if any of 'em ever made whoopie in bed with broke ribs?" Ethel Ann said one day. Then she leered at me. Then . . . frankly, I don't want to talk about it.

After more than a week, I was able to go back to work. It was a frightening experience. At odd moments I found myself wondering what Chuck Woolery was prying out of some woman about her date with the sleazoid of her choice, or whether the audience would vote for date number one, number two, or number three.

Occasionally, I would crave a brewski.

When I was getting about as scared of myself as I was of my wife, I called Raymond from work. "We've got to meet," I said.

He didn't like it, but he agreed. He was afraid of being seen with me.

We met on my lunch hour, in the third row of a movie theater, a place that showed third-run films for a dollar admission.

The theater was practically deserted, which was a good thing, since Raymond had no idea of protective coloration. He would have stood out in any crowd. It wasn't that he looked like his sister—quite the contrary. He was taller, and much thinner. Where her hair curled, his waved. Where she was coarse, he was refined. Except in the matter of proper dress.

It was too dark in the theater for me to tell what color his pants were, but his shirt was shocking pink. He was wearing an ascot of some dark color, and it was covered with tiny pink hearts.

My heart cries for you, I thought for some reason.

He sat down beside me. "I simply *adore* Paul Newman," he said. "He is just so *butch* with that little mustache."

So is Ethel Ann, I thought.

"But really, dear boy, we shouldn't meet like this. It's much too dangerous. What if someone should see us?"

My reputation would be ruined, I thought.

"I don't know why you're so *eager*," he went on. "If you could only be patient, I'm sure—"

"I can't wait," I said. "I think something's happening to me. Living with your sister is doing something to me. I . . . I can't explain it, but I don't think I like it."

He shook his head without taking his eyes off Paul Newman, who was stalking around a pool table in full color. "I know what you mean," he said. "I went out on my own early in life for much the same reason."

"Then *why*—" I stopped and started over, realizing I had raised my voice considerably. "Then why did you do this to me?"

"To be quite frank, I thought my father would have died by now. Surely you've *seen* him?"

I admitted that I had.

"Then you know what I mean. The strength of that man amazes me."

"But couldn't I kill her now and remain a grieving widower until you get the money? Why do I have to suffer like this?"

He managed to take his eyes off the screen and look at me. "I should think that would be quite evident," he said.

"It's sure as hell not—it's surely not evident to *me*."

He sighed theatrically. "Should she die too soon, too long before dear Father's own crisis, then he would have time to change his will. Don't you see? Why the old fool might do something *drastic*, like leaving his money to the Friends of the Earth or the Save the Whales Club. Not that I don't think that whales are quite *sweet* in their own way, but really I would much prefer to see the money go to a worthier cause. Such as myself." Then he gave me the old up and under. "And you, of course."

"Of course."

"So wait. Persevere." He pronounced it with the accent on the next-to-last syllable, so that it rhymed with *ever*. "You will be rewarded in the end."

"I'll try," I said.

He looked at me kindly. "Please do, dear boy. Please do. For both our sakes."

I left the movie then. Raymond said he thought he'd stay. "That Tom Cruise is just simply *gorgeous*," he said as I stepped into the aisle.

I looked back, and he was leaning forward in his seat. Drooling, probably.

■   ■   ■

Months went by.

Slowly.

So slowly.

Ethel Ann and I continued to visit her father. It was after one such visit that Ethel Ann said, "The old guy's lookin' better, don't ya think, hon?"

My pace faltered. She had confirmed my own suspicions. He *did* look better. Healthier, somehow.

"He's fillin' out, did ya notice? His color's better, too. He says his authur-itis"—as God is my witness, that's what she said—"is better, even. He can open and close his hands real good."

I must have shuddered then.

"What's 'a matter?" Ethel Ann said. "Is my sugar booger cold?"

Sugar booger. Holy shi—I mean, good grief.

It was a few weeks later that I noticed that I was eager to get home after work in time for *Wheel of Fortune*.

"That Vanna's such a doll," Ethel Ann was fond of saying. "If we ever have a kid"—she leered hopefully—"a girl kid, let's name her Vanna."

"I . . . uh . . . it's a lovely name," I said.

"And that Pat Sajak? A doll. Just a doll. Lucky for you ya got me when ya did. I could really go for a guy like that."

"Be quiet," I said. "You made me miss what letter that idiot asked for."

"It was an *m*," she said. "I thought it was a pretty good guess, myself."

"Hush," I said. "I'll miss the next one, too."

And it wasn't long after that when I realized that I was getting used to the filthy apartment. I tossed my towel on the floor right by Ethel Ann's, though I still used one more often than she did.

"After all, I hardly done a thing today," she said. "Why bathe?"

Why, indeed?

The dirty dishes piled up, the Budget Gourmet containers accumulated in the trash can, and there was actual grit on the kitchen floor. I saw roaches creeping and scuttling across the cabinets.

And at work I wondered: Who will sit in the center square on *New Hollywood Squares* today? And I wondered: Why didn't that fool take door number three yesterday? Anybody would have taken door number three. And I wondered: How could that nincompoop not have written down his answer in the form of a question? Does he have a death wish?

Worst of all was the time I thought, Gee, I wish I had me a brewski. It made my palms sweat, and my hands slipped on the smooth brown leather of the shoe I was trying to force onto the foot of a woman who obviously should have asked for a much larger size.

"What's the matter with you, fella?" she said. "Trying to feel me up?"

"You wish," I said. It slipped out. Honestly.

"What did you say, buster?"

"I . . . uh . . . said this *shoe* ish sized wrong. I'm shorry."

She looked at me with a great deal of suspicion, but she let it pass. She didn't buy any shoes, though.

I knew then that it couldn't go on any longer. I didn't care if Mr. Adams left his considerable fortune to Morris the Cat or the Liberace Museum. Something terrible was happening to me, and the longer I lived with Ethel Ann, the worse it got. I was crazy to have gone along with Raymond in the first place. For my own sanity, Ethel Ann had to go. And she had to go soon.

■ ■ ■

I didn't say anything about it to Raymond. There was no need for him to know, and I was sure he would have objected. He would have had good reason. Only two days before, Mr. Adams had gotten so much better that he had asked the doctor for an exercise program.

There was no doubt in my mind that he would live to be a hundred.

This time I made sure that nothing could go wrong. I planned everything carefully, even went over it in a practice run of sorts. This time was for keeps.

I waited until the perfect night—dark, cloudy, a little drizzle. I asked Ethel Ann if she'd like to take a drive.

"Gee, I don't know, hon. On *Lifestyles of the Rich and Famous* tonight, Robin Leach is gonna give us a tour of one of Wayne Newton's places."

"No kidding? Well—No. No. We really ought to get out more. All we do is watch the tube—the television set. A little drive is what we need. And you know?" I smiled at her in what I hoped was a provocative manner. "A drive in the cool night air just might give me some hot ideas."

She jumped off the couch. Well, actually, she more or less rolled off. At her size and weight, which must have been nearing 190 by then, jumping was more or less out of the question. "Why didn't ya say so the first time, sport? Lemme get some shoes on."

She did, and we left.

"Let me drive," I said. "I like to drive the Chevy."

"Fine by me, kiddo. That way I can snuggle-bunny on you."

Snuggle-bunny. Give me strength.

We drove around town for a while, nowhere in particular, listening to the radio. Ethel Ann had put a really good stereo in the old car, and a good set of speakers. Unfortunately, she usually insisted on playing her Slim Whitman tapes, but tonight she had forgotten them in her haste to get out to the car and make snuggle-bunnies.

Then I headed out toward Mount Granton.

She caught on fast. "I know where y're goin', big boy," she said. "Thinkin' about makin' a little time, huh?" She wormed her way even closer to me. "Well, I'll tell ya, ya got a good chance."

I held my gorge down and kept driving. Mount Granton was a popular spot for parking and engaging in sexual activity. It had quite a good view of the city, actually, and at night the lights could look quite attractive if you were in the right mood. Of course, on such a rainy night as this, there wouldn't be many couples there. The view was terrible, it was cold, and these days most people simply preferred to stay at home and do it in bed.

Or at least, so I hoped.

Near the top, there was a small turnout. As we neared it, I said, "Gosh, honey, I think there's something wrong with one of our tires."

There was, too. I'd let a great deal of the air out of it when I came home that afternoon. Not enough to be really bothersome, but enough to be noticeable if someone called your attention to it.

"It's in the back on my side, I think," I said. She raised her head as if that would help her to sense it. "Ya may be right," she said. "It's kinda bumping."

And that was true, too, not that I'd planned it. Just a little luck for a change. Things were at last about to go my way.

It was about time, after all.

"Why don't I pull up here," I said. "I can get out and check it." I gave a delicate cough. "I wish I didn't feel like I was coming down with a cold."

"If ya are, ya better not get your tootsies wet. I'll check it out for ya."

"How very thoughtful," I said.

I pulled into the turnout very carefully, just the way I had practiced it. Just the right angle. I stopped the car. Not a single automobile had passed us on the way up.

Goodbye, Ethel Ann, I thought. Or maybe I said it aloud. She laughed. "I'll be right back, ya big jerk."

That's what *you* think, my dear.

I could visualize myself talking to the police officer, tears of sorrow welling in my eyes. "It . . . it was terrible, officer. I suppose my foot slipped off the brake—God knows how!—just as she was crossing behind the car. It struck her, and the railing—the railing there is so low! There was nothing I could do to save her! Oh, my sweet darling!"

And at that point I would break down in body-shaking sobs, the drizzle in the night air blending with the tears that flowed down my innocent cheeks.

As a plan, it was perfect.

The execution of it, however, was flawed.

In order to be sure that I struck her hard enough, I was going to have to do a bit more than let the car roll backward. I was going to have to put it into reverse and give her a good, solid bump.

Even at that, I might have succeeded had I not been overly eager. I should have waited until she got right in the middle, but I didn't. I let her take one step behind the car, and shifted gears. She saw the backup lights and stepped back to the side.

I got my foot off the gas and back on the brake, but the surface was extremely slick, possibly oily. The guardrail was no help at all.

I remember hearing it splinter, my foot still frozen to the brake. I remember the rear end of the car tilting out over the ledge and the hood rearing up in the air.

I remember looking out the window at Ethel Ann's horror-stricken face.

And that's all I remembered for quite some time.

∎   ∎   ∎

When I woke up in the hospital, all I could think of was how cold it seemed and how thirsty I felt.

I tried to move, I think, but that proved to be impossible. I was encased in casts and had one leg suspended in some sort of medieval torture device. The pain was excruciating.

I fainted.

When I came out of it again, I felt better, though not much. There was a nurse in my room. I tried to say something to her, but I found I couldn't talk. It was as if my tongue had swollen until it filled my entire mouth. So I just lay there. Then I went to sleep.

I woke up more and more often, and the nurses and doctors seemed to be encouraged by my progress. Ethel Ann was there most of the time. I tried not to look at her.

One day she asked me how I was feeling. I surprised myself by being able to answer. After that we talked a little.

I had been in the hospital for three weeks. In another three I might be able to go home, if I behaved myself and was a good little boy.

"My itsy boogums will be good," she said. "I will take care wuv my itsy boogums."

It hardly bothered me.

I got better and was able to watch the tube. I watched all the game shows that came on, which meant that I got to see a few I'd missed because of work, like *The Price is Right*. I also got to see Donahue, and by the time I was ready to go home I knew I'd miss him when I had to go back to work, even if he was a little bit wimpy.

Then one day Ethel Ann came in crying. "What's the matter?" I said. "Have you talked to the doctor? He didn't say anything that he told you not to tell me, did he?"

And then an even more terrible thought struck me. "Ethel Ann—your father. He's not . . . he didn't . . ."

She looked at me and I could see that she wasn't sad at all. She was actually smiling, but the tears were running down her face and she was sobbing. "It's Daddy," she said. "It's Daddy."

I was out of traction by then, almost ready to go home. Just the casts here and there. One arm (the left) and one leg (the right), plus wrappings around my ribs (broken again, five this time). I sort of fell back in the bed in a collapse.

The old man was dead.

She was trying to keep a good face on things, but the tears gave it all away. He was dead, and that was that. If I killed Ethel Ann now, everyone would suspect me.

I tried to do the right thing. "I . . . I'm sorry," I said.

Ethel Ann wiped the back of her hand across her eyes and pulled at her nose with her fingers. "Don't be sorry," she said. "It's just that I'm so happy."

"Happy?" I said.

"That Daddy's doing so well."

"Uh . . . well?"

"Yeah. I was gonna surprise ya when ya got out of the hospital.

He's been just gettin' better and better ever' day. Strong as an ox. I just found out he's gonna run in the WonTon Marathon."

"He's . . . going to run . . . in a marathon?"

She rubbed her face, which made it look redder than ever. "Ain't it great? It's like, you know, a miracle. The doctor says he may live another hundred years."

Something came over me. I don't know what. I just knew that I had to do it then, no matter what. I came off the bed at her.

At least that's what I tried to do. I remember the leg with the cast hitting the floor and skidding. I remember the sound of the bedpan clattering across the floor. I remember falling.

I remember Ethel Ann telling the doctor, "He was so excited about my news that he tried to get up. I didn't know it would make him do that, honest I didn't."

And the doctor saying, "It's not your fault; don't worry."

■   ■   ■

So I had to stay in the hospital for a while longer, and watch a bit more television. I got real good at *The Wheel of Fortune*. Did a little more study for the bar exam with Judge Wapner. Ate hospital food.

Eventually I got to go back to the apartment. What it looked like after more than a month of Ethel Ann's care and hers alone, I can hardly tell you. There were piles of dirty clothes on the couch. The roaches had moved to the coffee table. There were coffee cups on top of the TV set. With cold coffee in them. Some of them had mold growing on the top of the coffee. It was yellowish, with green around the edges.

Ethel Ann shoved the dirty clothes from the couch to the floor and installed me on the Hide-A-bed. "This'll be fun," she said. "We can watch a lotta TV."

And we did. And we drank brewskis. And we ate Budget Gourmet. Drank Diet Pepsi. Ate ice cream. And watched TV.

Finally all the casts were gone. I could walk almost as well as I had before. I could have worked at the shoe store, but I had long since been replaced. They were very sorry, but that was all.

One day when Ethel Ann was out for more junk food, I called Raymond. I named the movie theater where we'd met before and gave him a time. I told Ethel Ann that I had to get out for exercise and some fresh air.

"Is it the Glade I've been spraying? I could change brands."

I assured her that the house smelled fine. It smelled like a gymnasium built in a pine forest, but I didn't say that part.

"What, then? Exercise? That stuff'll kill ya."

I assured her that I wouldn't be long, and I went.

Raymond showed up on time. He was a little bit put out that the movie was *Crimes of the Heart*. "Honestly, Diane Keaton should never have let herself go like that, even to get the part. And Jessica Lange? My dear, she should at least have used a little makeup."

I wasn't interested in his criticisms of the movie. I had Siskel and Ebert for that. And Harris and Reed. I had another thing entirely on my mind. I told him.

"Yes, it's really too bad that it turned out this way," he said. "It seemed like such a good idea at the time," he said.

"That's all you've got to say?"

"I'm sorry, dear boy. What else *can* I say?"

"How could you ever have come up with such a harebrained scheme in the first place?" I said.

"I've often wondered. I don't think I ever took it really seriously. I *did* hope to get the money, but I suppose that will never happen, not now. *C'est la vie.*"

"*C'est la vie?*"

"French, dear boy. It means—"

"I know what it means," I said. "What about me?"

"You?"

"Me. The man married to your sister. What about me?"

"Well," he said, "there's always divorce."

"Divorce," I said.

"I suppose she'd never agree to it. Well, one has to make the best of things."

I looked at him. It was dark, but I think he was laughing at me, quietly.

So I killed him.

It was quite easy, much easier than all my attempts with Ethel Ann. I simply stepped across him to the aisle, then looked back and bent down.

"That's a lovely ascot," I said.

He simpered. "Thank you. It's pure silk. You don't think the color is a trifle . . . much?"

"Chartreuse? Don't be silly." I reached out my fingers to touch it.

And before he knew it, I had it off, twisted around his neck, and tight, so tight that he could only gargle. On the screen, Sissy Spacek was trying to hang herself, and the two or three other customers were more interested in her troubles than in Raymond's. I sat in the seat behind him and slowly strangled the life out of him. Then I left him there.

·   ·   ·

When I got back to the apartment, Ethel Ann met me at the door. She had an envelope in her hand. "Do ya know what day this is?" she said.

"No," I said. "I don't believe I do."

"That's what happens when ya spend all ya time inside. I guess gettin' out is good for ya sometimes. Anyhow, it's a special day for us." She handed me the envelope.

Then I knew, of course. How sentimental. I hadn't really suspected her of being so sentimental.

She walked toward the kitchen. "I'll get us some brewskis to help us celebrate," she said. "Open it up. It's special."

I opened the envelope, though I already suspected what I would find inside. I was right. A duplicate of the valentine she'd given me exactly one year before.

I looked at the face on the heart, the downturned mouth, the tears.

I looked up at the apartment, the filth, the roaches, the coffee cups, the clothes in piles, the plates full of crusts and crumbs.

I opened the card.

My heart cries for you.

I saw Ethel Ann heading toward me with the brewskis.

And cries, I thought.

And cries.

THE BEST-FRIEND MURDER

Donald Westlake

Donald Westlake is probably the best suspense writer of his generation. Who has written so well in so many subcategories? Who single-handedly reinvented the comic mystery? Who created Parker, and in so doing pointed dark suspense in an entirely new direction?

His Levine stories are particularly good, American equivalents of the Maigret stories.

Here we see Levine in a particularly confounding tale, told in the somber and wily prose that shows yet another aspect of Donald Westlake's magnificent work.

DETECTIVE ABRAHAM LEVINE OF BROOKLYN'S FORTY-THIRD PRECINCT chewed on his pencil and glowered at the report he'd just written. He didn't like it, he didn't like it at all. It just didn't feel right, and the more he thought about it the stronger the feeling became.

Levine was a short and stocky man, baggily dressed from plain pipe racks. His face was sensitive, topped by salt-and-pepper gray hair chopped short in a military crew cut. At fifty-three, he had twenty-four years of duty on the police force, and was halfway through the heart-attack age range, a fact that had been bothering him for some time now. Every time he was reminded of death, he thought worriedly about the aging heart pumping away inside his chest.

And in his job, the reminders of death came often. Natural death, accidental death, and violent death.

This one was a violent death, and to Levine it felt wrong somewhere. He and his partner, Jack Crawley, had taken the call just after lunch. It was from one of the patrolmen in Prospect Park, a patrolman named Tanner. A man giving his name as Larry Perkins had walked up to Tanner in the park and announced that he had just poisoned his best friend. Tanner went with him, found a dead body in the apartment Perkins had led him to, and called in. Levine and Crawley, having just walked into the station after lunch, were given the call. They turned around and walked back out again.

Crawley drove their car, an unmarked '56 Chevy, while Levine sat beside him and worried about death. At least this would be one of the neat ones. No knives or bombs or broken beer bottles. Just poison, that was all. The victim would look as though he were sleeping, unless it had been one of those poisons causing muscle spasms before death. But it would still be neater than a knife or a bomb or a broken beer bottle, and the victim wouldn't look quite so completely dead.

Crawley drove leisurely, without the siren. He was a big man in his forties, somewhat overweight, square-faced and heavy jowled, and he looked meaner than he actually was. The Chevy tooled up Eighth Avenue, the late spring sun shining on its hood. They were headed for an address on Garfield Place, the block between Eighth Avenue and Prospect Park West. They had to circle the block, because Garfield was a one-way street. That particular block on Garfield Place is a double row of chipped brownstones, the street running down between two rows of high stone stoops, the buildings cut and chopped inside into thousands of apartments, crannies and cubbyholes, niches and boxlike caves, where the subway riders sleep at night. The subway to Manhattan is six blocks away, up at Grand Army Plaza, across the way from the main library.

At one P.M. on this Wednesday in late May, the sidewalks were deserted, the buildings had the look of long abandoned dwellings. Only the cars parked along the left side of the street indicated present occupancy.

The number they wanted was in the middle of the block, on the right-hand side. There was no parking allowed on that side, so there was room directly in front of the address for Crawley to stop the Chevy. He flipped the sun visor down, with the official business card showing through the windshield, and followed Levine across the sidewalk and down the two steps to the basement door, under the stoop. The door was propped open with a battered garbage can. Levine and Crawley walked inside. It was dim in there, after the bright sunlight, and it took Levine's eyes a few

seconds to get used to the change. Then he made out the figures
of two men standing at the other end of the hallway, in front of
a closed door. One was the patrolman, Tanner, young, just over
six foot, with a square and impersonal face. The other was Larry
Perkins.

Levine and Crawley moved down the hallway to the two men
waiting for them. In the seven years they had been partners, they
had established a division of labor that satisfied them both. Crawley asked the questions, and Levine listened to the answers. Now,
Crawley introduced himself to Tanner, who said, "This is Larry
Perkins of 294 Fourth Street."

"Body in there?" asked Crawley, pointing at the closed door.

"Yes, sir," said Tanner.

"Let's go inside," said Crawley. "You keep an eye on the pigeon.
See he doesn't fly away."

"I've got some stuff to go to the library," said Perkins suddenly.
His voice was young and soft.

They stared at him. Crawley said, "It'll keep."

Levine looked at Perkins, trying to get to know him. It was a
technique he used, most of it unconsciously. First, he tried to fit
Perkins into a type or category, some sort of general stereotype.
Then he would look for small and individual ways in which Perkins
differed from the general type, and he would probably wind up
with a surprisingly complete mental picture, which would also be
surprisingly accurate.

The general stereotype was easy. Perkins, in his black wool
sweater and belt-in-the-back khakis and scuffed brown loafers
without socks, was "arty." What were they calling them this year?
They were "hip" last year, but this year they were—"beat." That
was it. For a general stereotype, Larry Perkins was a beatnik. The
individual differences would show up soon, in Perkins' talk and
mannerisms and attitudes.

Crawley said again, "Let's go inside," and the four of them
trooped into the room where the corpse lay.

The apartment was one large room, plus a closet-size kitchenette and an even smaller bathroom. A Murphy bed stood open,
covered with zebra-striped material. The rest of the furniture consisted of a battered dresser, a couple of armchairs and lamps, and

a record player sitting on a table beside a huge stack of long-playing records. Everything except the record player looked faded and worn and secondhand, including the thin maroon rug on the floor and the soiled flower-pattern wallpaper. Two windows looked out on a narrow cement enclosure and the back of another brownstone. It was a sunny day outside, but no sun managed to get down into this room.

In the middle of the room stood a card table, with a typewriter and two stacks of paper on it. Before the card table was a folding chair, and in the chair sat the dead man. He was slumped forward, his arms flung out and crumpling the stacks of paper, his head resting on the typewriter. His face was turned toward the door, and his eyes were closed, his facial muscles relaxed. It had been a peaceful death, at least, and Levine was grateful for that.

Crawley looked at the body, grunted, and turned to Perkins. "Okay," he said. "Tell us about it."

"I put the poison in his beer," said Perkins simply. He didn't talk like a beatnik at any rate. "He asked me to open a can of beer for him. When I poured it into a glass, I put the poison in, too. When he was dead, I went and talked to the patrolman here."

"And that's all there was to it?"

"That's all."

Levine asked, "Why did you kill him?"

Perkins looked over at Levine. "Because he was a pompous ass."

"Look at me," Crawley told him.

Perkins immediately looked away from Levine, but before he did so, Levine caught a flicker of emotion in the boy's eyes, what emotion he couldn't tell. Levine glanced around the room, at the faded furniture and the card table and the body, and at young Perkins, dressed like a beatnik but talking like the politest of polite young men, outwardly calm but hiding some strong emotion inside his eyes. What was it Levine had seen there? Terror? Rage? Or pleading?

"Tell us about this guy." said Crawley, motioning at the body. "His name, where you knew him from, the whole thing."

"His name is Al Gruber. He got out of the Army about eight months ago. He's living on his savings and the GI Bill. I mean, he *was*."

"He was a college student?"

"More or less. He was taking a few courses at Columbia, nights. He wasn't a full-time student."

Crawley said, "What was he, full-time?"

Perkins shrugged. "Not much of anything. A writer. An undiscovered writer. Like me."

Levine asked, "Did he make much money from his writing?"

"None," said Perkins. This time he didn't turn to look at Levine, but kept watching Crawley while he answered. "He got something accepted by one of the quarterlies once," he said, "but I don't think they ever published it. And they don't pay anything anyway."

"So he was broke?" asked Crawley.

"Very broke. I know the feeling well."

"You in the same boat?"

"Same life story completely," said Perkins. He glanced at the body of Al Gruber and said, "Well, almost. I write, too. And I don't get any money for it. And I'm living on the GI Bill and savings and a few home-typing jobs, and going to Columbia nights."

People came into the room then, the medical examiner and the boys from the lab, and Levine and Crawley, bracketing Perkins between them, waited and watched for a while. When they could see that the M.E. had completed his first examination, they left Perkins in Tanner's charge and went over to talk to him.

Crawley, as usual, asked the questions. "Hi, Doc," he said. "What's it look like to you?"

"Pretty straightforward case," said the M.E. "On the surface, anyway. Our man here was poisoned, felt the effects coming on, went to the typewriter to tell us who'd done it to him, and died. A used glass and a small medicine bottle were on the dresser. We'll check them out, but they almost certainly did the job."

"Did he manage to do any typing before he died?" asked Crawley.

The M.E. shook his head. "Not a word. The paper was in the machine kind of crooked, as though he'd been in a hurry, but he just wasn't fast enough."

"He wasted his time," said Crawley. "The guy confessed right away."

"The one over there with the patrolman?"

"Uh-huh."

"Seems odd, doesn't it?" said the M.E. "Take the trouble to poison someone, and then run out and confess to the first cop you see."

Crawley shrugged. "You can never figure," he said.

"I'll get the report to you soon's I can," said the M.E.

"Thanks, Doc. Come on, Abe, let's take our pigeon to his nest."

"Okay," said Levine, abstractedly. Already it felt wrong. It had been feeling wrong, vaguely, ever since he'd caught that glimpse of something in Perkins' eyes. And the feeling of wrongness was getting stronger by the minute, without getting any clearer.

They walked back to Tanner and Perkins, and Crawley said, "Okay, Perkins, let's go for a ride."

They walked back to Tanner.

"You're going to book me?" asked Perkins. He sounded oddly eager.

"Just come along," said Crawley. He didn't believe in answering extraneous questions.

"All right," said Perkins. He turned to Tanner. "Would you mind taking my books and records back to the library? They're due today. They're the ones on that chair. And there's a couple more over in the stack of Al's records."

"Sure," said Tanner. He was gazing at Perkins with a troubled look on his face, and Levine wondered if Tanner felt the same wrongness that was plaguing him.

"Let's go," said Crawley impatiently, and Perkins moved toward the door.

"I'll be right along," said Levine. As Crawley and Perkins left the apartment, Levine glanced at the titles of the books and record albums Perkins had wanted returned to the library. Two of the books were collections of Elizabethan plays, one was the *New Arts Writing Annual*, and the other two were books on criminology. The records were mainly folk songs, of the bloodier type.

Levine frowned and went over to Tanner. He asked, "What were you and Perkins talking about before we got here?"

Tanner's face was still creased in a puzzled frown. "The stupidity of the criminal mind," he said. "There's something goofy here, Lieutenant."

"You may be right," Levine told him. He walked on down the hall and joined the other two at the door.

All three got into the front seat of the Chevy, Crawley driving again and Perkins sitting in the middle. They rode in silence, Crawley busy driving, Perkins studying the complex array of the dashboard, with its extra knobs and switches and the mike hooked beneath the radio, and Levine trying to figure out what was wrong.

■   ■   ■

At the station, after booking, they brought him to a small office, one of the interrogation rooms. There was a bare and battered desk, plus four chairs. Crawley sat behind the desk, Perkins sat across the desk and facing him, Levine took the chair in a corner behind and to the left of Perkins, and a male stenographer, notebook in hand, filled the fourth chair, behind Crawley.

Crawley's first questions covered the same ground already covered at Gruber's apartment, this time for the record. "Okay," said Crawley, when he'd brought them up to date. "You and Gruber were both doing the same kind of thing, living the same kind of life. You were both unpublished writers, both taking night courses at Columbia, both living on very little money."

"That's right," said Perkins.

"How long you known each other?"

"About six months. We met at Columbia, and we took the same subway home after class. We got to talking, found out we were both dreaming the same kind of dream, and became friends. You know. Misery loves company."

"Take the same classes at Columbia?"

"Only one. Creative Writing, from Professor Stonegell."

"Where'd you buy the poison?"

"I didn't, Al did. He bought it a while back and just kept it around. He kept saying if he didn't make a good sale soon he'd kill himself. But he didn't mean it. It was just a kind of gag."

Crawley pulled at his right earlobe. Levine knew, from his long experience with his partner, that that gesture meant that Crawley was confused. "You went there today to kill him?"

"That's right."

Levine shook his head. That wasn't right. Softly, he said, "Why did you bring the library books along?"

"I was on my way up to the library," said Perkins, twisting around in his seat to look at Levine.

"Look this way," snapped Crawley.

Perkins looked around at Crawley again, but not before Levine had seen that same burning deep in Perkins' eyes. Stronger, this time, and more like pleading. Pleading? What was Perkins pleading for?

"I was on my way to the library," Perkins said again. "Al had a couple of records out on my card, so I went over to get them. On the way, I decided to kill him."

"Why?" asked Crawley.

"Because he was a pompous ass," said Perkins, the same answer he'd given before.

"Because he got a story accepted by one of the literary magazines and you didn't?" suggested Crawley.

"Maybe. Partially. His whole attitude. He was smug. He knew more than anybody else in the world."

"Why did you kill him today? Why not last week or next week?"

"I felt like it today."

"Why did you give yourself up?"

"You would have gotten me anyway."

Levine asked, "Did you know that before you killed him?"

"I don't know," said Perkins, without looking around at Levine. "I didn't think about it till afterward. Then I knew the police would get me anyway—they'd talk to Professor Stonegell and the other people who knew us both and I didn't want to have to wait it out. So I went and confessed."

"You told the policeman," said Levine, "that you'd killed your best friend."

"That's right."

"Why did you use that phrase, best friend, if you hated him so much you wanted to kill him?"

"He was my best friend. At least, in New York. I didn't really know anyone else, except Professor Stonegell. Al was my best friend because he was just about my only friend."

"Are you sorry you killed him?" asked Levine.

This time, Perkins twisted around in the chair again, ignoring Crawley. "No, sir," he said, and his eyes now were blank.

There was silence in the room, and Crawley and Levine looked at one another. Crawley questioned with his eyes, and Levine shrugged, shaking his head. Something was wrong, but he didn't know what. And Perkins was being so helpful that he wound up being no help at all.

Crawley turned to the stenographer. "Type it up formal," he said. "And have somebody come take the pigeon to his nest."

After the stenographer had left, Levine said, "Anything you want to say off the record, Perkins?"

Perkins grinned. His face was half-turned away from Crawley, and he was looking at the floor, as though he was amused by something he saw there. "Off the record?" he murmured. "As long as there are two of you in here, it's *on* the record."

"Do you want one of us to leave?"

Perkins looked up at Levine again, and stopped smiling. He seemed to think it over for a minute, and then he shook his head. "No," he said. "Thanks, anyway. But I don't think I have anything more to say. Not right now anyway."

Levine frowned and sat back in his chair, studying Perkins. The boy didn't ring true; he was constructed of too many contradictions. Levine reached out for a mental image of Perkins, but all he touched was air.

After Perkins was led out of the room by two uniformed cops, Crawley got to his feet, stretched, sighed, scratched, pulled his earlobe, and said, "What do you make of it, Abe?"

"I don't like it."

"I know that. I saw it in your face. But he confessed, so what else is there?"

"The phony confession is not exactly unheard of, you know."

"Not this time," said Crawley. "A guy confesses to a crime he didn't commit for one of two reasons. Either he's a crackpot who wants the publicity or to be punished or something like that, or he's protecting somebody else. Perkins doesn't read like a crackpot to me, and there's nobody else involved for him to be protecting."

"In a capital punishment state," suggested Levine, "a guy might confess to a murder he didn't commit so the state would do his suicide for him."

Crawley shook his head. "That still doesn't look like Perkins," he said.

"Nothing looks like Perkins. He's given us a blank wall to stare at. A couple of times it started to slip, and there was something else inside."

"Don't build a big thing, Abe. The kid confessed. He's the killer; let it go at that."

"The job's finished, I know that. But it still bothers me."

"Okay," said Crawley. He sat down behind the desk again and put his feet up on the scarred desktop. "Let's straighten it out. Where does it bother you?"

"All over. Number one, motivation. You don't kill a man for being a pompous ass. Not when you turn around a minute later and say he was your best friend."

"People do funny things when they're pushed far enough. Even to friends."

"Sure. Okay, number two. The murder method. It doesn't sound right. When a man kills impulsively, he grabs something and starts swinging. When he calms down, he goes and turns himself in. But when you *poison* somebody, you're using a pretty sneaky method. It doesn't make sense for you to run out and call a cop right after using poison. It isn't the same kind of mentality."

"He used the poison," said Crawley, "because it was handy. Gruber bought it, probably had it sitting on his dresser or something, and Perkins just picked it up on impulse and poured it into the beer."

"That's another thing," said Levine. "Do you drink much beer out of cans?"

Crawley grinned. "You know I do."

"I saw some empty beer cans sitting around the apartment, so that's where Gruber got his last beer from."

"Yeah. So what?"

"When you drink a can of beer, do you pour the beer out of the can into a glass, or do you just drink it straight from the can?"

"I drink it out of the can. But not everybody does."

"I know, I know. Okay, what about the library books? If you're going to kill somebody, are you going to bring library books along?"

"It was an impulse killing. He didn't know he was going to do it until he got there."

Levine got his feet. "That's the hell of it," he said. "You can explain away every single question in this business. But it's such a simple case. Why should there be so many questions that need explaining away?"

Crawley shrugged. "Beats me," he said. "All I know is, we've got a confession, and that's enough to satisfy me."

"Not me," said Levine. "I think I'll go poke around and see what happens. Want to come along?"

"Somebody's going to have to hand the pen to Perkins when he signs his confession," said Crawley.

"Mind if I take off for a while?"

"Go ahead. Have a big time," said Crawley, grinning at him. "Play detective."

·   ·   ·

Levine's first stop was back at Gruber's address. Gruber's apartment was empty now, having been sifted completely through normal routine procedure. Levine went down to the basement door under the stoop, but he didn't go back to Gruber's door. He stopped at the front apartment instead, where a ragged-edged strip of paper attached with peeling Scotch tape to the door read, in awkward and childish lettering, SUPERINTENDENT. Levine rapped and waited. After a minute, the door opened a couple of inches, held by a chain. A round face peered out at him from a height of a little over five feet. The face said, "Who you looking for?"

"Police," Levine told him. He opened his wallet and held it up for the face to look at.

"Oh," said the face. "Sure thing." The door shut, and Levine waited while the chain was clinked free, and then the door opened wide.

The super was a short and round man, dressed in corduroy trousers and a grease-spotted undershirt. He wheezed, "Come in, come in," and stood back for Levine to come into his crowded and musty-smelling living room.

Levine said, "I want to talk to you about Al Gruber."

The super shut the door and waddled into the middle of the room, shaking his head. "Wasn't that a shame?" he asked. "Al was a nice boy. No money, but a nice boy. Sit down somewhere, anywhere."

Levine looked around. The room was full of low-slung, heavy, sagging, overstuffed furniture, armchairs and sofas. He picked the least battered armchair of the lot, and sat on the very edge. Although he was a short man, his knees seemed to be almost up to his chin, and he had the feeling that if he relaxed he'd fall over backwards.

The super trundled across the room and dropped into one of the other armchairs, sinking into it as though he never intended to get to his feet again in his life. "A real shame," he said again. "And to think I maybe could have stopped it."

"You could have stopped it? How?"

"It was around noon," said the super. "I was watching the TV over there, and I heard a voice from the back apartment, shouting, 'Al! Al!' So I went out to the hall, but by the time I got there the shouting was all done. So I didn't know what to do. I waited a minute, and then I came back in and watched the TV again. That was probably when it was happening."

"There wasn't any noise while you were in the hall? Just the two shouts before you got out there?"

"That's all. At first, I thought it was another one of them arguments, and I was gonna bawl out the two of them, but it stopped before I even got the door open."

"Arguments?"

"Mr. Gruber and Mr. Perkins. They used to argue all the time, shout at each other, carry on like monkeys. The other tenants was always complaining about it. They'd do it late at night sometimes, two or three o'clock in the morning, and the tenants would all start phoning me to complain."

"What did they argue about?"

The super shrugged his massive shoulders. "Who knows? Names. People. Writers. They both think they're great writers or something."

"Did they ever get into a fist fight or anything like that? Ever threaten to kill each other?"

"Naw, they'd just shout at each other and call each other stupid and ignorant and stuff like that. They liked each other, really, I guess. At least they always hung around together. They just loved to argue, that's all. You know how it is with college kids. I've had college kids renting here before, and they're all like that. They all love to argue. Course, I never had nothing like this happen before."

"What kind of person was Gruber, exactly?"

The super mulled it over for a while. "Kind of a quiet guy," he said at last. "Except when he was with Mr. Perkins, I mean. Then he'd shout just as loud and often as anybody. But most of the time he was quiet. And good-mannered. A real surprise, after most of the kids around today. He was always polite, and he'd lend a hand if you needed some help or something, like the time I was carrying a bed up to the third floor front. Mr. Gruber come along and pitched right in with me. He did more of the work than I did."

"And he was a writer, wasn't he? At least, he was trying to be a writer."

"Oh, sure. I'd hear that typewriter of his tappin' away in there at all hours. And he always carried a notebook around with him, writin' things down in it. I asked him once what he wrote in there, and he said descriptions, of places like Prospect Park up at the corner, and of the people he knew. He always said he wanted to be a writer like some guy named Wolfe, used to live in Brooklyn too."

"I see." Levine struggled out of the armchair. "Thanks for your time," he said.

"Not at all." The super waddled after Levine to the door. "Anything I can do," he said. "Any time at all."

"Thanks again," said Levine. He went outside and stood in the hallway, thinking things over, listening to the latch click in place behind him. Then he turned and walked down the hallway to Gruber's apartment, and knocked on the door.

As he'd expected, a uniformed cop had been left behind to keep an eye on the place for a while, and when he opened the door, Levine showed his identification and said, "I'm on the case. I'd like to take a look around."

The cop let him in, and Levine looked carefully through Gruber's personal property. He found the notebooks, finally, in the bottom drawer of the dresser. There were five of them, steno pad size loose-leaf fillers. Four of them were filled with writing, in pen, in a slow and careful hand, and the fifth was still half blank.

Levine carried the notebooks over to the card table, pushed the typewriter out of the way, sat down and began to skim through the books.

He found what he was looking for in the middle of the third one he tried. A description of Larry Perkins, written by the man Perkins had killed. The description, or character study, which it more closely resembled, was four pages long beginning with a physical description and moving into a discussion of Perkins' personality. Levine noticed particular sentences in this latter part: "Larry doesn't want to write, he wants to be a writer, and that isn't the same thing. He wants the glamour and the fame and the money, and he thinks he'll get it from being a writer. That's why he's dabbled in acting and painting and all the other so-called glamorous professions. Larry and I are both being thwarted by the same thing: neither of us has anything to say worth saying. The difference is, I'm trying to find something to say, and Larry wants to make it on glibness alone. One of these days, he's going to find out he won't get anywhere that way. That's going to be a terrible day for him."

Levine closed the book, then picked up the last one, the one that hadn't yet been filled, and leafed through that. One word kept showing up throughout the last notebook. "Nihilism." Gruber obviously hated the word, and he was also obviously afraid of it. "Nihilism is death," he wrote on one page. "It is the belief that there are no beliefs, that no effort is worthwhile. How could any writer believe such a thing? Writing is the most positive of acts. So how can it be used for negative purposes? The only expression of nihilism is death, not the written word. If I can say nothing hopeful, I shouldn't say anything at all."

Levine put the notebooks back in the dresser drawer finally, thanked the cop, and went out to the Chevy. He'd hoped to be able to fill in the blank spaces in Perkins' character through Gruber's notebooks, but Gruber had apparently had just as much trouble defining Perkins as Levine was now having. Levine had learned a lot about the dead man, that he was sincere and intense and self-demanding as only the young can be, but Perkins was still little more than a smooth and blank wall. "Glibness," Gruber had called it. What was beneath the glibness? A murderer, by Perkins' own admission. But what else?

Levine crawled wearily into the Chevy and headed for Manhattan.

■ ■ ■

Professor Harvey Stonegell was in class when Levine got to Columbia University, but the girl at the desk in the dean's outer office told him that Stonegell would be out of that class in just a few minutes, and would then be free for the rest of the afternoon. She gave him directions to Stonegell's office, and Levine thanked her.

Stonegell's office door was locked, so Levine waited in the hall, watching students hurrying by in both directions, and reading the notices of scholarships, grants and fellowships thumbtacked to the bulletin board near the office door.

The professor showed up about fifteen minutes later, with two students in tow. He was a tall and slender man, with a gaunt face and a full head of gray-white hair. He could have been any age between fifty and seventy. He wore a tweed suit jacket, leather patches at the elbows, and non-matching gray slacks.

Levine said, "Professor Stonegell?"

"Yes?"

Levine introduced himself and showed his identification. "I'd like to talk to you for a minute or two."

"Of course. I'll just be a minute." Stonegell handed a book to one of the two students, telling him to read certain sections of it, and explained to the other student why he hadn't received a passing grade in his latest assignment. When both of them were taken care of, Levine stepped into Stonegell's crowded and tiny office, and sat down in the chair beside the desk.

Stonegell said, "Is this about one of my students?"

"Two of them. From your evening writing course. Gruber and Perkins."

"Those two? They aren't in trouble, are they?"

"I'm afraid so. Perkins has confessed to murdering Gruber."

Stonegell's thin face paled. "Gruber's dead? Murdered?"

"By Perkins. He turned himself in right after it happened. But, to be honest with you, the whole thing bothers me. It doesn't make sense. You knew them both. I thought you might be able to tell me something about them, so it *would* make sense."

Stonegell lit himself a cigarette and offered one to Levine. Then he fussed rather vaguely with his messy desktop, while Levine waited for him to gather his thoughts.

"This takes some getting used to," said Stonegell after a minute. "Gruber and Perkins. They were both good students in my class, Gruber perhaps a bit better. And they were friends."

"I'd heard they were friends."

"There was a friendly rivalry between them," said Stonegell. "Whenever one of them started a project, the other one started a similar project, intent on beating the first one at his own game. Actually, that was more Perkins than Gruber. And they always took opposite sides of every question, screamed at each other like sworn enemies. But actually they were very close friends. I can't understand either one of them murdering the other."

"Was Gruber similar to Perkins?"

"Did I give that impression? No, they were definitely unalike. The old business about opposites attracting. Gruber was by far the more sensitive and sincere of the two. I don't mean to imply that Perkins was insensitive or insincere at all. Perkins had his own sensitivity and his own sincerity, but they were almost exclusively directed within himself. He equated everything with himself, his own feelings and his own ambitions. But Gruber had more of the—oh, I don't know—more of a *world-view*, to badly translate the German. His sensitivity was directed outward, toward the feelings of other people. It showed up in their writing. Gruber's forté was characterization, subtle interplay between personalities. Perkins was deft, almost glib, with movement and action and plot, but his characters lacked substance. He wasn't really interested in anyone but himself."

"He doesn't sound like the kind of guy who'd confess to a murder right after he committed it."

"I know what you mean. That isn't like him. I don't imagine Perkins would ever feel remorse or guilt. I should think he would be one of the people who believes the only crime is in being caught."

"Yet we didn't catch him. He came to us." Levine studied the book titles on the shelf behind Stonegell. "What about their mental attitudes recently?" he asked. "Generally speaking, I mean. Were they happy or unhappy, impatient or content or what?"

"I think they were both rather depressed, actually," said Stonegell. "Though for somewhat different reasons. They had both come out of the Army less than a year ago, and had come to New York to try to make their mark as writers. Gruber was having difficulty with subject matter. We talked about it a few times. He couldn't find anything he really wanted to write about, nothing he felt strongly enough to give him direction in his writing."

"And Perkins?"

"He wasn't particularly worried about writing in that way. He was, as I say, deft and clever in his writing, but it was all too shallow. I think they might have been bad for one another, actually. Perkins could see that Gruber had the depth and sincerity that he lacked, and Gruber thought that Perkins was free from the soul-searching and self-doubt that was hampering him so much. In the last month or so, both of them have talked about dropping out of school, going back home and forgetting about the whole thing. But neither of them could have done that, at least not yet. Gruber couldn't have, because the desire to write was too strong in him. Perkins couldn't, because the desire to be a famous writer was too strong."

"A year seems like a pretty short time to get all that depressed," said Levine.

Stonegell smiled. "When you're young," he said, "a year can be eternity. Patience is an attribute of the old."

"I suppose you're right. What about girl friends, other people who knew them both?"

"Well, there was one girl whom both were dating rather steadily. The rivalry again. I don't think either of them was particularly serious about her, but both of them wanted to take her away from the other one."

"Do you know this girl's name?"

"Yes, of course. She was in the same class with Perkins and Gruber. I think I might have her home address here."

Stonegell opened a small file drawer atop his desk, and looked through it. "Yes, here it is," he said. "Her name is Anne Marie Stone, and she lives on Grove Street, down in the Village. Here you are."

Levine accepted the card from Stonegell, copied the name and address onto his pad, and gave the card back. He got to his feet. "Thank you for your trouble," he said.

"Not at all," said Stonegell, standing. He extended his hand, and Levine, shaking it, found it bony and almost parchment-thin, but surprisingly strong. "I don't know if I've been much help, though," he said.

"Neither do I, yet," said Levine. "I may be just wasting both our time. Perkins confessed, after all."

"Still—" said Stonegell.

Levine nodded. "I know. That's what's got me doing extra work."

"I'm still thinking of this thing as though—as though it were a story problem, if you know what I mean. It isn't real yet. Two young students, I've taken an interest in both of them, fifty years after the worms get me they'll still be around—and then you tell me one of them is already wormfood, and the other one is effectively just as dead. It isn't real to me yet. They won't be in class tomorrow night, but I still won't believe it."

"I know what you mean."

"Let me know if anything happens, will you?"

"Of course."

■   ■   ■

Anne Marie Stone lived in an apartment on the fifth floor of a walk-up on Grove Street in Greenwich Village, a block and a half from Sheridan Square. Levine found himself out of breath by the time he reached the third floor, and he stopped for a minute to get his wind back and to slow the pounding of his heart. There was no sound in the world quite as loud as the beating of his own heart these days, and when that beating grew too rapid or too irregular, Detective Levine felt a kind of panic that twenty-four years as a cop had never been able to produce.

He had to stop again at the fourth floor, and he remembered with envy what a Bostonian friend had told him about a City of Boston regulation that buildings used as residence had to have elevators if they were more than four stories high. Oh, to live in Boston. Or, even better, in Levittown, where there isn't a building higher than two stories anywhere.

He reached the fifth floor, finally, and knocked on the door of apartment 5B. Rustlings from within culminated in the peephole in the door being opened, and a blue eye peered suspiciously out at him. "Who is it?" asked a muffled voice. "Police," said Levine.

He dragged out his wallet, and held it high, so the eye in the peephole could read the identification.

"Second," said the muffled voice, and the peephole closed. A seemingly endless series of rattles and clicks indicated locks being released, and then the door opened, and a short, slender girl, dressed in pink toreador pants, gray bulky sweater and blond pony-tail, motioned to Levine to come in. "Have a seat," she said, closing the door after him.

"Thank you." Levine sat in a newfangled basket chair, as un-comfortable as it looked, and the girl sat in another chair of the same type, facing him. But she managed to look comfortable in the thing.

"Is this something I did?" she asked him. "Jaywalking or some-thing?"

Levine smiled. No matter how innocent, a citizen always pre-sumes himself guilty when the police come calling. "No," he said. "It concerns two friends of yours, Al Gruber and Larry Perkins."

"Those two?" The girl seemed calm, though curious, but not at all worried or apprehensive. She was still thinking in terms of something no more serious than jaywalking or a neighbor calling the police to complain about loud noises. "What are they up to?"

"How close are you to them?"

The girl shrugged. "I've gone out with both of them, that's all. We all take courses at Columbia. They're both nice guys, but there's nothing serious, you know. Not with either of them."

"I don't know how to say this," said Levine, "except the blunt way. Early this afternoon, Perkins turned himself in and admitted he'd just killed Gruber."

The girl stared at him. Twice, she opened her mouth to speak, but both times she closed it again. The silence lengthened, and Levine wondered belatedly if the girl had been telling the truth, if perhaps there had been something serious in her relationship with one of the boys after all. Then she blinked and looked away from him, clearing her throat. She stared out the window for a second, then looked back and said, "He's pulling your leg."

Levine shook his head. "I'm afraid not."

"Larry's got a weird sense of humor sometimes," she said. "It's a sick joke, that's all. Al's still around. You haven't found the body, have you?"

"I'm afraid we have. He was poisoned, and Perkins admitted he was the one who gave him the poison."

"That little bottle Al had around the place? That was only a gag."

"Not anymore."

She thought about it a minute longer, then shrugged, as though giving up the struggle to either believe or disbelieve. "Why come to me?" she asked him.

"I'm not sure, to tell you the truth. Something smells wrong about the case, and I don't know what. There isn't any logic to it. I can't get through to Perkins, and it's too late to get through to Gruber. But I've got to get to know them both, if I'm going to understand what happened."

"And you want me to tell you about them."

"Yes."

"Where did you hear about me? From Larry?"

"No, he didn't mention you at all. The gentlemanly instinct, I suppose. I talked to your teacher, Professor Stonegell."

"I see." She stood up suddenly, in a single rapid and graceless movement, as though she had to make some motion, no matter how meaningless. "Do you want some coffee?"

"Thank you, yes."

"Come on along. We can talk while I get it ready."

He followed her through the apartment. A hallway led from the long, narrow living room past bedroom and bathroom to a tiny kitchen. Levine sat down at the kitchen table, and Anne Marie Stone went through the motions of making coffee. As she worked, she talked.

"They're good friends," she said. "I mean, they *were* good friends. You know what I mean. Anyway, they're a lot different from each other. Oh, golly! I'm getting all loused up in tenses."

"Talk as though both were still alive," said Levine. "It should be easier that way."

"I don't really believe it anyway," she said. "Al—he's a lot quieter than Larry. Kind of intense, you know? He's got a kind of reversed Messiah complex. You know, he figures he's supposed to be something great, a great writer, but he's afraid he doesn't have the stuff for it. So he worries about himself, and keeps trying to analyze himself, and he hates everything he writes because he doesn't think it's good enough for what he's supposed to be doing. That bottle of poison, that was a gag, you know, just a gag, but it was the kind of joke that has some sort of truth behind it. With this thing driving him like this, I suppose even death begins to look like a good escape after a while."

She stopped her preparations with the coffee, and stood listening to what she had just said. "Now he did escape, didn't he? I wonder if he'd thank Larry for taking the decision out of his hands."

"Do you suppose he asked Larry to take the decision out of his hands?"

She shook her head. "No. In the first place, Al could never ask anyone else to help him fight the thing out in any way. I know, I tried to talk to him a couple of times, but he just couldn't listen. It wasn't that he didn't want to listen, he just couldn't. He had to figure it out for himself. And Larry isn't the helpful sort, so Larry would be the last person anybody would go to for help. Not that Larry's a bad guy, really. He's just awfully self-centered. They both are, but in different ways. Al's always worried about himself, but Larry's always proud of himself. You know. Larry would say, 'I'm for me first,' and Al would say, 'Am I worthy?' Something like that."

"Had the two of them had a quarrel or anything recently, anything that you know of that might have prompted Larry to murder?"

"Not that I know of. They've both been getting more and more depressed, but neither of them blamed the other. Al blamed himself for not getting anywhere, and Larry blamed the stupidity of the world. You know, Larry wanted the same thing Al did, but Larry didn't worry about whether he was worthy or capable or anything like that. He once told me he wanted to be a famous writer, and he'd be one if he had to rob banks and use the money to bribe every publisher and editor and critic in the business. That was a gag, too, like Al's bottle of poison, but I think that one had some truth behind it, too."

The coffee was ready, and she poured two cups, then sat down across from him. Levine added a bit of evaporated milk, but no sugar, and stirred the coffee distractedly. "I want to know why," he said. "Does that seem strange? Cops are supposed to want to know who, not why. I know who, but I want to know why."

"Larry's the only one who could tell you, and I don't think he will."

Levine drank some of the coffee, then got to his feet. "Mind if I use your phone?" he asked.

"Go right ahead. It's in the living room, next to the bookcase."

Levine walked back into the living room and called the station. He asked for Crawley. When his partner came on the line, Levine said, "Has Perkins signed the confession yet?"

"He's on the way down now. It's just been typed up."

"Hold him there after he signs it, okay? I want to talk to him. I'm in Manhattan, starting back now."

"What have you got?"

"I'm not sure I have anything. I just want to talk to Perkins again, that's all."

"Why sweat it? We got the body; we got the confession; we got the killer in a cell. Why make work for yourself?"

"I don't know. Maybe I'm just bored."

"Okay, I'll hold him. Same room as before."

Levine went back to the kitchen. "Thank you for the coffee," he said. "If there's nothing else you can think of, I'll be leaving now."

"Nothing," she said. "Larry's the only one can tell you why."

She walked him to the front door, and he thanked her again as he was leaving. The stairs were a lot easier going down.

■　■　■

When Levine got back to the station, he picked up another plain-clothesman, a detective named Ricco, a tall, athletic man in his middle thirties who affected the Ivy League look. He resembled more closely someone from the District Attorney's office than a precinct cop. Levine gave him a part to play, and the two of them went down the hall to the room where Perkins was waiting with Crawley.

"Perkins," said Levine, the minute he walked in the room, before Crawley had a chance to give the game away by saying something to Ricco, "this is Dan Ricco, a reporter from the *Daily News*."

Perkins looked at Ricco with obvious interest, the first real display of interest and animation Levine had yet seen from him. "A reporter?"

"That's right," said Ricco. He looked at Levine. "What is this?" he asked. He was playing it straight and blank.

"College student," said Levine. "Name's Larry Perkins." He spelled the last name. "He poisoned a fellow student."

"Oh, yeah?" Ricco glanced at Perkins without much eagerness. "What for?" he asked, looking back at Levine. "Girl? Any sex in it?"

"Afraid not. It was some kind of intellectual motivation. They both wanted to be writers."

Ricco shrugged. "Two guys with the same job? What's so hot about that?"

"Well, the main thing," said Levine, "is that Perkins here wants to be famous. He tried to get famous by being a writer, but that wasn't working out. So he decided to be a famous murderer."

Ricco looked at Perkins. "Is that right?" he asked.

Perkins was glowering at them all, but especially at Levine. "What difference does it make?" he said.

"The kid's going to get the chair, of course," said Levine blandly. "We have his signed confession and everything. But I've kind of taken a liking to him. I'd hate to see him throw his life away without getting something for it. I thought maybe you could get him a nice headline on page two, something he could hang up on the wall of his cell."

Ricco chuckled and shook his head. "Not a chance of it," he said. "Even if I wrote the story big, the city desk would knock it down to nothing. This kind of story is a dime a dozen. People kill other people around New York twenty-four hours a day. Unless there's a good strong sex interest, or it's maybe one of those mass killings things like the guy who put the bomb in the airplane, a murder in New York is filler stuff. And who needs filler stuff in the spring, when the ball teams are just getting started?"

"You've got influence on the paper, Dan," said Levine. "Couldn't you at least get him picked up by the wire services?"

"Not a chance in a million. What's he done that a few hundred other clucks in New York don't do every year? Sorry, Abe, I'd like to do you the favor, but it's no go."

Levine sighed. "Okay, Dan," he said. "If you say so."

"Sorry," said Ricco. He grinned at Perkins. "Sorry, kid," he said. "You should of knifed a chorus girl or something."

Ricco left and Levine glanced at Crawley, who was industriously yanking on his earlobe and looking bewildered. Levine sat down facing Perkins and said, "Well?"

"Let me alone a minute," snarled Perkins. "I'm trying to think."

"I was right, wasn't I?" asked Levine. "You wanted to go out in a blaze of glory."

"All right, all right. Al took his way, I took mine. What's the difference?"

"No difference," said Levine. He got wearily to his feet, and headed for the door. "I'll have you sent back to your cell now."

"Listen," said Perkins suddenly. "You know I didn't kill him, don't you? You know he committed suicide, don't you?"

Levine opened the door and motioned to the two uniformed cops waiting in the hall.

"Wait," said Perkins desperately.

"I know, I know," said Levine. "Gruber really killed himself, and I suppose you burned the note he left."

"You know damn well I did."

"That's too bad, boy."

Perkins didn't want to leave. Levine watched deadpan as the boy was led away, and then he allowed himself to relax, let the tension drain out of him. He sagged into a chair and studied the veins on the backs of his hands.

Crawley said, into the silence, "What was all that about, Abe?"

"Just what you heard."

"Gruber committed suicide?"

"They both did."

"Well—what are we going to do now?"

"Nothing. We investigated; we got a confession; we made an arrest. Now we're done."

"But—"

"But hell!" Levine glared at his partner. "That little fool is gonna go to trial, Jack, and he's gonna be convicted and go to the chair. He chose it himself. It was *his* choice. I'm not railroading him; he chose his own end. And he's going to get what he wanted."

"But listen, Abe—"

"I won't listen!"

"Let me—let me get a word in."

Levine was on his feet suddenly, and now it all came boiling out, the indignation and the rage and the frustration. "Damn it, you don't know yet! You've got another six, seven years yet. You don't know what it feels like to lie awake in bed at night and listen to your heart skip a beat every once in a while, and wonder when it's going to skip two beats in a row and you're dead. You don't know what it feels like to know your body's starting to die, it's starting to get old and die and it's all downhill from now on."

"What's that got to do with—"

"I'll tell you what! They had the *choice*! Both of them young, both of them with sound bodies and sound hearts and years ahead of them, decades ahead of them. And they chose to throw it away! They chose to throw away what I don't have anymore. Don't you think I wish *I* had that choice? All right! They chose to die, let 'em die!"

Levine was panting from exertion, leaning over the desk and shouting in Jack Crawley's face. And now, in the sudden silence while he wasn't speaking, he heard the ragged rustle of his breath, felt the tremblings of nerve and muscle throughout his body. He let himself carefully down into a chair and sat there, staring at the wall, trying to get his breath.

Jack Crawley was saying something, far away, but Levine couldn't hear him. He was listening to something else, the loudest sound in all the world. The fitful throbbing of his own heart.